CHRONICLES
of
ALETHIA

CHRONICLES
of
ALETHIA
The Heir Comes Forth

R.S. GULLETT

Published in the United States of America
ISBN: 978-1-09041-037-5
1. Fiction / Christian / Fantasy
2. Fiction / Romance / Historical / Medieval
16.06.10

ACKNOWLEDGEMENTS

First and foremost, I wish to give honor and glory to Jesus Christ, my Lord and Savior. Without Him, this story would have no foundation. I also wish to thank my loving wife, Stephanie, for her encouragement and all the time she spent editing this book. Finally, I wish to thank my parents for always encouraging me to pursue my goals.

PROLOGUE: GALANOR

Oakwood, the largest and most mysterious forest in all the kingdom of Alethia. The night was dark, and thick clouds loomed ominously overhead, blocking out the faintest light of moon or stars. Even at midday, no light penetrated the dense foliage of the trees, leaving those under their great boughs in almost complete darkness. Galanor stood alone, wrapped in a dark-gray traveling cloak and hood, gazing up at the ancient fortress of Ardaband. The once proud fortress now lay in ruins, crumbling with age and neglect. Yet as he looked upon the ruins, Galanor shuddered as the memory of his last visit came rushing back.

It was fifty years ago. His apprentice had betrayed him and drawn the kingdom of Nordyke into a war with King Edward of Alethia. The battle had been won and Nordyke was defeated, but his apprentice had withdrawn to this stronghold, Ardaband. Galanor and his apprentice had used all their knowledge and powers to try and destroy one another. Yet in the end, his apprentice had fled, and King Edward had ordered the fortress destroyed. In the aftermath, Galanor had found a small chess piece lying on its side with a piece of parchment attached to it. He'd picked it up, recognizing the piece as the black king. The parchment read: "You've won this round." Galanor remembered standing in the ruins after the army had departed, wondering if the battle between he and his apprentice would ever be over.

He allowed the memory a moment and then pushed it from his mind. Though he was a student of the past, Galanor had to resist the temptation to remain there.

Suddenly, the underbrush to his right moved ever slightly. Galanor turned quickly and started as a pair of gleaming red eyes stared back at him.

"Wolves of Ardaband," he whispered, turning and pointing his staff toward the eyes. "Almighty God, please lend me your light!"

A brilliant bluish light flashed from the end of his staff, illuminating the area directly in front of it. A massive, gray wolf bared its teeth at him.

"You're foolish to come here, gray-beard." The wolf snarled as it shrank away before the light.

"Bodolf," Galanor gasped in surprise. "You're still alive.

"I still draw breath." Bodolf growled. "But you will soon draw your last. The master has come."

A sharp growl came from behind him. Galanor spun around just as a second wolf leapt toward him. He rolled out of the way and drove his staff into the ground, sending a burst of blinding light out into the darkness. Galanor gaped as the light revealed dozens of giant wolves all around him. He heard their cries of anger and pain as they shrank away and fled from the blinding light of his staff.

"Back!" he cried. "Back to the shadows, all of you!"

Galanor watched as all the wolves, including Bodolf, disappeared beyond the light of his staff. When the last of the wolves had gone, he turned his gaze back to the dark and empty fortress. As he did so, a faint light appeared in one of the main keep's upper rooms. It was the sign for which he'd been waiting. His apprentice had returned. Galanor made for the keep at once, ascending the many flights of stairs until he stood before the door leading to the only lit room. He made a motion with his right hand, and the door opened of its own accord. He stood for a moment on the threshold, gazing about the room, and then stepped inside.

Galanor removed his hood revealing a face lined and careworn. His head was covered in thinning gray hair, and he had a long gray beard that fell past his belt. Galanor's most remarkable characteristic was his eyes. They were a deep piercing blue, which gave them the seeming ability to penetrate the very walls of stone surrounding him. Galanor looked about the room, and his eyes fell on a small table with two chairs facing one another. An ornate chess set lay upon the table. He moved to examine the table more closely, but as he did so, another man entered the room behind him. The newcomer wore a black cloak and hood, and in his right hand he held a dagger glowing red as if it had just been drawn from a smith's fire. He moved silently across the room and stood for a moment behind Galanor. Then, swift as lightning, the newcomer thrust the dagger forward to stab the unsuspecting Galanor in the back. Yet the blade did not make contact but glanced off as if hitting an invisible shield and shattered into pieces.

"You will never learn, Methangoth," said Galanor softly. He did not turn or react but seemed unperturbed that the newcomer had just attempted to murder him in cold blood.

"I will never stop trying, Galanor." Methangoth growled, moving over to the hearth and pulling back his hood. The newcomer was younger than Galanor by at least thirty years. He had long black hair and black eyes that gleamed menacingly in the firelight. "So, what brings you so far from Elmloch?"

"That is my business," Galanor said, finally looking at Methangoth. He tried to hide it, but there was a look of disappointment and pity in his eyes when he looked at the other man.

"It's your move," Methangoth said, gesturing toward the chessboard.

"My move?" Galanor said, looking hard at the other man. "You think I came here to play a game of chess?"

"It's been so long since we've played, and I've missed the challenge," Methangoth said with an evil grin.

"What are you planning, Methangoth? Why have you come to Ardaband?" Galanor asked bluntly. He was in no mood for games.

"I decided a change of scenery was in order," Methangoth said smoothly. "As to the rest, that is *my* business."

"You tried this fifty years ago. It did not work then, and it won't work now."

"I know you have found the heir, Galanor," Methangoth said, continuing to smile. "It's your move."

"I will not play your games, Methangoth," Galanor said irritably. "I have warned you countless times to leave this path you keep choosing."

Galanor turned to leave.

"I know who your *knights* are, Galanor," Methangoth called after him, still smiling. "You'd be wise not to move them yet, which means you have a choice of which pawn to move first."

Galanor stood with his back to Methangoth, his anger bubbling beneath his calm exterior.

"Choose carefully, my old friend, for this is our last game."

Galanor glanced back at Methangoth for a moment and then left in a flurry of robes. His mind whirled with doubt and fear as he descended the stairs. If Methangoth was making a play for the book, he might also know the identity of the heir. He must visit Stonewall to ensure the book's safety. As for the heir...

Galanor had reached the ground floor and walked out into the courtyard. He knew that Methangoth must be watching, but Galanor knew there was no other choice. His old body groaned as he forced it to move faster than he had in years. He'd already passed through the ruined gatehouse and out into the forest, but he was forced to admit the difficult truth that he was growing old. He could hear the Ardaband wolves growling all around him, the light of his staff holding them at bay. It was going to be a long journey. The need to find a young apprentice was now apparent. Galanor now realized that his visit to Stonewall may prove productive for both tasks. Perhaps a suitable candidate would present themselves.

1

CORIN

As the sun rose in the eastern sky, two young men appeared on the road leading into the city of Stonewall. The first was Ardyn Thayn, the third son of Anson Thayn, who was the lord of Stonewall. He had blond hair, brown eyes, and the healthy build of youth. The second was Corin Stone. The generic surname of *Stone* marked him as one of the many orphans of the city. Corin had brown hair, brown eyes, and a leaner look than Ardyn, who was also several inches taller. Both boys were smiling broadly, clearly proud of themselves. They stopped and gazed back at the mountain rising up behind the city.

"Can you believe it?" Corin shouted to his friend.

"My dad said it was a myth, but we did it. We found the hidden stair!" Ardyn shouted in reply.

Mount Arryon rose majestically in the early morning light. Corin felt his heart racing with the exhilaration of returning from his first real adventure. The fact that it had been a success only increased his sense of satisfaction.

"Come on," said Ardyn, clapping him on the back. "Let's get you back before anyone at the academy realizes you were gone."

Corin nodded, and they both began the long trek up the winding streets to Stonewall Academy. The city of Stonewall was set on the side of Mountain Arryon, separated from the surrounding countryside by a great chasm. A large bridge spanned the chasm, providing the only way to reach the city. The gray stone walls and towers gave the city a somber appearance. Stonewall Academy was considered a national treasure of the kingdom of Alethia, founded by one of its kings over six hundred years ago. Ardyn and Corin climbed the street leading to the academy. The large gray stone building rose high, embedded into the side of Mt. Arryon. There were rumors of secret vaults filled with relics and hidden archives full of ancient tomes and records predating the first kings in and under the academy. Corin had never seen any, but he had to admit that the mystery of the ancient building fascinated him.

When they reached the great oak front doors, Ardyn and Corin stopped and shook hands.

"See you at the Eagle's Nest tonight for a pint?" Corin asked.

"Can't," Ardyn replied, his face downcast. "Father is leaving for Ethriel this morning and has demanded I accompany. He said something about 'securing my future,' or whatever."

At that moment, the doors of the academy flew open, and a man with a long gray beard, wearing black robes came storming out into the morning light. It was Markus Tolen, headmaster of Stonewall Academy. Ardyn and Corin stood rooted to the spot in surprise as Tolen walked straight at them. He was followed by another man whom neither Corin nor Ardyn recognized, though they were not paying much attention to anyone but the seething man coming toward them.

"Boy, you were to be here at sunrise," the headmaster said, glaring at Corin. His voice was quick and sharp, and Corin lowered his head in shame. "I told you this meeting was important."

"Yes, Headmaster Tolen," Corin said with a sigh.

Corin saw the headmaster glance at Ardyn then turned to the man who'd followed him.

"Master Galanor," Tolen said pompously. "May I present Ardyn Thayn and Corin Stone."

Corin's and Ardyn's eyes grew wide in astonishment as they surveyed the man in the dark cloak and hood.

"Pleased to meet you both," Galanor said with a slight nod of his head. Though his voice was quiet, Corin heard the power and authority in it. The man shook hands with Corin and Ardyn then abruptly turned and walked back inside.

"Well, come along Corin," Tolen said, rather flustered by Galanor's abruptness.

Corin and Ardyn exchanged a glance, then Corin and the headmaster entered the academy. They walked silently through the great halls, their footfalls echoing off the stone walls. No one else was moving about, giving the place a very lonely feeling. After several sets of stairs and adjoining corridors, they arrived at the headmaster's office. Tolen ushered Galanor inside. He glared at Corin for a moment before allowing him to enter also.

Corin had never before been inside the headmaster's office. It was a large room whose walls were covered with shelves and shelves of books of all sizes. Corin's eyes grew wide as he estimated how much knowledge this room alone contained. A large desk sat on the other side of the room, covered in parchments and even more select tomes that the headmaster was currently studying. The headmaster led them over to two chairs facing the desk, while he took the high-backed chair on the other side.

"It has been many years since you visited us, Galanor," Tolen said with a look of excited expectation. "I just wanted to say, welcome back to Stonewall Academy."

Corin glanced over at the man next to him. His expression was blank, though Corin thought he saw impatience in his eyes.

"I am curious as to why you asked for this meeting," Tolen said after a long silence.

"I asked to meet with Corin Stone, Headmaster Tolen. In private..." Galanor said, speaking softly but emphasizing the last two words.

"I, um, I thought," Tolen said, realization dawning on him.

Galanor nodded meaningfully.

"I see," Tolen said, clearly offended. He stood and moved toward the door, pausing briefly to look from Galanor to Corin, then left the room.

When the door had closed, Corin turned to the mysterious man next to him, a sense of anxiety and apprehension rising inside him.

"You work here at the academy?" the man asked in almost a whisper.

Corin nodded, trying to maintain eye contact. The man's gaze was piercing, and his deep blue eyes seemed to bore into his very soul.

"You know of me, yes?" the man asked after a brief pause.

"Yes," Corin replied.

"Then you know I am Galanor, a historian of Alethia. That much of what is known of our kingdom is due to my study and teaching," he said with no hint of arrogance in his voice.

"Yes, sir," Corin said quickly.

The man was silent for a moment, considering Corin carefully. Corin was very uncomfortable now and wished he was somewhere else.

"Corin Stone," Galanor said softly as if measuring the name to see if it was the correct weight. "The name *Stone* is given to orphans of Stonewall, yes?"

Corin nodded curtly. He did not like to be reminded of his lack of lineage.

"You know nothing of your mother and father?"

Corin shook his head, his mood shifting from fear to mild annoyance now. "I was found on the steps of the Stonewall Orphanage with this." Corin reached inside his tunic and pulled a tarnished silver chain with a ring hung on it. The ring was made of gold and had a rose imprinted on the top. He'd often wondered why someone would choose a rose as their symbol. He had kept it a secret from all except for his friend Ardyn. He was astonished by the recognition that crossed Galanor's face.

"You may not remember, Corin, but we have met before," said the man with a sad look. "Would it surprise you to know that I was friends with your parents, Marcus and Kaleen?"

"You knew my parents!" Corin asked, nearly shouting with excitement.

"Yes," Galanor answered. "It was a long time ago when you were very young."

Corin's mind was flooded with so many questions that he could not decide which one to ask first.

"But that is not why I asked to meet with you," Galanor said, interrupting Corin's thoughts. "I wish to instruct you concerning the history of Alethia. Will you allow me to teach you?"

Corin was torn between demanding more information about his parents and learning a secret history of Alethia. Galanor, famed throughout Alethia for much more than just being a historian, wanted to teach him. How could he refuse or risk this opportunity?

"What say you?" the man asked when Corin did not answer.

"Yes," Corin nearly shouted accidentally. He purposely lowered his voice then said, "Yes, sir. It would be an honor."

"Save the empty words, boy," the man said gruffly. "What I have to teach you will benefit you greatly in the future. I am afraid my time is limited, presently, but I will impart as much as my time here allows. Are you ready to begin?"

Corin nodded eagerly.

"Good," Galanor said, a small smile spreading across his face. "First, tell me what you know of Alethian history."

"I know that the House of Aurelia ascended the throne almost two hundred years ago," Corin began uncertainly.

"Yes, but before that," Galanor interrupted.

"I...I don't know anything before that," Corin admitted. He felt confused and slightly ashamed. The teachers at the academy never spoke of anything before the ascension of the Aurelian kings.

"As I knew, you would not," Galanor said with a grim laugh. "The history of Alethia before the House of Aurelia took the throne is not common knowledge. In fact, it is forbidden from being taught."

Corin looked at Galanor in amazement.

"I and few others know this history—the true history of Alethia. Even Headmaster Tolen does not know it in full because of the king's law. Do you still wish to know it?"

Corin nodded, his eyes wide in shock that this renowned historian wished to impart his knowledge to him.

"There is but one source for the true history of Alethia, the *Book of Aduin*, written down by the fabled historian following the War of Ascension two hundred years ago. The only known copy of the book is kept here within the academy in a secret vault known only to a few."

"Were there no other versions of the history written?" Corin asked, trying to mask his excitement.

"All histories written before the War of Ascension were burned or otherwise destroyed by the Aurelian kings."

"What's the War of Ascension? And why would the Aurelians want to destroy our history?" Corin asked earnestly.

"Sadly, we do not have the time to address that subject properly. We must press on," Galanor said firmly. "Today, I wish to enlighten you about our ancient history." Galanor cleared his throat and began.

"Alethia was once a minor province of the Atolnum Empire. Over a thousand years ago, the empire collapsed, and the lands were thrown into chaos."

"Why?" Corin asked quickly. Galanor looked angry at the interruption, and Corin hurriedly apologized.

"Seven houses arose from the ashes and established rule over the lands west of the Gray and Green Mountains. Yet the houses were unable to live harmoniously with their neighbors. The next two centuries were dominated by the Alliance Wars, where the houses bargained and blackmailed each other to war against one another."

Corin was enrapt in the story. He loved history in all forms, and since this was an unknown history, he was overwhelmed with excitement.

"Following the Alliance Wars—" Galanor continued, but Corin interrupted.

"Wait!" he said abruptly. "What happened during the Alliance Wars?"

"There is not enough time to delve into such details, Corin," Galanor snapped. "Now, around eight hundred years ago, the leaders of the seven houses were called to a council in Ethriel at the request of House Aurelia. The purpose of this council was to lay aside their issues and help unify the houses. Yet Farod and Noland refused to work with one another, and the council was disbanded.

"The following year, Farod attacked Nenlad, but this time the other five houses came to Nenlad's aid. Farod was forced to come to the city of Elengil, where the first Council of Lords convened, where the lord of each major house met to decide the future of Alethia. Following the crisis, the Council of Lords routinely met once a year in Elengil, where major issues could be discussed and solved without resorting to war. For almost a hundred years, Alethia knew peace."

"What happened that upset the peace?" Corin asked with interest.

"The land was invaded multiple times by Donia and Nordyke," Galanor said gravely. "Each time, only one of the seven houses was faithful to send aid to the others, House Aranethon."

Corin was confused. He'd never heard of House Aranethon. Galanor seemed to read his thoughts for he was looking intently at Corin.

"I see you are unaware of the Aranethons."

Corin nodded.

"It is not surprising since the house fell over two hundred years ago," Galanor said, still looking at Corin intently.

"Wait," Corin said, suddenly realizing something. "You said the War of Ascension occurred two hundred years ago, right?"

Galanor nodded with a twinkle in his eyes.

"Then the House of Aranethon must have fallen around the same time, right?"

"You are smarter than the headmaster gives you credit for," Galanor said with a small smile. "But back to the history. You see, Corin, before the days of the king, the houses would only send aid when an invader directly threatened them—all except one: House Aranethon. They were the only house to send aid regardless of the situation. Because of this, all the peoples came to love and respect House Aranethon. Finally, around six hundred years ago, the Council of Lords named Alfred Aranethon as Lord Protector of the Realm. During a time of war, each lord would send men to form a single army of Alethia to fight off the invaders. When Alfred Aranethon died, the Council of Lords elected his son, Henry Aranethon, to serve as Lord Protector. Henry had fought in several border skirmishes and had proven himself as a trustworthy protector."

"What about Eddynland?" Corin asked abruptly.

"What about it?" Galanor replied gruffly.

"Why haven't you mentioned Eddynland in your history?"

"The King of Eddynland forged an alliance with Henry Aranethon," Galanor replied. "They have been allies ever since."

"So if Aranethon had not fallen, they would still be allies?"

Galanor hesitated for a moment, looking intently at Corin. He then nodded and continued.

"For the next hundred years, the leaders of House Aranethon were always elected as Lord Protector by the Council of Lords. Finally, after much deliberation, the council voted to elect David Aranethon as King of Alethia."

"So, the first King of Alethia was David Aranethon," Corin said in almost a whisper. He sat staring at the stone floors, trying to piece all this new information together. It was too hard to accept that everything that his teachers had told him was false.

"I just can't believe it all," he said aloud.

"You must," said Galanor forcefully. His voice echoed off the office walls.

"Why?" Corin said, looking up quizzically at the old man. "Why must I believe all this?"

"All I have said is truth, Corin Stone," Galanor said gruffly.

"Yes," Corin said slowly. "But it is completely different from the history I have learned, the history that is common knowledge to all Alethians."

"Part of growing up is realizing you do not understand near as much about the world as you would like to believe," Galanor said, rising. He looked like he'd just realized something important. "I must go."

"What!" Corin exclaimed. "Right now?"

"Yes, Corin. I have other matters to which I must attend," he replied, moving to the door.

"But I still have questions," Corin said, almost pleading.

"They will have to wait."

"Please, Galanor," Corin said, standing up. "Before you go, can you tell me something of my parents?"

Galanor looked at him, and Corin saw a softness cross the old man's face. He shook his head.

"Another time, Corin," Galanor said, moving toward him. "Take this."

He dropped something in Corin's hand. It was a large black coin with a shield in the middle of it baring no sign or crest.

He turned the coin over to find the other side covered in an ancient script.

"It marks you as a member of the Shadow Garrison."

"The what?"

"They protect the survivors of House Aranethon as well as the kingdom."

"You mean there are still survivors?" Corin said, his mind racing.

"If someone shows you a coin like this one, do not hesitate to trust them."

Corin did not speak.

"Swear to me, Corin," Galanor said, and his voice was full of anxiety and earnestness. "Swear that you will trust anyone who shows you a coin like this one."

Corin eyed the old man with a mixture of fear and confusion.

"Okay, I swear," he said finally, and Galanor left.

Corin sat in the headmaster's office with a hundred questions floating in his mind. Foremost was why the old man had sought him out in the first place. Perhaps one day he'd see the old man again, and at least some of his questions would be answered. He stood and moved toward the door, but at that very moment the door opened, and Headmaster Tolen entered his office.

"Well, I hope you and Galanor enjoyed the use of my office for your private conversation," the headmaster said, glaring at Corin and advancing toward him menacingly. "What did you both talk about, I wonder."

"He just talked to me about the history of Alethia," Corin said quickly and backed away.

"Why?" Tolen asked, his eyes boring into Corin.

"I don't know," Corin answered honestly.

The headmaster continued to glare at Corin for a moment then jerked his head at the door. Corin was halfway out the door when he heard the headmaster call after him.

"I will find out, boy. Mark my words. I will be monitoring your every move from this moment on."

Corin ran for it and did not stop until he'd reached the main hall. He stopped to catch his breath and noticed Ardyn was standing at the other end of the hall. His friend waved at him. Corin smiled and walked over.

"So," Ardyn said with a hint of expectation. "What was that all about?"

Corin shrugged. "Aren't you supposed to leave soon?"

"Yeah," Ardyn said, nodding toward the entrance. "Just came to say 'bye' to my friend."

"Good luck in Ethriel," Corin said awkwardly and held out his hand.

"Thanks," Ardyn said, shaking his hand.

"Ardyn!" came the angry voice of Anson Thayn echoing through the hall. "Come now, boy! We must leave at once!"

Corin and Ardyn both looked toward the entrance and saw the silhouettes of several men standing at the front doors.

"Well," Ardyn said awkwardly. "See you later."

"See ya."

Ardyn left, and Corin watched his friend leave, then he realized he was late for his duties in the kitchen. He ran at a full sprint, hoping the cook would forgive his tardiness.

2

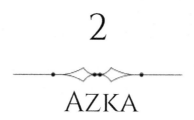

AZKA

The little room was dark save for the light emanating from a single candle in the center of the room. Next to the candle was a man seated on an ancient, faded, threadbare rug with his legs crossed. The man's face and most of his body was hidden under a weather-beaten traveling cloak. He sat unmoving with his head bowed in silent meditation.

Behind the man, in the far corner of the room, there was a large bag as weather-beaten as the man's cloak. There was also a plain sword in a cracked leather scabbard and an old bow and quiver with a few arrows. There was also an assortment of smaller items, but they revealed little about their owner.

The man sat facing the only door into the room. All was silent. Suddenly, the door burst open, and a figure carrying a torch emerged. The newcomer's features were blurred, as the light from the torch only allowed the figure's silhouette to be visible. Despite the sudden disturbance and the appearance of the stranger, the man seated on the rug did not stir.

"Are you Azka?" asked a gruff male voice.

The man on the rug remained silent.

"Are you Azka?" the stranger asked, a little louder and taking a step into the room.

"I am he," the seated man said without looking up. His voice was deep and impassive.

"I am here to give this to you," the stranger said, holding out a roll of parchment and a small bag of what sounded like money. "The Guild has a new mission for you."

When Azka remained silent and unmoving, the stranger became frustrated and said, "Did you hear me, Azka?"

"I hear your words, messenger," Azka said, lifting his head to reveal his face. His skin and eyes were as dark as pitch. No emotion showed on his face, which caused the other man to falter and step backward. "Leave it on the floor and go."

The man dropped the parchment and money bag in front of Azka, bowed, and disappeared. Azka picked up the money bag first and weighed it in his hand. Based on the number of coins, he deduced that the target must be local. He knew that the way an assignment worked was the Guild provided an amount they felt reasonable to complete the mission, including travel, room and board, etc. The assassin's fee was whatever was left after expenses.

Azka then picked up the parchment and unrolled it. He read the contents carefully, which confirmed his theory about the target, then placed the end of the parchment in the candle's flame. He pocketed the money bag and stood to gather his possessions, carefully rolling up the ancient rug. He buckled the sword to his belt and hoisted the bow, quiver of arrows, and bag onto his shoulders. Then he turned, blew out the candle, and walked out into the night.

✳   ✳   ✳   ✳

The city of Nenholm was dark and silent. The windows and doors of the shops and houses were closed tight against the darkness without. Azka moved silently through the shadows, avoiding any patrols by the City Watch. Nenholm was one of the most corrupt cities in Alethia, but that also meant the guards were corrupt also. Azka considered this as mere child's play when compared to his other missions.

It had been several days since he'd received his mission. His target was a low-ranking city official whose actions were bankrupting the city. Although greed was never in short supply in Nenholm, unbridled it could spell disaster, especially when acted upon by those in power.

One life for a thousand, Azka thought. *Undeserving...perhaps.* He did not care about how others justified or condemned his actions. Despite his loyalty to the Guild of Assassins, he was no fool. His many years of being an assassin had taught him to distrust the Guild's reports. When he took on a mission, he studied his target carefully before taking a life. It was his decision and his blade that would change the course of history. Yet it was not just directing the course of history that caused him to take care in which lives he decided to take. It was his concern in the condition of his soul that often stayed his blade. His own code, outside the normal Code of Assassins, dictated that he never harmed the innocent.

Movement on the road ahead brought Azka out of his contemplative state. He waited. Three people emerged from the shadows, two men in chainmail with swords at their sides and a smaller man in a bright-colored robe. The moonlight shined on the silver lines that ran along the hem of his robes, marking the man as a low-level official. His target had arrived, but Azka was patient. His mission was to eliminate the official, not the guards. Though the guards of this city were seldom free from the corrupt influences of Nenholm, Azka never took a life without need. In addition, Azka had studied this target for many days and learned he was a predictable man of habit.

The target was a frequenter of a local bar, where he often became inebriated. Around midnight he would stagger down to the brothel at the end of this street, where he took the same harlot each night. Azka learned much from this harlot, with whom he had spoken many times. He paid his fair, but he himself never took the woman. Though she tried to entice him each time, he resisted her advances.

After his trip to the brothel, he and his guards would walk to the corner of the street where a larger house stood. This was the home of the captain of the City Watch. Azka guessed that the man had some sort of grudge against the captain for the official made a point to stop and relieve himself on the captain's back doorstep, which was down the alleyway. The official's guards never accompanied the man down the alley when he did this, so Azka knew this was his opportunity.

The official was nearing the alley. Azka moved further down into the shadows, his muscles tensed. The man was staggering toward him. Azka readied his blade. The man stooped to pull up his robes clumsily. Azka moved fluidly and silently. In two lightning-fast moves, Azka hit the man in the side of the neck, incapacitating him and preventing any noise from leaving the man's lips. Then, he brought his blade through the right side of the man's back. Azka held him there for a moment and then pushed him forward. The man crumpled in a heap at Azka's feet.

Azka slipped from the alley and moved silently through the shadows. He knew that in a few movements the guards would investigate the long delay in the official's return. He was several streets away when the cry went out...

* * * *

Several days later, Azka sat crossed-legged in his little room, meditating in front of a small candle. He sat unmoving, with his head bowed in apparent prayer. He sat in the same place, facing the only door into the room. His thoughts were on the last man he'd killed. He had no doubts that the man was guilty and deserved to die for his crimes against the people of this city, but there were hundreds of greedy disreputable men in this city.

Azka wondered why this man was so dangerous. Despite his best attempts to learn the truth, his informants had only been able to reveal the man's habits, not his background or any of his activities that would justify the Guild's death sentence.

After many long hours pondering and meditating, light and sound interrupted his silent reflection. It was night again, and a figure holding a torch stood in his doorway. The figure's features were blurred again, as the light only allowed his or her silhouette to be visible. As before, the sudden disturbance and the appearance of the stranger did not faze Azka. He remained seated on the rug, head bowed.

"Azka?" the newcomer asked, this time quietly and reverently. The voice was female, and though it caught Azka by surprise, he did not outwardly show it. He simply looked up at her with mild interest.

"I am here to deliver a message," she said, stepping into the room and pulling back her hood to reveal long brown hair and piercing blue eyes. She held out roll of parchment. "The Masters demand your presence at once."

"What is your name?" Azka asked bluntly.

"A-Annet," she replied nervously.

"Very well, leave the roll of parchment," Azka said, studying her carefully.

"Will...will you be coming then?" she stammered, setting the parchment down in front of him.

"I will, thank you, messenger," he said. His voice was measured, but his eyes conveyed his whole meaning—*leave now.*

The woman bowed and disappeared. Azka stood and once again gathered his possessions, blew out the candle, and walked out again into the night.

His direction was aimed at a large building in the middle of the city. The building was old and decaying. A single tower rose from its midst. Most people believed the building was a blight upon the city's landscape, but the owner of the building refused to sell the property to anyone. In fact, anyone who made any attempt to purchase the building and property often disappeared. Because of this, the building decayed in peace.

A group of people were conversing near the building, so Azka waited patiently until they moved down the street. He then slid out from the shadows and into the building. He moved a rug to reveal a trapdoor, opened the door, and descended a dark stairwell that led out onto a long corridor lit with many torches. Azka walked the length of the corridor and opened a thick wooded door at its end. He found himself in a large dimly lit room. Across the room and hidden in the shadows sat four hooded figures behind a long stone table—the Masters of the Guild of Assassins.

Azka waited patiently, for he knew to enter without leave was forbidden. After a long moment, one of the hooded figures spoke.

"Enter, Azka," said a solemn voice. The voice was clearly a woman's. "We've been expecting you."

Azka walked to the center of the room and stood upon a small circular dais positioned there. He bowed low but did not speak.

"Rise, Azka," said a man's voice coming from the figure on the far right. "It is good to see you. I trust your most recent mission was a success?"

"Indeed," Azka said, inclining his head toward the man.

"We knew, of course, but we also wished to congratulate you."

Azka was confused but did not allow that feeling to reach his face. His expression remained vague. Why would the Masters summon him here only to issue their congratulations for what he believed was a simple assignment? Azka, ever patient, waited and hoped that their reason for this summons would reveal itself.

"Azka," the woman, who had been the first to speak, said. "You have served the Guild well for many years, and you have never failed to complete an assignment." Azka did not speak, so the woman continued. "A matter of greatest importance has arisen, which must be dealt with promptly and without fail. We cannot trust this task to anyone but our best assassins. That is why we have chosen you, Azka and Annet, to handle these assignments."

Azka turned and saw the same young woman who'd visited him earlier enter the chamber. When she reached the center dais, she bowed low and glanced briefly at Azka.

He regarded her with great interest, wondering how one so young could be trusted with the Guild's greatest tasks.

Azka asked, calmly turning back to the Masters, "Who is the target?"

"You will find the information you need and your fee on the table to your left. Annet, you will find the same on your right," said the woman, gesturing toward the table. "We know that you seek news of your sister, Aylen."

"Aylen?" Azka asked, his normally emotionless façade supplanted by concern for his sister.

"You may find information during this assignment that will lead to her," the Master continued, unabashed. "Azka, know that we are giving you a choice this time. Should you take this assignment, you will be bound to its completion. Know this also that if you fail, your life is forfeit. If the choice comes down to your sister or the target, you must choose wisely."

"I understand," Azka said, bowing yet again.

"Then each of you must make your choice," the woman said as the door to the chamber opened. "You may accept the assignment or leave the chambers."

Neither Azka nor Annet hesitated but went straight to the tables. The only items sitting upon them were a single lit candle, a small roll of parchment, and a large bag of money. Azka weighed the bag, which was very heavy. He opened it and, to his surprise, he found it filled with golden crowns. The contents of this bag could buy a small castle, lands, and soldiers to protect it for the rest of his life. He did not need to read the parchment to know who his target must be—a king.

3

RINIEL

"We praise thee, O God, for the blessings Thou hast bestowed upon us. We thank Thee that we are better than the infidels who sin against Thee. Let our good works save us from Thy wrath," the archbishop said in a ringing voice.

Riniel Aurelia opened her deep brown eyes and raised her head up ever so slightly. Everyone had their heads bowed and their eyes closed. The chapel was silent save for the voice of Archbishop Julius Durante. He was filling the air with words as usual, and Riniel could not help disdaining the man for his pompous attitude. If Christ calls his followers to humility, why did every bishop she had ever met act as if everyone else was a sinner except himself. As if everyone was born in sin except those destined to become bishops or archbishops or popes. She hated coming to mass not because she didn't believe in God but because so many of the Church's leaders spoke and behaved contrary to what Christ taught his followers. She came only because she was the Princess of Aurelia and her father wished it. He was very devout and believed that the royal family must set the example for the rest of the kingdom. She sighed and wished she was somewhere else. This, of course, made her feel guilty because she did want to please her father.

She had so many questions regarding "his faith." She called it so because she was not sure that she shared it anymore. *If God was so gracious and merciful,* she thought, *why did bad things happen? If God wants what is best for us, why did He allow so much pain and misery to happen in the world? If God loves me, why did He allow my mother to die?* As she asked herself that last question, a tear began to run down her cheek. She quickly brushed it aside and dabbed her eyes with her handkerchief. She hated crying because once she started, it was hard to stop; plus it always gave her a headache afterward.

Everyone lifted their heads and said "amen" in unison. Riniel didn't because she hadn't listened to a thing the old man had said. The mass goers rose and began to leave. Riniel remained seated until everyone was gone. She sat in silence for several minutes, then she bowed her head and began to pray.

"God," she said, her voice barely more than a whisper. "You know I have my doubts and that I am no saint. You know that I am still angry with You because You took my mother from me, but please bring my father back to me. Please don't take him from me too." Riniel sat silently in the chapel for several more minutes then rose and walked out.

✳   ✳   ✳   ✳

When the trumpets sounded from the watchtowers on the walls of the city of Ethriel, Riniel was quietly reading a book in her chambers. The ringing triumphal resound echoed off the walls of the room, causing her eyes to jump from the page she was reading and turn toward the nearby window. She jumped to her feet and threw down the book she'd been reading. Her light-brown, waist-length hair flew behind her as she ran to the window. Looking down across the city of Ethriel, she saw a column of men on horseback, over a hundred strong, riding up the Citadel Way.

Even from this distance and minus the shining crown of Alethia upon his brow, she recognized the man leading the column. Her father, King Greyfuss Aurelia, had finally returned.

Her face broke into a smile as she watched the column make its way up the street. She turned and ran to the door of her chambers. She threw it open to find a familiar face. Her guardian, Sir Jordan Reese, stood in the doorway smiling down at her. For the brief moment she stood there she noticed that, despite his age, Sir Jordan's smile seemed to melt away the years from his face.

"Princess," he said with a bow.

"My father has returned!" she exclaimed, breaking protocol and hugging him around the middle.

He did not return the hug, but Riniel did not care. She had not been this happy since her father's departure two months ago. She released Sir Jordan and ran past him to the spiral staircase. Her descent lacked the poise and grace of a princess, but Riniel did not care at the moment. All the lessons concerning etiquette and protocol drilled into her head by her instructor when she was younger were forgotten in her feeling of exuberance.

She reached the courtyard as the citadel gates opened to receive the king.

"Father!" she shouted, forgetting herself.

She stood there blushing as many eyes looked at her, laughing. Her father dismounted and began walking toward her. What little restraint she had left broke, and she found herself running full sprint toward him. He opened his arms just before she collided with him. He stumbled backward a step, chuckling deeply as they embraced.

"Daughter," the king said in a deep, rich voice. "You act as though I'd been gone a year instead of two months."

"I had heard news of your battle on the northern frontier but nothing of its outcomes," she said, looking up at him with tears of joy glistening in her eyes. "Why was there no word of your coming?"

"I am sorry, daughter, for worrying you," he said with a smile. "Lord Kinison suggested sending no rider for fear of ambush on our way home."

A man in his late twenties stepped forward. Riniel looked up into Kinison Ravenloch's intense blue eyes and fought back a smile. Riniel had known Kinison since childhood and regarded him as an older brother.

"So it is you I am to blame for weeks of worry," she said, glaring at Kinison. Her facial expression was one of anger, but her eyes were smiling.

"It was I who convinced the king. Pray, dear Princess, grant this poor soldier your pardon," he said, winking and bowing low.

She released her father and embraced Kinison.

"I am forgiven, I take it?" he asked, laughing and hugging her. "I figured you'd harbor resentment against me for at least a month."

"I suppose I should be grateful," Riniel said, releasing him and hugging her father again. "You did bring my father back to me."

"All right, daughter. I cannot have you smothering me and the Lord Commander of the Guardians," he said, still smiling. Then turning to his men, he said, "Men, we have returned victorious from battle. Tonight we shall feast and be merry in the Great Hall."

A cheer went up from the men that followed them as they walked out of the courtyard and into the Great Hall.

✳   ✳   ✳   ✳

It was nightfall when the celebration began. The Great Hall had not looked this decadent since Christmas. The walls were hung with the banners of every great house in Alethia; the largest was blue with a large golden lion representing the House of Aurelia. Musicians serenaded the guests, filling the hall with rhythms in which to dance and enjoy. Five long wooden tables ran the length of the hall, each piled high with every food dish imaginable.

Torches hung along the walls, and six great chandeliers hung from the ceiling, giving light to the entire hall.

Riniel stood in the doorway, gazing at the spectacle. She was wearing a purple dress with silver flowers sewn into it. Her eyes followed the long tables to the high dais, which held the great white marble throne of Alethia. On it sat her father, Greyfuss Aurelia. Next to the king stood Kinison Ravenloch, in his place of honor as Lord Commander of the Guardians. When she caught his eye, they exchanged smiles. Riniel sighed, thinking how relieving it felt to have her father and childhood friend back home.

She turned her eyes to the other guests, purposely avoiding Kinison's gaze. She saw many lords and ladies mingling about the room as well as servants and cupbearers weaving in and out of the small groups clustered around the tables. Archbishop Julius Durante was following the food, as usual. Though he'd been appointed only a few months ago, Riniel already disliked the man.

"Good evening, Princess," said a voice from behind her.

Riniel started and turned quickly around. Her eyes fell upon a man with black hair and eyes just as dark. He was wearing a black cape and a red tunic, which bore the crest of a black wolf.

"Lord Noliono!" she exclaimed, stepping back. A momentary panic and fear gripped her heart. Noliono's face wore a pleasant smile, yet Riniel always felt alarmed and guarded when she was in Noliono's presence. The feeling often faded but never disappeared completely.

"Pardon me for startling you, my Princess," he said, smiling and taking Riniel's hand, kissing it gently. "It is so lovely to see you here tonight."

"The pleasure is mine," she said stiffly but politely.

"I know that you must be even happier than I am that King Greyfuss has returned safely from the frontiers."

"I am indeed."

"It is truly fortune who favors our bold king. Any lesser man would have perished if so many foes had fallen upon him. Your father is a great man," Noliono said.

Riniel could not help noting a hint of disappointment in Noliono's voice. *Was he disappointed that her father had survived the battle? Surely not...*

"Good evening, Princess Riniel," said a jovial voice from her right.

Riniel turned away from Noliono to see an older man and a younger man walking toward her. She recognized the older man as Lord Anson Thayn. He was short, stocky, and had short graying brown hair and brown eyes. The younger man was unknown to her. He had blond hair, brown eyes, and the healthy build of youth. He was taller than Lord Anson by several inches, but he was sullen and slouched, so his height appeared less. Apart from his demeanor, Riniel thought the young man quite handsome. Both Lord Anson and the young man wore tunics of blue with a great white eagle on it, the crest of the House of Thayn.

When Lord Anson reached Riniel, he took her hand and kissed it gently.

"My dear princess, please allow me to..." but Lord Anson faltered as his eyes fell upon Lord Noliono. "Lord Noliono, I am pleased to see you as well."

Riniel could tell by the change in Lord Anson's tone that this was not true.

"Lord Anson," Noliono said, extending his hand. Lord Anson shook it once and let go. "And you were just about to introduce your companion?"

"Yes," Lord Anson said, turning to the young man. "This is my third son, Ardyn Thayn."

Riniel turned and looked upon Ardyn. He had blond hair and brown eyes. He was nice-looking but, to Riniel, he seemed timid. When Riniel held out her hand, Ardyn took it and kissed it, but he seemed nervous and reluctant.

They locked eyes for a moment, and Riniel thought she saw a hint of attraction in his eyes. She looked away quickly, blushing slightly.

"A pleasure, princess," Ardyn said, though his voice was shaky.

"And what brings you and your son to Ethriel, Lord Anson?" Noliono said, eyeing Ardyn with peculiar interest.

"I am meeting with Sir Ramond Kludge in the morning in the hopes of obtaining a position with the Guardians for my son," Lord Anson said proudly. "The boy must be good at something other than book learning and chasing after old fairytales."

Riniel looked at Ardyn and noticed that the young man's countenance fell at his father's words. He hung his head as if ashamed.

"The Guardians of the Citadel is a noble order of knights and soldiers who protect the king and his citadel. They would be well to accept him, I'm sure," Lord Noliono said then moved away from them.

Lord Anson sniffed then bowed to Riniel and moved away in the opposite direction. Ardyn followed in his wake, though he looked back at Riniel more than once.

Riniel's eyes followed Noliono as he made his way over into a far corner of the room, where he joined another man who appeared to be waiting for him. As they stood whispering, curiosity got the better of her, and she made her way over toward them. She slipped behind a pillar that was between her and the two men and listened closely.

"Is all in place, Sir Kludge?" came Noliono's voice.

"All is ready except for finding a scapegoat, my lord," said the harsh and the grisly voice of Sir Ramond Kludge.

"I may have just met someone who would serve this purpose for us, Sir Kludge, provided you allow him into the Guardians."

"Who?" Kludge asked eagerly.

Riniel's heart was beating fast. A conspiracy plan was being revealed right now, and she was eavesdropping on it's architects.

She never found out what Noliono was planning or who Noliono intended to blame, for at that moment a voice behind her said, "Here you are!"

Riniel jumped backward into someone's arms, and she might have screamed had she not recognized Lord Kinison's face.

"Are you all right?" he said, concerned.

"Fine, fine," she said, trying to catch her breath. "What is it?"

"I came over to ask you something, if you are willing?" Kinison asked playfully.

"Yes, of course," Riniel said, still trying to compose herself.

"May I have this dance, my Princess?" he said kindly and held his outstretched hand toward her.

She looked up and smiled at Kinison, all thoughts of what she had just overheard driven out of her mind. "Wouldn't you rather dance with your wife, Sarah?"

"Yes, I would," Kinison said with a small chuckle, but unfortunately she is sick and decided not to come."

"Oh, I'm so sorry to hear that. I will be sure to look in on her tomorrow."

"I'm sure she would like that," Kinison said, smiling. "Now I ask again, would you like to dance?"

"Very well, Lord Kinison, I'd be honored to dance with you," Riniel said, laughing and curtsying. She took his hand and followed him out onto the dance floor.

They slowly danced around the room in silence for a time.

"I'm sorry that Sarah couldn't be here," Riniel said at length.

"As do I," he said, a look of sadness on his face.

"I want to thank you for bringing my father home safely," she said.

"You're most welcome, princess." He smiled.

"I feared for you and father. Sarah and I went to the chapel daily to pray for your safe return."

"Well, the Almighty must have heard your prayers for we are both safely home."

"I know she will be happy to see you," Kinison said, his smile returning.

A moment later the music stopped, and a hush fell on the room. Kinison and Riniel broke away from each other and both looked toward the dais. Her father was standing, and Lord Noliono was whispering something in his ear. Her father's continence fell. The king's eyes rested on Kinison. Without a word, Kinison immediately crossed the room, climbed the dais, and stood at the king's side. The king shot him a meaningful glance then turned to the crowd.

"Honored guests," the king began, a smile on his face again. "I am afraid that you must continue this celebration without me for I must attend to a few affairs of state."

Even from across the room, Riniel noted that her father's smile did not reach his eyes. There was a general murmuring that ran throughout the room, but the king, the members of the Council of Lords, and several Guardians left without another word.

Riniel remained, mingling about and smiling as she knew she must. Behind the smile, she wondered what had been so important that the king and the Council of Lords had to meet on the night of the king's return. She sighed as the two most important men in her life were absent yet again.

4

NOLIONO

The chamber of the Council of Lords was full of the noise of heated debate, yet Noliono Noland sat silently surveying the room over the tips of his fingers. His elbows rested on a large and ornately carved circular table made of oak. The din around him did not faze Noliono in the slightest. The truth was that he'd expected as much and more by the end of this meeting.

His eyes moved to a large and intricately drawn map displayed on the wall opposite him—a map of the kingdom of Alethia, perfectly represented except that this map had been drawn before the annexation of the island of Nendyn. What a shame, yet that was the nature of maps. Even before they are finished, they can already be outdated.

His eyes returned to the inhabitants of the room. There were two guards at each of the two doorways leading from the chamber: the large front entrance with its great double-hinged oak doors and the small side door toward the back of the chamber. One of the guards was Ramond Kludge, a lieutenant in the Guardians of the Citadel and his inside source. The Kludge family owed its allegiance to the House of Noland since his ancestor granted Symon Kludge the Barony of the Eastern Wastes. Since then, a

Kludge has remained at the side of every lord of the House of Noland. They exchanged a knowing look, then Noliono turned his gaze to the other inhabitants. There were around a dozen people in the room, but he concentrated on the eight who were wearing golden rings. He included himself in this group, for these were the High Lords of Alethia. Each ring, he knew, bore the family crest of a ruling House of Alethia. He turned for a moment to his own ring, which bore the Great Black Wolf of the House of Noland, marking him as high lord and member of the Lords' Council. His gaze turned to the short, stocky figure of Lord Anson Thayn. House of Thayn ruled a large area of land north of the River Vedmore and west of the Mountains of Eodar. Noliono loathed the man, and his loathing only grew more every time he saw him.

To Lord Anson's left was Lord Renton Myr. The House of Myr controlled the lands south of the Mountains of Eodar, west of the River Rockwicke, north of the Iron Hills, and east of the Forest of Oakwood. Lord Renton Myr was a tall, older man with a gray beard and a fiery temper. Noliono smiled as he mused about how easily Lord Renton could be manipulated by simply angering him or appealing to his pride.

Next to Lord Renton and on Noliono's right sat the king's nephew, Gefric Aurelia. Since King Greyfuss was the true head of the Aurelian family, it was tradition for the elected king of Alethia to name the closest male relation as Lord Regent of the house and lands. Lord Gefric was a young and arrogant man, with brown hair and hazel eyes. In Noliono's opinion, Gefric was a dull and predictable man; easily manipulated by the slightest appeal to his honor or by questioning his family's historical importance. The House of Aurelia ruled over the lands between the River Ryparian in the west and the Gray Mountains in the east. On the southern border of the lands of Aurelia, beyond the Forest of Whitewood and the River Belwash, lies the Pass of

Stenc, which divides the kingdom between north and south. The pass is the only way to reach northern Alethia by land.

On Noliono's left sat Gaven Soron. Gaven Soron was originally the head of a minor house, but when the head of the Farod family died, Gaven became Lord Regent of the House of Farod. The House of Farod controlled the lands north of the River Waterdale and east of the Sea of Farod, including the Forest of Elmwood. It stood to reason that the Farod family would soon be supplanted by the House of Soron, but only time would tell. Lord Gaven was a large and portly man, with dark-brown hair and a stern face. Noliono found that Lord Gaven was often of the same mind as himself when it came to ruling the kingdom.

To Lord Gaven's left stood Lord Atton Nenlad, ruler of the island of Nendyn, which translates to "westernmost." Lord Atton and the other members of the House of Nenlad were all darker skinned than the rest of Alethians, with eyes like pitch, and stern faces. His was a reserved people who long resisted joining the rest of Alethia long ago. Next to Lord Atton sat Lord Wesley Rydel, head of the House of Rydel. The House of Rydel ruled over the lands west of Oakwood Forest, south of the River Vedmore, and north of the River Westmore. This land was given to Reese Rydel over five hundred years ago by Lord Ardys Thayn. Since then, the Rydel Family had prospered and has become a prominent member of the great houses of Alethia.

Finally, on Lord Rydel's left sat Lord Markus Eddon, leader of the House of Eddon. This house was also a young house, who ruled over a narrow strip of land between the Iron Hills in the south and the River Westmore in the north, which was given to them over two hundred years ago by the House of Myr following the War of Ascension.

These eight men comprised the Council of Lords, whose purpose was to elect a king and advise him as he ruled the kingdom. Although the election of a king for life was the initial and primary purpose of the Council of Lords, several centuries ago the Council adopted an advisory mandate to the king. The king, once elected, held the absolute final decision; however, since the Council of Lords was made up by the leaders of the most powerful houses in the kingdom, the kings of Alethia have been forced to listen to their counsel. Each lord was attended by a page, at least until the meeting began.

Noliono turned to his own page to demand a glass of wine. He tried not to show it outwardly, but the stress of this situation was causing many ailments in his digestive tract. Everything must go right or—he dared not consider the consequences of failure. The page returned quickly, and Noliono took a long draft. Just as he was placing his cup on the table, the great oaken front doors opened, and the king entered along with Lord Kinison Ravenloch and Julius Durante, the Archbishop of Alethia, and another man with his hood covering his face. The various conversations stopped abruptly, and the lords clapped their hands while taking their seats. The rest of the room's occupants cleared out, and the guards exited also, pulling the doors closed behind them.

King Greyfuss seated himself and surveyed the silent room. In particular his gaze fell on Noliono. Kinison, Julius, and the stranger stood to the side of the king.

"I apologize for the lateness of this session, my lords, but Lord Noliono impressed upon me the need for urgency," the King said with obvious disdain and exasperation. "Lord Noliono, please proceed."

"Your Majesty, my words are for yours and the Council members' ears only. May I inquire the name of this man you bring into our midst?" Noliono said, rising from his seat and pointing to the man under the hood and cloak.

"You may indeed, Lord Noliono," the king answered gruffly. The man removed his hood, and every lord in the room gasped in surprise. "This is Galanor, renowned historian of Alethia. He is here to advise me regarding the current situation."

"You invite this wandering old storyteller to advise you, sire?" Noliono said, glaring hard at Galanor. "He is a charlatan and a fool."

"Watch your tongue, my lord," Greyfuss growled. "He is here at my request, and you will respect him in my presence."

Noliono bowed but kept this gaze on Galanor.

"Proceed, Lord Noliono," the king ordered, sitting back in his seat. "The hour grows late."

"Your Majesty and fellow lords of the Council," Noliono began, turning his gaze on the rest of the room. "You have been made aware of the attack on the king's company on the northern frontier. What you may not know is that this attack was merely a foray into our kingdom to test our defenses by the kingdom of Nordyke."

"Lord Noliono," Lord Anson Thayn said, interrupting. "We know that the attack on the king was planned and executed by trained soldiers, but what proof do you have that these other incursions are anything more than raids made by outlaws and renegades?"

"I have this." Noliono gestured to a piece of parchment lying on the table in front of him.

"And what is that?" Lord Anson asked with clear disdain in his voice.

"Galanor, you are a master of lore and writings. Would you please authenticate this document?" Noliono said, passing the document over to the older man. Then turning to Lord Anson, Noliono said, "This is a report from Peter Astley, Baron of Ironwall Fortress, and Alastor Warde, Baron of Ytemest Fortress. In it, Baron Astley and Baron Warde reported seventeen separate incursions by raiders from Nordyke in the last two months. The last raid occurred when the king's company was attacked near the foothills of the Gray Mountains."

Noliono turned back to Galanor, who was studying the document carefully. After a few long moments, he looked up and nodded.

"Let me look at that!" Lord Anson demanded.

Galanor looked momentarily affronted but held out the parchment, which Lord Anson snatched from him.

"It has both Baron Astley's and Baron Warde's seals and signatures, Your Majesty," Lord Anson said after several long moments of scrutinizing the document. "I believe this report to be genuine."

"Why did neither of these men report this to me when I was last at Ironwall and Ytemest?" King Greyfuss asked, his right hand massaging his forehead.

"The report indicated that they wished to wait and receive more information first," Lord Anson replied, summarizing the document.

"Does he indicate why he believes the number of raids have increased and to what purpose?" the king asked.

"He states that the number of raiders in each incursion has grown with their successes. He also predicts that a major incursion is coming soon, and he begs for reinforcements," Lord Anson replied.

"What do you make of this, Galanor?" Greyfuss asked, turning to the older man.

"Your Majesty knows the history of war between Alethia and Nordyke. These raids may be the precursors of war, but they may just be the actions of opportunistic men looking for a cause for violence."

The king nodded and was silent for a moment.

"Your Majesty, please do not heed this old man's counsel. It is clear from the evidence that a war is coming," Lord Noliono began, but the king cut across him.

"No, Lord Noliono, it is not clear," King Greyfuss said with a heavy sigh and straightened in his seat. "What is clear to me is that bandits are raiding into Alethia, and Baron Astley cannot keep them at bay. Nothing more."

"Your Majesty..." Noliono began.

"Enough!" the King shouted, pounding his fist on the table. "There has been peace between the kingdoms of Alethia and Nordyke for fifteen years, and I have received no word of hostile intentions from Prince Ivan or any of the lords of Nordyke. I will heed the Barons' request and send an additional hundred men to augment their garrisons at Ironwall and Ytemest so that these outlaws may be dealt with, but I will not risk open war with Nordyke."

The king stood as if to leave, and the lords rose in respect.

"Please, Your Majesty, reconsider this report," Noliono said earnestly.

"I have given you my decision, Lord Noliono. This is not the first time that Baron Astley or you, Noliono, have beaten the war drums unnecessarily," King Greyfuss said sternly and turned toward the front entrance. "This Council is now in recess."

Noliono glared hard at Galanor as he waited for the king and his advisors to depart; then he turned to the other lords who were gathering their papers to leave.

"My fellow lords, please remain," Noliono said with his head bowed. "We have much to discuss."

✳   ✳   ✳   ✳

The throne room was dark and empty save for the lone man— the man seated on his throne. All his advisors and courtiers had left, and as the sun set beyond the beautiful stained-glass windows, all the light and life seemed to drain from the room. As the darkness fell, the king remained upon his throne reading, or rather staring at a piece of parchment reporting strange troop movements south of the Pass of Stenc. Noliono watched from the shadows as the king let the parchment fall to the floor and leaned forward in his seat. The torchlight, which had been held at bay by the great blue canopy overhead, now fell on the king's lined and careworn face. He placed his face in his hands and began rubbing his eyes.

Noliono moved slightly, and the king did not stir. The torches, which lined the hall, left small gaps of darkness between each of them. The sun had now set, and no other light came from the windows overhead. Noliono watched cautiously as the king's right hand moved ever so slowly to the hilt of his sword. Noliono knew the king had heard his footfalls and chose to reveal himself. From the shadows, he emerged slowly with his hands to his sides, his long black cape barely moving behind him. He watched the king's face emerge from behind his hands and saw recognition in his eyes. The king's eyes narrowed, and Noliono noted that the king's hand remained on the hilt of his sword. Noliono moved to the center of the room near the dais and held his hands outstretched to the sides as a sign of peace.

"I beg your pardon, Your Majesty," Noliono said softly and bowed slightly. "I did not mean to startle you."

"What brings you to my hall at this hour, Lord Noliono?" King Greyfuss asked with a hint of sarcasm.

"I come to you, King Greyfuss, to somehow sway you from the decision you made earlier this evening," Noliono replied.

"Oh?" the king said in mock surprise.

"Yes, sire, regarding the recent problems on the northern frontier," Noliono said. "The other members of the Council of Lords feel that your Majesty's handling of the current situation with the raiders from Nordyke is...how shall I say...overly cautious."

At this Greyfuss stood and took several steps forward off the dais on which the throne sat. Noliono watched gleefully as the king's face reddened and his eyes flashed, yet Noliono did not allow his feelings to show on his face.

"Take care with your words, Lord Noliono," the king said softly yet threateningly.

"But sire," Noliono said smoothly and bowed again. "The Council of Lords is unanimous in its position, which, I need not remind Your Majesty, is quite unprecedented."

"I will hear no more of this!" Greyfuss shouted, waving his left hand vaguely. "Your words have been heard in council, and I have endeared your arguments, as well as those of the other lords, already. I do not need to hear them again. My decision is made."

The king turned to climb back onto the dais, but as he did so, Noliono drew out his own sword, the sharp ringing of steel unsheathed echoing off the walls. The king turned quickly back toward Noliono.

"You dare draw your sword in my hall!" Greyfuss asked incredulously.

"Your Majesty will pardon me, but it seems my arguments require a stronger point," Noliono said, smiling darkly at his own small joke.

"You are a greater fool than I realized, Noliono. For challenging me, I will have you executed. Guards! Guards!"

The king's words echoed through the hall but quickly fell silent. The anticipated sound of expedient footfalls and the clatter of spears and swords were not forthcoming. Greyfuss's gaze darted to each of the four entrances leading into the Great Hall, but no sound came from beyond them.

"I am afraid Your Majesty's men will not be joining us as they are indisposed at the moment," Noliono said, now unable to conceal his glee.

"What have you done?" Greyfuss asked. The king's fear and anger were now betrayed in his voice.

"When Your Majesty refused to heed my warnings and the warnings of the Council earlier tonight, it became clear that a change in leadership might be necessary to protect the realm."

"Protect the realm?" Greyfuss said with a laugh. "You mean you saw a chance division between myself and the Council, and you chose to take it."

"Aptly put, Your Majesty," Noliono said, his smile gone and his eyes narrowing in anger. "Yet my ambitions are tempered by the desire for the good of the realm."

"Your words are meaningless, for I see your true purpose. You seek power and your own glory, Noliono. Do not pretend what you do is anything but for your own gain!"

"Your leadership will lead us to ruin. A new king must rise!" Noliono shouted.

His anger was boiling over now, and he lunged halfheartedly at the king. Greyfuss fell back and drew his own sword.

"Your intent is now clearly stated, Noliono...treason!" Greyfuss yelled.

"If it must be so...then let it *be* so!"

At this Noliono leapt forward onto the dais and made a broad swipe at the king's head. Greyfuss parried the blow and pushed Noliono's blade aside, kicking him off the dais. Noliono felt himself falling backward and the pain of landing on the hard stone floor. Yet he righted himself just as the king ran forward, bringing his sword down hard at Noliono's head. Noliono righted himself just in time to block the king's blade. The two men broke apart and began circling one another, each looking for the other's weak point.

"Your Majesty's wits are not as slow as he pretends in Council. Your strength also remains despite your years."

"And your reflexes and stamina are also keen, Noliono, despite your slow mindedness" the king retorted jeeringly.

"Despite your wits, Your Majesty, you will feel the bite of my blade because you refuse to see reason."

"Reason!" Greyfuss shouted incredulously. "For over a hundred years, the House of Aurelia has led Alethia. Those kings, Greyfuss Aurelia among them, were elected by the Council of Lords, each in their own right, to guard this kingdom from its enemies without...and within its borders."

At these words, Noliono dropped his guard ever so slightly, and he felt the sting of doubt. Greyfuss took advantage of this and flew at Noliono. Yet Noliono's reflexes sprang to life, and he blocked the king's attack. He then grabbed the king's tunic and hurled him into a nearby pillar. Greyfuss slammed into the pillar, which knocked the wind out of him, and fell to the floor. A moment later, Noliono brought his sword down on Greyfuss's undefended head, yet the king brought his sword up just in time to block the blow. Greyfuss stood shakily and pushed Noliono away from him.

The two men began circling one another again, each searching for an opening in the other's guard. Noliono began to panic as he began to doubt whether he could defeat the king before the Guardians returned. This was supposed to be a quick duel, and he was supposed to emerge victorious. He took some comfort that Greyfuss was limping slightly and seemed out of breath.

"You will not succeed, Noliono," he stammered between gasps. "I will not allow you to lead my kingdom down the path to war. I will live solely to prevent that."

"We are already at war, sire. It is *you* who will not accept it. If Your Majesty refuses to defend this kingdom, then I will," Noliono retorted.

He made a feigned jab, causing Greyfuss to move his guard, but before Noliono could take advantage of the king's mistake, several things happened at once. Both he and the king heard a sharp twang and a hiss. Then Greyfuss grunted as the crossbow bolt struck him in the back. The king lurched forward and fell onto his knees, his blood spilling onto the floor of the Great Hall. Noliono stared in disbelief. The king looked up at him for a moment then began to fall forward. Noliono dropped his sword and caught the king as he fell. He cradled the king's broken body in his arms and looked down into Greyfuss's eyes. Defeated, Noliono watched as Greyfuss's spirit began to slip away. Tears were welling up inside Noliono's eyes. It was not supposed to end this way.

ARDYN

Ardyn Thayn was riding fast on his white war horse. The wind whipped his riding cloak, the sun shining on his armor, and his drawn sword shone like a beacon of light. He was nearing his destination. His heart was beating fast, but not from fear. Excitement flooded his veins as he brought his horse to a stop before the dark fortress, which rose up out of the steep cliff face. High above him in the tallest tower stood Princess Riniel Aurelia, his love. He called to her as he dismounted. She smiled and waved at him. He ran to the gates, and just as he was about to force them open, he woke up.

Ardyn looked around and found that he had been dozing at his post on the ramparts above the gates leading to the Citadel of Ethriel. He shook his head and looked at himself. As a member of the Guardians, he wore the traditional blue cloak fastened by a golden brooch shaped like the head of a roaring lion, the symbol of the House of Aurelia. For over a hundred years, the symbols and colors of the House of Aurelia had been worn by those guarding the Aurelian kings. Though these trappings did not distinguish him as a member of the Guardians, it was the silver shield pinned on his outer cloak. The simple silver shield was adopted by the Guardians of the Citadel as a means to distinguish them and as an attempt to prevent any allegiance to a particular house. Under the cloak Ardyn wore a shirt of metal rings over a broiled leather tunic.

As he stood there in the cool night air dozing, his grasp on the spear he was holding must have slipped ever so slightly, causing him to stumble forward. When he had awoken with a start, Ardyn cursed as he realized where he was. He turned his angry gaze out on the city. The sun had set behind the horizon, and the city was growing dark and quiet. He looked down both sides of the wall to make sure that no one was looking then sat down on a stool nearby and leaned his back against the cold stone wall. He closed his eyes and let his mind begin to brood over the events that had left him in his current situation. Only a few weeks prior, he had been living in his lordly father's castle, waited on by an army of servants and doing whatever his heart desired. Now he was sitting out in the cold night guarding the wall.

Ardyn was the third son of Lord Anson Thayn, ruler of the House of Thayn, which meant that his older brothers would inherit land or be made a marshal of the provincial armies. For the third son, the laws of Alethia offered no inheritance and no guarantee for their future. Many third sons studied to become priests within the Church, which offered the chance for advancement and prestige. The Archbishop of Alethia was a powerful influence in the kingdom. Ardyn could remember several archbishops who were also third sons. The most recent was the current Archbishop Julius Durante. Others chose to join groups of knights who swore to protect important religious and historical sites in Alethia. Yet still others chose the life of an itinerant knight, wandering the lands seeking adventure.

For Ardyn, the choice had been made for him by his father. Lord Anson had brought his third son Ardyn, who had just celebrated his seventeenth birthday, to the city of Ethriel, the capital city of the kingdom of Alethia. Lord Anson had arranged for Ardyn to meet with Sir Ramond Kludge, a lieutenant in the Guardians of the Citadel, earlier that evening. Under pressure from Ardyn's father, Sir Kludge had grudgingly permitted Ardyn to join the illustrious group of men charged with guarding the Citadel of Ethriel and ensuring the wellbeing of the king. Kludge had sent Ardyn to the outfitters and ordered him to report for the night watch that very evening. That was the last time Ardyn had seen his father.

As Ardyn sat there thinking, his head began to droop, and it became difficult to stay awake. Just then there was movement to his right. Ardyn grabbed his spear to defend himself. A hooded figure emerged from the darkness and stopped in front of Ardyn. He took off his hood to reveal a pleasant face. The man had brown hair that fell to his shoulders, a short brown beard, and Ardyn would have sworn the man's face glowed slightly. His eyes were brown, and there was a kindness in them.

"Good evening," the man said pleasantly. "May I sit with you awhile?"

Ardyn lowered his guard and nodded. Somehow he felt he could trust this stranger, yet he had no evidence to support his assumption. They sat down, and neither of them spoke for a long while.

"Who are you?" Ardyn finally asked, unable to contain his curiosity.

"You and I have never met, but your father has spoken of me on occasion. You are Ardyn Thayn, are you not?"

"Yes," Ardyn answered suspiciously. "How do you know my name?"

"Oh," said the stranger with a small chuckle. "I know a great deal about you, Ardyn. I know that you are the third son of Anson Thayn, who brought you here so that you could make a future for yourself. I know that you and your father are on bad terms and that you feel rejected by him."

Ardyn's jaw dropped.

"I also know," the stranger continued, "this has made you doubt yourself. You must find your courage and strive to do right, Ardyn. Remember this when you awaken."

Ardyn found himself falling forward. His face smashed against hard stone. Ardyn opened his eyes to find that he had fallen sideways out of his chair. He picked himself up and dusted himself off. The cold night air blew across his face. He then remembered and looked around for the stranger but found no sign of him. *Was it all a dream?*

A sudden noise caught his attention. A horn was sounding from within the citadel. Three long blasts echoed off the stone walls. Ardyn stood there for a moment, racking his brain and trying to remember what three long blasts meant. He counted it out on his fingers.

One blast meant a general call to report to guard stations, Ardyn thought. *Two blasts meant the city was under attack, and three blasts...*

Ardyn's eyes widened as he remembered that three blasts meant that the king was in danger. He nearly tripped over his feet as he ran down the ramparts to the nearest stairwell. The horn sounded the alarm again as he reached the bottom and sprinted across the empty courtyard. As he was running, Ardyn recognized the sound of other Guardians responding to the horn blasts coming from all around him. When he reached the doors, he found them already opened, and other Guardians were pouring into the hall from every doorway.

Ardyn turned out to be one of the last to respond to the alarm, so the hall was packed with men, and Ardyn had no idea what was going on. He tried to peer over the shoulders of the men in front. What he saw caused him to stumble backward in bewilderment. Lord Noliono was kneeling beside the body of King Greyfuss Aurelia. The king was lying face down, and a crossbow bolt was protruding from his back.

The men fell silent at the sight of the pierced body of their king. Eventually, Lord Noliono stood, and Sir Kludge joined him. They whispered together for a moment, and then Kludge turned to address the room.

"My fellow Guardians, King Greyfuss Aurelia has been murdered," he said.

A wave of murmuring and whispering began, and Sir Kludge waited for it to subside.

"Lord Noliono had come to meet with the king when he found him as you see him now," Kludge continued after the room had gone silent again. "Men, we have failed our king once tonight, but we must not fail twice. Your orders are to search the whole of the citadel and find the king's murderer. Go and bring our vengeance upon this coward!"

At that the men exited the room en masse, breaking off into small groups to search the Citadel. Ardyn, utterly stunned by the news, had shrunk back into the shadows and did not notice the mass exodus until he was alone in a dark corner of the hall. A soft whispering wakened him from his stunned state. He looked up and saw Lord Noliono speaking again with Sir Kludge. Their faint words echoed off the stone walls, enabling Ardyn to overhear their conversation.

"I thought you were going to challenge the king to single combat, my lord?" came the gruff voice of Sir Kludge.

"I did challenge him," Lord Noliono's voice retorted. "But we were interrupted by someone else."

"So you didn't hire the assassin?"

"No, Kludge. I did not."

"Well then, who was he, and who hired him, my lord?"

"I don't know, Kludge!" Noliono said, clearly annoyed by the questions. "I was as surprised as Greyfuss was to find a crossbow bolt in his back."

"Could it have been Methangoth?" Kludge asked with anxiety in his voice.

"I said I don't know, Kludge!" Noliono snapped.

"He said something about using a 'pawn' to distract the Guardians," Kludge said quickly. "Some of our men and I followed him to an apothecary in the upper city, but he gave us the slip. I questioned the stupid boy behind the counter...I think his name was Rad."

"None of that matters now, Kludge!" Noliono hissed. "I need to meet with the Council of Lords and head this thing off. Rumors of the king's death will spread with the Guardians. The other lords will want answers, and I aim to give them the answers that will further our cause."

"What about Kinison Ravenloch?"

"The Lord Commander of the Guardians? What about him?"

"You know he will want to investigate this further. What should be done about him?"

There was silence for a moment, and Ardyn held his breath for fear of being discovered.

"You are right, Kludge," Noliono said at length. "He should be dealt with quickly, but how should we do it?"

"Well, the king died on his watch. Might we place the blame on him?" Kludge suggested.

"Hmm...you might have something there, Kludge. But we must move quickly. Once Kinison is aware of this, he will quickly complicate things for us. Alert your men not to speak with the Lord Commander and post guards outside his quarters to prevent anyone from alerting him. Go quickly, and I will meet with the Council of Lords. If we can gain control of this, I will be King of Alethia by morning, and you, my loyal Kludge, shall be rewarded for your service to me."

"I will do all you ask, sire," Kludge said.

Both men exited the hall, leaving Ardyn questioning what he should do with what he just heard. After several moments, he made up his mind and began walking quickly toward the exit. As he walked, he tried to piece together what he was going to do—

find the Lord Commander and inform him of all that he had heard from Lord Noliono and Sir Kludge. As he walked through the corridors, he saw groups of Guardians racing past him or ahead of him, searching the rooms and the halls of the citadel.

After climbing several more staircases and passing through even more corridors, Ardyn finally reached the other side of the citadel and entered the corridor leading to the Lord Commander's quarters. About halfway down the corridor, he saw something that caused him to freeze in his tracks. Standing on either side of the door leading to the Lord Commander's chambers were two members of the Guardian, and they were both looking at him with their weapons drawn. One held a crossbow and the other a drawn sword.

"Are you Ardyn Thayn?" the one holding the crossbow asked gruffly.

Ardyn knew if he tried to run or fight, he'd be killed by the man bearing the crossbow before he could turn or unsheathe his own sword. He knew he was caught and surrendered to his fate.

"I am," Ardyn finally squeaked.

"Sir Kludge wants to see you. You are ordered to come with us right now," the man said, moving forward.

Ardyn allowed the men to disarm him and march him to the end of the corridor to the stairwell leading to Sir Kludge's office. Yet when they got to the stairwell, instead of going up in the direction of Kludge's office, he was forced to descend the stairs to the lower parts of the citadel. Ardyn knew enough about the layout of the Citadel to know where they were now taking him— the dungeons.

They bypassed the floors with regular cells and forced Ardyn to continue down the stairs to the Dark Cells. These cells were placed far below the citadel, where no light was present save the torchlight of the guards. These normally reserved for murderers and traitors. The two men marched him into a cell and locked the door behind him. Ardyn watched through the bars of his cell as the light of the torches retreated, leaving him in total and complete darkness. He sank to the filthy stone floor and placed his face in his hands. He had failed in his duty to protect the king, and now he had failed to bring justice on the king's killers. He eventually let the darkness claim him. He drifted in and out of dreams where the king was killed before his eyes over and over again. No matter what he did, he failed to stop the killer every time.

6

NOLIONO

Noliono Noland sat in his chambers behind a large desk. The room was dark save from the lamps burning on either side of a large bookcase behind the desk and a smaller lamp upon the desk. Noliono sat in silent thought, going over all his plans. His thoughts were interrupted by a knock at the door.

"Enter."

The door opened, spilling light into the darkened room. A man in a dark cloak and hood stood silhouetted in the doorway. The figure's presence was menacing and filled Noliono with a sense of dread. The figure entered, closed the door, and removed his hood, revealing a man with long black hair and black eyes that gleamed in the light of the lamps.

"Methangoth," Noliono said, his voice shaking slightly. There were few things in life that frightened Noliono, but the man that stood before him was at the top of the list.

"You know why I am here," Methangoth said sharply. It was a statement, not a question.

"Yes," Noliono said, swallowing hard. "He will be here shortly."

Methangoth growled softly but said nothing else. He moved

behind Noliono's desk into one of the dark corners. Noliono glanced back at Methangoth and was surprised that even from this distance, he could only barely see him. There was another knock on the door.

"Enter," Noliono said with a hint of irritation in his voice. The fact that Methangoth was standing behind him was unnerving.

The door opened, spilling light into the room once again. This time, Sir Ramond Kludge stood in the doorway, accompanied by another man.

"My lord," he said with a bow. "I have brought the man you requested."

"Show him in, Kludge," Noliono said calmly.

Kludge and the stranger entered, and Noliono was briefly struck by the man's hat. It was a vibrant red with a long red feather sticking out of it. The man crossed the room and sat down without a word.

"Leave us," Noliono said to Kludge, who bowed and left, closing the door behind him.

"Silas Morgan," Noliono said, taking in the man's sharp eyes and black goatee. "Your reputation precedes you, though you are much younger than I expected."

Silas looked at Noliono but remained silent.

"You *are* the Silas Morgan that fought against the kingdom of Donia and captured its king, are you not?" Noliono asked, irritation rising in his voice.

"No, that was my grandfather," Silas said, not even attempting to hide his annoyance.

"Then are you the Silas Morgan who sailed across the Sea of Aear to rescue the Princess of Eddynland from the evil tyrant Rydnalt?"

"No, that was my father," Silas said, looking even more annoyed. "We Morgans like to pass our names down to our sons. It allows the name to live on and earn more glory."

"Then you are the Silas Morgan that stole the ancient Tapestry of Hurn from the Castle Elmloch."

"Ah, now that I can take credit for, depending on who was asking, of course?" Silas said with a sinister smile.

"Then you are the Silas Morgan that I need."

"I take it you need something that someone else possesses, yes? Something that the other person is unwilling to sell?"

"You are correct," Noliono said, standing and opening an ancient tome in front of Silas. "Are you familiar with the *Book of Aduin*?"

"Supposed to be the only true history of Alethia," Silas replied, showing his interest. "You sure have an eye for the rare and unobtainable. This book is supposed to be locked away in the city of Stonewall, isn't it?"

Noliono heard Methangoth move slightly, and a soft barely audible grumble reached his ears. He paused for a moment before continuing.

"It is in the Stonewall Academy, yes," he said, regaining his composure. "I need you to obtain it for me and bring it back here."

"Done," Silas said, slamming a hand on the desk. "So all we need to discuss now is my price."

"I will pay you fifty golden crowns for this book."

Noliono watched with much satisfaction as Silas's mouth fell open in surprise.

"F-fifty gold crowns? That's almost fifteen years' wages!"

"I can offer more if you can get the item here by the end of the month."

"I'll leave at once," Silas said, standing and moving toward the door.

"Mr. Morgan," said Noliono in a menacing tone. "Don't fail, or there will be dire consequences."

Silas looked at him seriously for a moment then broke into a smirk and left.

"You're sure he can obtain the book?" Methangoth asked, moving out of the corner.

"He's supposed to be the best thief in the land," Noliono said, rearranging a stack of parchments.

"Just make sure *you* don't fail me, Noliono," Methangoth said, moving to the other side of the desk to face Noliono. "You will become king today, but there will be dire consequences for *you* also if you fail to deliver the book."

Noliono looked up into Methangoth's dark face and nodded silently. Methangoth glared down at him for a moment then turned and left.

Noliono took a deep breath to settle his nerves. What had he been thinking when he had made a bargain with Methangoth?

✳   ✳   ✳   ✳

Several hours later, Noliono stood at the entrance to the Council of Lords's chamber, listening to the words of the other lords in attendance. His herald had reported the news that King Greyfuss Aurelia was dead. The whole room was staring at the man in disbelief. Seven men, who represented seven of the eight most powerful houses in Alethia, sat in a large room around a circular table. All of them the ruling lords of their respected lands: Lord Anson of House Thayn, Lord Renton of House Myr, Lord Gefric of House Aurelia, Lord Gaven Soron of House Farod, and Lord Atton of House Nenlad, Lord Wesley of House Rydel, and Lord Markus of House Eddon. Only he, Lord Noliono of the House of Noland, was not present.

Although each one was the leader of an entire house themselves, each one of them were looking at the others for direction. Lord Gaven Soron stood to speak. Lord Gaven was a large and portly man, with dark-brown hair and eyes, and a stern face. His voice was tempered and firm.

"My fellow lords," he began. "I feel that I must speak my mind on this matter. I am deeply grieved by the king's untimely death. Yet it is also clear that we do not yet know how the king died, and we must reserve our judgment."

Lord Gefric Aurelia, nephew to the late king, rose from his seat to speak. He was a young man, tall and slender, with brown hair and dull hazel eyes.

"Reserve judgment, say you? He was our king and my kin," Lord Gefric said, pointing at himself. He then slammed his fist on the table, getting attention of all the room's occupants. "We must find the assassin and bring justice upon him!"

"Yet we do not know what happened, my Lord Gefric," Gaven retorted. "Your uncle was old, and it is possible..."

"Not so old..." Gefric said with a dark look at Gaven.

"Age notwithstanding, you cannot rule out natural causes..." began Gaven.

"Where is Lord Noliono?" asked Lord Anson Thayn abruptly. "Was it not Noliono whom we sent to persuade the king? Would it not be he who would know how the king died?"

As he listened to these men prattle on, Noliono's mind returned to the scene of King Greyfuss's death. He had looked disbelieving at the king's dead body as it lay there, blood still spilling from the wound. He had quickly come to his senses, and his eyes darted around the room. In the dim light, he had thought he had seen a shadow move in between the torchlight.

"Show yourself, fiend!" he had shouted.

The figure had not answered but darted through a door and was gone.

Noliono had knelt beside the king's body and felt for a pulse. There was none. He remembered the words he had uttered just before the members of the Guardians had entered the room.

"I meant to kill the king myself," he repeated quietly to himself and shook his head. "I would have had Greyfuss die honorably in combat, not assassinated by some coward." Noliono could not bear to listen any longer.

"There was nothing natural about the king's murder, my Lord Gaven," said Noliono as he burst through the chamber's doors and assumed his place at the table.

Sir Ramond Kludge entered with him and stood at his side.

"Welcome, my Lord Noliono," Lord Gaven said, bowing slightly. Then all those who had been standing seated themselves. "Please tell us what news you bring of my uncle's death?"

There was a general murmur of agreement from the council.

"My lords," Noliono began, leaning forward and placing his hands upon the table. "I spoke with His Majesty before his death, and when the king would not see reason, I challenged him to single combat."

There was a sudden intake of breath echoed around the chamber. Several of the lords rose from their seats.

"You admit that you killed my uncle in cold blood?" Gefric said as he rose, placing his hand on the hilt of his sword.

"Stay your blade, my Lord Gefric. It was not I who killed the king. I attacked his grace with drawn swords, but His Majesty was slain by a crossbow bolt."

"So you say," Gefric said disbelievingly. "Where's your proof?"

"Right here." Noliono threw a piece of parchment on the table and sat himself in his chair.

The paper fell in front of Lord Gaven, who took and read it.

"The document is a sworn statement that the king was assassinated with a crossbow bolt," he said, still staring at the page.

"Sworn by whom?" Gefric asked, still staring at Noliono.

"The signatures of eleven members of the Guardians are here, my lord. Here is Sir Ramond Kludge, Sir Ethan Graymore, Sir Edward Highman..."

"Very well, my Lord Gaven," said Gefric, turning back to Noliono. "So he was assassinated by a crossbow bolt, but by whom?"

"I did not see his face. He shot from the shadows. Before I could ascertain from where, the assassin had fled," Noliono replied calmly.

"Did you know the man?" Gefric asked.

"I just said that I did not see him," Noliono replied impatiently.

"I did not ask you if you saw him," Gefric said through gritted teeth. "I asked if you knew him."

"Just what are you implying, my Lord Gefric?" Noliono asked, his voice rising in anger, although he knew already where Gefric was going.

"I would think it would be obvious," Gefric said, leering slightly.

"Why would I challenge the king openly and then pay to have him assassinated!" Noliono shouted incredulously.

"Your purpose may have been to attack the king to keep him off guard while your assassin waited for a chance to strike. Then when the opportunity presented itself, your man then murdered my uncle!"

Noliono rose and slowly looked around the room at each lord in turn. "My lords," he said, keeping his voice and his temper in check. "I will not deny that I intended to kill the king, but I did so in accordance with our laws."

"You dare profane the just laws of Alethia by manipulating them to suit your purposes," Gefric said, his rage rising to the surface once more.

"How do you mean, my Lord Noliono?" Lord Anson Thayn asked, rising from his seat in turn. "The Council of Lord requested that you convince the king to reconsider his decision. We could not and would not authorize you to execute the legitimate ruler of the realm."

Noliono motioned for his aid to approach him. Anson and Gefric sank back into their seats as the man came forward and handed Noliono a roll of aged parchment. He unrolled the parchment and began to read its contents to the room.

"By order of His Majesty the King of Alethia, henceforth, the King of Alethia shall be deposed only by the unanimous position of the Council of Lords that His Majesty has, by either his action or inaction, placed the whole of the realm in jeopardy. His deposition shall be determined by single combat at the request of the Council of Lords. Should the king prevail, His Majesty may consider the actions of the Council of Lords treason and may require the lands and lives of the Council of Lords. Signed in the tenth year of his reign: Justus Aurelia, King of Alethia, Lord of Aurelia, Steward of the City of Ethriel, Lord Protector of the Northern Wilds and High Marshall of the North."

None of the members of the Lord's Council spoke as Noliono finished reading, and rolled up the royal decree. After looking around the room at the blank faces of the lords at length, he spoke again.

"My fellow lords of the realm, as you have heard the decree, you must now judge my actions, and yours, in accordance with the law."

Again the lords remained silent.

"Also," Noliono said slowly. "I believe the decree and the sanctioning of the assassination of the king by the Council of Lords should be kept hidden from the people."

"We did not sanction the death of the king!" Gefric shouted angrily. "You took action that the Council of Lords did not authorize!"

"The Council of Lords was in agreement that the king's decision would lead to the ruin of us all. Once word of the death of the king reaches the people, they will demand that someone pays for his death. If you try to place the blame upon my head, my lords"—at this, Noliono gazed darkly around the room—"I will make this decree public, and once the people hear of this decree, they will assume the Council of Lords ordered the murder of the king. They will rise up in rebellion and kill us all. Then who will defend our kingdom from the threats rising up against it?"

The lords all looked at each other and shifted nervously in their seats. Gefric opened and shut his mouth several times before sinking back into his seat. Noliono waited for the reality of the situation to sink in then spoke again.

"We have a decision to make, my lords," he said, looking around the room. We must decide upon which is more important—our kingdom or our conscience."

When a long silence had passed, Noliono spoke again. "So, my lords...who shall be our new king?"

7

KINISON

The next day dawned crisp and beautiful. The inhabitants of the city of Ethriel awoke and began going about their normal routines, none the wiser of the startling events that had transpired the previous night. By midmorning, however, rumors began spreading through the city like wildfire. Shops and businesses closed at noon save the pubs and mead halls, which were busier than ever, becoming centers from which new information, whether true or false, flowed.

By evening, the heralds and town criers had proclaimed throughout the city, calling for the city's inhabitants to gather at the gates of the citadel at noon the following day. The entire city was filled with anxious anticipation. The pubs and mead halls remained open well into the night and into the next morning, for the gossip and rumors were now on the verge of the unthinkable: that King Greyfuss might be dead.

Within the citadel, the news of what had happened caused much alarm and fear. From the king's advisors and courtiers to the stable boys, all the inhabitants of the citadel were terrified at the news that King Greyfuss Aurelia had been assassinated in his own hall. When they learned that many members of the serving staff at the citadel had been dismissed by the Council of Lords for asking too many questions, the overall feeling that something very suspicious and sinister was occurring within the city gripped the people.

Yet neither Kinison nor his beautiful wife, Sarah, were aware of any of the previous night's events. Kinison was one of the youngest men to be appointed Lord Commander of the Guardians of the Citadel. He also had the manner of one whose soul is much older than his body. His wife, Sarah, also carried herself with wisdom beyond her age. She was tall and slender like a willow branch. She had dark-brown hair and eyes and a sweet, kind voice. Kinison considered himself blessed to have a woman like Sarah as his wife.

For both Kinison and Sarah, the morning had dawned just as any other. Sarah had risen early, like she always did, while Kinison had lain in bed a bit longer. He eventually got out of bed, washed, and dressed for his day. But before leaving, he knelt beside his bed to say his morning prayer.

"God, bless us this day as we go forth to do Your will. Thank You for my loving wife, Sarah, and the life we have together. Give us strength and courage to..."

Kinison stopped short because at that moment, there was a loud knock at the door. Kinison opened the door and found Princess Riniel Aurelia standing in the doorway.

"Kinison, Sarah!" she shouted, running over to Sarah and throwing her arms around her.

"What's wrong?" Kinison said, standing up in alarm. He looked at Sarah, who looked back, bewildered.

"Something has happened," Riniel sobbed. "They say my father has been murdered!"

"Murdered!" Kinison shouted. "How? When?"

"I don't know!" she wailed. "The Council of Lords will not grant me an audience! No one will tell me anything! I don't even know if it's true or a lie!" Riniel nearly screamed.

"Neither of us know any more than you do," Sarah said softly. "I'm sure it's all just a misunderstanding."

"Riniel," Kinison said, coming over and gently turning her around to face him. "Please tell me everything you *do* know."

✳   ✳   ✳   ✳

Kinison was half walking and half running down the corridor. He stopped short just outside the Council of Lords' chamber. In front of the door stood two guardsmen in red tunics baring the crest of the black wolf, and nowhere on their tunics was the traditional crest of the Guardians, a small silver shield usually pinned just below the left shoulder.

Kinison realized that something was wrong because neither one of the guardsmen demonstrated any sign of respect toward him. Instead of standing at attention and saluting, the two men were leering at him.

"Open the doors," Kinison said in a commanding voice.

The men exchanged amused glances before one of them spoke.

"The Council is in session, Lord Kinison," he said in a mockingly respectful tone.

"I do not care. I must speak with the Council. I repeat, open the doors," Kinison said calmly but firmly.

"I am afraid we have strict orders not to allow anyone to enter for any reason," the other guard said.

"I see," Kinison said. Then he gave a loud and distinct whistle; in a moment half a dozen men appeared, all wearing the silver shield of the Guardians. Kinison never took his eyes off the two men in front of him. "Now, gentlemen, stand aside, or you are under arrest."

The two guardsmen glared at Kinison but reluctantly moved aside. Kinison moved forward, placed his hands on each door, and thrust upon them. The doors flew open, slamming into the walls on either side with a reverberating boom. The members of the Council of Lords jumped to their feet, outraged, as Kinison entered the room.

"What is the meaning of this, Lord Commander?" demanded Lord Gaven Soron.

"My lords," Kinison began with a bow. "I have heard a grievous rumor that the king has been killed. I have come hoping to confirm the truth of these rumors and inquiring as to why I was not made aware immediately after these events transpired."

The lords were silent, and they all sank back into their seats, save Lord Gaven.

"Lord Kinison, the Council of Lords is thoroughly investigating the events of last night. We can confirm that King Greyfuss was slain. As to why you were not alerted immediately," Gaven said with a hint of disgust in his voice, "you might ask your guardsmen on duty last night since it was they who failed to protect the king. Let them explain their actions."

Kinison's anger burned at Gaven's response, but he controlled his temper. "My lord, I request that the Council allow me to lead the investigation so that I may learn how this deed was accomplished."

"Request denied, Lord Kinison. Your lack of ability to protect the king has called into question the wisdom of allowing you to retain your title and office. See to your duties as Lord Commander of the Guardians and protect the new king. Leave the investigation to us," Gaven said.

"New king, my lord?" Kinison asked, momentarily confused. He looked over at Lord Gefric Aurelia, who refused to meet his gaze.

"Yes, King Noliono Noland," Gaven said irritably as Kinison turned back to look at him. "Let us see if you can do a better job protecting the new king."

* * * *

An hour after his meeting with the Council, Kinison was back in his chambers, staring blankly at the wall, waiting. He had left the

Council's chamber in a tempered fury. *How could the Council expect him to fulfill his duties and obligations without any information?* It was at that moment, while he was storming through the corridors, that he resolved to start his own investigation into the king's murder regardless of the Council's orders. He was the Lord Commander of the Guardians, which meant that he and his men had failed last night, and he wanted to know why.

He summoned his two lieutenants: Sir Ren Gables and Sir Ramond Kludge, as well as Sir Mikel Greyvan, the captain of the City Watch. Even if the Council refused to provide him with answers, one of these men would provide him with what he sought. Now he found himself waiting. He hated waiting. Of all the virtues he possessed, waiting and patience were not among them.

Half an hour later, all three men entered his chambers. Ren Gables, a short, stout, middle-aged man who had been the former captain of the City Watch, entered first. After him came Sir Mikel Greyvan, a slightly slimmer man than Ren but of the same age and height, who had been a former member of Lord Gefric Aurelia's personal guard. Finally, Sir Ramond Kludge entered. Kludge was a tall and dark-haired man, with shifty eyes and a devilish grin. He had been a former marshall of Noland, and Lord Noliono had been instrumental in Kludge's appointment as a lieutenant in the Guardians of the Citadel.

They all seated themselves around Kinison's table and looked expectantly at him.

"Men, a tragedy has struck this citadel that has not occurred in over a hundred years. A plot to murder the king was carried out in his own hall, and as leaders of the Guardians of the Citadel and the City Watch, we failed to prevent it," he said, looking at each man in turn. "Which of you was on duty last night?"

"I and my men were on duty in the citadel, Lord Commander," Kludge said, raising a hand.

There was something in the look that Kludge gave him that was very unsettling to Kinison. He thought he caught the curl of the man's lip in a brief sneer.

"Report," Kinison commanded him.

"I and my men reported for duty an hour before dusk. We all reported to our posts, and all was silent. Then a call went out that an intruder had been sighted in the northwest tower."

"The one on the other side of the citadel from the Great Hall?" Kinison asked.

"Affirmative," answered Kludge. "I assembled some men and went to investigate, but we found nothing. When I returned to the Great Hall, I saw a large man in a dark cloak and hood dart out of one of the side doors. We gave chase, but the figure eluded us in the passages. I called for more men to perform a more thorough search of the area, but word came of a disturbance near the Great Hall. I immediately returned with my men to find that the king had been assassinated by a crossbow bolt in the back and Lord Noliono kneeling beside the body."

"Did Lord Noliono explain what had happened?" Kinison asked.

"He said that he and the king had been arguing in the Great Hall when a dark figure shot him in the back and then fled," Kludge answered.

"The same figure that you had pursued?" Kinison asked urgently.

"I am not sure, my lord. We never caught him or the other, if there was indeed two," Sir Ramond said.

Kinison thought for a few moments, leaving the other men in silence, then spoke again.

"Sir Ren," Kinison said, turning to him. "Your men are currently on duty?"

"Yes, my lord," Ren said.

"Good," Kinison said, then turned to the others. "Sir Mikel, return to your duties in the city. Sir Ramond, send to me every man who was on duty near the Great Hall. I wish to question them personally. Then wake the rest of your men and tell them to assemble in the citadel courtyard in one hour. Dismissed."

"As you command, Lord Commander," all three men said, rising to leave.

"Ren, remain a moment," Kinison said quickly as the other two were leaving the room.

"Lord Commander?" Ren asked, standing in the doorway, looking confused.

"Close the door and come sit down," Kinison said.

Ren obediently closed the door and returned to the table, looking expectantly at Kinison, who waited a moment before speaking.

"I have reason to believe that Sir Ramond is lying," he said bluntly.

"My lord?" Ren said, looking alarmed. "That is a serious accusation."

"I know," Kinison said, laying his hands on the table. "I am not sure about what, but his story strikes me as only partially true."

"Why do you suspect him though? Do you have any evidence to prove your theory?"

"Not yet, but I am going to investigate this thoroughly. The king is dead, and Sir Ramond was on duty. That means these actions are in question. When the king is in the Great Hall, every door is supposed to be guarded by two men. In addition to that, at least one member of the Guardians should have been in the hall with the king. That means there should have been at least eleven men guarding the king last night. Sir Ramond must have called some of his men away from the Great Hall just in time to allow the assassin to slip in unnoticed. The question is, did Sir Ramond call those men away with the purpose of leaving the king unguarded, or was it a simple lapse in his judgment. Either way, I will learn the truth."

"What do you need me to do?" Ren asked, shifting uneasily in his seat.

"Ren," Kinison said, looking intently at the man, "You are my closest friend. If Sir Ramond did purposely allow the king to be murdered, he was not acting alone. I need to know whom I can trust."

"Who do you suspect would try to assassinate King Greyfuss?" Ren asked, somewhat bewildered.

"Whoever stood to gain most from his death," Kinison replied.

"You mean..." Ren began.

"Yes, I do," Kinison said in a whisper. "If Kludge did purposefully allow the king to be assassinated, I do not believe he did it for his own ambition. No, he was told to do so by someone poised to gain the most from the king's death. You and I both know who, but do not utter anything I have shared with you to anyone. If I can prove it, I will need your support."

"For what, my lord?" Ren asked, looking slightly alarmed.

"To bring the true murderer to justice," Kinison replied.

"You cannot be serious!" Ren exclaimed, standing up in protest. "Do you really think that the Council, the city of Ethriel, the people of Alethia, would believe that King Greyfuss was murdered by...?"

"It does not matter, my friend," Kinison said, standing and placing a hand on Ren's shoulder. "Whatever they choose to believe, King Greyfuss was murdered, and I will not allow the person responsible to escape justice."

At that very moment, Kludge came through the door with half a dozen men of the Guardians. He bowed slightly when he entered.

"Lord Commander, your presence is required in the Council's chambers immediately," he said with a sinister smile.

"Why are your men not at their posts guarding the king, Sir Ramond?" Kinison asked, his temper rising.

"I have been ordered by the king to bring you to the Council chamber, my lord," Kludge answered with a slight sneer.

Kinison looked at Ren, who nodded and left.

"Very well," Kinison said, turning to Kludge and rising from his seat. "Lead the way."

✳ ✳ ✳ ✳

Kinison was marched through the corridors to the Council of Lords's chamber. He was ushered into the chamber room, and the first thing he noticed was that the only person in the room was King Noliono. He was seated on the far side of the room in the king's seat, and Kinison was tempted momentarily to draw his sword and challenge him for his crime. Noliono rose when Kinison entered and motioned for his guards to leave. They bowed and closed the door behind them. Noliono turned his gaze on Kinison and waved his hand to the seat opposite him.

"No, thank you, Your Majesty. I prefer to stand," Kinison said, trying to keep his face and voice emotionless.

"Very well," Noliono said, seating himself. "I suppose you were wondering why I have summoned you."

It was not a question, so Kinison remained silent.

"It concerns me gravely, Sir Kinison, that under your watch King Greyfuss Aurelia was slain," Noliono said after a brief pause. "Not in a hundred years have the Guardians failed to protect the king, which begs the question—was the king left unguarded deliberately, or was it simply inept leadership?"

"Is Your Majesty questioning my loyalty?" Kinison asked, his anger rising.

Noliono did not respond immediately but simply looked at Kinison.

"This is your chance to defend yourself, Sir Kinison. I suggest that you speak clearly and concisely," Noliono said with a dark look.

"I have already begun my investigation into the matter of King Greyfuss's murder. I believe that I have already identified the guilty parties."

"Oh?" Noliono asked, leaning forward and raising an eyebrow. "Tell me what you have found and on whom you are placing the blame."

"As I said, sire, I have begun my investigation, but I need time to gather more evidence before I am ready to bring accusations. I ask to be allowed to continue my search for the *truth*," Kinison said calmly, emphasizing the last word.

"That will not be necessary, Lord Kinison," Noliono said, sitting back in his chair again. "The Council has already conducted their investigation and have discovered the culprit."

"May I ask upon whom are *you* placing the blame?" Kinison asked snidely.

At this Noliono rose from his seat and knocked three times on the table. The chamber doors opened, and the guards came and stood beside Kinison on either side. Noliono then picked up a roll of parchment that had been sitting next to him. He unrolled it and began to read the document.

"On this day, the first day of the month of April, in the first year of the reign of King Noliono Noland, by the findings of the Council of Lords, I, King Noliono do hereby charge Sir Kinison Ravenloch, Lord Commander of the Guardians of the Citadel, hereafter known as the accused, with negligence and dereliction of duty as evidenced by the murder of King Greyfuss in the Great Hall of the Citadel of Ethriel. The accused is found guilty of the charge and sentenced to death."

Before Kinison could react, the guards on either side had grabbed his arms and were dragging him backward. He looked to either side and noticed that these men were not members of the Guardians but bore the crest of the House of Noland.

"Take him to the citadel courtyard," Noliono said to his men.

They dragged him out the door and through the corridors to the courtyard, where Sir Ren Gables, Sir Ramond Kludge, and all the other members of the Guardians were assembled.

When Noliono's men threw him onto the ground before the doors of the Great Hall, Kludge actually laughed. Kinison looked, and there on the steps above him he saw King Noliono. Noliono spoke to the men assembled before him.

"Kinison Ravenloch is accused of unintentionally causing the death of King Greyfuss Aurelia," he began in a grand fashion and looked out upon the assembly. "However, as the crime was not committed intentionally, let the record show that I, King Noliono, commute the sentence of death. The accused will instead face the rite of 'The Exiled Guardian.'"

His guards picked him up, and Ren stepped forward. He came up to Kinison but would not look him in the eye. He reached up and took the silver medallion and chain off Kinison's neck, which was the badge of rank for Lord Commander. He also unpinned the silver shield of the Guardians. Finally, he ripped the crest of the House of Aurelia from Kinison's tunic. Ren then walked up the steps toward the king and stood at his side.

"Sir Ramond Kludge, step forward."

Kludge moved forward and knelt before the king, who took the chain and medallion from Ren and hung the chain around Ramond's neck.

"Arise, Ramond Kludge, Lord Commander of the Guardians," Noliono said. Then he turned and moved toward Kinison. "Kinison Ravenloch, you are henceforth and forever stripped of all your titles and privileges and banished from this city. You are forbidden from returning under pain of death."

Kinison turned to the king and considered many actions he could take and many obscene gestures he could make, but he refrained from them all. He resolved to simply stare incredulously up at this man who had murdered the true King of Alethia.

"You will not long sit on the throne of Alethia, Noliono," he said, so quietly that none but Noliono could hear. "I know what you did, and I will avenge the king's death."

"You know nothing. That much was obvious from our conversation in the Council chamber. Go, Kinison, and do not return, or your wife, Sarah, will suffer for it," Noliono said, smiling. Then turning to Kludge, he said, "Take Kinison away for the rite. Make sure he is unharmed by any until he is outside the city."

"With pleasure, my King," Kludge said with relish, and he seized Kinison's arm.

At first Kinison struggled as they dragged him out of the citadel gates and through the city, but he soon gave up. It was no use. He had failed King Greyfuss not only once but twice.

8

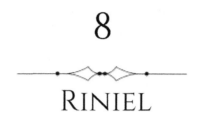

RINIEL

Riniel had never cried so hard in her life. She was kneeling beside her bed; the bed clothes were soaked with her tears. It felt as if her heart would burst. She almost wished that it would. Perhaps in death, the pain would simply evaporate. *Why? Why did this have to happen? Why!*

"Why God?" she cried out in a loud voice then buried her face into the bed once more, tears streaming down her face in torrents.

She looked up suddenly, overcome with the feeling that someone was watching her. A man in a dark cloak sat in the corner of the room. Riniel would have cried out except she was baffled by the look of deep concern on his pleasant face.

"I am here, Riniel," he said softly.

His voice was soothing somehow, and Riniel was somehow comforted by it.

"Who are you? Why are you in my chambers?" she asked, wiping her face. "I should call the guards."

"It is not surprising that you do not recognize me," the man said as if pained by what he was saying. "You know of me, Riniel. Even my name is familiar to you, but despite your knowledge, you do not know me."

Riniel was silent. She felt confused. *And what was this other feeling? Was it shame?*

The man seemed to know her thoughts.

"I am here now, Riniel. You called out to me, and I have answered."

"But who are you?" Riniel asked.

"Do you still not realize who I am?"

Riniel shook her head slowly.

"You called out to me in your distress, and I answered."

"What do you mean, I called out to you?" she asked irritably. "I didn't call out to anyone."

"Didn't you?" the man asked calmly. "All your life, I have reached out my hand, yet you will not take it."

"I am sick of your riddles and cryptic responses. Tell me plainly, or I shall call the guards."

"I have told you no riddles. I have come to bring you comfort in your distress and answer your question."

"What question?"

"Why your father was taken from you?"

"No. I want to know why God took my father from me!"

"You blame God?"

"Of course I do!" Riniel nearly shouted. "If God is all-powerful and controls everything, then He is responsible for every good and evil deed." Riniel's voice trailed off at the end for she noticed the man's kind face had grown stern.

"God is not evil, nor did he create evil," he said firmly.

"Then why is there evil in this world? If God created everything, he must have created evil too," Riniel said, her voice trailing off again as the man's face grew sterner.

"You cannot understand for you do not truly wish to understand. You only wish to assign blame, just as you do not truly wish to know me," the man said, his voice like distant thunder. Riniel was struck by the power in the man's voice, yet the self-control he must also possess. "God is holy, just, righteous, pure. He is love. He is unchanging. In Him, there is neither darkness nor evil."

"Then why is there evil in the world?" Riniel asked, her eyes blurring with tears again.

"Man's rebellion."

"What?"

"Man's rebellion against God brings pain into this world."

"You mean God is punishing us?"

"No, child," the man said, his voice softening. "God desires to bless you. He wants to guide you on the right path, a path that leads to joy and knowledge of Him. When men choose to rebel against him and go their own way, it leads to pain and suffering. Your father was murdered by rebellious men seeking their own evil desires apart from God. Place the blame on the right person, Riniel."

"Shut up! Just shut up!" Riniel screamed at the top of her lungs. "I don't believe you! I don't believe any of this! Get out! Get..."

But she stopped short for the man had vanished before her eyes. Riniel stared bewildered at the place the man had sat. A shaft of light from the window fell upon the chair, casting a shadow on the wall behind it. She looked intently then burst into renewed sobs for the shadow had the appearance of a cross.

✳ ✳ ✳ ✳

The funeral for Greyfuss Aurelia was the largest and grandest in Ethriel's long history. Over three hundred lords and ladies crowded into the Great Hall to pay their last respects to Alethia's beloved king. Black banners hung from the ceiling, and the throne had been moved to the side on the dais. In its place sat a table, and upon the table lay the body of Greyfuss Aurelia. The silent stillness was only disturbed by the occasional sobbing of one of the ladies. The men sat stoically, facing the dais, their eyes downcast.

Riniel was sitting on the front row, just below the dais. She looked up at the table where her father's body lay but could not long endure the pain of seeing him like this.

Her cousin, Lord Gefric Aurelia, stood and delivered the eulogy. He was followed by many others who stood and spoke of her father that day, but Riniel could never remember a single thing anyone said. Everything was a blur, as if everything else had continued moving forward but she remained fixed in this moment of grief and misery.

She shook her head in disbelief. Only yesterday she had been overjoyed at her father's return and been looking forward to spending time with him after such a long time apart. She would never see his smiling face. She'd never see him standing at her chamber door, waiting to surprise her with a gift or with a horseback ride through the country. She would never be able to sit and talk with him late into the night, as they often had done. She would never hear his rich laugh or feel him hug her tight. The sense of loss was overwhelming her. She tried to hold back the tears, but it was no use.

Suddenly, people all around her got up and began leaving. She watched as the lords and ladies paraded out of the Great Hall until it was just her and her father. She sat in the silent stillness until her cousin, Lord Gefric Aurelia came over and sat down beside her.

"I won't ask you if you are all right," he said softly. "And I will not pretend that I feel the same pain you do, though my heart is broken by your father's death."

"His murder you mean," Riniel said indignantly.

"You know that's what I mean, Riniel," Gefric said patiently. "Your father *was* murdered, and I will not rest until his killer is brought to justice."

"Justice!" Riniel nearly shouted. She looked up at Gefric, her tear-streaked face burning with rage. "You think justice is what I want?"

Gefric was silent. He simply looked at her with quiet compassion, which Riniel regarded with both appreciation and annoyance. She felt her anger ebb as despair began to overwhelm her.

"You heard about what happened to Kinison then?"

"No," Riniel said, looking up in alarm.

Gefric hesitated then said, "Kinison has been relieved of duty and sent into exile."

"What!" Riniel nearly shouted, standing in her outrage.

"He was found guilty of dereliction of his duty to protect the king. Guardians are often executed for this, Riniel, but he was exiled instead."

"I don't understand," Riniel said, shaking her head in disbelief. "How could you let the Council do this?"

"He was Lord Commander of the Guardians, charged with protecting the king's life at all costs," Gefric answered, his face downcast. "He failed to protect your father from being murdered. That has to be punished, Riniel."

Riniel sat back down and was silent for a long time. At length, Gefric got up and kissed her on the head.

"If you need anything, cousin, let me know," Gefric said, then he left her alone in the Great Hall.

Riniel placed her face in her hands, the frustration and emptiness overwhelming her. She broke down, tears pouring from her eyes. For a long time, she sat there alone in the Great Hall, her sobs continuing to echo off the cold stone walls. Never before had she felt so empty and alone.

✳   ✳   ✳   ✳

After her father's body had been laid to rest in the tombs of the Aurelian Kings, Riniel wandered aimlessly through the citadel wondering what to do next. She wanted to conduct her own investigation, but she had no idea of where to start. Her face was tearstained and her eyes red from her constant weeping, but for the moment her face was emotionless. The corridors of the citadel were full of people, and she passed countless servants, guards, and courtiers. They bowed before her, offered their condolences, and asked her if they could do anything for her.

Despite the turbulence in her heart, Riniel always summoned the strength to respond in the expected courtly manner in each instance. Yet after a dozen or so encounters, she was desperate for solitude. Riniel fled to the citadel gardens and wandered among the flowers. Eventually she found an empty bench in a lonely corner of the gardens. She knelt down beside it, and all the emotion that she had been holding in broke through to the surface, and she wept bitter tears.

It was not until several hours later as evening was approaching that someone came upon her place of solitude. Her back was to the intruder, and her eyes were still clouded with tears.

"Who's there?" she said, wiping her eyes and dusting off her dress.

The man did not respond but continued to slowly walk toward her. When he had come closer, Riniel recognized him as Lord Noliono, her father's chief opponent on the Council of Lords. Although she felt like sending him away at once, she remembered her courtly manners, and it was a good thing she did.

"My lord, I am sorry. I mistook you to be..." but she stopped short, for the glint of gold was upon Noliono's brow. She stared at her father's crown as it sat upon Noliono's head, and anger began to build within her. She struggled to remain calm. "What is my father's crown doing upon *your* head?"

Noliono looked at Riniel with pity and sorrow. He spoke softly and calmly. "I am deeply sorry for your loss, Princess Riniel, and I am deeply troubled by this turn of events."

"You did not answer my question, *my lord*," she said, her eyes flashing and voice rising. "What is my father's crown doing upon your head?"

Noliono waited a moment and again spoke calmly. "I would think that obvious, princess. The Council of Lords elected me king upon your father's death this morning."

"My father's murder, you mean?" Riniel said sharply.

"Indeed, I do, princess. I was present when the assassin murdered your father. I saw what happened to our king," Noliono said.

"And yet you did nothing to save him?" she asked again sharply.

Noliono hesitated and then said, "I could not."

"Could not or would not?" she said, fire now leaping from her eyes.

"I will not pretend that your father and I were friends, princess. Neither will I say that we saw eye to eye on most matters. The truth be told, your father and I were very different men, yet I respected him and honored him to the last. Were it my will, he would have died by my hand in honorable combat, not by the crossbow bolt of a cowardly assassin."

Riniel listened to Noliono and examined his face carefully, looking for any sign or tell of falsehood. His eyes never wavered but continued to gaze into hers. When she found no sign of falsehood, the fierce fire that had burned inside her began to falter. For the moment, as Riniel looked into Noliono's eyes, she believed him. Riniel watched as a single tear slid down his stolid face, and her disposition softened more. She sat down upon the bench, her own tears clouding her eyes again.

"I wish to know everything regarding my father's murder...Your Majesty," Riniel said guardedly.

"All your wish shall be done, princess," Noliono said quietly.

He sat down beside her but did not offer any physical condolence. For a long time, they both simply sat there on the bench in a lonely corner of the gardens. Not a single word was heard for a long time. Finally, at length, Noliono spoke.

"Come," he said, rising and offering his arm.

It was a request, not a command. She rose slowly and took his arm. Then the two of them walked out of the gardens. Neither spoke a word as they walked toward the Great Hall of the citadel. When they stood in front of the massive doors at the entrance of the Great Hall, Noliono stopped short and looked at Riniel for a moment. She returned his gaze, expecting him to speak. He did not. At length he simply nodded and turned toward the guards standing to either side of the doors.

"Open," he said, and the guards obeyed.

The two giant oak doors swung inward to reveal the entire court assembled to either side of a long red carpet that ran all the way to the dais at the far end, on which sat the throne. When the courtiers closest to the front doors saw Noliono, they immediately fell to one knee. Riniel watched as the movement at the front of the hall caused the entire room to react, causing a human wave all the way to the dais, on which sat the throne. Riniel followed the wave to the dais, and as her eyes fell onto the throne, she steeled herself to keep from tearing up again.

"Hail, King Noliono!" the court shouted.

The king moved forward with Riniel on his arm. As they walked toward the dais, Noliono waved his hand slowly over the crowd on either side, who rose to their feet. Upon reaching the foot of the dais, Noliono turned and spoke.

"My lords and ladies, advisors and leaders of Alethia, knights and defenders of the realm, and honored guests, I welcome you to the Citadel of Ethriel," he said somberly. "I wish it was under happier circumstances that you came to my hall this day, yet the passing of Greyfuss Aurelia is not cause for celebration. A good and just king is an abundant blessing. Tomorrow at noon, we will pay our final respect to our former king.

"Many of you have heard, and I now will confirm, that King Greyfuss was murdered in this very hall."

Here Noliono paused and, without thinking, looked at the very spot where Greyfuss died.

"It was a cowardly act," he said softly. "An act that will be brought to justice."

Riniel watched Noliono, as did every person in the Great Hall. For several long minutes there was silence, and then the king spoke again.

"The man responsible has been discovered and dealt with accordingly," the king said gravely. "I will not reveal his name at this time. Instead, I would also like to take this moment to honor Princess Riniel Aurelia. Although her father is no longer king, I would like to invite her to stay here in the citadel as my honored guest and twice welcome."

The crowd may have cheered at Noliono's words, but Riniel was dumbfounded by the king's offer. *Why would Noliono want to keep a member of the House of Aurelia in his own citadel,* she wondered. *There must be some reason behind it.* As the cheering began to subside and the crowd's eyes shifted to her, Riniel realized that she was expected to speak. She longed to be away from Ethriel, to escape the place where her father had died, but she also felt drawn to this place. A desire to know the truth about her father's death was overwhelming her. At last she turned to Noliono and spoke.

"You honor me, Your Majesty. I am especially grateful to you and to the people of Alethia for allowing me to remain here at the citadel. In this place are many memories of my father, and I pray that these memories do not quickly fade for me or for anyone who knew King Greyfuss," she added pointedly.

Thunderous applause came from the crowd, and Noliono reached out and kissed Riniel's hand. She knew that there was more to this ploy of Noliono's than she knew at the moment, but she now had access to the citadel indefinitely, where she would be privy to information known only within its walls.

As the court was dismissed, her cousin, Lord Gefric Aurelia, came up to her with a smile on his face. He hugged her, but as he did so he whispered in her ear: "I hope you know what you are doing."

"As do I," she whispered in response.

9

KINISON

Beneath the shade of a tree standing beside the road some five miles from the city of Ethriel sat Kinison Ravenloch. His back was against the tree, and his countenance was clearly fallen. If a casual observer had looked at him, they would have seen a humble traveler, not the former Lord Commander of the Guardians. He wore simple traveling clothes: a green tunic without any sign or crest, a pair of plain brown pants, a dark-gray hood and cloak that was pulled over his face, a belt with a sword and dagger, and large brown boots. He sat there reflecting upon the past two days. *That's right, the former Lord Commander of the Guardians*, he thought.

His dismissal from his post had come because of his investigation of King Greyfuss's death. He had been arrested, brought before the new king, Noliono, and dismissed from his position. Now he was banished from the city of Ethriel on pain of death. As was customary when a member of the Guardians was dismissed for any reason, Kinison was given a horse, a set of plain clothes, his weapons, and bag containing five golden coins with a crown stamped onto each side. Alethian currency consisted of three coins: golden crowns, silver lions, and bronze shields. A golden crown is equal to twenty silver lions, a single silver lion is worth fifty bronze shields, and ten bronze shields were usually considered a day's wage for a common laborer. So, a bag of five golden crowns was considered a small fortune. It was enough money to take Kinison anywhere in Alethia. But where should he go?

Kinison had left at once, riding hard and fast so as to put the distance of an archer's shot between himself and the city walls. After that, he rode slowly and aimlessly until he stopped for the night several miles west of the city. There he had spent the night under the stars, unwilling to try an inn for fear that he was being followed. He arose early the next day and traveled several more miles before noon when he stopped for a rest under the tree in which he now sat—a dismal tale and a crushing blow to Kinison. He now wondered where he might go. Investigating the death of Greyfuss Aurelia was now out of the question. All the evidence was back in Ethriel. He dared not go back there for fear of endangering Sarah. He knew that the more distance he placed between the capital and himself, the better. He could not go to his father, Henry Ravenloch, at Estelhold for fear of Noliono seeking retribution on his family. No, he knew that from this point onward, the name Kinison Ravenloch would not be safe to use. He would have to change his name, change his habits, and change his home. He just did not know where to begin his new life and what that life might resemble. He shook his head, disillusioned by the last two days. How could he possibly live his life with the shame of leaving his wife behind and leaving that monster to rule over Alethia?

He sat in silent thought for a long time. As the hours passed, the day grew warmer. Kinison was grateful for the shade of the tree. He looked out toward the road and saw a man walking toward him.

"May I join you?" the stranger asked when he came up on Kinison.

THE HEIR COMES FORTH

Kinison nodded but did not speak. The man walked up under the tree and sat down facing Kinison. He took off his hood to reveal a pleasant face. The man had long brown hair to his shoulders and a short brown beard. Kinison looked at the man's face, which seemed to glow slightly even in the shade of the tree.

"You are Kinison Ravenloch, formerly of the Guardians, are you not?" the man asked abruptly.

Kinison jumped to his feet and drew his sword.

"Peace," the man said, holding a hand out. "You have no need of your weapon. I am not here to harm you."

"You seem to know me, but I know nothing of you?" Kinison said, sheathing his sword and sitting back down almost as commanded to do so.

"You already know me, Kinison, but you believe that I have abandoned you," the stranger said, looking hard at Kinison.

"Well then, remind me who you are then," Kinison said irritably.

"Why do you think I am here?" the man asked calmly.

"If you really are my friend, which I doubt, then how did we meet?"

"I will caution you, Kinison. You cannot go through life without trusting people."

"If you know me so well, then you know what I have just endured at the hands of those in whom I trusted."

"I do."

"Then how can you ask me, after all that I have been through, to trust people?"

"You have only suffered a blow to your pride, Kinison, nothing more. Yet you now question your faith in everything, including God."

"What god?" Kinison said derisively. "If there is a god, why does he allow good men like me to suffer? And if there is a god, why does he raise up men like Noliono to become kings?"

"You have lost your faith in God because you face hardships in life? Tell me, Kinison, where does it say that faith in God will guarantee you a perfect life?"

Kinison was silent.

"You blame God for your problems, but in truth it was not His fault but yours."

"My fault?" Kinison said, standing up and clenching his fists. "How is any of this my fault! My friends betrayed me, my wife is being held hostage, and if I try to return to Ethriel and rescue her, Noliono has threatened to kill her! My life has fallen apart, and there is nothing I can do about it. Yet you say this is all my fault!"

"Ah, it was you who chose to confront Noliono so quickly. It was you who put Sarah at risk."

"I was trying to do the right thing!" Kinison protested. "I was trying to bring justice upon those who killed the king!"

"You may tell yourself that, but the truth is that you wanted to save face. After all, the king was killed on your watch. You wanted to rectify your mistakes. You wanted revenge. You wanted to look like a hero. Even now, your pride blinds you to the truth."

Kinison was silent again.

"Pride cometh before the fall, Kinison," the man said. "Beware of your pride."

* * * *

Kinison started awake and found himself alone under the tree. He sat there for a long time pondering all this in his mind. As the sun began sinking low in the west, he began collecting his things and remounted his horse. He rode for several hours well into the night until he came to a small town nestled in a little valley. In the middle of the town, which consisted of a smattering of small shops and houses, was an inn. The inn consisted of two relatively comfortable-looking buildings. The main building was a large two-story structure made of gray stone with many windows and a wooden roof. The other building, which served as a tavern, was to the left and adjacent to the main building. The tavern was built of wood and a simple thatched roof.

As Kinison rode closer, he noticed that the main building was dark and quiet, whereas light and music poured from the windows and door of the tavern. Wishing to avoid the many eyes and ears of the tavern, he approached the door of the main building first. His hand was almost on the door handle when he saw the notice posted on the door:

NOTICE:
ALL THOSE WHO SEEK LODGING
AT THE DANCING LION
MAY INQUIRE NEXT DOOR.

Kinison sighed. It looked like he would be joining the crowd next door after all. He pulled his hood back over his head and entered the tavern.

The tavern consisted of a single large room brightly lit by lamps and a roaring fire in hearth. Many people were gathered at the bar and around the many tables drinking, talking, and laughing. The air was hazy with smoke from the dozens of pipes, and the smell of tobacco, ale, and body odor nearly knocked him off his feet. Kinison gazed about the room and noticed several men in red tunics that bore the crest of a black wolf. Most of them were gathered in a far corner of the room, and they were now watching him closely. He pretended to take no notice and proceeded to the bar. The man behind the bar was short, stocky, and had squinted eyes that seemed to stare unblinkingly. He was now looking at Kinison as he approached the bar. Kinison locked eyes with the man, and they stared at one another for a moment.

"Help ya?" the man finally asked.

"I need a room for the night, a private room if you've got one."

"It'll be a silver lion," the man said gruffly.

Kinison took out his money bag and laid a golden crown in the man's hand. The man shifted his gaze several times between

Kinison and the coin that he had been given. He turned it over several times in his hand, scrutinized every surface of the coin, bit the edge, and finally placed it in his pocket.

"A moment, sir," he said, grinning slightly and bowing. The man disappeared into the back, and reemerged with another larger man, who had red hair and mutton chops and friendly blue eyes. The newcomer stood for a moment as the first man whispered something to him then faced Kinison.

"Sam Brandyman, at your service, sir," he said pleasantly and smiled broadly. "Welcome to the Dancing Lion."

Kinison now saw that the man had a kind face, and he felt that this man could be trusted, at least to a point. Mr. Brandyman pulled a large book from under the bar and opened it.

"My man Biff here says you want a private room?" Brandyman asked, still looking at the book.

"Yes, if that is possible."

"Yes, we have many private rooms, mister?" Brandyman looked expectantly at Kinison.

Kinison hesitated before speaking. He knew that this was the moment he had been pondering about all afternoon. If he used his real name, those men in red tunics would certainly recognize the name and come over to talk, or worse, they may have been sent to kill him because of his investigation into the former king's murder. He had to think fast.

"I go by the name Cas, Cas Olan," Kinison said quickly.

"Of course," said Brandyman, writing the name and closing the book. "Payment?"

"Your man there has my payment," Kinison said, pointing at Biff.

Brandyman turned to Biff, who reluctantly handed him the coin. He took it, looked hard at it, and nodded at Biff, who walked off sulkily. Brandyman watched Biff until he was farther down the bar, then he turned back and motioned Kinison to lean in closer.

"You'll have to forgive me, sir, but not many of these fall into my hands," he whispered, holding up the golden crown.

"I take it not many men dressed as I do come in with coins like that either, eh?" Kinison said in a whisper.

"No, indeed," Brandyman replied, still whispering. "Which begs the questions of who are you really, and do I even want to know."

"Probably not," Kinison said, giving Brandyman a meaningful look.

"You are probably right," Brandyman said.

He then straightened up and motioned for Kinison to follow him. Kinison moved to follow, but as he did so, he cast a look behind him at Biff, who was now talking to the men in the red tunics. All of them were still watching him intently. He had a bad feeling about this.

He walked behind Brandyman into a hallway connecting the tavern to the main building and then up a flight of stairs to the second floor. Brandyman unlocked a room to the right of the stairs and held it open for Kinison to enter. He then shut the door and locked it behind them. The room was large and very dark, save for the light coming from a fire in the hearth. Two chairs sat near the fire.

"So, who are you really?" Brandyman asked, sitting down in the chair closest to the door and motioning for Kinison to take the one opposite him.

Kinison sat down but did not speak. After a few long moments, Brandyman spoke again.

"Look, I may look like a simple barkeep, but do not take me for a fool. A man in simple garb enters my bar and hands me a golden crown, and I am expected to accept this at face value?" Brandyman asked, leaning back and giving Kinison a knowing smile. "Appearances can be deceiving, and yours is transparent to me. You are, or were, a member of the Guardians, and you've been exiled for something. Probably something related to the death of King Greyfuss."

Kinison tried to hide his surprise. The man's guess was unnervingly correct, and for the moment he forgot to pretend to be ignorant of the events of the previous few days.

"How do you know this?" Kinison asked before he could stop himself.

"As a barkeep, I am made aware of many things. I have perfected the art of listening, and I often overhear things that others mean to keep secret. I am also perceptive. Take those men wearing the crest of Noland, the crest of our new king, who arrive a mere hour before you do, asking for information on an escaped criminal wearing simple garb. Then you walk into my bar and throw down a golden crown." Brandyman continued with a small laugh. "Am I to take all this as mere coincidence? If you were intending to slip away into exile without being followed, you are not succeeding, my friend."

"So you intend to hand me over, I take it?"Kinison asked, his hand going immediately to his sword.

"On the contrary, I have no love for King Noliono. I do, however, wish to know more about you, Kinison Ravenloch."

At the speaking of his name, Kinison stood up and drew his sword.

"Stay your weapon, Kinison," a voice commanded from a dark corner of the room.

Kinison turned toward the sound to see a dark figure in a black hood and cloak leaning on a long wooden staff. This gave Brandyman time to draw a hidden blade and knock Kinison's sword from his hand. Brandyman then pushed Kinison back into his chair and pointed the blade at his heart.

"Put away your blade, Brandyman," the figure said, moving into the light and removing his hood. "He was never a danger to me."

Brandyman obeyed, and Kinison finally took a hard look at the newcomer's face. It was lined with age. His hair was gray and thinning, and he had a long gray beard that fell all the way to his belt. He stood clutching a staff with a strange blue stone embedded at the top. The most notable aspect of the man was his eyes, which were a deep piercing blue. The man sat down opposite Kinison and surveyed him for a long time before speaking. As the man gazed intently at him, Kinison felt as if the man could see right through him and he could not long bear the intensity of the man's gaze.

"You have nothing to fear from us, Kinison Ravenloch," he began with a stern look on his face. "Do not be surprised, for I have known you for some time."

"You may know me," Kinison said, finally looking at the man with bewilderment and anger. "Yet I do not know you."

"I am Galanor," the man said. "Doubtless you have heard of me, or at least that name?"

"I have heard of Galanor, yes, but what proof do you have that you are him?" Kinison asked.

The man struck his staff on the floor, and the stone at the top of it shone brightly for a moment. The fire left the hearth and moved to hover over the man's staff. He struck the staff again, and the stone grew dim, and the fire returned to the hearth.

"Satisfied?" Galanor asked.

Kinison stared in utter shock at what he'd just seen.

"There is much in this world that a man claims to understand, but he does not even come close," Galanor said ominously.

"Indeed," Kinison said, regaining some of his composure. "What do you want with me?"

"Much," Galanor said. "As you may have guessed, you have been exiled for your investigation of King Greyfuss's murder. Please do not ask me how I know this, just accept that I have my ways of gleaning information. You do not know who was truly behind the murder."

"I do know," said Kinison. "The man who murdered King Greyfuss is the man who gained most from his death, Noliono Noland."

"You are correct that the murderer is the man who gained the most, but Noliono did not murder Greyfuss, although he meant to do so," Galanor said matter-of-factly.

"Who was it then?" Kinison asked disbelievingly.

"A man much worse than a scheming lord with a desire for power, but I will not yet reveal him to you. I have come here tonight to make you an offer," replied Galanor.

"And what might your offer be?"

"I think I am correct in assuming you have lost your purpose in life," Galanor said matter-of-factly.

Kinison looked back at Galanor in amazement. "Yes," he said quietly.

"I have a task for you," Galanor said, looking even more intently at Kinison than before. "If you should succeed, I can give your life a purpose again."

"What do you want me to do?" Kinison asked uncertainly.

* * * *

Kinison felt angry and indignant as he rode. Galanor had sent him west to a homestead on the edge of the Forest of Roston. There, Galanor had told him, a woman and her three children lived. It was his task to go and check on a flower. *A flower!* He fumed at the humiliation of this menial task. How far had he fallen to be sent as an errand boy to check a flower?

It only took an hour to reach the Forest of Roston, and there on the edge of the trees lay the small homestead. All the windows were dark as he dismounted and walked up to the front door. He stood there on the threshold for a moment, wondering what he was going to say. *Hello, I was sent here to check on a flower...in the middle of the night.* Yes, that isn't strange or creepy at all. He shook his head and knocked on the door. There was no answer. He knocked again. When there was still no answer, Kinison began to wonder if Galanor had sent him to the right house. He knocked a third time, harder this time, and the door opened a crack.

"Who are you?" said a small voice from below him.

Kinison looked down in surprise and saw a young girl peeking at him from behind the door.

"Is your father or mother home?" Kinison asked kindly.

The young girl shook her head.

"Are you here all by yourself then?"

She nodded, a tear falling down her cheek. "My parents went into the forest for food three days ago."

"Does anyone else live here besides you and your parents?"

She shook her head.

"I heard the wolves howling and some people yelling last night," she said, more tears streaming down her face.

Kinison realized what must have happened to the girl's parents, and he was overcome with compassion and concern for this small child.

"My name is Kinison," he said, kneeling down so that he was eye level with the young girl. "What's your name?"

"Rose," she said, rubbing her eyes.

"Rose," Kinison said, and understanding hit him. "I need you to come with me, okay?"

"My parents said to stay in the house," she said, starting to close the door.

"Rose," Kinison said, holding the door open and searching for the right words. "I don't think your parents are coming back."

"They're not?"

"I don't think so, sweetie," he answered, shaking his head sadly.

She looked at him for a moment, tears welling up in her dark-brown eyes, then she opened the door and flung her arms around Kinison. He held her for a moment then picked her up and walked away from the house.

"I will take you somewhere safe," he said, carefully sitting her astride the horse.

❋   ❋   ❋   ❋

"Galanor, Brandyman," Kinison said, carrying Rose into the room at the tavern.

Galanor and Brandyman were standing by the fire talking when they entered. They turned and looked at Kinison. There was a look of deep concern on Brandyman's face.

"Rose," Brandyman said, and Kinison saw a tear in the corner of his eye.

"Uncle Sam!" Rose exclaimed as Kinison sat her down on the floor. She ran over to Brandyman, who caught her up in his arms and hugged her tightly.

"Oh, I was so worried about you!" Brandyman said, a tear sliding down his face.

Kinison looked in surprise at Galanor.

"There is no such thing as a menial task, Kinison," he said in answer to Kinison's look.

"I hadn't heard from my brother or his family in over a week," Brandyman explained. "There are no horses in this village, so I have been unable to go myself. Thank you so much."

Kinison nodded, a feeling of empathy overcoming him.

"You have completed the task, Kinison," Galanor said, beaming. "You overcame your pride and rescued a young girl. Do you wish to hear my offer?"

Kinison nodded.

Galanor grabbed Kinison's wrist and forced something into his palm. Kinison looked down to see a large black coin with a shield in the middle of it baring no sign or crest. Kinison turned the coin over to find the other side covered in an ancient script.

"What is this?" Kinison asked.

"Illumina. Tueri. Inducas," Galanor said in a strange tongue. "It means 'Enlighten. Defend. Lead.' We wish to induct you into the Shadow Garrison."

Kinison looked hard at the older man questioningly. There was silence for a long time.

"Who or what is the Shadow Garrison?" Kinison asked finally.

"We are a secret group of men who protect the realm from its enemies from without...and from within," Galanor replied.

10

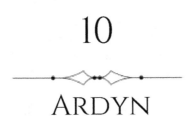

ARDYN

Ardyn Thayn awoke to the complete and utter darkness of his cell. At first the complete lack of light and the amplified sounds of scurrying rats had terrified him. Yet as time wore on, he grew more and more numb to everything. Even the perception of the passage of time had eluded him. Ardyn could not tell if days or even weeks had passed while he wasted away in this cell. The guards fed him so inconsistently that meals were unreliable as a means of measuring time. He drifted in and out of sleep and waking, and Ardyn even began wishing he could go to sleep and never wake just to escape the endless darkness. His mind had at first only worried about events transpiring above in the citadel and stopping Noliono, but now his only desire was some form of release.

"Hello, Ardyn," said a voice out of the darkness.

Ardyn started as he realized there was someone else in the cell with him.

"Who...who's there?" he asked, his voice shaking slightly.

"I am a friend."

"Who are you?" Ardyn's eyes frantically tried to pierce through the blackness.

"In the past, I have been a mere acquaintance to you, Ardyn, but I am here to become a friend to you and to bring you comfort in the midst of your suffering."

"What do you mean, you are here to bring me comfort?" Ardyn asked. "Are you not a prisoner also?"

"Am I?" the voice asked ominously. "I am the light in the darkness."

At once the room was filled with a blinding light, as if the sun had suddenly found a way to break through the thick stone walls and bring its light and warmth to Ardyn's cold, dark cell. Ardyn shielded his eyes as they struggled to adjust. When he was finally able to see again, he found a man seated across from him in the cell. Ardyn recognized him at once as the man from his dream.

"I know you," he said quickly. "You were in a dream I had just before...before all this happened. Who are you?"

"As I have told you, I am here to be your friend and to help you through this trial."

"Yes, but..." Ardyn began, but the man held up a hand, and Ardyn was rendered silent.

"Listen to me, Ardyn. You must remain strong in the coming hours. Do not allow other men to manipulate you. Remain strong and find your courage through faith."

"Faith? Faith in what?" Ardyn asked, confused.

"Faith in me."

"How can I have faith in someone I do not know?" Ardyn asked irritably.

At once the room faded, and Ardyn started awake and found himself back in the blackness of his cell.

He sighed and rubbed his eyes. What was going on? Who was this man who kept appearing in his dreams or visions or whatever they were? And what did he mean by "remain strong and find your courage through faith." Courage for what?

As he sat there thinking, he looked up and saw a dim light dancing on the far wall of the cell. He stared at it for a few moments, and as he did so, the light grew brighter. Ardyn stood up and moved toward the cell door. His stomach growled as he peered down the corridor, hoping that the guards were going to finally feed him. He continued watching as the light came closer, becoming ever brighter. As the guard came closer, the light from the lantern began to blind Ardyn, so he could not see who it was carrying the light. He backed away from the door toward the far side of the cell. Ardyn heard the rattling of keys, the soft click of the lock, and the creak of the cell door as it opened.

"Ardyn Thayn?" came a voice from the doorway.

Ardyn did not speak but shielded his eyes from the light.

"Ardyn Thayn?" came the voice again.

"Ye...yes," Ardyn said weakly.

The sound of the door opening further and footsteps echoing off the stone floor was deafening after the long silence. A hand reached out and grabbed Ardyn's tunic, forcing him into the light of the lantern. It was then that Ardyn's eyes finally fixed on the guard, and he recognized the figure as Sir Ramond Kludge.

Ardyn jerked himself free and backed into the far wall.

"Oh no, you don't, boy!" Kludge shouted, grabbing Ardyn and pulling him out of the cell.

Kludge forced Ardyn down the corridor leading to the upper halls. Ardyn would normally have been petrified with fear, but his long incarceration had numbed him to it.

"Where are you taking me?" he said, turning around in the middle of the dark corridor and facing Kludge.

"Shut it, boy!" Kludge said, shoving him forward again. "You'll get your answers soon enough. Now get moving before I gut you right here."

When they reached the upper halls, Kludge dragged Ardyn into a well-lit corridor leading to a large ornate door that Ardyn recognized at once as the entry to the chambers of the Lord Commander of the Guardians. He was totally confused now and his mind raced, trying to make some sort of sense of this. Kludge burst through the door without knocking.

"Sit down and keep quiet!" Kludge ordered as he forced Ardyn into a nearby chair.

He had just enough time to wonder what was going to happen to him when another man entered the room. It was Noliono, and he was wearing the crown of Alethia. Ardyn was shocked speechless, and fear began creeping back into him.

"What?" was all he managed to say before he felt the pain of Kludge smacking him on the back of his head.

"I told you to shut it, boy!" he yelled.

"Now, now, Lord Kludge," Noliono said smoothly, taking a seat opposite Ardyn. "There is no need for violence. The boy is obviously curious about why we've brought him here."

Ardyn made note of the different title given to Kludge by Noliono but said nothing. He watched as Noliono surveyed him, apparently sizing him up.

"Ardyn Thayn, son of Lord Anson Thayn, am I right?" Noliono asked.

Ardyn nodded, wanting to avoid speaking and, by correlation, another blow from Kludge.

"Yes, yes. I see it now in your eyes," Noliono said, continuing to survey him. "Your father's passion and pride is present. Yet I also see fear. Tell me, young Ardyn, how long have you served with the Guardians?

Ardyn eyed him for a moment but dared not remain silent.

"I had just been assigned to the night watch before I was arrested, *sire*," Ardyn said, emphasizing the last word in the hopes to engender favor. It seemed to work, for he noticed the pleasure on Noliono's face upon hearing a reference to his title.

"You were on watch the night Greyfuss Aurelia was murdered, correct?"

Ardyn nodded again.

"Can you tell me what happened during your watch?"

"I was supposed to be on watch on the ramparts overlooking the gate of the Citadel—" Ardyn began.

"Supposed to be on watch?" Noliono said, interrupting him. "What do you mean 'supposed to be,' Ardyn?"

"I fell asleep just after dusk and only awoke again when I heard the alarm, sire."

Noliono stood up and walked to a nearby painting of the citadel. He seemed to be making up his mind about something.

"Ardyn Thayn," he said, quickly turning to face Ardyn once more. "Did you know that allowing a spy or an assassin into the citadel carries the penalty of death?"

Ardyn's eyes widened in shock.

"Sire, you don't think?" Ardyn began but was silenced with another blow from Kludge.

"After careful consideration of the evidence and events of the night Greyfuss Aurelia was murdered, it is the conclusion of the Council of Lords and the Lord Commander of the Guardians that the only gap in the Citadel's defenses on the night in question occurred around dusk near the gates of the citadel. Owing to this, it has been determined that the king's assassin could only have entered the citadel at this point. Therefore, Ardyn Thayn, you are hereby charged with aiding in the assassination of Greyfuss Aurelia and will be sentenced to death at dawn!"

Ardyn was dumbstruck, his heart in his throat. The two men whom Ardyn knew were responsible for the king's death were now going to frame him for the murder. He was about to try and make a break for the door and hope to outrun Kludge when Noliono spoke again.

"However, if you would be willing to sign this confession"— Noliono held up a piece of parchment—"your crime will be pardoned, and you will receive a promotion to lieutenant in the Guardians, effective immediately."

"Wh-what?" Ardyn said, unable to contain himself. "I don't understand."

"What do you mean?" Noliono said with a smile.

"You place the blame for the king's death on me, and then you give me a promotion? If I confess to this, the people will demand my death," Ardyn said shakily.

"The people will not be told everything. It is simple, Ardyn," Noliono said silkily. "You will confess to dereliction of duty, and I will pardon you then promote you and charge you with finding the king's true killer, which you will do in a few weeks when Lord Kludge and I will provide you with a proper scapegoat. You will be declared a hero of the kingdom. All you have to do is sign the confession."

Ardyn did not know what to say. He could only stare at Noliono in disbelief.

"Lord Kludge and I will be waiting outside for you, Ardyn," Noliono said laying the parchment on the desk and motioning Kludge to exit with him. "The choice is yours—be a hero or be hanged."

The two men left the room and shut the door. Ardyn placed his face in his hands. *What should I do?* He wondered. If he refused to sign the confession, he would simply be framed for the king's murder and executed. If he signed the confession, he would save his own neck, but he'd be forced to implicate someone else to take his place. In the meantime, the true killers would get away with murdering the king. He got up and walked over to the desk. Ardyn stood staring down at the offending piece of parchment for a long time before slowly picking up the quill and then signing the document.

Ardyn put the quill down and stared at the confession. He knew what he would have to do. He would use his new position as a means to prove that Noliono and Kludge were the real culprits behind Greyfuss's murder and present the evidence to the Lord's Council. He walked to the door and knocked softly. The door opened, and Kludge looked down at him menacingly.

"Did you sign the confession?" Kludge asked, leering at him.

Ardyn nodded and handed the parchment over to him. Kludge looked at it and laughed suddenly.

"Take him back to his cell," he said to the guards with him. "But take care not to harm him. The king has special plans for this one."

"But...but I signed it," Ardyn squeaked as Kludge continued to laugh.

Ardyn considered fighting but thought better of it. He lowered his head and allowed the guards to drag him slowly down the corridor, the laughter of Lord Kludge echoing down the hall after him. It was then that Ardyn realized that Noliono's promises were all a sham just to get him to sign the confession. His countenance fell further when he realized that he'd just handed in his own death sentence and the true murderers—Noliono and Kludge—would now get away with murdering the king. Hopelessness overwhelmed him as the guards threw him back into his cell, slammed the door, and left him to despair in the blackness.

11

NOLIONO

It was working. Noliono thought as he sat in the Council of Lords's chamber, gazing across the table at the livid face of Gefric Aurelia and Renton Myr.

"What is the meaning of this, Noliono?" Gefric shouted, waving a piece of parchment.

"I will ignore your insolence this once, Lord Gefric," Noliono said darkly. "But do not test my patience."

"This parchment contains a report that an army of Noland soldiers is marching north into the Pass of Stenc and into Aurelia lands."

"The soldiers marching north have been summoned at my command, Lord Gefric, or have you forgotten that I called the banners of all Alethia this morning?" Noliono said stoically and rested his chin on his laced fingers.

"It takes days if not weeks to muster an army of this size!" Gefric shouted, clearly exasperated. "This army began marching even before Greyfuss Aurelia was murdered."

"They began marching in anticipation of the former king's decision to go to war with Nordyke," Noliono replied.

"King Greyfuss never indicated to any of us that he intended to go to war, despite our arguments," Lord Anson Thayn interjected.

"Which is why the Council of Lords made its decision to remove King Greyfuss, as I recall," Noliono said coolly.

"That was your decision, Noliono, not ours." Gefric said, his rage continuing. "I will not allow Noland soldiers to blatantly enter Aurelian lands."

"Are you refusing to allow soldiers who are honoring the summons of their rightfully elected king from obeying his command?" Noliono asked, standing and glaring at Gefric. "There is a word for that, Lord Gefric—*treason*."

A wave of murmuring went up from the Council, but Noliono stood his ground.

"Lord Gefric," Noliono said at length. "You will allow my troops to cross your lands, and all of you will call your banners and bring them north to the Last Pass by the end of the week."

At this Lords Gefric Aurelia, Renton Myr, Welsey Rydel, and Markus Eddon left the Council chambers. After watching them go, Noliono sat down again. The lords who remained were Lords Gaven Soron of House Farod, Atton of House Nenlad, Anson of House Thayn, and Baron Kaleb Jorrah, the newly appointed representative of House Noland.

"My loyal lords," Noliono said, trying to sound as if this was a surprising betrayal. "The war with Nordyke will have to wait. I believe Houses Aurelia, Myr, Rydel, and Eddon have chosen to revolt against the rest of Alethia."

"It seems so, my King," Baron Kaleb Jorrah said, barely hiding his smirk.

"Lord Gaven and Lord Atton, I will need your fleets ready to sail in two days to blockade the port towns lying along the Bay of Ryst. Above all, the port city of Abenhall must be captured," Noliono ordered. "Lord Anson, I need your troops to march on the city of Vedmore within the week. We must be prepared to hit the enemy on all sides."

At once, Lord Atton and Lord Gaven proclaimed that their fleets were at the king's disposal, but Lord Anson merely nodded.

"My lords, we face a hard situation. If these men choose war, we must be prepared. Bring your army from Farodhold and lay siege to Abenhall as soon as possible, Lord Gaven. Noland's army will seize Aurelian lands before turning west toward the city of Elengil."

"Sire," Lord Anson began weakly. "You act as if Lord Gefric and the rest have already declared open rebellion against Alethia. May I remind Your Majesty that all they have done is leave the Council chambers."

"I am only preparing for the worst, Lord Anson," Noliono sneered. "Lords, I give you leave to do what is necessary."

The lords moved to leave, but as Lord Anson reached the door, Noliono called him back.

"Lord Anson," Noliono called. "I wish you to remain."

Lord Anson turned, nodded, and returned to his seat. When the rest of the lords had left, Lord Kludge closed the door, and Noliono spoke.

"Lord Anson, I noticed, though you did not express it verbally, a reluctance to march your army south to take Vedmore."

When Lord Anson said nothing, Noliono continued. "What troubles you, my lord?" he asked, keeping his voice calm and cool.

"I believe Your Majesty knows why I am reluctant to wage war on my fellow Alethians," Lord Anson said, unable to keep his voice from breaking with anger. "There hasn't been a full-scale civil war between the great houses since the War of Ascension, when the House of Aranethon was destroyed nearly two hundred years ago."

There was a pause.

"Go on," Noliono said, continuing to remain calm.

"Yet within a fortnight of your coronation, the realm begins to splinter. So I ask you, sire, what do you suppose the catalyst is for this dissension?" Lord Anson continued, clearly becoming agitated.

"My Lord Anson, I suspected you harbored such thoughts so I took certain precautions to ensure your loyalty," Noliono said, motioning toward Kludge, who opened the door.

Two guards brought a man, bound, whose face was covered in a dark hood. The guards dumped the man in a chair across from Lord Anson and removed the hood.

"Ardyn!" Anson said, rising from his seat and staring at his son.

The shock was apparent on Anson's face. His son looked bloodied and beaten.

"Your loyalty to the crown will determine Ardyn's fate, my lord," Noliono said with a sneer. "He has signed this confession, stating that his negligence led to the death of King Greyfuss."

Noliono allowed a moment for Lord Anson to interpret the meaning of his statement.

"You will send your army to seize Vedmore within the week, or your son will be executed."

Noliono watched with satisfaction as Anson's resolve faltered.

"I will send word at once," Anson said meekly, still looking at his son.

"Good. Your son will remain here as a member of the Guardians, but be warned that we are watching your actions closely, my lord. If you betray the crown, Lord Kludge will not hesitate to end your son's life."

"I understand," Lord Anson said.

"Then take your leave, and send word to your forces at once."

Lord Anson nodded and left the Council chambers.

"Lord Kludge," Noliono said, turning to his new Lord Commander, "Please take Ardyn to the armory and see that he is prepared for duty by morning."

"At once, my King," Kludge said, bowing and leading Ardyn out of the room.

Noliono was left with his thoughts. Yes, all his schemes were coming together perfectly. His enemies were seen as traitors, and he now controlled the largest armies and fleets in Alethia. Nothing could stop his plans now.

12

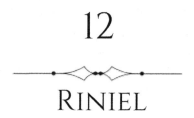

RINIEL

It was night, and the dark corridors seemed foreboding as Riniel Aurelia ran across the hard stone floors. The air was stuffy, which meant she must be in an interior corridor. She looked this way and that, but nothing seemed familiar. Just then, she heard a voice behind her calling her name. She turned. The dim torchlight illuminated a lone figure at the end of corridor. It was her father. She ran toward him, tears running down her face.

"Father, I've missed you so much!" she said, sobbing.

Then she stopped short. A dark figure was standing behind her father, raising a shining silver dagger. She tried to yell out but found that she could not speak. She watched helplessly as the figure plunged the dagger deep into her father's back.

"*No!*" Riniel screamed, waking and sitting up suddenly in a cold sweat.

She scanned the dark room, but all she saw was the dimly lit walls of her bedchamber. She covered her face with her hands and began to sob uncontrollably. She might have continued like this for some time, but at that moment her chamber doors burst open, startling her. Two people rushed into her chambers. The first was

Sir Jordan Reese, a member of the Guardians and Riniel's personal bodyguard. He was a middle-aged man with brown hair flecked with gray. He was tall, broad shouldered, and very muscular; the perfect build for a protector in Riniel's opinion. Sir Jordan had been Riniel's bodyguard when her father had been king, and King Noliono had insisted that he remain Riniel's ever-present protector.

The other person was Sarah, Kinison's wife. Since Kinison's banishment, Noliono had forced Sarah to serve as Riniel's chambermaid. Riniel had been glad of this because Sarah was a person who never made you feel uncomfortable. Since Riniel often felt out of place in the citadel now that her father was gone, Sarah had become her closest friend.

"My lady," Sarah said, softly coming to the edge of the bed and bowing. "Are you all right?"

"I'm fine," Riniel said, wiping her eyes as she hugged Sarah tightly. "Just a nightmare."

Sarah looked up at Sir Jordan, whose face showed concern.

"This is the fourth night this week, my lady," he said, his deep voice ringing off the chamber walls.

"I know," Riniel said, releasing Sarah and moving to the water basin. She splashed the cold water on her face and then covered her face with the towel. She knew they were still watching her and only removed the towel at length.

"Really, I am fine," she said with a weak smile.

"My lady," Sarah began.

"Please, Sarah, stop with the 'my lady,'" Riniel said, coming over and hugging her again. "Noliono may consider you a chambermaid, but you will always be my friend."

They stood in silent embrace for a few moments, then Riniel released her and stepped back.

"You should get some rest," Sarah said, still looking concerned. "You are to have breakfast with the king in the morning and the Guardians ceremony after that. Shall I change the bedsheets for you?"

Riniel sighed. She had forgotten all about her schedule. The dreams had begun taking their toll. She shook her head though.

"No. I think I need some air. The garden is always quiet at this hour."

"As you wish," Sir Jordan said, bowing and leaving, while Sarah brought out some clothes and a wrap for Riniel to wear.

A quarter of an hour later, Riniel was wandering about the citadel gardens. It was just beginning to grow lighter in the eastern sky, as the sun began its long journey. A light mist was about the gardens, producing a light fog. This plus the absence of any sounds from birds or insects gave the gardens an eerie sort of atmosphere. Yet the quietness of the gardens did bring her solace from her nightmares.

For about half an hour, she wandered aimlessly along the lanes of gardens, which were divided by hedges. The sun rose higher along the horizon, and her thoughts turned to the events that this day held. In a few hours, she'd be sitting in the great hall eating breakfast with King Noliono. She loathed the man, and she suspected that his letting her remain here at the citadel had not been a simple kindness. She often wondered if he might have feelings for her. The very thought repulsed Riniel.

The citadel felt like more of a prison since word had come to her that Kinison Ravenloch had been exiled. She'd always considered Kinison to be like her older brother and Sarah, Kinison's wife, to be her best friend. According to the king, Kinison had fled the citadel when he was accused of dereliction of duty leading to the death of her father. Riniel would not believe it. When she could not find Kinison anywhere, she confronted Sir Ren Gables about Kinison's absence. Sir Ren confirmed what the king had said, and she wept bitter tears for many nights. Noliono had sent Sarah to be her chambermaid. The combination of her father brutally murdered, her cousin abandoning her, Kinison's flight into exile, and Noliono overturning all that had made the citadel homelike to Riniel had left her shaken and hollow inside.

As she continued walking, her thoughts returned to her dreams, or rather nightmares, of the previous few nights. She already knew why she'd been having them. For the past three weeks, Riniel had been subtly trying to gather information regarding her father's murder, but so far she'd found nothing but hints and rumors. She'd begun to despair now of ever finding the truth about her father's murder. That was when the dreams began.

She sat down on a nearby bench and placed her face in her hands. Just as the first tears were gathering in her eyes, a strange sound caught her attention. She looked up and listened hard. The sound was a young man's voice, and it sounded as if he was just around the corner of the hedge dividing the two lanes of the garden. By the sound of his voice, he was arguing with someone. The odd thing was Riniel never heard a second voice. She could not help herself. Her curiosity got the better of her, and she rose and walked down to the corner of the lane. Peering around the corner, she saw a young man sitting on a bench with his face in his hands. She looked around for the second person but failed to find anyone. She turned back to the young man and looked hard at him.

He looked young, of average height and build, with short blonde hair. She thought he looked like a kind person and was just steeling herself to speak to him when he shouted suddenly.

"I can't do it!" he shouted, shaking his head violently. "I just can't!"

Riniel cleared her throat, causing the young man to jump to his feet suddenly and reach for his sword.

"Who's there? Where are you?" he shouted, looking around.

Riniel stepped out from behind the hedge, and the young man stood frozen, gaping at her. Out of nowhere Sir Jordan emerged, placing himself between Riniel and the young man.

"Take your hand off that sword, boy!" he shouted in a commanding voice. "Kneel before Her Majesty, Princess Riniel Aurelia!"

The young man obeyed immediately and knelt with his face to the ground.

"Who are you, sir?" Riniel asked quietly.

"Not a 'sir,' my Princess. I am Ardyn Thayn, son of Lord Anson Thayn. I am his third son, so I am now a Guardian of the Citadel," Ardyn Thayn said without looking up.

"Please rise, Ardyn Thayn, honored Guardian of the Citadel," Riniel said kindly. Then turning to Sir Jordon, she said, "You may go, Sir Jordan."

"But Princess," Sir Jordan protested.

"Sir Jordan, I doubt very much that a member of the Guardians of the Citadel bears me any ill will. Or are you saying that other members of the Guardians cannot be trusted?" Riniel said. Although there was playfulness in her voice, she knew he would get the point.

Sir Jordan bowed away, leaving her to talk with Ardyn privately.

"So, Ardyn Thayn," Riniel said once Sir Jordan had gone. "What brings you out here at this hour?"

"Perhaps the same reasons as princess," Ardyn said sheepishly. "I came for the quiet atmosphere and to think."

"You were thinking rather loudly," Riniel said, grinning.

Ardyn turned away.

"I wonder if you might reveal what is troubling you, Ardyn?" Riniel said, sitting down on a nearby bench.

"It's none of your concern!" he shouted, forgetting himself.

There was a moment of silence, and Riniel thought that she caught a brief glimpse of Sir Jordan peering around the corner of the hedge.

"I'm sorry, Your Highness," Ardyn said quickly and bowed. "I am not myself."

"Please sit," Riniel said, gesturing to the seat beside her.

Ardyn looked awkward and backed away a step.

"I won't bite," she said.

"As Your Highness wishes," Ardyn said, taking a seat and looking, if possible, more awkward.

"Now tell me what troubles you, Ardyn."

"I...I can't say."

"Why not?"

"It is a personal matter," he said timidly. "I do not wish to say, Princess."

"Oh?" Riniel said, becoming very interested.

An awkward silence passed before Ardyn spoke again.

"If I tell you, Your Highness, can you keep it to yourself?" Ardyn said as respectfully as possible.

"Ardyn Thayn," Riniel said, rather insulted by the young man's question. "As a princess, I am privy to many secrets, and I am very good at keeping them."

"Yes, well," Ardyn said with clear trepidation. "Can I trust you to keep this one? I must have your confidence, my lady, for it concerns you. I do not wish you to come to harm."

Riniel eyed Ardyn suspiciously but nodded.

Ardyn moved in close and whispered in Riniel's ear.

"I know who killed your father."

"Who?" Riniel asked, her eyes widening.

"His name is Meth—" but Ardyn stopped short.

There was sudden noise from behind her. She turned around but saw nothing. As she turned back to Ardyn, she saw his expression had changed. In his eyes there was a mixture of fear and anxiety.

"Are you all right?" she asked, concerned.

"Yes!" he said sharply, standing up suddenly. "I have to go. I'm on duty soon."

Riniel stood up, staring as Ardyn ran from the gardens at a full sprint.

"Wait!" she called after him. She turned to Sir Jordan, who shrugged. Riniel shook her head, wondering if this boy really knew who had killed her father, or was he just a fool trying to feel important?

* * * *

Riniel's head was still spinning when she returned from the citadel gardens. Her conversation with Ardyn concerning her father's murderer had left her shaken and bewildered. Sir Jordan Reese was by her side and eyeing her thoughtfully.

"My Princess," Sir Jordan finally said. "Forgive my bluntness, but I pray that you will not take the words of that boy seriously."

"How can I not, Sir Jordan?" Riniel asked, keeping her eyes forward and refusing to look at him.

"Princess, he is just a boy. He is a little older than seventeen—a foolish age, which..." Sir Jordan stopped when Riniel shot him a look of deep offense.

"Sir Jordan, may I remind you that I too am only seventeen," she said in a measured voice.

"Yes, Princess, but you are more educated and mature for your age," Sir Jordan contended. "Most young people your age are foolish and gullible. They believe any rumor they hear and spread it like truth, even going so far as to include themselves in the rumor in order to satisfy some need for attention. This boy strikes me as no different."

Riniel was quiet for a moment, then she said, "I value your counsel, Sir Jordan, yet I did not see deceit in Ardyn Thayn's eyes. Though I do not know him well, somehow I trust what he said."

They remained silent as they approached the Great Hall, and as Sir Jordan opened the side door for Riniel to enter, the sound of harsh whispering resonated off the stone walls. The hall was dark save the torchlight. Riniel moved into the shadows and gestured for Sir Jordan to close the door and join her. She edged closer to the voices and began catching some of the words.

"So the plan is set, my King," said a harsh and raspy voice.

"Very good, Lord Kludge. I will speak to her tonight," King Noliono said, his voice clear and recognizable now. "By proposing marriage to Riniel Aurelia, it will stabilize my claim to the throne of Alethia and ensure the loyalty of the Lords's Council."

Riniel gasped suddenly, unable to contain her surprise and fear. The two men stopped talking for a moment as if to listen then continued talking, apparently believing the noise was of no concern.

"What if she refuses, sire?"

"If she refuses, I have means to deal with her," the king replied.

"My men tell me that she has been investigating King Greyfuss's murder," Lord Kludge said, a hint of fear in his voice.

"It is of no consequence," the king said. "I would have expected nothing less of the headstrong daughter of Greyfuss Aurelia, yet she will never discover the truth. Come, let us make the final preparations in case the princess chooses wrongly."

The sound of two men's footfalls echoed off the stone floor. The sound of a door opening and closing came, and then there was utter silence. Riniel stood overwhelmed by what she had just overheard. Sir Jordan placed a tentative hand on her shoulder and turned her toward him.

"My Princess, I am sorry I doubted you and Ardyn."

"Wha...what do I do, Sir Jordan?" Riniel said, her voice shaking.

Sir Jordan did not speak but gently drew her back to the side door and out into the courtyard. They walked across the courtyard, back into the corridors leading to the princess's chambers. As they walked, Riniel looked about her. The new day had dawned, and the sky was turning bright blue. People were beginning their daily routines, completely unaware of the crisis going on within the walls of the very place they worked every day. They climbed the stairs and entered Riniel's chambers. Sarah was waiting on them and smiled as they entered.

"Sarah," Sir Jordan said earnestly. "Go stand in the hall outside. If you see the king or any of his men coming this way, you are to come back in here and warn us immediately. Do you understand?"

Sarah nodded, the smile falling from her face. She walked out into the hall, and Sir Jordan shut the door behind her.

"Now," Sir Jordan said, turning back to Riniel, "we must make preparations for your escape, my Princess."

"Escape?" Riniel asked, confused. Where can I go?"

"Your cousin, Lord Gefric, has departed the city for the ancient stronghold of your House, Rockhold."

"Gefric left?"

"Yes, Princess. Word has spread through the Guardians that there was a major disagreement between King Noliono and some of the members of the Council of Lords. The Lords Aurelia, Myr, Rydel, and Eddon have all left the city in protest and returned to their own lands. A war may be coming, yet I believed you would be safe here in the citadel. Now that is not so certain."

"How do I get to Rockhold without being noticed?"

"I do not know, but we must think of something."

At that moment, Sarah burst into the room. Her face was stricken, and fear was apparent in her voice.

"The king is coming!"

13

KINISON

The northern reaches of the lands belonging to the House of Myr were sparsely populated in those days. Small farms, tiny towns, and hamlets of no more than fifty people dotted the landscape between the edge of the Gray Mountains in the east and the Forest of Oakwood in the west. The only purpose these hamlets truly served was to offer hospitality and shelter to those traveling between the cities of Elengil and Stonewall.

Yet the closer one wandered to Oakwood, the fewer towns there were along the way. Most travelers, who were forced to travel through Oakwood, chose to cross its northern arm, for it was the narrowest and presumed the least dangerous. That is why the town of Castel existed.

Castel, a quaint little town situated on the northeastern bank of the River of Westmore, was the only sizeable town between the cities of Elengil and Stonewall. Many travelers chose Castel as their last stop before braving the dangers of Oakwood, which explained the town's importance and relative prosperity. Situated on a frontier of sorts, the danger of Oakwood Forest prompted the townspeople of Castel to build a palisade wall around the entire perimeter of the town long ago. Every male child born in the town was trained from a young age as a defender on the wall. It was around nightfall that these defenders saw a lone rider, shrouded in a black hood and cloak, approaching the town gates.

"Halt, stranger!" the guard captain shouted as he stood on the ramparts over the town gates. "Declare yourself."

The rider was within fifty yards from the wall, moving forward slowly and silently.

"Answer, stranger, or you will be considered an enemy!" the captain shouted again.

Still not speaking, the figure continued forward. The captain grabbed a bow from a nearby guard and fitted an arrow in the string.

"Speak, stranger, or die!" the captain shouted, bending back his bow and aiming at the figure. "This is your last warning!"

The figure was now only twenty yards from the gate, well within the light of the torches.

"I am a friend of Castel," the stranger said, pulling back his hood and revealing the face of Kinison Ravenloch, though none recognized him.

"What is your name and business here?" the captain asked with his bow still bent.

"I am Cas Olan," Kinison replied, holding up his right hand in sign of peace. "I am journeying north and seek shelter from the night."

"Are you armed?" the captain asked, eyeing the stranger.

"I am," Kinison replied.

"Dismount your horse and place your weapons on the ground in front of you," the captain said.

"I mean Castel no harm, but I will not relinquish my arms," Kinison said firmly. "Then you are not welcome here. Be off at once, or you will be killed," the captain said,

motioning for his men to bend their bows.

"Ambulavero in umbras, sed lucem facies mea afferat (I walk in the shadows, but light shines from my face)," Kinison said.

There was a long silence.

"Luceat lux vestra coram hominibus (Let your light shine before men)," the captain said, as if in reply, then turning to his men, he ordered them to open the town gates.

Kinison dismounted and led his horse through the now-opened gates, ignoring the stares from the other guards. The captain met him on the other side and motioned for Kinison to walk with him.

Kinison approached the captain, noting that intermixed with his dark hair was some gray. He held out his hand to Kinison, who took it with a small smile.

"Well met, brother," the captain whispered once he and Kinison were out of earshot of the other guards. "I am Captain Jon Grehm of the Castel City Watch. And you, brother?"

Kinison responded hesitantly. He was still unaccustomed to complete strangers calling him "brother." "I am Kinison Ravenloch, though I go by the name Cas."

Kinison had only been a member of the Shadow Garrison for a week, and he'd been surprised at how many of its members he'd already met during his journey from Ethriel. In every village there was a safe house, in every city a small contingent of men watching over the other citizens. He'd often wondered how such a large association of men had remained so organized yet so secret for so many centuries.

"What brings you to Castel?" the captain asked.

"I am journeying north to Stonewall," Kinison replied then stopped and looked at the man for a moment before continuing. "I am being pursued by the king's men for a crime I did not commit. Any help you can provide will be much appreciated."

"Some men arrived earlier today bearing the crest of the House of Noland. They inquired around town concerning an escaped fugitive fitting your description," the captain said, eyeing him. "They said that this futigive murdered King Greyfuss."

"Do not believe it!" Kinison nearly shouted in anger. He paused a moment to calm himself before continuing. "There is but one kingslayer, and he now sits on the throne of Alethia."

The captain's eyes grew wide for a moment. Then he said, "My men and I will be on the watch for them. Should they reach the gates tonight, I will send word to you at once."

"Are the men here trustworthy?"

"Some are, but be on your guard, brother," the captain said, looking worried. "My watch is over at midnight. I will join you shortly after. In the meantime, watch what you say in here and trust no one."

The captain left Kinison standing by the entrance to the local inn. The building was three stories tall and constructed entirely of dark-gray stone. The building was so large that it was easily the largest building in the small town. The size and stone workmanship of the building had heavily influenced the structure's importance in the community. The inn's original name had been forgotten long ago. The townspeople referred to the inn as the Castle of Castel, or the castle for short.

Because of the late hour, the only light emanating from the inn came from the ground floor. All the upper floors were dark, and the shutters were drawn over the windows. Kinison pushed open the bulky wooden doors and entered.

He found himself in a large and dimly lit room with a bar along the far wall. The few patrons still in the room glanced momentarily toward the newcomer but then returned to their drinks. Kinison moved to the bar and stood there looking for the innkeeper. He found the man talking to someone at the other end of the bar. The innkeeper, noticing Kinison, moved over and eyed him suspiciously.

"Help you?" he said curtly.

"I'm looking for a room for the night."

"Name?" the innkeeper said, pulling out a large book from under the bar.

"Cas Olan," Kinison said.

"Payment?" the innkeeper asked, putting the book away.

Kinison pulled out a silver lion and placed it on the bar. Before leaving, Brandyman had exchanged his five golden crowns with one hundred silver lions so as not to be so conspicuous. The innkeeper pocketed the coin and motioned for Kinison to follow him. He led him out a side door onto a creaky wooden stairwell leading up to the upper floors. Upon reaching the third floor, the innkeeper led Kinison through a dark hallway until reaching the last room. He opened the door and motioned Kinison into the room.

Kinison entered the shabby room, wondering if the bedsheets had ever been changed. The smell was barely tolerable. There wasn't even a window to bring in fresh air.

"Do you have any other rooms?" Kinison asked, turning to the innkeeper.

"None 'til tomorrow," the man said, closing the door behind him.

Kinison sighed and sat down on the bed. His thoughts drifted to Sarah. His heart sank as he again reflected on the fact that he might never see her again. The thoughts were like daggers in his heart. A sharp knock at the door brought him back. He opened the door to find Captain Jon Grehm standing there.

"Quickly, follow me," the captain whispered in earnest.

Kinison stood eyeing the captain suspiciously. The captain reached in and grabbed Kinison's tunic.

"Quickly!" he whispered, pulling him out the door and down the hall.

The captain pushed open a door on his left and pulled Kinison in after him. He turned and locked the door. Kinison looked about the room in surprise. This room was much nicer than the one he'd just left. It was larger, the furnishings were finer, and a handsome fire was crackly in the grate.

"Well, Kinison, you've wasted no time getting yourself into trouble," said a voice from the corner nearest to the fire.

Kinison turned to see Galanor wrapped in a traveling cloak and looking careworn.

"You picked a fine way to begin your service to the Garrison. You've been followed all the way from Elengil by soldiers of the House of Noland," Galanor said chidingly. "Had it not been for the knowledge and wits of the captain here, you would have been murdered in that room tonight. As the former Lord Commander of the Guardians, I expected you to be more cautious and observant than this."

Kinison said nothing but glared resentfully at Galanor. He was in no mood to be chastised.

"Who is this innkeeper, Jon?" Galanor said, turning to the captain. "Is he in the employ of the king or worse?"

"No, Galanor. Sam Muddberg is only an opportunistic simpleton," the captain said with a sigh. "Two days ago a messenger of the new king came to the inn and proclaimed that a fugitive named Kinison Ravenloch, who was charged with treason, had escaped and was on his way here. The messenger said that if anyone brought news concerning this man, leading to his capture, the king would reward him with ten golden crowns. The capture of the man would earn him a hundred golden crowns. Sam and many others in town seemed very interested in the reward."

"Then why did you send me to the inn?" Kinison said exasperatedly at the captain.

"You forget yourself, Kinison," Galanor said in retort. "The good captain here just saved your life. Had he been idle or lost his wits, you would be dead now."

Kinison paused a moment then turned to the captain with his hand outstretched. "Thank you, Captain. I owe you much, it seems. Forgive my outburst as well. I am unused to relying on others for help."

"A brother does this and more for another," the captain said, shaking Kinison's hand and smiling.

"What of the innkeeper?" Galanor said quickly. "Word of Kinison's whereabouts must not reach the ears of the king."

"My men have already dealt with Sam only moments ago," the captain replied. "One of my men is already in place to pose as the inn's new owner in the morning. We will spread a rumor that Sam took advantage of our man and sold the inn at a nice profit. That should satisfy any who knew Sam well."

"Good," Galanor said, sighing with relief. "It brings me some comfort knowing the new king will be none the wiser."

"This new king could be a major problem for us, Galanor," the captain said, rubbing the back of his neck. "His goals are not yet known, and his contacts seem to stretch well beyond the borders of his lands and the capital."

"He also seems to want no loose ends," Galanor said with a meaningful look at Kinison. "You, Kinison, are in grave danger. This new king will not stop until you are found."

"Do you think the king is in league with Methangoth?" Jon began to ask, but Galanor cut him off.

"This is not the time, Jon," he hissed.

"Who is Methangoth?" Kinison asked, looking at the two men in confusion.

"There is more, Galanor," the captain said earnestly and ignoring Kinison's question. "I have heard rumors of a mass mustering of men from Castel to Elengil. Word has spread that Lord Renton Myr is mustering his army. For what purpose, I do not know."

"I have heard as much from other members of the Garrison from Farodhold to Stonewall," Galanor said gravely. "War is brewing between the various great houses in Alethia. I fear that a full-scale civil war is near at hand."

"Turning back to the matter at hand," Kinison said impatiently. "What do you suggest I do?"

Galanor sat in deep thought for a moment and then said, "I think you should continue on the mission I set you. We are near the borders of Oakwood, and few brave the dangers of that forest without great need."

"But Galanor, this is the main route from Elengil to Stonewall. If any pursuit arrives here, they will assume Kinison entered the forest," the captain said.

"You are correct, of course, Jon. Therefore, we must take measures to throw off pursuit. Kinison will take a longer, more dangerous course, and he must leave before sunrise," Galanor replied intently. "Jon, you must journey across these northern lands, gathering the other members of the Garrison. I will return to Elengil and meet with Lord Myr and convince him to join us. We must all meet back at Elengil."

"Galanor, what of Methangoth?" Jon asked, obstinately breaching the subject again. "If Kinison is journeying near Ardaband, he needs to know about him and take precautions."

Kinison looked at Galanor, who sighed deeply.

"Very well," he said, acquiescing. He looked intently at Kinison, as if studying him, before he spoke again. "Methangoth is a dark sorcerer who, last we knew, resides at Ardaband."

"What is Ardaband?" Kinison asked impatiently.

"Do not interrupt," Galanor said irritably. "Ardaband is the ruins of a great fortress that lies deep in the Forest of Oakwood. It is an evil place with an even more evil history. Just know you must avoid that place at all costs, especially after you have obtained the *Book of Aduin* and the boy."

"But who is Methangoth?"

"I told you, he is a dark sorcerer," Galanor replied, clearly losing patience. "An evil genius who desires ultimate power. He has already put his plan in motion, and his followers are already working to achieve his goals. King Noliono is one of his key pawns."

"But how will obtaining this book help him obtain ultimate power?" Kinison asked, shaking his head in confusion.

"Methangoth believes the *Book of Aduin* contains spells and enchantments that will give him this power. He will do anything to obtain it."

"Does it?" Kinison asked, his interest peaked.

"No, it contains within its pages something much more powerful," answered Galanor vaguely. "I have revealed enough, Kinison. You have a long and dangerous journey ahead of you, and you need rest if you are to leave before the sun rises," Galanor said, getting up and moving to the door. He hesitated then turned and looked intently at Kinison. "Beware of Ardaband, Kinison. There are creatures in the forest born of darkness that few have the power to defend against. They are the wolves of Ardaband, gifted with the mind and speech of humans by Methangoth. You must protect the boy and the book, Kinison."

"What about Sarah?" Kinison said earnestly. "You promised that you knew a way to rescue her from the citadel."

"A plan is in motion, Kinison," Galanor said after a moment's hesitation. "I cannot say more just now."

The old wizard and the captain left Kinison feeling frustrated. He knew that Galanor was right and he needed more rest but resented the fact that Galanor had not revealed all he knew about the book and this mysterious sorcerer. He lay down in the bed, but it was a long time before he finally felt sleep take him.

14

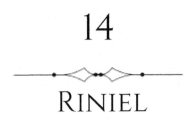

RINIEL

Riniel was overwhelmed with worry. It had been a week since Noliono had visited her and proposed marriage. She pretended to be shocked and told him that she still needed time to grieve her father's death, but seeing the dangerous look in his eyes, she said that she would consider his proposal. Meanwhile, she and Sir Jordan had still not thought of a way for her to escape. Her days were busy with appearing at Noliono's side as he dealt with affairs of state, yet she suspected that he merely wanted her there to legitimize his claim to power and, of course, the throne.

Her nights were spent in her chambers where she spent hours pacing back and forth. She had to think of a way to escape before Noliono forced her to marry him. A knock at the door brought her out of deep thoughts.

"Enter."

The door opened, and Sir Jordan Reese entered, followed by Ardyn.

"My lady," Sir Jordan said, bowing. "This young man craves an audience."

"That is fine, Sir Jordan, and please stay also. We have much to discuss," Riniel said, gesturing to a small table and chairs nearby.

They all sat silently for a moment before Ardyn spoke.

"Princess," he said hesitantly. "The king plans to formally propose to you at the feast in three days."

"Then that means I must flee...tonight," Riniel stated anxiously.

"Flee where?" asked Sir Jordan. "Noliono is now king, and reports have come in telling of an army of over three thousand men of Noland have crossed the River Belwash. I have also heard that the Council of Lords has been dissolved. Noliono has declared your cousin, Lord Gefric Aurelia, in open rebellion, as well as Lords Myr, Rydel, and Eddon. Whom can we trust, and where can we go?"

Riniel looked at Ardyn, who was staring at her.

"Princess," Ardyn said softly. "I think I have an idea. There is a passage out of the citadel that is unguarded except by members of the Guardians."

"I have not heard of this passage," Sir Jordan snapped.

"It is a recent discovery," Ardyn protested. "Lord Kludge and Sir Ren Gables believe it was made before the War of Ascension."

"Fine," Sir Jordan said grudgingly. "How does it help us?"

"Since few know about it, the passage is not guarded. We can be out of the city before anyone notices."

"We?" Sir Jordan asked suspiciously. "Why do you wish to accompany us?"

"Sir Jordan, please, Ardyn is a friend. Please remember that," Riniel said chidingly. Then turning to Ardyn, she said, "Ardyn, please tell us everything."

✳ ✳ ✳ ✳

After discussing at length how they were to escape the citadel and arrive safely at Rockhold, Ardyn and Sir Jordan left to make preparations. Before leaving, Sir Jordan had cautioned Riniel yet again about trusting Ardyn. She had to admit her doubts, but she had no alternative. Now came the difficult time of waiting. She hated waiting. She tried to occupy her mind with reading, but she never got beyond a few pages before she realized that she had no recollection of the pages she had just read. A knock at the door caused her to jump to her feet.

"Enter," she said and was surprised by the shakiness in her voice.

The door opened, and Noliono entered the room. Two members of the Guardians entered after him. He wore an expression of triumph, though he was obviously trying to hide it.

"Your Majesty," Riniel said, curtsying. "What brings you to my chambers?"

Noliono turned to his guards and motioned for them to go. After they had closed the door and they were alone, he spoke.

"My Princess," Noliono bowed to her in an uncharacteristic display of honor and respect toward her, which he had neglected during their time spent with the Council. "I have come to see if you are well."

"If I am well?"

"Your behavior of late and rumors telling of your discontent have not gone unnoticed by your king, Princess Riniel," Noliono said, a gleam in his eye, as he looked hard at Riniel, making her insides squirm.

"I am well, Your Highness," she said, not meeting his eyes.

Noliono crossed the room and took her hands in his.

"My Princess," he said, his voice soft and gentle. "This was your home long before it was mine. Please know that I will do all in my power to make you happy and comfortable here."

Riniel met his eyes, and a part of her wanted to believe him, but the rest of her wanted to reach out and strangle the man.

"I know, Your Majesty," Riniel said, lowering her eyes.

He placed his hand under her chin and gently raised her gaze back up to his again. "I care for you deeply, Riniel. You must know this."

Riniel did not speak but stood there, trying to control her rage and fear. Noliono turned and walked to the door but stopped with his hand on the handle.

"Princess," he said in an almost pleading tone. "Please do not do anything rash."

He left the room and closed the door. At that moment, fear gripped Riniel's heart like a python. *Does he suspect? Does he know?*

✳   ✳   ✳   ✳

Ardyn and Sir Jordan returned late that evening to find Riniel seated and silently staring out of the window.

"Princess? Are you all right?" Sir Jordan asked.

"Noliono came to see me earlier," she said without looking at him.

"What did he want?" Sir Jordan asked.

"I...I think he knows something," she said, finally turning.

"What do you mean?"

"He asked some questions that made me wonder."

"How could he know? Only the three of us know about our plans, and Ardyn and I have been together all day."

"There isn't time for this," Ardyn said softly.

"He's right," Sir Jordan said, helping Riniel to her feet. "If we are to attempt escape, it must be now."

Riniel was silent and thoughtful for a moment then nodded.

"Good. Now put this on," Ardyn said, stepping forward and handing her a dark weather-stained hood and cloak.

Riniel took them and suddenly realized that Ardyn and Sir Jordan were not wearing their usual Guardian's uniform but instead were wearing common clothes and a hood and cloak similar to hers.

"Quickly," Sir Jordan said, helping her put it on and pulling the hood over her face. "Now for it."

"No, wait," she said, turning to Ardyn. "Please, tell me who killed my father."

She saw a look of discomfort cross Ardyn's face before Sir Jordan interrupted them.

"There is no time, Princess," he hissed. "We must go!"

They all left her chambers and made their way through the citadel by side passages and less-frequented corridors. There were still several times when a servant nearly spotted them, but they quickly disappeared into a nearby room or corridor. Riniel's heart was pounding in her chest. She felt faint but steeled herself and would not admit it to the two men with her. She wanted to be strong.

What seemed like hours later, they reached the corridor leading to the secret gate. Riniel breathed a small sigh of relief but realized it was premature. Standing on either side of the "unguarded gate" were two Guardians with drawn swords. Riniel turned to retreat and found two more Guardians behind them, walking up the corridor toward them.

A trap! she thought.

"Well done, Ardyn," came the voice of Noliono.

Riniel turned back to see the king, Sir Kludge, and several more Guardians emerging from the gate.

"Arrest Sir Jordan," the king commanded. "He is charged with attempting to abduct Princess Riniel."

The men charged forward and seized Sir Jordan before he could draw his weapon. He tried to fight and swore vengeance on Ardyn and the king, but in the end he was dragged away to the dungeons.

Riniel was overcome with panic and grief.

"How could you!" she screamed at Ardyn, who looked at his feet guiltily. "You liar! Everything you told me was a lie! You betrayed us! You betrayed me!"

"Princess, please calm yourself," Noliono said consolingly. "The danger has passed. You are safe."

Riniel lunged forward to get at Ardyn, but two Guardians restrained her.

"Let me go!" she screamed.

"Take the princess back to her chambers," Noliono ordered. "She is distraught by the betrayal of her personal Guardian. She needs rest. See to it that she is not disturbed nor visited by anyone."

"No! Release me! No!" Riniel screamed as the Guardians carried her back up the corridor toward her chambers.

Was all lost? she asked herself as tears poured from her eyes.

15

CORIN

It was late and unusually quiet for the end of the week. Barely ten patrons were in the Eagle's Nest, a local tavern in Stonewall so called because it sat so high on the western slope that it gave a clear view of the surrounding countryside. Many travelers and city dwellers considered the Eagle's Nest a second home, frequenting the establishment often. Yet for some reason, the tavern was quiet.

Corin sat at his usual table, sipping his ale and thinking. Coming to the Eagle's Nest had become a weekly ritual for him after he began working at the Stonewall Academy. He'd just turned eighteen a few weeks ago, and since the departure of his best friend, Ardyn Thayn, he'd taken to visiting the Eagle's Nest. Unfortunately, his weekly vigil only made him miss his friend all the more. He'd spent most of his days working at the academy sorting books, working in the kitchens, and various odd jobs the headmaster gave him. His nights were spent reading through the many ancient tomes and books that filled the academy's endless bookshelves. Although Corin enjoyed his time among the shelves, something inside him always yearned to venture outside the stone walls of the academy and explore the lands described in his books.

Corin's visits to the Eagle's Nest also stirred his desire to venture beyond his usual haunts. Although Stonewall was the largest city in the region, Corin still could not help yearning to see other places and meet other interesting people. The Eagle's Nest was frequented by travelers from all over the kingdom, bringing new tales of their adventures abroad. Corin loved to sit and listen to the travelers' tales and looked forward to visiting the tavern each week. Yet listening to all the interesting stories also had a downside, as they often forced Corin to consider the monotony of his own life. He began to yearn for adventure and a life beyond the walls of Stonewall. He would allow the stories to wash over him, and he would begin making plans to leave Stonewall and set out for anywhere else; yet when he returned to his room at the academy, he felt guilty for wanting so badly to break away from his obligation to the only home he remembered.

Since it was so quiet, Corin had been sitting and staring at his mug, pondering what he would do if he was free of his obligations and had enough money to leave Stonewall. He had just taken a long draft of his ale and was considering going home earlier than usual when a man sat down abruptly at his table.

"You look as if you could use some good conversation," said the stranger.

Corin looked at the man, taking in his sharp eyes, black goatee, and red hat with a long red feather sticking out of it. His first impression was that this man was not to be trusted.

"I was just leaving," Corin said, starting to stand up.

"Pity," the man said. "There is such a scarcity of interesting people here tonight, and I thought you might enjoy a tale or two about Oakwood Forest."

Corin stared at the man and sat back down in his chair.

"How's about another ale, on me, of course?" the man said, snapping his fingers.

As if the bartender had been waiting for the man's signal, two fresh mugs of ale appeared on the table. The man handed the bartender a silver lion, which made Corin gape in astonishment. He realized that he would have had to work a week to earn a single silver lion, and here this man was handing them out like it was Christmas.

"Who are you?" Corin asked abruptly.

"Oh, forgive my rudeness," the man said, taking off his hat. "My name is Silas Morgan."

"The Silas Morgan?" Corin asked, gaping at the man again. "The man who fought against the kingdom of Donia and captured its king?"

"No," the man said with a chuckle. "That was my grandfather, also known as Silas Morgan."

"Then are you the Silas Morgan who sailed across the Sea of Aear to rescue the Princess of Eddynland from the evil tyrant Rydnalt?"

"No," the man sighed. "That was my father."

Corin looked questioningly at the man.

"We Morgans like to pass our names down to our sons. It allows the name to live on and earn more glory," Silas said, apparently trying not to look annoyed. "And you are?"

"Oh," Corin said, coming to himself and extending his hand. "I am Corin Stone."

"A Stone, eh?" Silas said. "You must be one of Stonewall's many orphans. The only people named *Stone* are those with no known family."

Corin looked down at his mug in shame.

"Hey now!" Silas said abruptly, making Corin look up. "A name is nothing unless you make it something. My father's name has followed me since birth, but his name is not mine any more than his life is mine. My name is my own, and my life is my own, which brings me to a point I wish to make to you, young Corin."

Silas leaned forward, causing Corin to lean forward also.

"I've noticed you come in here every week and listen to the travelers' tales of far-off lands. I know you long to travel and experience the wide world. So why don't you?"

"I stay because I have an obligation to my job."

"To the academy?" Silas asked forcefully. "Says who? You don't owe anyone anything. Lord Thayn pays to support the academy. You don't owe them anything."

"They took care of me and raised me," Corin protested.

"And for that be grateful, but don't let a sense of misplaced obligation drive you to give up on your dreams," Silas said, staring as if to burn his point into Corin's head. "It's your life!"

"I also have no money."

"But if you did, what would you do? Where would you go?" Silas asked with a mischievous grin.

Corin shrugged.

"Aren't you tired of simply reading about adventure?"

"How do you know so much about me?" Corin asked suspiciously.

"As I said before, I have noticed you come to the tavern every week. I've asked around about you and learned much."

"Why?" Corin asked, a sense of foreboding growing in his gut.

"Well, I think I know of a way to help you leave Stonewall and help support the academy like you want."

"Why do you want to help me?"

"Because I believe helping you will help me."

"How?"

Silas motioned him closer then whispered, "Are you familiar with the restricted collections in the chambers beneath the academy?"

✳ ✳ ✳ ✳

Corin shook his head in disbelief as he entered the main hall of the academy. He could not believe he was actually doing this. It was midnight, and there was only silence. Most of the scholars and archivists were gone. Only the night guards and headmaster were still there. Most of the lamps were dark, and Corin walked quickly and quietly through the dimly lit corridors. The only sound came from his footfalls, which echoed off the cold stone walls. He was alone and about to do something against his better judgment.

"Why am I doing this?" he kept asking himself over and over again.

A sound at the other end of the hall made him dart into a nearby recess in the wall. He waited in the shadows, hardly daring to breathe. A light danced on the walls of the corridor. Someone was coming down the corridor toward him. Corin knew that when the person reached him, they would see him, and he had no reasonable excuse for his presence at the academy at this late hour. They were now only ten feet away. Then just as Corin had given up hope and was about to declare himself, the light disappeared down a side corridor. Corin peered around the corner and then sprinted down the hall to the far doorway. He descended the spiral staircase, taking them three at a time. He was three floors below the main hall before he stopped to catch his breath.

He stood panting and arguing with himself over whether he should go on or not when he saw what lay at the other end of the corridor. A lamp hung from the ceiling, illuminating a large iron-bound door. Corin walked slowly toward the door, noticing that his steps were disturbing the dust that covered the floor. He reached for the large handle and pulled. The old door creaked loudly, echoing back up the dark passage. Corin froze and listened for the sound of footsteps descending the staircase behind him. He waited and listened for what seemed like hours but heard no sound. He pulled opened the door wide enough for him to squeeze through and entered the room beyond.

Corin blinked as the light from the room momentarily blinded him. When his eyes finally adjusted, he found himself in a well-lit room filled with shelves upon shelves of ancient tomes. His heart skipped a beat as he cast his gaze around the room, wondering how old these books were and how much gold each one was worth.

After a few minutes of staring, Corin remembered why he was there. Silas had told him to look for a book entitled *The Book of Aduin*. The book, Silas had told him, was worth fifty golden crowns, and Corin's share would be ten crowns for retrieving it. This was the equivalent of almost five years' pay. It was enough money to support the academy and give him the chance to break free and travel the world.

Corin wandered through the selves, searching for the book. Many of the books were written in the old tongue of Alethia, which Corin had never learned to read proficiently. He could make out a few words, but none of the books resembled the title he was searching for. This was taking forever, and the fact that this room was so well lit made Corin suspect that someone could return at any moment. He moved toward the back of the room until he came to the end of a row of shelves and noticed a lone book sitting on a reading stand. He walked toward the stand to get a better look. The book was of regular size but very thick. Many of its pages were old, yet other pages looked brand-new. He closed the book to get a look at the front cover, which read in peeling gold letters: *The Book of Aduin*. He had found it. Corin's heart was racing as he picked the book up from its stand. All at once, every light in the room went out, and Corin heard the crash of something large and metal falling to the floor. He groped his way back down the row of shelves to the door, which he found barred by a small iron portcullis.

Corin sunk to the floor, knowing he'd been caught and there was no way out of this. After a while, a light appeared at the other end of the corridor leading to the upper floors. Many voices and the sound of many booted feet came echoing down the corridor. Corin looked up to see the face of Markus Tolen, the headmaster of Stonewall Academy, gazing down at him with a look of malevolent triumph. Corin hung his head in dispair.

✳ ✳ ✳ ✳

The door closed with a deafening slam. Corin was seated in the headmaster's office, his hands bound and his heart beating fast. Suddenly he found himself face down on the floor, the side of his head throbbing in pain. Stars floated before his eyes.

"That's enough," came the sneering voice of Markus Tolen, headmaster of Stonewall Academy. "Pick the boy up, gentlemen."

Corin felt strong hands grasp his arms and hoist him back into the chair. His head felt fit to burst, the pain intensified by his being jerked up from the floor. The room spun for a few more seconds, then Corin looked up to see the snide face of Markus Tolen smiling down at him from behind his desk.

"So," the headmaster began, grinning at him malevolently. "You thought to come into *my* academy and steal a priceless tome from its shelves?"

Corin looked down in shame.

"Just tell me, boy. Why did you try to steal the book?"

Corin was about to answer when he felt another sharp blow to the side of his head. He was on the floor again, staring at the cold stone.

"Pick him up!" Tolen shouted, and once again Corin was hoisted back into the chair.

The room swam before his eyes, and he felt faint.

"Answer me, boy!" came the headmaster's voice from what seemed to Corin like a great distance.

Corin watched uncomprehendingly as the figure of the headmaster came from behind the desk. He felt the old man's hands grab his tunic.

"Answer me, boy, or I'll..." the headmaster yelled but stopped short for there was a loud knock on the door.

All turned to see the door open, and a short, overweight man with a grim face entered, followed by four armed guards in chainmail. All the guards wore the traditional blue tunics with a white eagle emblazed on their chest, the colors and symbol of House Thayn. The short man also wore a blue tunic but without the white eagle. He also wore a black cape that fell almost to the floor.

The headmaster stood dumbstruck, staring bewildered at the newcomers.

"Leave us!" the short man commanded. His voice was high pitched and whiny.

"At once, my lord," said the headmaster, bowing and leaving quickly.

When the door was closed, the short man turned to Corin.

"Do you know who I am?"

Corin shook his head.

"I am Zul Voss, the advisor to Lord Anson Thayn. In his absence, I am Lord of Stonewall," Voss said, a sense of pride in his whiny voice. "It has come to my attention that a priceless Alethia treasure was nearly stolen tonight, and I understand that you are the thief."

Voss bent down over Corin and grinned malevolently down at him. Corin instantly despised the small man.

"I know who you are, boy," Voss said in a whisper that only he and Corin could hear. "Have you heard the name Methangoth?"

Corin shook his head slowly.

"Well, he's heard of you," Voss said, his eyes flashing maliciously as he backed away and walked around the headmaster's desk. "So, you thought that you'd just walk into the academy and steal the *Book of Aduin*, did you? Well, my master has been trying for years, as have I, to lay hands on the book."

"Your master?" Corin asked, confused. "I thought you served Lord Thayn."

"I serve the true master of Alethia," Voss said with a wicked laugh. "He has been seeking the *Book of Aduin* for many years. The book has been hidden for years by the fool, Galanor, but thanks to you, we now know where it lies. My master will be pleased, for I have found the book and the heir."

"The heir?" Corin asked, feeling more and more uneasy by the man's stare.

"The last of the Aranethons," Voss whispered as he leaned over so that only Corin could hear him. "Tell me where the book lies, boy," Voss said, wearing a dangerous smile.

Corin did not want to tell this man anything, let alone where the book was hidden.

"Tell me now willingly, or I shall force you to tell me," Voss said, coming back around the desk and getting right in Corin's face so that he could smell the short man's breath. Corin and Voss stared at one another for several moments, then Voss straightened up and motioned to one of the guards, who came over and picked Corin up.

"Take him to one of the city prisons," Voss ordered with a nasty look at Corin. "See that he is *taken care of.*"

✻　✻　✻　✻

An hour later, Corin found himself locked in a jail cell on the lower south side of Stonewall. In the dismal cell filled with other lowlifes and ruffians, Corin sat condemning himself.

Why, oh, why did I listen to that conman? Corin asked himself over and over again.

He sat in silent thought until his personal interrogation and condemnation was interrupted by one of his bored cellmates.

"Eh, little man!" came a gruff voice from the far corner. "Whatcha in for?"

Corin remained silent.

"Whatsa matta?" the man said, standing up and moving toward him. "Someone cut out your tongue?"

Corin looked up and noticed not only the alarming size of the man but also the gleam in his eyes. The man's eyes screamed murderer, and Corin's heart began to race.

"Oh, I get it," the man said, pretending to come to some profound conclusion. "You think you're better than me, eh?" The man stooped and picked Corin up, slamming him to the wall. "You got something to say, little man?"

Corin stared at the man in silence. After considering him for a moment, the man suddenly punched Corin in the face. The force of the punch knocked Corin to the ground. His head was spinning, and his eyes saw stars. He heard the sound of the jail door opening.

"Back off," said a familiar voice.

Corin looked up and saw Silas standing over him. Two jailors with drawn swords were forcing the other prisoners away.

"Come with me," Silas said, helping Corin to his feet. "I've paid your fine."

Silas led Corin out into the street and down several blocks to a shabby building that looked abandoned.

"Come on," Silas said, opening the door.

Corin obeyed, and upon entering the room, he saw a shabby one-room apartment with a small fire crackling in the grate. Several chairs encircled an old wooden table, and a few empty plates and mugs littered its surface.

He turned to thank Silas when he noticed two strangers standing beside him. The two newcomers were big burly men. Silas shut the door and motioned Corin to sit down. Corin did so, and Silas and the two men joined him at the table.

"So," Silas said. "Where is the book?"

"I...I don't have it," Corin mumbled.

"Where is it then?" Silas said, still trying to sound calm.

"I don't know. The headmaster took it and..."

Silas slammed his fists on the table, cutting Corin off. He stood and began to pace the room while his goons glared menacingly at Corin.

"So you did find the book?" Silas asked, stopping to look at Corin.

Corin nodded.

"So, you can go back tomorrow?"

"What?"

"You will go back for the book tomorrow," Silas said, this time more of a statement than a request.

"I...I can't. The headmaster told me to never come back."

Silas ran over and struck Corin across the face, knocking him to the floor.

"Stupid boy!" Silas screamed. "You had a simple task to retrieve a book!"

"It was a trap!" Corin yelled in retort. "When I tried to pick up the book, it triggered some kind of hidden switch. I was caught..."

"But you will try again!" Silas shouted.

"I...I can't."

Silas grabbed Corin by his tunic and pulled him up. "Is that your final word?"

Corin nodded fearfully.

"Then there is no further use for you," Silas said, releasing him and walking to the door. Silas opened the door and closed it behind him.

"Wait!" Corin shouted as the two men stood and began moving toward him.

Suddenly, the door burst open, and Silas came hurtling in and crashed to the floor.

Corin and the other two men looked over as another man in a gray traveling cloak and hood entered the room. The two men pulled knives from their belts and rushed at the newcomer, who unsheathed his sword. In a flash of steel, the two men now lay dead at the newcomer's feet. Corin gaped at him. The man came over to him and looked at him closely.

"What is your name?"

Corin looked at him in shock.

"What is your name!" the man asked, seizing Corin by the tunic and shaking him violently.

"C-C-Corin. C-Corin Stone," he stammered.

"Do you recognize this?" the man asked, pulling out a large black coin with a shield in the middle of it baring no sign or crest.

Corin stared then pulled out the same coin that Galanor had given him. They matched perfectly. Corin looked up at the stranger in wonder. The man released Corin and pointed his sword at Silas. "Follow us and you die too."

Silas glared back him angrily.

"Come on," the stranger said, pulling Corin out the door and into the dark street. "Follow me closely."

They darted from street to street for what felt like hours, always staying in the shadows. Finally, they reached the city walls, which towered up on their left. Corin looked up in awe at the great stone boundary protecting its namesake city. The man led Corin to a small unguarded gate and motioned Corin to follow him as he darted toward it. Corin hesitated.

"Do you really want to stay and let Silas find you again?" the stranger whispered.

Corin shook his head and followed the stranger. In a few moments, Corin and the stranger were outside the walls and running across the great stone bridge that transverse the massive chasm, which separated the mountain on which Stonewall was built and the rest of the plains beyond. It was because of the chasm that the city was built, for it provided ample protection from raiders and invading armies. In the centuries since its founding, Stonewall had never been taken by an enemy force. Corin looked back for a moment at the vast city that was built on the mountainside and knew he may never see it again. He shook off the feeling and met up with the stranger at the other end of the bridge. They continued on until the stranger stopped in a wooded area not far from the bridge, and they sat down together. The man handed Corin a water skin, which he took gratefully.

"Thank you," Corin gasped between gulps.

When he had drank his fill, Corin looked at the stranger carefully. The sun was beginning to rise and in the dim light. Corin thought he saw a kind face. He finally summoned the courage to ask the man who he was.

"My name?" the stranger said, appearing to hesitate. "You may call me Cas Olan, or Cas for short. And you are Corin Stone."

Corin nodded.

"That was a foolish thing you did, joining up with thieves and attempting to steal from the Stonewall Academy. Why would you do this?"

"Who are you to criticize me for my actions?" Corin asked in indignation. "You killed two men back there."

"They attacked me, and I defended myself," Cas replied calmly. "But do not sidestep my question: why would you do this?"

"I...I wanted out!" Corin finally said. "I wanted to leave the academy, leave this city, and maybe even leave the kingdom."

"Why?"

"I wanted to live my own life!" Corin said, his voice exposing his emotional exhaustion. "I wanted to explore the world, but I needed money."

"So you conspired with known criminals to steal one of the most important books in the entire kingdom?"

Corin looked at Cas questioningly.

"Surely you know why the book you were going to steal is so valuable?"

"How do you know so much about me and my doings?"

"I know many things, Corin Stone. I have been told much about you and your doings," Cas said, interrupting. "The *Book of Aduin* is the last surviving book that includes the history of Alethia before the War of Ascension, which you know occurred about two hundred years ago."

Corin's eyes grew wide in astonishment.

"All our other histories only go back to the rise of the House of Aurelia and the Aurelian line of kings, but the *Book of Aduin* goes back over eight hundred years to the rise of the first king of Alethia, and it is the only record of the lost House of Aranethon."

"I've heard of House Aranethon, but I've not been told its true significance."

"The House of Aranethon ruled Alethia for four hundred years until the War of Ascension and the fall of the house."

"So if the house fell, why is it so important to have a record of it?"

"The House of Aranethon fell, but was not destroyed," Cas said, shifting slightly and leaning back against a nearby tree. "The House of Aranethon survived through Gideon, third son of King Gregory Aranethon, who escaped and settled in the foothills of Eodar, near the beginnings of the River Westmore. Later he and his family traveled west through Oakwood and settled in the city of Stonewall. There the family thrived for several generations, though they had lost all political influence or military power. Then seventeen years ago, a group of mercenaries hired by some unknown lord found them. Markus and Kaleen Aranethon were killed, but not before hiding their one-year-old son in an upstairs cupboard. A wandering city watchman found the door broken and the house in shambles some hours later. He found the young boy crying in the cupboard and brought him to the academy."

Corin's brow broke into a sweat. He had no memory of his parents or any idea of who they were. When he had asked the headmaster, the man had told him that a guard had brought him in with no other information except that his name was Corin. He looked up and saw Cas watching him closely.

"You know, don't you?" Cas asked.

"Know what?"

"You know who you really are?"

"Who I really am?"

"Yes," Cas said, pointing at him. "You are Corin Aranethon, the last survivor of the House of Aranethon and the true heir to the throne of Alethia."

"What!" Corin said, standing up and backing away. "That's crazy! You're crazy!"

"It is not crazy. It *is* the truth," Cas said, opening his bag and pulling out a book. "Let me prove it to you."

"Is that..."

"It is," Cas answered. "*The Book of Aduin.*"

16

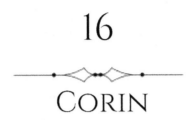

CORIN

Corin could hardly believe it. Even after five days, he still could not truly believe that he, Corin Stone, was a direct descendant of the Aranethon kings. Even when Cas had shown him *the Book of Aduin* and his ancestry, he still wondered if this was just a hoax. He had been fooled before, and he promised himself that he would not allow it to happen again.

They had been traveling for three days in the blackness of the Forest of Oakwood. During the day, the forest was in a gray half-light; the forest fell into near complete darkness beneath the towering trees. Yesterday, they had crossed a river that Cas called the Vedmore River. Corin, who loved maps and had spent hours studying the maps at the Stonewall Academy, knew they were entering the deepest and darkest part of the forest. Corin had also heard many stories of the perils of Oakwood, most of which ended badly.

One story, in particular, frightened Corin more than any other—the story of the Dark Magician and his dark fortress deep within Oakwood. Corin tried to push the memories of that story from his mind, but with the darkness and the strange noises all around him, it was hard to keep his imagination in check. Suddenly, Corin felt his foot catch on a root and he fell forward into the hard earth.

"You all right?" came the voice of Cas through the darkness ahead of him.

"Yeah, I'm fine." Corin grunted, taking Cas's outstretched hand.

"For a decendant of kings, you aren't very graceful." Cas said, with a smirk that even the darkness could not hide.

"Shouldn't you call me 'Your Majesty' or something." Corin threw back with a weak smile.

"Not unless you've got the Crown of Alethia in your back pocket. With balance like that, I'll certainly never call you 'Your Grace'." Cas said, helping Corin to his feet.

They both shared a laugh. Corin was growing to like Cas, though he realized he still knew very little about the man.

They walked on for a few minutes in silence, then Cas stopped suddenly and turned toward Corin. His face was grave.

"Did you hear that?" He whispered.

"Hear what?" Corin asked, becoming very alarmed.

"Nothing. The forest is silent." Cas answered, peering into the darkness. "There isn't so much as a stray gust of wind."

They stood in silence for several minutes, both listening intently.

"Come on," said Cas, finally.

They walked through the underbrush, trying to minimize any hint of their passing; the forest remained silent. Corin felt a growing sense of uneasiness. He felt like eyes were watching him from within the gloom surrounding them. They entered a small gully where the river had once run long ago; the far side rose up to create a steep, near-impassible ridge. When they had reached the bottom, Cas held out his hand to stop him. Corin was about to speak, but Cas held up a finger to silence him. He was scanning the ridge above them, looking for something. Corin strained his eyes to pierce the gloom on the other side of the gully.

"Something is hunting us." Cas whispered, slowly.

"What?" Corin asked, his heart beginning to beat very fast.

"I'm not sure." Cas said, still scanning the ridge.

Corin's mind immediately went back to the story of the Dark Magician, who, according to legend, enchanted the wolves of Oakwood with human intelligence and even enabled them to speak. The thought made him shudder as he scanned the far side of the gully. Wolves were bad enough, but wolves with human intelligence...Corin's eyes darted all along the ridge line, looking for something he hoped he wouldn't find.

After several tense minutes, Cas pulled Corin along the gully until they found a place where they could climb out. Cas had just helped him climb up when he grabbed Corin's shoulder unexpectedly.

"Look," he said, and Corin followed Cas's gaze to the other side of the gully where several pairs of red-glowing eyes stared back at them.

"Wh-what are they?" Corin whispered.

"Wolves of Ardaband!" Cas exclaimed. "Run! Run for the River Westmore!"

Corin turned and ran, his legs moving faster than he had ever run in his life. The darkness slowed Corin down only slightly as he dodged trees and brambles. The thought of those wolves chasing him through the blackness made him continue even when his sides began to ache and his every breath was a struggle. In what seemed like hours later, Corin found himself on the west bank of a river that he assumed was the River Westmore. Either the darkness hid the far bank or this point of the river was extremely wide. He stopped, panting hard. He listened carefully, trying to hear over the sound of his wheezing and puffing. The forest was still silent.

Where was Cas? Corin thought, suddenly realizing he was all alone. He straightened up, looking wildly about the gloom surrounding him. There was no sign of another living thing. His heart was still beating fast; fear was beginning to overwhelm him.

Not wanting to leave Cas behind, he began moving quietly

along the riverbank, trying to blend with the trees. He walked downstream for a long time, but caught neither sight nor sound of Cas or any other living thing. He paused to rest by a large oak, which he felt sheltered him from unseen watchers in the gloom. After half an hour had passed, Corin felt fear rising up in his chest again. What if Cas had been caught or even killed? How could he get out of the forest without him? Should he go back and look for Cas, or was there no point? All these thoughts came rushing into Corin's mind. He began to panic and was just about to call out Cas's name when he saw movement on his right. Corin looked to see a massive gray wolf emerge from the gloom, followed by several others. Corin was overcome with terror. All the wolves were looking straight at him, their eyes glowing red in the darkness. He hesitated for a moment, but the lead wolf started toward him.

"It's him," the wolf snared to the others.

Corin froze, gaping at the wolf in surprise.

"Wh-who are you?" Corin stammered.

"I am Bodolf, and there is no escape," the wolf growled with an unmistakable grin. "No matter where you run, I will find you."

Corin had no other option, so he turned and plunged into the river.

The water was ice cold, stealing Corin's breath. He felt momentarily stunned, but the howling of the wolves behind him brought Corin quickly back to his senses. He swam as fast as possible, trying to reach the far bank. He felt himself making progress, but as he neared the river's center, Corin felt the swiftness of the current. He was dragged downstream at a rapid pace. Corin swam with all his might; yet when he finally got to the other side, the river had carried him several miles downstream.

Corin climbed out of the river and onto the eastern bank and looked about him. There was nothing to be seen or heard except the monstrous oaks rising up out of the gloom and the creaking of old limbs catching a scarce breeze. Corin noticed it was even darker now than it was earlier and realized that the sun must be setting. He turned to scan the far bank but could not even make it out in the growing darkness. Corin quickly realized the need to find shelter for the night.

He stood up, brushed himself off, and began walking east, or at least what he thought was east. What Corin did not know was that while he was being pulled downstream, the river had bent southeastward. He was now actually walking northeast and into the darkest part of the forest.

*   *   *   *

Several hours passed, and the darkness had become almost complete. Corin was beginning to succumb to his fear again as he continued walking. His heart was now beating so fast that he felt it might burst. Out of the gloom, a solid stone wall suddenly appeared, and Corin nearly walked right into it. He stepped back and placed a hand on it. The cold stone was very old. Corin could feel the decades of erosion that wind and rain had inflicted upon it. He walked to the left, keeping his right hand on the wall, and he soon found an opening, where the stones had collapsed and fallen outward.

Corin walked through the opening, picking his way through the ruined stones, and saw a glorious sight. Before him, stretching out several dozen yards, was a stone courtyard. High above, illuminating the entire area, the full moon shone brightly. Corin stared for several moments, drinking in the welcome moonlight, and actually smiled despite his circumstances. After pausing for a moment, he slowly began to make his way across the courtyard to the crumbling remains of what was once the great hall. The roof had caved in, but the walls were still intact. Corin slipped inside and found a corner near one of the windows and sat down. For the first time in days, he felt a small sense of security. Corin yawned then slapped himself awake. He knew he could not fall asleep, so he looked about the hall. It was aged stonework much like the outside wall. The furnishings had long been pillaged or rotted away. None of the long tables or chairs remained. It was difficult to imagine why any lord would want a castle here in the midst of Oakwood.

It was not long after he'd sat down that Corin heard the faint sound of footsteps. He froze, listing intently as the sound grew louder and nearer. A few moments later, a dark figure wearing a dark hood and cloak emerged from the entrance on the far side of the hall. The figure did not pause or look around but walked resolutely toward Corin. Despite the figure's mysterious appearance, Corin did not feel a sense of fear. About ten feet away, the figure stopped and removed his hood. Corin saw that it was a man with a pleasant face. The man looked straight at him and smiled warmly. Corin saw a kindness in those brown eyes that put him at ease, despite his circumstances.

"May I join you?" the man asked in a loud voice.

Corin looked about as the man's voice echoed off the walls.

"Oh, don't worry," the man said as if in answer to Corin's thoughts and fears. "We are safe."

As the man sat down, his cloak opened, and Corin saw a white robe underneath. The robe shone like the sun, and for a moment the entire hall was as bright as a sunny day. Corin was blinded, but the man quickly drew his cloak back over his robe, and darkness returned.

"Sorry about that," said the man. "Most people can't handle the light. They try to hide from it. In darkness such as this, however, its power is felt more intensely."

Corin was confused, and so many questions filled his mind. He wondered which to ask first.

"Who are you?" he finally asked. It seemed like a good place to start at any rate.

"Who am I?" the man asked as if considering carefully before he replied. "I am he who has come to bring a *light* to your situation."

"Huh?" Corin said, now even more confused. "I don't understand."

"Few do," the man said gravely. "I have come to help guide you out of here, Corin."

"How do you know my name?" Corin asked suspiciously.

"I know much about you, yet you know very little of me," the man said sadly. "I have come so that you would believe what I tell you and do what I tell you."

Corin was baffled by this whole situation.

"When you awake, the wolves of Ardaband will find you," the man continued.

"When I awake? You mean this is a dream?" Corin asked disbelievingly.

"Of a sort, yes," the man replied simply. "You must not run."

"What?" Corin asked incredulously. "If I don't run, the wolves will kill me."

"No, they will not kill you," the man said reassuringly. "A man will appear who will defend you *if* you do not run. You will not know him, and he certainly does not know Me, but he will help you."

"So...you don't know him, and I don't know him, yet I'm just supposed to trust you both with my life?" Corin nearly shouted.

"You must surrender to him and obey him without any resistance," the man replied firmly.

Corin stared at the man in disbelief. How could he trust this man...this dream...this...whatever it was.

The man looked back at him, and Corin saw something in the man's eyes. He did not know what to call it, but somehow he knew he must believe what the man was telling him. Corin nodded, and the man stood up.

"Remember to obey the stranger, no matter what. Do not despair, for I am with you. Now awake."

✳   ✳   ✳   ✳

Corin woke up with a start. He looked about the great hall, searching for any sign of the strange man, but found nothing.

Corin shook his head, wondering what to make of his dream or whatever it was. Just then, the sound of sniffing and scuffling came from just outside the hall. Corin was suddenly brought back to the reality of his situation. He got into a crouching position and tried not to make a sound. His heart was racing as he looked about the far wall for something—anything that might help him. He saw on the far side of the hall a door partially hidden by an old tattered tapestry. He was about to make a break for the door when the words from the stranger in his dream reentered his mind. *You must not run.*

Corin shook his head. He was being stupid. How could he trust a dream? The wolves would eat him alive if he sat there obeying the instructions a *stranger* told him in a *dream*. Then a thought came to him. *What if I don't run, but instead I creep quietly across the hall? That is still obeying the spirit of the dream's instructions right?* He hesitated for another minute and then decided to go for it. Corin crept slowly and cautiously across the hall. Somehow he made it to the far side of the hall without make a sound. He was just about to pat himself on the back when something big and gray came at him from out of a dark corner. Corin was knocked to the ground. Dazed for a moment, he was brought back to reality by a sharp stabbing pain that erupted from his leg. Corin looked down to see the shredded remains of his left leg in the jaws of an enormous wolf; its eyes glowing red in the darkness. Corin was seized with terror and pain. He screamed as the wolf bit down harder on his injured leg. He saw a broken staff lying on the floor next to him. He seized it and swung it as hard as he could at the wolf's head, but all he got was a hateful look from the beast tearing his leg to shreds. Corin seized the wolf's jaws and tried to pull them open, but its jaws were too strong. Panic grew inside him as he grabbed the staff again and swung it at the wolf's head over and over again until his arm felt like it would fall off. He was about to give up when out of the shadows, a large hooded figure bounded into the fray.

The figure pulled back his hood, drew out his sword, and cut off the wolf's head before the brute was even aware. Corin felt the wolf's jaws instantly release, and he pulled his leg out of the dead wolf's jaws. He turned toward his rescuer, but in the darkness, Corin could not make out the man's features, save that man had a shaved head. A snarl drew Corin's attention as three more wolves emerged from the shadows and surrounded the figure.

"Give us the boy," the wolf in front growled, and Corin instantly recognized him as Bodolf.

The man held out a torch that Corin had missed at first. The wolves shrank away from it and snapped at it in anger. The three wolves growled at one another for a moment, as if deciding a strategy, and then all attacked at once. Corin knew the wolves had actually planned the attack because they managed to knock the figure down and caused him to drop his sword and torch. The man righted himself, but the wolves were on him in a moment. Corin shut his eyes. He knew that both he and the newcomer were dead. There was the sound of snarling, the singing of a sword slicing through the air, scuffling of feet and claws on the hard stone floor, a sharp yowl, a whimper, and then silence. It was the silence that made Corin open his eyes. He stared in disbelief as the man rose. In his hand was a dagger dripping in blood, and all three wolves were dead at his feet.

"H-how?" Corin stammered, but the pain in his leg was too much.

The man did not speak but knelt down beside him. He took off his hood, revealing a darkskinned face and eyes. Corin was afraid of the eyes. He then remembered his dream, but somehow this was not what he had expected. The man moved toward Corin and went straight to his left leg. Corin watched as the man inspected the leg carefully and then shook his head. The man went to his sword, picked it up, and cleaned it thoroughly. He then walked back over to Corin and put a hand on his shoulder.

"You will feel this," the man said in a deep and solemn voice.

"F-feel w-what?" Corin stammered through the pain.

"Prepare yourself."

Then the man swung his sword high, and it came slicing down

near Corin's leg. Corin looked down at where the lower half of his left leg had been, looked at the man, felt an intense wave of pain, and then knew no more.

17

AZKA

Azka had traveled for weeks, stalked his prey for days, waited for his chance to strike for hours, and now he had only minutes to save the life of a young man who had been marked for death. The boy's leg was bleeding badly. He quickly found some spare bandages in his pack and bound them tightly on the boy's leg. He then turned and built a fire, waiting impatiently for the fire to burn hot enough to cauterize the wound.

The boy, though unconscious, shivered and called out into the night. Azka bathed the wound in hot water hourly, watching and waiting for a sign. Night became day, and he waited. Day became night, and still he waited. Another day and night passed, and yet the boy remained unconscious. His forehead burned though he shivered under Azka's blankets. Finally on the fourth night, the young man's fever broke, and he finally woke up. Azka was mopping the young man's forehead, when the young man awoke and started at the sight of the large dark man kneeling over him.

"Who? What?" the young man stammered.

"Rest," Azka said in his deep voice, relieved to see the boy finally awake. "You are safe."

The young man looked at Azka in the face, then his eyes rolled back, and he fell back asleep.

Azka got up and walked outside of the circle of firelight. He stopped and sat down about fifty paces away. The worst was over, yet he could not get over the irony of the situation. Here he was, sent to assassinate this boy, and instead he was saving his life. This boy was his target—or was he? How could he be sure? Azka had never made a mistake and taken the life of an innocent, and he would not start now. He had argued with himself for the past four days, and now it came to it.

A scream echoed off the walls of the ruins coming from the direction of the fire. Azka crossed the courtyard to find the boy staring at his left leg, or rather the stump where his leg had been.

"You...you...how?" the young man gasped, clearly overwhelmed.

Azka remained silent.

"Why did you? How could you? My leg! *What have you done to my leg!*" he screamed at Azka.

"The wolves of Ardaband had torn your flesh and shattered the bone. You would have died had I not..."

"*No!*" the young man raged. "You were sent to rescue me, but you...how could you...what have you done?"

Azka was silent, while the young man sobbed uncontrollably. He was struck by the young man's words: *You were sent to rescue me.* It was indeed quite the opposite, yet Azka remained silent for a long time.

"What is your name?" Azka finally asked.

The boy simply glared at him through tear-filled eyes.

"I saved your life from wolves and from bleeding to death," Azka said calmly. "The least you owe me is to tell me your name."

"My name is Corin Stone," the young man said gruffly.

"I see," Azka said then got up abruptly and walked away.

"Where are you going? Come back!" Corin yelled.

Azka ignored him. So this boy was his target. He knew what he should do, but for some reason he could not do it this time. He went a dozen or so yards from the fire and sat down. The sun was rising in the east, and the darkness was fading to dim morning. He decided to meditate on this issue, hoping that the solution would come to him.

He closed his eyes, but a sound caused them to reopen almost immediately. Sitting opposite him was a man with a pleasant face, dressed in a dark-gray robe. The man smiled at him, but Azka jumped to his feet and drew his sword.

"All those who take up the sword shall perish by the sword," the man said.

Azka dropped the sword quickly for it felt like the metal had suddenly grown white hot. He looked down at the pool of liquefied metal that was all that was left of his sword.

"Now sit with me," the stranger said, sitting down opposite Azka.

Azka obeyed almost without thinking. It was as if the stranger's words could not be resisted or ignored.

"Who are you?" Azka asked, a sense of fear growing in his heart—a sensation that he had not felt for a long time.

"I am a stranger to you. Where you are from, they do not know me nor do they speak my name. You have lived in ignorance of me, so I am here to enlighten you."

Azka was silent. He studied the man, who returned his gaze. He soon found he could not long endure the eyes of the stranger. He dropped his gaze and remained silent.

"You have done much evil in your life, Azka."

Somehow Azka was not surprised that the stranger knew his name.

"You have killed many people. Why?"

Azka tried again to look up but found it impossible to meet the stranger's gaze.

"Why are you silent, oh, man?"

"The lives I have taken were for the greater good," Azka said almost in protest.

"Whose good?"

"The good of the people who suffered from the selfish actions of the individuals I killed."

"How do you know that the people you *helped* are better off now?"

"What?" Azka asked, surprised by the question. "The men I killed were corrupt or brutal."

"Yes, but did you consider who would replace them?" the stranger asked calmly. "Consider your last victim. Yes, he was a corrupt city official who stole from the people and squandered it on his lusts, but would you be surprised to know that the man who replaced him is worse."

Azka was silent, taking in what the stranger said. The words were ringing true in his heart somehow.

"Not only does this new man demand more from the people, but he kills any who cannot pay. Since you killed the first man, eighty people have died in Nenholm."

Azka's eyes grew wide, and his heart was pierced to the core. He began to question every action he had ever taken, every decision made, every life he had taken. He had been so sure that taking those men's lives would bring peace and restoration, that somehow he was making a positive difference in the world. Now he knew that eighty innocent people had died because of him. He could not bear it.

"You cannot change the past," the stranger said softly. "What is done is done. But you can change yourself and what you will do presently."

"How?" Azka asked, but the stranger was gone.

He stood up and instinctively reached for his sword. It was still in its sheath. He looked down where the pool of molten metal had been, but there was nothing there. He drew it his sword and noticed that the blade seemed warm to the touch. He returned it to his scabbard and remained in silent thought for a time. *Was it all a dream or vision?* he wondered. Even if it had been, did that matter? Somehow Azka knew that the stranger was telling the truth, and based on that fact, he now had to make a decision—would he kill the boy or not?

Azka returned to the fire. The young man was still weeping over his leg and did not look up. Azka watched him for a long while and then made his decision.

"We must go."

"Go? Go where?" Corin said absentmindedly. He seemed barely aware of Azka. He only stared at his leg.

"I will take you to your companion."

"Cas?" Corin asked, looking up finally. "You know where he is?"

"Come," Azka said, helping Corin up and giving him a tree limb, which was shaped perfectly to serve as a crutch. "He is not far."

Azka gathered his belongings and supplies, doused the fire, and he and Corin began making their way out of the courtyard.

❊ ❊ ❊ ❊

After several grueling hours, Azka and Corin stopped to make camp. The sun was setting and Azka knew that Corin's wound would need bathing and warmth. He made a fire and tried to make Corin comfortable, but the young man was inconsolable.

"Not far, eh?" Corin said sarcastically. "So how do you measure distance?"

Azka ignored the boy. If he had been quick-tempered, the young man would be dead. Azka had endured many slights and offenses from the young man over the course of the day. He clearly did not understand that Azka could kill him in a moment. *Let him vent*, Azka thought. *It is probably the pain talking.*

After heating the water, Azka soaked a rag and moved to clean Corin's wound.

"Give me the rag," Corin demanded with a glare. "I'll do it."

Azka looked hard at him, but Corin stared back in defiance. After a moment, Azka handed him the rag and settled back against a tree. The forest was black again. The only light came from their little campfire. Azka listened carefully, but there was no sound save the burning wood and Corin's wincing.

"Who are you anyway?" Corin asked, finally throwing the rag down in anger.

"I am Azka," he replied, taking the bloody rag and washing it in the hot water.

"That's a strange name. Where are you from?"

Azka closed his eyes. "I come from the south, many hundreds of leagues south of Alethia, where the seas are warm and summer never ends."

"So why are you here?" Corin gasped as a sharp, stabbing pain emanated from his leg.

"I was brought to this land as a child with my younger sister to escape the wars of my people," Azka said sadly.

"Your family brought you here?"

"No," Azka sighed. "We were brought to Nenholm by my uncle, who sold us into slavery."

"You're a slave?"

"I was freed many years ago by a man named Galanor."

"Galanor? You know him?"

Azka merely nodded.

"What about your sister?"

"She was sold to another man who took her far away. I have been searching for her for many years, but I have yet to find her," Azka said, bowing his head.

"I am sorry," Azka heard Corin mumble.

They were silent for several moments, then Corin spoke again.

"So what brought you to Oakwood?"

"I came on a journey seeking you, Corin Stone."

"That's interesting. You are the second person to tell me that in the last few days," Corin said, looking alarmed. "So, why were you seeking me?"

Azka looked hard at Corin, considering what telling him the truth would do.

"You need rest. Perhaps I will tell you more in the morning."

It was clear that Corin wanted to protest, but Azka's expression was stone.

✳ ✳ ✳ ✳

When Corin's breathing became more rhythmic, Azka stole away into the forest. He knew what he must do—find the boy's companion and lead him back to Corin. The problem was that before he did not know where to start looking. By happenstance, Azka had noticed a trail of footprints during their day's journey. Guessing by the tracks that a man had passed the same way recently, Azka deduced that it must be Corin's companion.

After about an hour of tracking, Azka saw a faint glimmer of light in the distance. He made for it and found a lone traveler sitting beside a fire. He gauged the situation carefully, noticing the loaded crossbow lying next to the traveler. The man was focused on the fire at the movement, which meant that if Azka simply appeared in the firelight, the man might shoot him. Azka knew what he must do.

Skirting around the edge of the firelight, Azka managed to get behind the man. Without making a sound, he crept up behind him. In a sudden fluid motion, Azka grabbed the man and subdued him.

"Do not fear," Azka said, restraining the man without injury. "You have nothing to fear from me."

The man struggled for several seconds but could not break Azka's hold. Finally, the man nodded, indicating his surrender.

"Before I release you, answer me this: are you searching for someone?"

The man hesitated and then nodded.

"Are you searching for Corin Stone?"

The man nodded again.

"Last question, are you Cas?"

At that, somehow the man broke free and drew his sword, but Azka was now holding the crossbow.

"How do you know that name?" the man asked warily.

"I have been searching for a man by that name because I know he was traveling with a young man named Corin Stone."

"Do you know where Corin is?"

"That depends...are you Cas?"

The man hesitated then nodded.

"Good. Gather your things, and I will lead you to him."

"Is he all right?" Cas asked.

"He was injured, but I think he will be fine."

Cas grabbed his things, snuffed out the fire, and Azka led him back to his camp.

＊ ＊ ＊ ＊

About an hour later, Azka and Cas arrived back at his camp. Corin was snoring softly, and the fire was low. When Cas saw the young man, he ran over and gasped when he saw Corin's leg.

"What have you done to him!" Cas cried out.

"The wolves of Ardaband attacked him, and his flesh was torn and broken. If I had not taken the boy's leg, he would have died," Azka replied calmly.

Azka watched as Cas checked Corin's condition.

"Where did this happen?" Cas asked, finally turning back to Azka.

"In the ruins of Ardaband."

"Ardaband?" Cas gasped. "What madness drove Corin into that cursed place?"

"The boy sought shelter there," Azka said plainly. "Little did he know that many wolves have gathered there. For what reason, I know not."

"So you both walked all this way?"

"Indeed. The boy's strength is remarkable in one seemingly so frail. He should recover in a few more days."

Cas nodded absentmindedly. Azka heard him whisper, "But will Alethia accept him now as king."

"If he is indeed the last son of Aranethon, the people will flock to his banner regardless of his physical condition," Azka said, slipping into the darkness.

"How do you..." Cas began to ask but stopped when he realized Azka was gone.

18

KINISON

"Hey, Cas, what city is that?" Kinison heard Corin ask. He was sitting astride a horse that Kinison had acquired in a village near the eastern edge of Oakwood. They had just come over a hill that overlooked the plains to the east of Oakwood, giving them a clear view of the surrounding countryside. A large city lay to the east, built on a large hill, and shone in the morning sun.

"That is the city of Elengil," Kinison replied, stopping for a moment to gaze out at the plains below. The city was still leagues away, yet its tall white walls and gleaming towers shone in the early morning sun so that the city was especially prominent on the horizon. "And I told you last night, my real name is Kinison."

"Sorry, I forgot," Corin said quickly. Then Kinison heard Corin murmur, "Elengil."

"It is the city of the ancient kings of Alethia, and some call it the true capital of the kingdom."

"Why do they say that?" Corin asked, unable to hide the eagerness in his voice.

"Because the kings of Alethia ruled from Elengil until the War of Ascension. The House of Aranethon ruled these lands until the war," Kinison replied, leading the horse down the hill.

"Who rules them now?"

"The House of Myr became 'stewards' of these lands after the war, but as I understand our history, they were always truly loyal to the House of Aranethon."

"I have never heard what caused the War of Ascension or what actually happened. How did my ancestors fall? How did the House of Aurelia claim the throne, and why is Ethriel the capital now?" Corin asked.

"You ask many questions, Corin, and you will find the answer is a long story," replied Kinison with a sigh. "I cannot tell you the tale in full just now, but there are those who know the whole history of Alethia waiting for us in Elengil. These scholars can tell you much more than I will ever know. What I do know is that the War of Ascension completely changed the kingdom. Following the war, the great houses of Alethia came together to form the Council of Lords and began electing the kings of Alethia, and until Noliono, they were all from the House of Aurelia."

"Why?"

"Who knows," Kinison said with a shrug. "Tradition is hard to break. Though the Council of Lords could elect any lord to be king, it's hard to break tradition or a line of kings."

They were silent for several hours. Kinison did not like to break the silence as he believed the young man needed time to process this information.

"But how *did* the war start?" Corin said, finally breaking the silence.

"I can only tell you what I've heard. It is well known that the War of Ascension began during a feud between the houses of Aurelia and Noland over the Pass of Stenc. There has always been bad blood between these two houses. It is said that the House of Noland seized control of the pass and began seizing control of Aurelian lands south of the River Belwash. Lord Kelbrandt Aurelia mustered a large host and marched on the Noland Army. Meanwhile, King Gregory Aranethon declared House Aurelia and

Noland in violation of the King's Peace. He summoned a host of over ten thousand men from the other great houses to subdue the two rebellious houses. When the king crossed the Belwash, he found the Aurelian Army encamped. The king rode out to meet with Lord Kelbrandt, who submitted to the king and promised to return to Ethriel with his host.

"During the night, a raiding party from Noland *mistook* the king's camp for the Aurelian camp. They managed to kill the king, and his army was scattered. Some of the lords joined Lord Noland and others joined Lord Aurelia. A civil war would have soon followed, except that the following day word arrived that the kingdom of Nordyke had invaded Alethia. The invaders had seized control of Elengil and slaughtered the king's family and the entire House of Aranethon. Lord Aurelia and Lord Noland joined forces and marched north to defend the kingdom and seek revenge for the killing of the king's family. The armies of Alethia and Nordyke met at the River Rockwicke, where a fierce battle ensued lasting several days. In the end, the invaders were destroyed, but it seemed a hollow victory for Elengil was sacked, and the king and his family were dead."

"So the lords met in Elengil to elect a new king, right?" Corin interjected.

"Indeed. Since Lord Noland had been killed and his son was only a child, there was no opposition to Lord Kelbrandt Aurelia from being elected king. And so the tradition of electing a king from House Aurelia began."

"But now the House of Aurelia is in danger, and Noliono is seizing control of the kingdom?"

"Yes," replied Kinison.

Corin was silent for a long time. Kinison knew he was trying to make sense of everything, so he refrained from speaking. They were now reaching the bottom of a long hill. The city still loomed up on the horizon, but it was steadily growing larger as they made their way across the countryside. They crossed a small bridge, spanning a stream that cut across the road. Kinison noted that there were few travelers on the road. The war must have driven them inside the city for protection. He wondered when Noliono would make his move to take Elengil. Almost as a prayer, Kinison thought that if ever they needed a miracle, now was the time.

"So how is it that I am to be made king then?" Corin asked, interrupting Kinison's thoughts.

"That is for the Council to decide," he answered vaguely.

"Council?" Corin asked, confused. "I thought Noliono disbanded the Council of Lords."

"There will be a new council formed, and you will lead it." Kinison noted Corin's sudden silence. "The hope of a free Alethia rests upon you, Corin Aranethon, but you do not have to bear the burden alone. There will be many others alongside you to help you, myself included."

They both fell silent for they were now nearing the city gates. Despite his grandiose statement, Kinison wondered if the others would follow this young man so easily, especially now that the heir was less than whole. *I guess we will find out*, he thought.

✳   ✳   ✳   ✳

As Lord Renton Myr refused to live in the old castle atop the hill, preferring to live in his own manor house within the city below, the Castle of Elengil had fallen into disrepair over the past two hundred years. Years and years of disuse and neglect had taken its toll, leaving only small areas of the castle habitable. As Kinison and Corin neared the city, they gazed up at the crumbling old fortress, which appeared little more than a ruin.

"This was the king's castle?" Corin asked.

"Two hundred years ago, this was the stronghold of the king," said a voice from behind them.

Kinison turned, and a look of surprise spread across his face. It was Galanor.

"Pleased to see you, Kinison," Galanor said, ignoring Kinison's expression.

"Galanor, this is Corin Stone," Kinison said, regaining his composure.

"We've met," Galanor said curtly.

"Why didn't you ever return to Stonewall?" Corin asked almost accusingly.

"Recent events have occupied my time, young Corin," Galanor said somberly. "I apologize for not returning to continue your lessons."

Galanor glanced toward Corin's left leg then grabbed hold of Kinison's tunic.

"What happened!" he exclaimed, shaking Kinison slightly. "You were instructed to keep him safe!"

"Release me!" Kinison said, shaking loose of Galanor's grip and retreating a few paces. "It's a long story, and perhaps we'd better find a place to rest. It's been a long journey for both of us," Kinison said with a meaningful glance at Corin.

"Indeed," Galanor replied gruffly. "This way."

They entered the city, and Galanor led them up the hill and through the ruined gates of the castle. The only building still standing was the great hall, which looked like it had been recently restored. The stonework looked new, and the windows were polished and shone in the sunlight. Even the oaken front doors were newly reinforced with iron hinges.

"My lord," Galanor said, opening the door and bowing. "Welcome to *your* hall."

Kinison helped Corin dismount and into the great hall.

A slew of people greeted them within the hall. Some were dressed like vagabonds while others were dressed as noblemen. They all became silent when Kinison and Corin entered.

"Hail, Corin Aranethon, the true heir to the throne of Alethia!" Galanor exclaimed.

The entire room echoed Galanor, and all dropped to one knee, except three men standing in front of the dais leading to the throne. Kinison looked at the three defiant men and recognized them as Lord Renton Myr, Baron Peter Astley of the Fortress of

Ironwall, and Baron Alastor Warde of the Fortress of Ytemest.

"Sire," Galanor said, still bowing. "These are the leaders of the Shadow Garrison, as organized by your great-great-great grandsire two hundred years ago."

"Shadow Garrison?" he heard Corin whisper.

Kinison understood the young man's surprise as he gawked at the number of men in the room. If these were the leaders of the Shadow Garrison, he had greatly underestimated their numbers and influence.

"We are charged with protecting the realm from threats without and within its borders, and to protect the House of Aranethon," Galanor said, motioning for the rest to rise. "We have gathered now to protect and serve the rightful heir of Alethia."

Galanor led them past the three men to the top of the dais and helped Corin into the empty throne. He motioned toward everyone else to take a seat at once at one of the five long tables below. Kinison noticed that Lord Myr and the two barons were eyeing Corin and himself.

"I recognize you, Kinison Ravenloch. So you kill one king only to appear at the side of a usurper," called Baron Astley.

"I did not kill King Greyfuss," Kinison said, turning toward him and stepping off the dais. His face contorted with rage. "And I will be avenged upon any and all who say otherwise!"

"Peace," Galanor said firmly. "Baron Astley, we have already spoken of this at length. Kinison Ravenloch was falsely accused of killing Greyfuss Aurelia. You know this and already accepted it. Why do you insist on provoking him?"

Astley tilted his head forward in a mock bow, but his eyes were full of mistrust. The man then turned away and said nothing more to Kinison.

"This man is of no consequence regardless of his guilt or innocence, Baron Astley," said Myr. "The true point is whether or not this boy is the heir to the throne of Alethia. It is all well and good for Galanor to call this boy a son of Aranethon, but where is the proof?"

"It is here," Kinison said, pulling out the book. "This is the *Book of Aduin*, the only trusted source of Alethian history beyond the War of Ascension and the only record of the House of Aranethon."

Kinison watched as Myr's gaze darted between the book, Corin, and back again.

"He is the last son mentioned in the book—meaning he is the last true heir to the throne." Kinison continued, "I have seen it, Galanor has seen it, Corin has seen it, and all here who wish to see it may do so."

"And why does the House of Aranethon come forth now?" asked Warde. "Our history records that the house was destroyed over two hundred years ago, yet you parade this boy in here as an heir of Aranethon, and a cripple no less. Where have the Aranethons been, and why now does the heir come forth?"

"My Lord Warde," Galanor answered stiffly. "Your question is just and will be answered. The true tale of the War of Ascension shall now be told in full. It was recorded in the *Book of Aduin*, but all other histories were destroyed by order of King Kelbrandt Aurelia.

"To what end would the Aurelias wish to hide their history? They were heroes of the war, and their ancestry predates the kingdom," Astley protested.

"Yes, the Aurelias are an ancient house but hardly noble, for it was they who began the war," Galanor replied.

A murmur went up from the room. Kinison stared at Galanor in disbelief. *Could this be true? Could the Aurelias, a house that had uplifted his family and himself to nobility and power, be responsible for the last great war? No. It couldn't be.*

"Outrageous!" Myr shouted, giving voice to Kinison's thoughts. "My house and House Aurelia have been allies for centuries. We have never hidden the truth from one another. It is absurd, I tell you!"

"My lord, your ancestors were also involved," Galanor replied calmly. "It was treachery and treason of the vilest kind. We were

THE HEIR COMES FORTH

led to believe that Noland attacked Aurelian lands, beginning the war. We were also led to believe that during the fighting, the kingdom of Nordyke invaded Alethia and destroyed the House of Aranethon. Yet it was Aurelia and Myr who plotted and killed the king and his family."

"*Lies!*" Myr shouted. "You would slander my family's honor in my own city?"

"This is not your city, or have you forgotten where you stand?" Galanor replied in kind. "This is the Castle of Elengil, the stronghold of the House of Aranethon and the seat of power for the kings of Alethia for hundreds of years. Have you never wondered why this castle has never been inhabited by your family but allowed to decay?"

Myr stared, a look of outrage mixed with confusion on his face.

"It is because Lord Gerrod Myr and his descendants could not face what they had done. So they allowed the evidence to decay."

"This is ridiculous, Galanor!" Astley protested.

"Indeed. I have heard nothing but lies and absurdity from these three," Warde said, pointing at Galanor, Kinison, and Corin.

"How can you know this to be true?" Myr asked, a hint of doubt in his voice. "An ancient book written and edited over two hundred years is your only source to defend these claims."

"This book has only been read and added to by the headmaster of Stonewall Academy for the past two hundred years," Galanor replied. "He was loath to let me read it and outraged when I demanded it be returned to Elengil."

"Returned to Elengil?" asked Myr incredulously.

"The Hall of Records, which was burned on the night that the soldiers of Aurelia and Myr attacked this castle, resided just across the courtyard."

"So you say, Galanor, but where is the proof?" Astley protested.

"Right here!" Galanor shouted, opening the book. He began to read. "Listen to the words recorded by Aduin, the greatest loremaster of Alethian history:

I, Aduin, Protector of the Hall of Records and Loremaster of Alethia, do record herein the truth regarding the so called War of Ascension. I write this in the hopes that one day the truth will be revealed. Alethia was not invaded by the kingdom of Nordyke, nor did the House of Noland attack the House of Aurelia. The War of Ascension is a farce, a ruse to hide what really happened.

"Thirty years ago, in the ninth year of King Gregory Aranethon's reign, Lord Kelbrandt Aurelia and Lord Gerrod Myr paid a group of bandits to stage raids against Alethia along its border with Nordyke. These lords then misinformed the king that Nordyke was raiding our settlements along the border. When the king summoned troops to deal with the raiders, Myr and Aurelia were the first to answer. A great many soldiers were gathered in Elengil in less than a fortnight, for these troops had been mustered before the king summoned them; then began the most heinous crime in our history. The soldiers of Aurelia and Myr fell upon the king and his unsuspecting family. All of Aranethon were murdered save Gideon Aranethon and his wife.

"Only I and a few others know of their escape, and no word will ever reach the conspirators. Once the deed was done, Lord Aurelia and Lord Myr shifted the blame on Noland and Nordyke. The Council of Lords was convened, and Kelbrandt Aurelia was made king. Lord Myr was granted stewardship over Elengil, and Lord Noland was given control of the Pass of Stenc in exchange for his silence. A war with Nordyke was begun by declaration, and the rest fell into place.

"I am grieved to know that so few know these truths, and I wonder if ever the people know, will they believe the truth or adhere to the lies? It is my hope for those who read these things will believe and teach others the truth."

Kinison let out a heavy sigh that was echoed by many in the

hall. This was a lot to process. The history of Alethia that they knew to be true earlier this morning was, in fact, false propaganda written and spread by those who had killed the entire House of Aranethon.

"If you require further proof, Lord Myr"—Galanor closed the book and pulled from within his robes an old piece of parchment—"then hear the words of Lord Geremy Myr, son of Gerrod Myr, written in his own hand some fifty years after the murder of King Gregory Aranethon and his family.

> In the thirteenth year of King Alfred Aurelia, I, Geremy Myr, Lord of House Myr and all its holdings, desire to write herein the truth regarding my family's actions. Doubting that these words will ever be read by another soul, I must confess to my father and my family's sins. It grieves my heart and soul to know that my own blood plotted and committed treason against our rightful king and murdered him and his family. May God forgive us for what we have done and pray He shows us grace and mercy in spite of our sins.

"You will remember, Lord Myr, that Lord Geremy Myr died not a year later, while on the road to the Council of Lords in Ethriel," Galanor said with a meaningful glance.

"It was always suspected that bandits fell upon him and his company while they were traveling," Myr said, gazing off. It was clear to Kinison that Myr was troubled by his ancestor's letter.

"He was, no doubt, killed by House Aurelia in order to silence him before he revealed the truth," Galanor said firmly. "I located this parchment ten years ago while, by your leave, I was searching through your records. I have chosen my own time to reveal my findings."

"So you stole a letter written by my ancestor, confessing his part in the death of King Aranethon?" Lord Myr asked incredulously. "How can I believe all this?"

Kinison had to admit that all this was a lot to take in, and it flew in the face of all he had thought he knew about the House of Aurelia.

"Can you really still doubt?" Galanor asked impatiently.

"What of Lords Warde and Astley?" Myr asked, clearly flustered by all this.

Kinison turned to the other two men, who both seemed perturbed by all they'd heard.

"We have seen the *Book of Aduin*, and we have heard the words of Loremaster Aduin and the confession of Geremy Myr," Astley began with a heavy sigh. "I acknowledge the actions of House Aurelia and House Myr so written in Aduin's account. These accounts fit with our own family history and what our fathers have told us—that there never was an invasion by Nordyke. But you have still not proven the boy is the lost heir."

"Corin!" Galanor shouted angrily, turning to face the young man. "Show them the ring."

Kinison and everyone else in the hall turned toward Corin as the young man pulled from under his tunic a silver chain. Upon the chain was a golden ring baring the crest of a rose."

"Behold," Galanor exclaimed. "The signet ring of House Aranethon, baring the symbol of the rose."

The hall was suddenly filled with exclamations of shock and awe.

Astley looked hard at Corin for a moment then bowed and said, "I must, therefore, pledge myself and my house to Corin Aranethon."

"Hail, Corin Aranethon!" Warde exclaimed, also bowing.

At this, the whole hall, led by Astley and Warde, knelt before Corin. Kinison noticed how uncomfortable Corin looked and stifled a chuckle. He then turned to Myr, whose gaze was scanning the hall.

Lord Myr looked at Corin, fell to his knees, and kissed Corin's hand.

"Forgive me, my King, for my sins and my house's sins against you and your family," he cried, continuing to kiss Corin's hand.

Corin looked at Kinison, who nodded.

"I...I forgive you, Lord Myr," Corin said quietly, looking thoroughly uncomfortable. He pulled his hand away.

"Behold, all of you are witnesses. Our king has mercifully granted clemency to Lord Myr and his family for their ancestors' crimes," Galanor said in a commanding voice. Then turning to Lord Myr, he said, "May your family never again forget where their loyalties lie."

Kinison looked on as Myr nodded fervently, while the rest of the hall knelt and continued to praise Corin. He smiled and nodded to Corin. And so it begins.

❋　❋　❋　❋

Kinison was pacing back and forth in his chambers, which Lord Myr had graciously provided to him and Corin. Despite the lavish decorations or the comfortable furniture, his mind could not rest or relax. He was focused on family and his wife, Sarah. He wanted to hear word of them. He wanted to know if Galanor had kept his promise to rescue Sarah from Noliono. He wanted to hold his wife in his arms again. He wanted to know they all were safe.

A sudden knock at the door drew Kinison's attention.

"Enter."

Galanor entered followed by a man whom Kinison recognized but could not remember from where. His face was pleasant, and he was dressed in a dark-gray robe that seemed to hide an inner light.

"You wished to see me?" Galanor asked.

"Yes," Kinison said, unable to hide his anxiety. "What word do you have regarding my wife?"

Galanor looked at the man who had entered with him.

"She remains a prisoner of Noliono," the man said softly.

Kinison began to pace back and forth, trying to control his

fury—his outrage.

"There is more, Kinison," Galanor said gravely. "Noliono has destroyed Estelhold."

"I pledged my service to you, and you promised to save my wife and family. Now my father and all his men are dead, and you have done nothing?" Kinison almost shouted. "I trusted you, found your heir, and brought him here. Yet you have failed to uphold your end of our bargain."

"I admit that my efforts to rescue her have failed, but I assure you that I have not been idle," Galanor said with measured speech. It was clear that he was becoming angry.

"Yet my father is still dead, and my wife remains Noliono's prisoner!" Kinison began to gather his belongings.

"What will you do? Rescue her alone?" Galanor asked, bemused.

"I will," Kinison said, buckling his sword to his belt and picking up his pack.

"You will lay aside your oath then?" Galanor asked with a hint of outrage in his voice.

"Which oath is that?" Kinison asked, rounding on Galanor.

"The oath you swore to the Shadow Garrison and to your king!" Galanor shouted.

"I made a vow to my wife to provide and protect her long before I swore an oath to the Shadow Garrison or this new king!" Kinison retorted. "Now stand aside."

Galanor and the other man stood their ground.

"I know you fear for your wife, Kinison Ravenloch, and that is good that you care for her so much," said the other man calmly. "Yet you worry in vain. She is safer where she is than if she was with you here and now."

"How can you know this?" Kinison said, beginning to lose his temper.

"You must learn to trust me."

"Why should I trust you? I don't even know you?"

"You know me, Kinison, but you have forgotten who I am,"

the man said, and Kinison suddenly remembered where and when he had met this man.

"You, you are the man from my vision or dream or whatever it was...that day on the road from Ethriel."

"I am," the man said. "You trusted me before. Trust me now. If you leave and go to save Sarah on your own, I will not stop you. But if you choose your own path, one of you will be killed in the coming events."

"But I can't just wait here and do nothing!" Kinison said as if pleading with the man.

"You must trust what I say is true," the man said. "Stay and defend your new king, and you will see your wife alive again."

Kinison was silent as his mind told him to ignore this stranger and go rescue his wife. So what if he himself died in the attempt. If he had to die, at least he'd die trying to save his wife. Yet his heart told him to trust this man and do what he said. Kinison shook his head several times before speaking.

"I can't just wait here and hope everything will be all right," he said then pushed past the two men and jogged down the corridor toward the stables. He just could not wait any longer.

"Sarah, I'm coming for you."

19

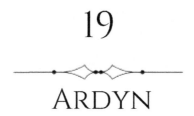

ARDYN

Do you still remember the shame? his mind asked.

Yes. His heart answered.

Ardyn was sitting in his chambers; his face was in his hands. Not many men could boast of being made a lieutenant in the Guardians of the Citadel within two months of taking his oath, yet upon his left shoulder was his badge of office. As if that was not enough, one of the privileges of being a lieutenant afforded Ardyn his own private quarters and a personal servant. Yet Ardyn could not enjoy any of these things. His mind and body were both replete with guilt and shame.

He looked up and saw his reflection in the mirror hung on the far wall. His tear-stained face stared back at him, his own eyes looking back accusingly. Why had he done it? He knew exactly why he'd done it. It was because he didn't want to lose her, and now she was Noliono's prisoner. Ardyn turned away and shook his head violently. He could not long hold the condemning gaze of his own reflection. He looked toward the window. The sun was beginning to set. Soon he'd have to go down to the feast. It was in his honor after all.

He got up and went to the washbasin beneath the mirror to refresh himself. He splashed the cold water on his face twice then dried himself off. He looked up in the mirror again. It was all a charade, he thought. A proverbial mask to be worn when I am around others in order to hide my true self...my true character. How I loathed myself now. He turned his eyes away again, unable to withstand the accusation in his own eyes. Yet looking away did not stem the tide of shame and sorrow that flooded his being. There was no avoiding the truth. It was indeed all his fault. It was his failure, his weakness, his sin.

Ardyn left his chambers several minutes later and crossed the grounds to the Great Hall. He started for the main doors but then decided upon taking the side entrance. He remained in the passage off the main corridor leading to the Great Hall for several long minutes, pacing and muttering to himself. The Great Hall, he knew, would be full of people from all over the kingdom—people who had been misled into believing that he, Ardyn, was some kind of hero. Ardyn knew he could handle his own self-loathing, but to be paraded around as if he was the complete opposite, that he could not stomach.

"Ardyn?" said a raspy voice behind him.

Ardyn turned to see Archbishop Julius Durante and several other members of the Church walking toward him.

"F-Father?" Ardyn stammered, bowing and averting his eyes from the old man and those with him.

"What are you doing out here, my son?" the archbishop asked, amusedly motioning Ardyn to rise. "Your presence is required at the feast. The door is open, but you must enter in order to receive your reward, my son."

"I am unworthy of such an honor, Father," Ardyn said, wondering if he should tell the old man the truth. He was the Archbishop of Alethia, after all. If anyone would know how he could make amends for his sin, the archbishop should.

"Unworthy?" the archbishop said before Ardyn had time to

wonder for long. "My son, your humility is touching, but your actions are worthy of praise. The king has told me of your deeds, and you would be a fool not to accept his gratitude."

The old man held out his hand, and Ardyn noticed that every finger was adorned with a jeweled ring made of the purest gold. He gazed at them for a moment before realizing the old man was staring expectantly at him. Ardyn quickly bowed and kissed the old wrinkled hand, which seemed to appease the archbishop and the others with him.

"Come, my son," the old man said, placing a glittering hand upon Ardyn's shoulder and ushering him forward. "Your feast awaits."

※　※　※　※

The Great Hall was indeed full of people from all over the kingdom. The stone walls echoed with the din of so many voices. A herald, positioned near the door, announced their arrival when Ardyn and the archbishop entered the hall. All eyes turned toward him, and Ardyn's heart began beating very fast. It felt as if these people could see through his façade and were judging him harshly. His eyes perceived all the smiles, and his ears heard them cheering his name, but all this translated in his mind to unwanted attention and heightened shame.

Despite his inner turmoil, Ardyn strived to maintain his façade, knowing that he could not disappoint the king no matter how he truly felt about the whole affair. If he revealed the truth, they all would hate him. So he smiled at each person as they came up to talk to him. He shook each of their hands in turn, laughed at their jokes, gave sympathy to their woes, and yet the whole time Ardyn continued to silently wrestle with his deep inner conflict that threatened to crush his very soul. The guilt and the shame was overwhelming his very being as he stood there trying to keep a smile on his face and pretending to enjoy himself. This celebration was supposed to be for him after all. If they only knew what I have done, Ardyn thought, smiling and nodding at another lame jest.

Finally, Ardyn moved to sit down at a table near the side entrance. The king had not arrived yet, which only gave Ardyn more time to further ponder his transgressions. He looked out across the crowded hall and noticed the splendor of those present. Lords representing all the ruling houses were in attendance, along with their wives and even some of their older children. The high steward, Robert Grayhall, and Chancellor Reginald Wolsey were seated at the high table. The chancellor had kept trying to engage him in conversation earlier, but Ardyn was not interested in contributing much. The chancellor became bored and left Ardyn soon after.

Several barons were also present, and even his father's adviser, Zul Voss, was here. This seemed rather odd to Ardyn that Voss would make the long journey across half the width of the kingdom just to attend a feast. He turned to his right and found Chancellor Wolsey standing next to him again.

"Chancellor?" Ardyn said, bowing.

"Ardyn, my lad," Wolsey said jovially. "Enjoying the festivities, I hope."

"Yes, my lord."

"Your fame has spread quickly. Some of these lords and ladies have journeyed many days in order to celebrate your valor."

"Is that so?" Ardyn said, uninterested.

"I know Princess Riniel must have been grateful for you coming to her rescue," the Chancellor said with a wink that made Ardyn cringe. "And how did she reward her young savior?"

Ardyn did not know what to say, so he remained silent.

"Your father must be very proud of you," the chancellor continued unabashed. "I have not seen him lately. Is he here this evening?"

"No, he isn't," Ardyn said, trying his best to contain a renewed surge of shame that was washing over him.

The last Ardyn had heard, his father was near the city of

Vedmore, an important city for it was founded where the River Vedmore met the Sea of Aear. Now that half the realm was in open rebellion, the entire host of House Thayn had marched on the city and laid siege to it. Two nights ago, word had arrived by messenger that Lord Anson had been critically wounded in battle. Ardyn felt his eyes welling up and made a conscious effort to push the thought from his mind.

He was thankful a few moments later when his attention was diverted by the entrance of the king. The noise in the room reached new heights as everyone in the Great Hall stood and began clapping and cheering all at once. Ardyn imitated the others, but the look of jubilation on his face was only a front.

Within his very core, he felt the need to run from here. He wanted to escape from the citadel, the Great Hall, the very situation and circumstances that he found himself. Yet he knew that to run was folly. There was no escaping the guilt, the shame, the knowledge of his sin. He watched as King Noliono made his way across the crowded hall and stopped in front of him.

"Here is the man of the hour, my friends," Noliono said, placing his hand on Ardyn's shoulder. "Were it not for this brave lad, Princess Riniel might have been lost to us. Thank the heavens that he was there to save her."

The room burst into renewed cheers as the king embraced Ardyn.

"Smile, my boy," Noliono whispered in his ear. "The girl's life depends on it."

The king released Ardyn and turned to address the crowd.

"This is a momentous day, my fellow Alethians," Noliono began, smiling broadly. "We celebrate the courage of this young man and the safe return of Princess Riniel. Few men in the history of the Guardians could boast such valor." The king paused for effect, and then continued. "You all know that less than a week ago, there was an attempt to abduct the princess here within the very walls of the citadel. Three men gained entry to the princess's chambers and attempted to make off with her into the night. One of them was none other than Sir Jordan Reese, the princess's personal guard and member of the Guardians."

There was a gasp from the crowd at the mention of Sir Jordan Reese, and a wave of murmurings moved across the room. With every word, Ardyn felt as if the very fibers of his being were snapping one by one. He did not know if he could take much more. He felt his mask beginning to crack and fall away.

"Young Ardyn heard the princess's scream and rushed to her aid," Noliono continued, unabated. "He bravely subdued all three men and rescued the fair maiden from their clutches. Though he may appear to you subdued and meek, this young man has a fierceness about him when those he has swore an oath to protect are threatened. So let us drink a toast."

Noliono called for wine to be brought, and servers appeared from every corner bearing trays of goblets and wine bottles. When everyone was provided with a fresh goblet of wine, Noliono turned to Ardyn.

"To Ardyn Thayn, the bravest Guardian of the Citadel in living memory!" the king shouted.

"To Ardyn!" the crowd echoed and cheered.

Ardyn gazed around the hall, watching the smiling faces of all those people. He knew they were all expecting him to speak, but his voice was not working.

Finally, Ardyn found himself saying aloud, "Please, Your Majesty. You are too kind, but I am undeserving of this outpouring of praise."

"Nonsense!" the king said, shooting him a meaningful look. "You saved the princess's life! I find that is something worth throwing a feast over. Now that I think on it, this deserves no less than a week of feasts!"

The room erupted in laughter and cheers as the hopeful crowd waited to see if the king was serious about the week of feasts. After all, there is no table like the king's table. Ardyn did not join in with the festivities but excused himself and left the hall. He felt the eyes of the king on him until he left. He'd played his part, and now he needed a respite from the praise. He walked for a while until he found himself in a deserted corridor on the other side of the citadel. He knew that the king or Kludge would be looking for him, but this time his guilt was overpowering his fear. He knew what he had to do and was about to screw up his courage when a door to his left opened. A short, stout man emerged in a dark traveling cloak; the hood was pulled up over his face.

"Ardyn Thayn?" the man said in a whisper.

Ardyn stood bewildered for a moment, but remembering his sword, he drew it and turned to face the man.

"You have no need for that, Ardyn. Please come," the man said, holding the door open.

"Who are you?" Ardyn asked in a weak voice.

"I am a friend. You have few enough of those now. Can you afford to turn away one such as I?" the man asked.

Ardyn dropped his guard slightly and walked toward the man. "Who are you, though?"

"As I said, I am a friend," the man said, pulling back his hood. Ardyn started as he recognized the man as Sir Ren Gables.

"Please," Sir Ren said, motioning toward the door. "We are waiting for you."

"We?" Ardyn said, becoming more and more confused.

"Just come on!" Sir Ren hissed and pulled him inside, shutting the door behind them.

Ardyn looked around and saw Sir Jordan Reese, Princess Riniel, and another woman whom he had not met. He stood speechless as Sir Jordan, upon seeing Ardyn, crossed the room and sucker-punched him in the face. Ardyn fell to the floor, stunned and disorientated. When he came to his senses, he realized that his nose was bleeding.

"You're lucky I'm holding back, traitor!" shouted Sir Jordan's voice. "I owe you much for your betrayal!"

Ardyn looked to see Sir Ren holding Sir Jordan back.

"Sir Jordan!" Sir Ren roared "Have you forgotten what I revealed to you?"

Just then, someone came up and slapped Ardyn hard across the face. Already on the ground, his nose bleeding, the blow caught Ardyn off balance. The impact drove him into the hard wooden floor, causing his head to ring.

"Princess!" Ardyn heard the others cry out.

He looked up with eyes watering, the pain in his now-throbbing head reaching new heights.

"Let go of me, Sarah!" Ardyn heard Riniel exclaim.

"Princess Riniel, nothing good will come of this," said Sarah.

"You don't know that!" Riniel retorted, struggling to get her arms free.

Ardyn looked up and saw Sarah holding Riniel back. She was breathing heavily, and her hand was raised as if ready to strike. She glared at Ardyn in such a way that all that remained of his self-worth seemed to dissipate like a mist before the blazing noonday sun.

"Ardyn Thayn," Riniel said, obviously making great effort to keep her voice even and calm. "Had I the power, you would suffer greatly for the disloyalty you have demonstrated. You have disgraced the name of House Thayn and the name Guardian. Were it not for our great need, I would have nothing more to do with you."

Ardyn looked at her dumbly. He did not know what he could say to express his grief and desire for repentance.

"I am sorry," he managed to utter.

"Sorry? You're sorry! That is all you can say?" Riniel shouted, slapping him hard again.

Ardyn took the blow and prepared for more, but that was the last one. Apparently, the others felt he was not worth their effort. Ardyn tended to agree with them.

"Enough!" Sir Ren said loudly. "Ardyn is the only one who can get us out of the citadel without raising the alarm."

"Me?" Ardyn asked, looking at Sir Ren in utter confusion.

"You, boy," he answered, grabbing his arm and pulling him up. "You hold the rank of lieutenant in the Guardians. You can order the men out of position on the south wall long enough to allow our escape."

"Why can't you, Sir Ren? You are also a lieutenant," Ardyn argued.

"I can't because Noliono has my family hostage," Sir Ren retorted irritably. "I already risked more than I should releasing Sir Jordan from the dark cells."

Suddenly, within Ardyn, the battle between his fear and the desire to make amends for his treachery was won.

"Quickly, follow me," he said, moving toward the door.

"Why should we trust him!" Sir Jordan shouted in anger.

"You have no choice," Ardyn said with a quick look outside. "You can trust me once more or remain in this room and be caught again."

"Go with him," said Sir Ren, pulling the cloak back over his head. "I will try and create a diversion on the other side of the citadel to draw them away."

Sir Jordan glared at him but nodded curtly. Ardyn turned to Riniel, who refused to catch his eye. He gave up and led the way out of the room.

❊ ❊ ❊ ❊

The grounds of the citadel were empty and dark. The revelers in the Great Hall and half the members of the Guardians were still too busy celebrating and toasting their absent would-be hero to notice anything going on outside. Ardyn led the princess and her party across the shadowy courtyard toward the south wall. It was here that a lone door stood that was originally made to serve as a servant entrance to the lower city. It was normally guarded by four men at a time, but tonight's festivities had required more security elsewhere.

When Ardyn and the rest of them reached the corridor leading to the servant door, they realized that there was only one man on duty that night. Ardyn knew that he and Sir Jordan could subdue the lone guard quickly, but would they be quick enough to avoid an alarm? Ardyn turned to Sir Jordan, who took his meaning.

They moved quickly and silently toward the guard. Sir Jordan managed to catch the man off guard, knocking him unconscious. The fight was over in a moment. They all breathed a sigh of relief until Sir Jordan yelled in alarm. Ardyn turned to see Lord Kludge and a slew of Guardians running toward them from the Great Hall.

Ardyn grabbed Riniel's arm and pulled her toward the door. Sir Jordan drew his sword, and prepared fight.

"No!" Ardyn yelled at them. "The door! Flee!"

At that moment Ardyn heard the sharp twang of a crossbow. He saw, in a split second, that the bolt was headed for Riniel. He only had a moment to act. Ardyn threw himself in front of the princess, receiving the full impact of the bolt in his chest. The pain was overwhelming. Someone was screaming his name. He hit the ground in a daze. He reached down at his chest and felt warm blood on his fingers. He looked up at the princess, whose face was twisted in anguish and whose eyes were full of tears. He tried to say something, but the princess was being pulled away by someone. He tried to move, but he could not feel his arms. He was cold. Ardyn wondered if this was what it felt like to die, and then knew no more.

20

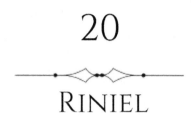

RINIEL

Once escaping the citadel, Riniel and Sir Jordan had stolen some horses and rode hard and fast until reaching a small town a full day's ride from Ethriel. Riniel's mind was full of remorse and regret, lamenting the recent turn of events. Only they had escaped. Sarah had been captured, and Ardyn was dead. He'd given his life to save hers, and all she could think about were all the hateful things she'd said to him.

They rode through the small town until they reached an inn. Riniel looked up at the sign displaying what appeared to be a dancing lion. She smiled for the first time all day at the funny figure of the lion. Riniel had never stayed in an inn before, but she found the Dancing Lion quaint and charming. It was night, and as Sir Jordan helped her dismount, she suddenly realized how comforting the warm light emanating from the windows was to her as she stood shivering in the cold night air. While Sir Jordan led the horses away to be stabled, Riniel walked up to the inn doors. She hesitated for a moment then pushed the door open. The smoky air and light from the fire overwhelmed her at first. She coughed and blinked for several seconds, trying to adjust. A hand on her shoulder made her start and turn sharply. She squinted up at the owner of the hand. He was a tall man with kind blue eyes, red hair, and mutton chops. The man smiled at her, and Riniel smiled back despite the coughing.

"Sam Brandyman, at your service, my lady," he said pleasantly and smiled more broadly. "Welcome to the Dancing Lion. What can I do for you?"

"I...uh...that is..." Riniel stammered. She'd never felt so flustered. This was all so new to her.

"A room, perhaps, and stabling for two horses?" Brandyman offered, continuing to smile.

Riniel stared up at him, stunned.

"Little happens in these parts that gets by ol' Brandyman, my lady," he said with a wink. "And here's your companion."

Riniel turned to see Sir Jordan entering the inn.

"Just the one room then?"

"Brandyman!" Sir Jordan exclaimed, running over and embracing the man.

Riniel was taken aback. She'd never seen Sir Jordan react like this. He was often so cool and stoic. To see him smiling was a pleasant change.

"It's been too long, my old friend!" Brandyman replied, clapping Sir Jordan on the shoulder.

"Too long indeed," Sir Jordan said smiling.

"So who is this?" Brandyman asked, gesturing toward Riniel.

"This is my wife, Rebecca," Sir Jordan replied, putting his arm around Riniel.

She tried not to look shocked by the sudden news of her nuptial to her bodyguard.

"Bit young for you, Jordan," Brandyman said with a twinkle in his eye. "Ah, no need to explain. Follow me, and I'll take you to your room."

"Ambulavero in umbras, sed lucem facies mea afferat," Sir Jordan said quietly.

"Brandyman had started to turn but stopped and looked hard at

Sir Jordan. Riniel looked back and forth between the two men, confused to why Sir Jordan was speaking the old tongue of Alethia to an innkeeper.

"Indeed," Brandyman said after a long pause. "Come on then."

He led them up a flight of stairs, onto the second landing, and into a nearby room. Riniel was struck at how comfortable the room looked, though the furnishings were of lower quality than she was used to enjoying. Still she thought the room nice and cozy. A fire burned in the hearth, with two chairs sitting in front of it. Two blankets were thrown over the tops of the chairs, and it was all Riniel could do not to run over and curl up in one of the chairs near the fire, wrapping herself in one of the blankets. Instead, she looked expectantly at Sir Jordan.

"Well, Jordan, what's this all about?" Brandyman asked, also looking at Sir Jordan expectantly.

"I seek shelter for myself and—"

"Don't say she's your wife," Brandyman interrupted. "The look she gave you when you said it earlier made it clear to me and everyone in the room that you two are not married."

Riniel looked at her feet, blushing with embarrassment.

"Tell me the truth," Brandyman demanded.

"Fine," Sir Jordan said after a pause. "Brandyman, meet Princess Riniel."

"The last of the Aurelias," Brandyman said, his eyes growing wide.

"The last!" Riniel asked, her voice rising. "What do you mean the last!"

"You haven't heard then?" Brandyman said, his face grave.

"Haven't heard what?" Riniel asked, her voice becoming more of a shrill.

"The army of Noland besieged and destroyed Rockhold no more than two days ago. Rumor is that everyone inside the castle was slaughtered.

"Oh god!" Riniel exclaimed, her head beginning to swim. She was overwhelmed. First her mother, then her father, then her entire family? The room grew suddenly dim.

"Princess!" someone said, but Riniel had fainted.

When Riniel awoke, she found herself lying on a bed. It took a moment for her to remember where she was and everything that had transpired. She turned toward the hearth and found Sir Jordan and Brandyman sitting and talking in low voices. The firelight was the only light in the room, causing both men to cast sinister shadows across the room. She tried to sit up, but the room began to spin again. Noticing her stir, Sir Jordan was at her side in a moment.

"Princess?" he said, helping her sit up and steadying her.

"I'm all right," she said, noticing the concern etched in the older man's face. "Truly I feel fine. Please, tell me of my family."

"Princess, you are fatigued by our long journey. Please rest."

"I am well enough, Sir Jordan, to hear news of my family," she said sharply. "Mr. Brandyman, tell me your news."

"Castle Rockhold was sacked by the army of Noland six days ago," Brandyman said with a long sigh. "The soldiers who passed through here boasted that they left none alive."

Riniel was silent for a long time. Her heart was beating fast. She knew what the stranger said must be true, but somehow she needed to see it for herself. What did it matter anyway? It was just a dream, right?

"I need to see it for myself," she said finally.

"See it?" Brandyman asked disdainfully.

"If what you say is true, then I am the last survivor of House Aurelia. I wish to be taken to Rockhold and see if I am truly alone."

"Foolishness!" Brandyman exclaimed.

"Watch your tongue, Brandyman!" Sir Jordan chided. "This is Princess Riniel."

"What you propose will get you killed and anyone foolish

enough to accompany you as well," Brandyman said without regard for politeness or protocol.

"You are too bold, Brandyman," Sir Jordan said, rising from beside Riniel, his fists clenched. "If we were not such good friends..."

"Peace, Jordan," Brandyman said apologetically. "Pardon my outburst, Princess Riniel. I only fear for your safety and for my friend's as well."

"We leave at first light," Riniel said firmly.

"If it pleases you, Princess," Brandyman said, trying to remember his manners. "If you are to embark on this journey, which I caution you to forsake, it would be best to travel by night. From what Jordan tells me, the last thing you need right now is to run into a Noland patrol.

"Agreed," Sir Jordan said, looking intently at Riniel.

"Very well," she said after a moment's consideration. "Saddle the horses. We leave now."

✳ ✳ ✳ ✳

The Castle of Rockhold was a smoldering ruin. A large gaping hole compromised its once proud walls. What remained of the keep was a fuming pile of stone and rubble. From their vantage point within the Forest of Roston, Riniel fought the overwhelming urge to scream in anger and dismay. It had taken two days for them to reach Rockhold, dodging patrols of Noland soldiers and traveling only under the cover of night. Now Riniel wished they'd never have come. To see the stronghold of her family as a pile of rubble and to know that it represented the fall of her house was almost too much for Riniel to bear. She had lost everything.

"Now you see," Brandyman said softly and gravely. "Our hope can no longer be in House Aurelia."

"Where do you suggest we place our hope then?" Sir Jordan said gruffly.

"In House Aranethon."

Both Riniel and Sir Jordan stared at Brandyman with a mix of cynicism and bewilderment. *Surely this man was jesting*, Riniel thought. *And at such an inappropriate time as well.*

"I have received word that a council of the Garrison has been convened in Elengil and that the heir of Aranethon has come forth."

"Impossible," Sir Jordan said in derision. "The last Aranethon was murdered almost twenty years ago."

"Yes, but his son survived," Brandyman protested.

"Who told you of this?" Sir Jordan snapped.

"Galanor."

Sir Jordan fell silent.

"Galanor the Loremaster?" Riniel asked quietly.

"Indeed," Brandyman replied quietly. "He visited the Dancing Lion less than a month ago. He and I inducted a new member to the Shadow Garrison."

"Who was the new member?" Sir Jordan asked, continuing to watch for any sign that they'd been spotted.

"Kinison Ravenloch."

"Kinison!" Riniel nearly screamed. Sir Jordan hastened to her side and covered her mouth.

"Princess, please calm yourself, or we'll be caught," he said soothingly.

"Where is Kinison now?" Riniel whispered, pushing Sir Jordan away.

"Galanor sent him to Elengil to do something for the Shadow Garrison," Brandyman replied quickly.

"What is the Shadow Garrison?" Riniel asked, confused.

"Long ago, the last king from House Aranethon organized a secret group of soldiers to guard the realm from its enemies."

"Isn't that what the army is for?" Riniel asked smugly.

"The army can protect the kingdom from invasion, yes, but what about treason? What about the War of Ascension?" Brandyman asked knowingly.

"Silence!" Sir Jordan whispered harshly, forcing Riniel down.

They all fell silent as a slew of Noland soldiers rode past on horseback.

"Respectfully, this is neither the time nor the place for this, Princess," Brandyman said after the riders were out of sight.

"Agreed," Riniel said shakily. "Where shall we go now?"

"We should make for Elengil with all speed," Sir Jordan said, rising and helping Riniel to her feet.

"Lead on then, Sir Jordan."

21

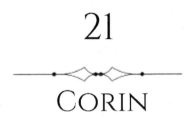

CORIN

It was still dark. The sky was only now beginning to brighten over the Gray Mountains, which were mere phantoms on the eastern horizon. Corin stood at the window in his chambers, gazing thoughtfully out over the lands east of Elengil. He had been unable to sleep. So much had happened in the last two weeks that he could not quiet his mind. To make matters worse, he was also plagued by the constant pain in his left leg. A knock at the door drew his attention from the window.

"Enter," he said quietly.

The door opened, and Galanor entered.

"I thought you might wish to talk, Your Majesty," he said, quietly shutting the door and sitting down in a nearby chair.

"Don't call me that," Corin said, turning back to the window. "I'm not a king."

"But you are the heir to the throne," Galanor protested calmly. "And at noon today, you shall be crowned King of Alethia."

Corin remained silent.

"What is troubling you, sire?" Galanor asked in a fatherly manner.

"What is troubling me!" Corin nearly shouted, rounding on Galanor. "I'll tell you what's troubling me! I'm an orphan from the streets of Stonewall! I've been a nobody all my life! And now, suddenly, I'm supposed to be the heir to the throne of Alethia? How am I supposed to feel?"

"Most people would be thrilled to suddenly find out they are royalty," Galanor suggested.

"Most people are fools. They have no idea what they want out of life," Corin retorted, collapsing into a chair facing Galanor.

"You speak wisdom beyond your years," Galanor said with a soft chuckle. "Since the throne is not enough, what is it that you desire, Your Majesty?"

"Please stop calling me that!"

"Very well, what shall I call you?"

"Corin. Call me Corin."

"As you wish, Corin," Galanor consented with a slight smile. "What is it that you desire?"

"Two weeks ago, I wanted to be free. I wanted to go on adventures and see the world, to leave responsibility behind me."

"And now you find yourself with even more responsibility," Galanor said knowingly.

Corin nodded.

"What's worse," Corin began after a long pause, "is that the only person that I was remotely acquainted with and trusted, Kinison, has abandoned me. If I cannot get men like Kinison to follow me loyally, what hope do I have of leading a kingdom? And on top of everything else, I'm a cripple."

They were silent again for several minutes.

"True leadership is more about submission than it is about great deeds of valor or charisma," Galanor began after a long period of silence. "Men think that to be a leader, you must demand others to submit to you and your will. You must make others do what you want them to do, yet true leadership is about denying your wants and desires and submitting to the needs of others."

"How do I do that?"

"When you show the people that you care more for their well-being than you do for yourself, then they will want to follow you," Galanor replied, getting up and moving toward the door. "Not everyone feels this way, but the majority of people do. You did not seek power, yet it has been thrust upon you nonetheless. What you do with that power, Corin Aranethon, is up to you."

Corin watched as the older man left and closed the door. He sat in silence for a long time, pondering all that had happened to him for the past two weeks. His silent contemplation was finally interrupted by a knock at the door.

"Enter," Corin said, rising.

A man wearing a dark hood and cloak entered. He removed his hood, and Corin immediately knew him.

"You?" Corin gasped. "You're the man from the vision I had while in Oakwood."

"I am."

"You're the reason I lost my leg."

"I'm the reason?"

"Yes. You told me that a man would appear and protect me from the wolves. You told me to do what he said, and I'd be safe. I did all that you said, and that same man cut off my leg!"

"Neither I nor Azka caused you to lose your leg, Corin Aranethon. Yes, I told you to surrender to Azka, but you have forgotten the first thing I told you: 'You must not run.' You chose to run from the wolves instead of trusting my words."

"So I am to be punished for not doing it exactly the way you told me?"

"You made a choice. I tried to give you guidance so that you would be safe and whole. You *chose* to deviate from that path. Your actions and decisions always have consequences...in this case, the loss of your leg."

"So you are saying that if I had done exactly as you instructed, I would still have my leg?"

"You are never told what would have been. Azka also had a

choice to make that night. He could have left you to die, but he chose to save you, though you may not be grateful for it. He now must face the consequences of his actions."

"What consequences does he face?" Corin asked incredulously.

"I am here to tell you your story, no one else's."

"Who are you?" Corin asked, unable to contain his frustration.

"I am the still, small voice that guides you. I have come to give you life."

"I don't understand. What do you mean?" Corin asked, his frustration continuing to build.

"Those who seek wisdom need only ask for it. For you, Corin, the need for such wisdom quickly approaches."

"Please, give me a straight answer! Tell me what to do, like before!" Corin nearly shouted.

"Learn to forgive. As king, that will be your first challenge," the man said, his voice a mere whisper.

"As king? You want me to be king?" Corin asked but gaped as the man vanished before his eyes. He sat staring at the empty chair. *Who is this man who kept appearing in my dreams and now my waking mind? Why is he interested in me? Am I going crazy?* All these things kept going through Corin's mind. He sat in silence for over an hour, trying to make sense of all that had happened to him. It all seemed connected somehow; like some greater being was laying out the events of his life for some purpose. Corin had heard of God but considered the question of God's existence to be irrelevant to his life. *If God did exist, why did He allow so many hardships to befall me?* he often thought. Yet after the events of the past two weeks, Corin was now forced to reconsider everything he once thought to be true. Could this visitor be a messenger from God sent to help guide him or even an incarnation of God Himself? Corin was forced to admit that all the things he was once sure of, he could no longer rely upon with any certainty. How could he rule with such uncertainty? Weren't rulers supposed to know everything and be completely certain of their decisions? Corin wondered if his preconceived notions about, well, everything were, in fact, naive and misguided.

Corin got up, walked to the door, and laid his hand upon the knob. He hesitated for a moment and then pulled it open.

"I wish to speak to Galanor and Lords Myr, Astley, and Warde," Corin said in his best regal voice.

"At once, Your Majesty," one of the guards said, bowing and disappearing down the corridor.

"Do you require anything else, Your Majesty?" the other guard said, bowing.

"No, thank you, ah..." Corin hesitated when he could not remember the guard's name.

"Kaden, sire," the guard said helpfully. "Kaden Ridgeshire from Castel. I came with the garrison under Captain Jon Grehm.

"Right, of course," Corin said, realizing that he and the guard were about the same age. "Thank you, Kaden. That will be all for now."

Corin closed the door and returned to his seat. He only had to wait a few minutes before there was a knock at the door.

"Enter," he said, rising with an effort.

Lord Myr and Barons Astley and Warde entered, followed by Galanor.

"You summoned us, sire?" Galanor asked.

Corin looked at each man in turn. They all had anxious and expectant faces. "My lords and Galanor, I have decided to accept my rightful place as your king."

*　　*　　*　　*

Several hours later, Corin was still sitting in his chambers. The only real change was that he was now dressed in his royal regalia. Everything from the tassels to the long velvet robes made Corin feel ridiculous. His tunic bore the crest of House Aranethon—a rose on a field of white. Corin had snickered at this. *Of all the symbols, why a rose?* He'd asked Galanor about the crest, to which the old man said that the ancients considered the rose as a symbol of purity and passion—two things that a ruler should possess.

The three lords and Galanor had been thrilled upon his decision to ascend the throne. Plans had already been in motion prior to his decision, and his coronation was now only an hour away. Corin sat, his face in his hands, feeling as if his world was spinning out of his control. Despite this, he also felt that this was the right decision; if not for him, then for the kingdom.

A tap on the window drew his attention. He got up and unlatched the windowpane to look out. It was a fine morning, and a light breeze brought up wonderful smells from the kitchen below. Corin shook his head and was just returning to his seat when a cloaked figure jumped through the open window. Corin tried to stand but overcompensated and fell. The figure was upon him in a moment, but not to harm him, as Corin feared. The figured held out a hand, which Corin took suspiciously.

"Guards always forget about windows," said a familiar deep voice from within the hood. "Are you injured?"

"Who are you?" Corin asked once he was standing again.

The man threw back his hood to reveal a dark familiar face. Corin know it at once.

"You!" he said with a mixture of anger and relief.

"Yes, it is I, Azka," he said with a bow.

"I never thought I'd see you again."

"Indeed," Azka said, eyeing Corin's attire. "I never thought to see you in such splendid regalia."

"Why are you here?" Corin said sulkily.

"I have two reasons for coming here," Azka said, sitting down across from Corin. "First, I have come to protect you."

"Protect me from whom?" Corin asked suspiciously.

"From the Guild of Assassins," Azka said firmly. "Those who sent me to kill you will not stop until you are dead. Now that I have failed to kill you, they seek to kill me as well."

"How will you protect me? Engaging a wanted man as a bodyguard does not seem logical to me."

"As a former member of the Guild, I have insights into their way of thinking. I will be able to foresee their plans and efforts."

"What will you want in return?" Corin asked after a few minutes consideration.

"My second reason for coming here—my sister. I wish for your help in finding her."

"How can I help find your sister?"

"As king, you have men and supplies enough to search the whole kingdom. I will pledge to protect you if you swear to help me find my sister after this war is over. Will you swear?" Azka finished, holding out his hand.

"Yes, Azka, I swear to help you find your sister," Corin said, taking Azka's hand and shaking it.

At that moment, the door burst open, and Galanor entered, followed by several guards.

"Your Majesty, are you all right? We received word that one of the guards spotted a cloaked figure sneaking into your chambers," one of the guards said, eyeing Azka suspiciously.

"I'm all right, Galanor," Corin said, standing with an effort and holding up a hand. "This is my new bodyguard, Azka. He will be protecting me for the foreseeable future."

"If that is your wish," Galanor said. Then turning to the guards, he said, "Please leave us."

They waited until the guards had left and the door was closed before speaking again.

"Caught climbing in a window? Azka, you're getting sloppy," Galanor chided with a smile.

"And you, Galanor, have grown more gray hair since last we saw each other. Pray your mind has not aged as much as your body," Azka retorted, smiling and embracing Galanor.

"You know each other, I take it?" Corin asked, taken aback.

"A long time ago," Galanor said.

"Fifteen years, my old friend," Azka corrected. "Galanor rescued me from the streets of Nenholm."

"Though I still do not approve of your chosen profession, Azka. If you remember, I tried to teach you about God's word..."

"I have heard your reasons before, Galanor," Azka said grumpily. "Despite my choice to abandon my previous profession, I still have little use for your god."

"I am glad you remember my lessons," Galanor said at length. "Though I had hoped you would have learned more from them."

"I have learned much in my travels, yet all I have learned from you and elsewhere has not helped me find my sister."

"Is that why you came here? To find Aylen? I have heard no news from you or your sister for years. Why come here, and why now?"

"I was sent to kill the last son of Aranethon. I chose to spare and protect him instead in the hopes that he would help me find her," Azka said plainly. "I hope my deeds have warranted a little favor."

"A life for a life?" Galanor asked, his anger flaring. "You have not changed, Azka!"

"I chose to spare his life before coming here, but I do not demand anything. Only now do I ask for help."

"And I granted his request, Galanor," Corin interjected. "What better person to protect me than someone who knows the best ways to kill me?"

"I suppose a king will have his way," Galanor said, apparently not convinced.

A sudden knock at the door drew their attention. Corin bid them come, and a guard entered.

"Your highness," the guard began, looking very anxious. "A young lady and her two companions beg an audience with you."

"Did they give their names?"

"Yes, sire," the guard said, looking even more anxious.

"Well, speak, man!" Galanor said irritably.

"She claims to be Princess Riniel Aurelia, sire," the guard said.

Corin and Galanor exchanged looks of bewilderment.

"And the others?" asked Galanor quickly.

"A Guardian named Sir Jordan Reese and an innkeeper named Sam Brandyman."

"What shall we do?" Galanor asked, turning to Corin.

"Arrest them and place them in separate rooms. Do not mistreat them. I will summon them to the Great Hall after the ceremony," Corin said after a moment's consideration.

"Your Highness, if I may..." began Galanor.

"Not now, Galanor," Corin snapped. "Leave me, all of you. I need to think."

The others left Corin to his thoughts. He had to admit that this was a choice turn of events. The daughter of his family's greatest enemy was in his custody. He knew that how he treated her would define his reign as king. He sat thinking on this until the guards came to take him to the Great Hall. He stood and went with them still asking himself: *Should I be merciful or should I exact revenge?* He could not say.

*   *   *   *

As Corin entered the Great Hall, he found the room packed with people. They stood upon his arrival, and Corin wondered if he would ever get used to it. The trumpets sounded, announcing his arrival, and the chapel bells rang midday across the courtyard from the Great Hall. He stood in the doorway, Galanor and Azka on either side followed by Lord Myr and Barons Astley and Warde. Corin looked toward the dais on the far side of the hall, where the bishop of Elengil stood holding a crown. This crown was, of course, a substitute, for Noliono still possessed the real one. Galanor had told Corin that this crown was made of gold donated by the people of Elengil. It was humbling for Corin to think that already there were so many who wished to follow him.

Silence gripped the hall, and Corin knew it was time. Using the staff given to him by Galanor, he began the long walk forward. Galanor and Azka followed in his wake. He did not flinch but kept limping forward. Finally, after what seemed like an hour, Corin reached the foot of the dais. He turned toward the crowd and, with a struggle, knelt down. Galanor, Azka, and the others remained facing him.

"Corin Aranethon," the bishop began as he came and stood beside Corin. "Do you solemnly swear to govern the peoples of the kingdom of Alethia and all its territories according to its laws and customs?"

"I swear," Corin said, trying to sound more regal than he felt.

"Do you swear to cause law and justice, in mercy, to be executed in all your judgments?"

"I swear."

"Do you swear to do all within your power to maintain the laws of God and to promote and protect the free worship of His name, so help you God?"

"I swear, so help me God."

"Rise, then, and ascend the throne of Alethia."

Leaning heavily on his staff, Corin stood and turned to climb the steps leading to the dais. Atop the dais sat the throne. It was a simple high-backed chair gilded in shining gold. The banner of House Aranethon was draped over it. Corin looked at his family crest for the first time, which was a crimson rose with an emerald-green stem and two adjoining leaves upon a white background. Corin reached the throne and sat down with an effort. The bishop came to his side.

"I crown you, Corin I, King of Alethia," the bishop said, placing the crown upon Corin's head. "May your reign be long and just. Long live the king!"

The last phrase was echoed by all those in attendance, and as one, they all knelt before Corin, their king. Corin had never felt so awkward. The chanting and praising went on and on. He tried to hide the unworthiness he felt and smiled meekly at the crowd. Finally, Lord Myr held up a hand, and the crowd became silent.

"People of Alethia, I thank you for your kind words. I am grateful to be your king," Corin said shakily then looked at Galanor. "As my first act as your king, I declare the usurper, Noliono, fashioning himself as King of Alethia, and all those who follow him to be guilty of high treason and other crimes too many to recount."

The crowd cheered in approval. Again, Lord Myr held up his hand for silence.

"I also declare the once king Kelbrandt Aurelia as a traitor and usurper. He is guilty of high treason, as are all his descendants."

The crowd seemed conflicted, but most shouted their approval. Corin turned to Lord Myr and nodded.

"Bring in the prisoners," Lord Myr ordered.

The great doors opened on the other side of the hall, and the crowd turned to see those accused. A young woman and two older men, bound in chains, were brought to the foot of the dais and made to kneel. Corin's eyes fell on the young woman and was struck by her beauty. Even as she looked up at him in anger and fear, Corin was mesmerized by her deep brown eyes and long brown hair. Her appearance was disheveled, probably due to her struggle against arrest, yet Corin found her absolutely stunning.

"Your Majesty?" Galanor whispered softly.

"Yes?" Corin said, shocked to find him standing by his side.

"Sire, we await your pleasure to begin."

"You may proceed, Lord Myr," Corin said, again attempting to sound more regal than he felt.

"Thank you, Your Majesty," Lord Myr said with a bow and turned toward the prisoners. "State your names for the record."

"I am Sam Brandyman, owner of the Dancing Lion," Brandyman said, bowing.

"Sir Jordan Reese, formerly of the Guardians of the Citadel," Sir Jordan answered.

"And the young lady we all know," Lord Myr said with a sneer. "This is Princess Riniel Aurelia, daughter of the late Greyfuss Aurelia."

A wave of murmuring swept across the hall at this, and the three prisoners looked uncomfortable.

"For the record," Galanor interjected. "What house do the Guardians serve, Sir Jordan?"

"No house," answered Sir Jordan. "We owe our allegiance only to the king and to Alethia."

"But to which king are the Guardians now loyal, Sir Jordan?" Lord Myr interrupted.

"Currently, the Guardians are loyal to King Noliono." Sir Jordan answered. The anxiety on his face was apparent.

"You say you are formerly of the Guardians, Sir Jordan?"

"Yes, I forsook my oath in order to help Princess Riniel escape from Ethriel."

"So you are not loyal to Noliono, but loyal to House Aurelia?"

"I am the sworn protector of Princess Riniel," Sir Jordan said, looking at the young woman.

"So you broke your oath in order to protect the princess?" Lord Myr said accusingly.

"I swore an oath to protect the king and his family. When King Greyfuss died, my oath transferred to Princess Riniel. I never swore fealty to Noliono and would have left the Guardians were it not for the princess."

"And you, Sam Brandyman," Lord Myr said, turning toward the other man. "To which king are you loyal?"

"I am a member of the Shadow Garrison. I admit it freely in the presence of many of its other members. I have sworn loyalty to the people of this kingdom and have never served nor swore allegiance to any king."

"The Shadow Garrison swore to protect the House of Aranethon. The last remaining heir sits before you," Lord Myr said, pointing at Corin. "Will you both swear your allegiance to him now?"

"We will," both men said, nearly in unison.

"Then I declare you pardoned," Corin said, remembering Galanor's earlier instruction of Alethia law and court procedure. "Rise, Sam Brandyman. You will prove your loyalty in battle. Report to Captain Grehm for assignment. Sir Jordan Reese, you are hereby stripped of your title. You will also prove your loyalty in battle. If after proving your loyalty you are found worthy, I will restore your titles and rank."

"Your Highness," both men said with a bow. The guards removed their chains, and the two men were led out of the hall.

Once the two men had gone, all eyes turned toward the young woman.

"Princess Riniel Aurelia," began Lord Myr. "Your ancestor, Kelbrandt Aurelia has been found guilty of high treason, and the king has declared your entire family guilty as well. How do you plead?"

"Not guilty," Riniel said, her voice shaking.

Corin looked hard at the young woman and was struck by her composure. Despite her terror, her eyes and facial expression remained resolute. He was moved with compassion for her, yet struggled with his previous decree.

"Are you familiar with the *Book of Aduin* and its account of the War of Ascension?" Lord Myr asked.

Riniel shook her head.

"Then you do not know that your ancestor, Kelbrandt Aurelia, plotted and murdered the House of Aranethon?" Lord Myr asked, his voice rising.

"What!" Riniel shouted incredulously. "That's absurd! It was the kingdom of Nordyke who murdered the Aranethons."

"No, dear princess," Galanor interjected kindly. "The commonly known history of the War of Ascension is a lie. The only true account is found within the *Book of Aduin.*"

"I refuse to believe these lies about my family!" Riniel shouted.

"Enough," Corin said calmly, looking hard at Riniel. "Give her the book, and let her read the truth for herself."

Riniel looked questioningly at Corin but took the book when Galanor handed it to her. Corin kept watching her the whole time. Her countenance fell, and her face paled as her eyes continued to dart across the pages.

"As you can see," Lord Myr began after Riniel had finished. "The kingdom of Nordyke had nothing to do with the murder of the Aranethons. It was actually a plot by the Aurelias..."

"What of House Myr?" Riniel asked defiantly. "What of your

guilt?"

"I have already accepted my ancestors' guilt and pledged my undying loyalty to my king!" Lord Myr shouted in retort. "The question is, do *you* continue to deny your ancestors' treason?"

"I...I don't know," Riniel said, her face falling once more. "I guess not."

Corin watched as Lord Myr and Galanor exchanged looks. He rose, and the entire hall's attention shifted to him. He looked down at Riniel, and his heart was suddenly filled with compassion for her. Then he remembered the strange visitor's words: "Learn to forgive." He knew what he had to do. He cleared his throat.

"I declare the House of Aurelia stripped of its titles, and all its lands shall be returned to the crown as recompense for the two hundred years of exile my family has suffered. Princess Aurelia, I give you a chance to save yourself. If you will renounce your title and your house, I will grant you clemency and absolve you of any crime your ancestors committed against my own," Corin said. "However, if you refuse to renounce your house, you will be executed for the crimes of your family."

Riniel looked up at him in bewilderment as the crowd murmured its approval. She seemed overwhelmed and struck dumb by his decree.

"You have until tomorrow to decide," Corin said when Riniel appeared unable to respond. "Take her somewhere where she can consider my offer and see that she is left undisturbed."

"Sire, if I may object," Lord Myr began.

"You may not, Lord Myr," Corin said calmly. "Now do I need to repeat myself?"

Lord Myr bowed and issued orders to the guards. As Riniel was taken out of the hall, Corin wondered if he was doing the right thing. It seemed so, but as this was his first day as king, he had no idea what consequences his actions would hold. He continued to watch Riniel, and he began to wonder what kind of person she was. She was obviously attractive, and Corin could not help but wonder if she was married or betrothed to anyone. Of course, this was all pointless speculation. If she chose not to renounce, he would be forced to execute her; and if she did renounce, he would take her titles and lands anyway, which would make her hate him. In either case, she would never consider him anything more than her judge.

22

RINIEL

After leaving the Great Hall, Riniel was taken to a room and locked inside. She paced back and forth, her anger bubbling and churning within her. Never in her life had people treated her so disrespectfully. *It is an outrage,* she thought. *An absolute outrage. How dare some common boy sit in judgment of me and my family. Heir of Aranethon indeed!*

There was a knock at the door. An old man entered the room and closed the door behind him.

"Riniel Aurelia," he said with a bow. "It has been far too long."

"Do I know you?" Riniel asked, trying to remain cordial.

"I am Galanor. I was a friend of your father's for a long time."

"If that is true, why then do you align yourself against his house?" Riniel asked, her anger boiling. It was all she could do not to shout.

"The House of Aurelia has fallen, Riniel," Galanor said bluntly. "Its lands conquered by Noliono, and all its members are slain save you."

"You think I don't know this!" Riniel shouted, tears beginning to stream from her eyes. "I have seen with my own eyes the smoldering ruins of Rockhold. I have heard the reports of my family members' deaths."

"Then you must realize that what King Corin asks of you is merely to acknowledge the truth," Galanor replied kindly.

"He slanders my family and my father!" Riniel shouted, turning her back on Galanor. "How can I let that pass?"

"The charges against your family are brought by history, Riniel," Galanor answered, placing a hand on her shoulder and turning her around. "The true history found in the *Book of Aduin*."

"What makes his account true and the others false?"

"For one, Aduin lived during the events. For another, his is the only source of history from before the War of Ascension. Your ancestors saw to it that all other records were burned to prevent the Aranethons from proving the truth and reclaiming the throne. Only Aduin's account survived. Thus, the Aranethonian kings became more myth than fact."

"I won't believe it," Riniel said, turning away again.

"If you do not accept this, King Corin will have no choice but to execute you," Galanor said grimly.

"He wouldn't dare hold me responsible."

"He has declared all of House Aurelia guilty of treason. If you don't renounce your house, you will share their guilt and their fate."

"I don't care!" Riniel shouted.

"Very well, I will leave you to your thoughts," Galanor said, opening the door to go. Before he left, he turned to Riniel and said, "Please think carefully, Riniel, before you decide. Is honoring the dead really worth your life?"

Sometime later, for Riniel had lost all track of time, she awoke in the now-darkened room, lying atop the small bed. Rising up, she rubbed her tear-stained face sleepily then started, looking wide-eyed at the man sitting in the corner.

"You!" she said, recognizing him at once.

"Yes, dear Riniel, I am here," the man said tenderly. "The last time we spoke, you told me to leave."

"Then why are you here?" Riniel asked meekly.

"I have come because you called out to me. I always answer when my children call."

"Will you please stop speaking cryptically and just tell me who you are?" Riniel asked exasperatedly.

"You know who I am, Riniel."

"No, I really don't!" she nearly shouted.

"I am the still, small voice who whispers guidance to those who know me and are willing to listen," the man responded calmly. "I have come to guide you. Will you listen?"

Riniel considered for a moment then slowly nodded.

"Do you remember that day in the citadel chapel when you told me that you were still angry with me over your mother's death?"

"Yes, but how do you know that? I thought I was alone," Riniel asked, taken aback.

"You are never alone, for I am always with you."

"If you are who I think you are claiming to be, then why did you let my father be murdered?" Riniel asked, her voice shaking with suppressed anger.

"As I said before, your father's death was the actions of men. You value the freedom to choose and deny the sovereignty of God until your choices lead to pain and suffering. You cannot have it both ways. You must either surrender to God's will and guidance or be prepared to face the consequences of *your* actions and decisions," the man gently retorted. "Your father was murdered, and the one responsible will face the consequences of *her* actions."

"Her actions!" Riniel shouted in disbelief. "But I thought that Noliono murdered my father?"

"No, Riniel. He did not, though he did want to be king," the man said, infuriating Riniel with his calm demeanor. "Your father was a good man of faith. He was a just king, yet he has passed on from this life as have the rest of your family. Clinging to them will not bring them back nor will it save you from a similar fate."

"What should I do, Lord?" Riniel asked, and for the first time she realized that she was asking sincerely. A tear slid down her cheek.

"Put your faith in me," the man replied simply. "Let go of all the rest."

※　※　※　※

Riniel awoke, lying on the very same bed, and immediately looked to the same chair where the man had been sitting. He was gone, yet Riniel felt that He was still with her somehow. She got up, went to the door and knocked.

"My lady?" The guard asked after opening the door.

"Please tell King Corin that I have made my decision."

"Yes, my lady."

"And please bring me some water so I may make myself presentable," she added quickly.

The guard closed the door and hurried off. Riniel sat in silent thought for a long time, interrupted only by the guard's reappearance with a basin of water and a summons to the Great Hall in half an hour. She knew what she had to do, but part of her still rebelled against it.

When guards returned for her and they began their trek back to the Great Hall, Riniel's stomach began to writhe with anxiety. As they passed onto one of the battlements, Riniel saw that the sun was rising in the clear morning, just above the distant mountains. *A new day and a possible new beginning*, she thought.

Within moments, they stood before the doors of the Great Hall. Riniel took several deep breaths to steady herself; then the doors opened, revealing the crowded room, and on the other side of the room sat the new king upon his throne. Riniel was paraded down the hall as the crowd murmured around her. When she reached the foot of the dais, she bowed to the king, who inclined his head toward her.

"Princess Riniel Aurelia," Lord Myr began. "Have you made your decision?"

"I have," Riniel said, her voice shaking. "I have decided to renounce my titles, lands, and my house."

The crowd became alive, and the din filled the hall. Some hissed while others cheered, but nearly all were shocked by her decision.

"Riniel Aurelia," the king said, his voice echoing off the stone.

Both the crowd and Riniel noticed the immediate absence of her title. A part of her felt a sudden loss, but that was quickly swept aside as she focused her eyes on the king.

"I hereby strip you of any titles, lands, and privileges you previously possessed, and I declare you pardoned from any crimes you or your former house has committed against me or my family. I release you from royal custody and declare you free to go where you will."

The crowd became alive again, but Riniel didn't care. She bowed and allowed herself to be led from the hall. When they reached the courtyard, Riniel had only a few moments to wonder what would become of her when one of the king's pages ran up to her.

"My lady," the young man said with a bow. "The king requests you dine with him this midday."

"Uh...okay. I mean, yes...I accept," Riniel stammered.

"Excellent. I will tell him at once," the page said and ran back into the hall.

Riniel's head was spinning

"Would you like to freshen up before meeting with the king?" one of the guards asked.

Riniel nodded, and they walked back to her room, where she found a tub with hot water and some fresh clothes for her to wear. She sat down on the bed for a moment to gather herself. Her head was still spinning with all that had happened. She wondered what would happen to her and why the king would wish to dine with her after all that had transpired. Pardoned or not, she was still Aurelian born.

After sitting in silent thought for a while, Riniel finally got up, undressed, and got into the tub. She enjoyed the feel of the warm water. She let out a long sigh and drifted off for a moment. A knock at the door brought her swiftly back.

"Just a moment," she said, hurriedly getting out and covering herself with a towel. "Okay. You may enter."

The door opened, and the king entered. He stopped short and averted his eyes.

"My lady, I apologize. I can return later," he said, backing out and pulling the door partly closed.

"No, I uh,...what brings you here, Your Highness?" Riniel stammered, dripping water all over the floor.

"I came to see if you needed anything," he said, still averting his eyes.

"No, I'm fine. I mean, thank you for the bath and clean clothes."

He looked at her, and they locked eyes for a moment. She saw kindness in his dark eyes, and something inside Riniel leapt with excitement. Her heart was racing, and she was shaking.

"I...I only wish to make you comfortable here," he said, looking away again.

"Thank you," she said, also looking away and moving her hair from her face.

"I will see you later?"

"Yes."

"Until then...then," he said, bowing and closing the door.

Riniel stood dumbstruck, the past few minutes racing through her mind. The king had come to check on her; the king himself had come to see her. And what was that feeling that had leapt inside her when they had looked at each other. Riniel dried herself and dressed, going over the short interaction word by word, wondering what was going to happen next.

❋ ❋ ❋ ❋

A few hours later, Riniel found herself seated alone at a table in the king's chambers. She gazed about the sparsely furnished chambers, hardly believing a king lived here. When the door opened, she stood and watched as the king entered. As he slowly made his way across the room, Riniel felt a pang of sympathy for him, despite all that had transpired.

"Thank you for agreeing to dine with me," he said, taking the seat across from her.

"It is my pleasure, Your Majesty," Riniel said awkwardly.

"I apologize for interrupting you earlier."

"Oh, no harm done, Your Majesty."

"Please, call me Corin."

"I, um..."

"Unless that makes you feel uncomfortable?"

"No. I just...okay, Corin."

Corin smiled at her, and that same excitement leapt inside her again, causing her to look away and blush profusely.

"If I may be so bold, Corin, how did you...um?"

"Lose my leg?" Corin finished for her. He sat thoughtfully for a moment then said, "I ignored the advice and guidance of God."

Riniel studied his face for any sign of jest or sarcasm; there was none. She was amazed at the king's openness with her.

"Do you believe in God?" she asked inquisitively.

"Not until just recently," he said with a meek smile. "You?"

"I'm not sure," she said, her mind turning to the recent dreams or visions she kept having.

"What aren't you sure about?" he asked.

"She looked at this young man hard and wondered if she dared share her visions with him. Would he understand, or would he think she was crazy?

"It's complicated," she said finally. "It's something I don't feel comfortable discussing just yet."

This wasn't wholly true. For some reason, Riniel felt she could be open with Corin. There was something in those kind eyes of his that just made her feel safe, and it scared her; that was what held her back.

"Fair enough," Corin said, leaning back in his seat. "I understand your reluctance to trust me or anyone here in Elengil after everything you've been through today. Just know that I meant every word I said in the Great Hall. I have pardoned you and will not seek any vengeance against you or what happened in the past. I may also add that any who try to hold you responsible or try to hurt you will face my judgment."

She studied his face but found not even a hint of subterfuge.

"I believe you," she found herself saying. "At least, I want to believe you."

There was silence between them for several minutes. The servants brought their food, and they both focused on their meals. Riniel's feelings and emotions were in turmoil. Nothing made sense. She should hate this man and yet...and yet...

"There is a banquet this evening in honor of my coronation," Corin said, interrupting her thoughts. "I was hoping that...if you wanted, that is, if you weren't busy..."

His voice drifted off, and he simply looked at her expectantly. Then it suddenly hit her.

"Are you asking me to go with you?"

"I, uh...yes, I am."

"Oh,...I, uh..." Riniel stammered, her mind whirling with thoughts and emotions. What nerve this young man had! To strip her of her pride and family honor then ask her to a banquet? It was outrageous! Yet his eyes were so kind and gentle...

"I'm sorry, but I don't, well..." she said, standing. "Please excuse me, Your Highness." She saw the disappointment on his face, but he nodded. Riniel hurried to the door, and the guards walked her back to her chambers. Her emotions were in an uproar. In less than a few days, she'd lost her entire family, renounced her father and ancestors, lost her titles and lands, and now the man who'd taken her father's place was trying to court her. She was filled with excitement and dread at the same time, sending her mind whirling in every direction. She worried if she'd just blown it with Corin and at the same time was hoping she had blown it.

When they arrived back at her chambers, Riniel thanked the guards and closed the door. She walked over to the bed and fell to her knees, weeping confused tears. Saying a silent prayer for guidance, Riniel wondered where all this might lead her.

23

KINISON

For the first time in his life, Kinison Ravenloch had dreaded the sight of Ethriel. The city that had been his home for years now appeared daunting and mysterious. Kinison had entered the city the previous morning disguised as a trader and had spent the hours since making his way toward the citadel. Several times he thought someone had recognized him or had a close call with one of the members of the City Watch, and he darted into a dark alley or corner.

Now night had fallen, and Kinison was searching along the walls of the citadel for the ancient hidden passage. Not even the reigning king knew of it; only the Lord Commander and his lieutenants knew of this passage for obvious security reasons. Built long ago by some long-forgotten king or lord, it was the only way into the citadel besides the main gate. Since only a few knew of its location, Kinison had hoped the passage was still left unguarded.

Kinison stooped and ran his hand along the stonework beside the wall until he found a small indentation only the length of a man's finger. Anyone who happened upon this indentation would think it was an accident of the stone masons. Kinison looked down both sides of the street; seeing no one nearby, he pushed his hand into the indentation, and the stone slab at his feet rose slightly. Kinison pulled the slab up, revealing a set of stone steps leading beneath the citadel walls. He entered the passage, taking care to pull the slab back into place. A small click told him that the slab was now back in place, leaving no sign of his passing. He was now alone in the pitch-black passage leading into the citadel.

Kinison pulled open his pack and felt around for his tinderbox and the torch he'd brought. In a few moments, the bright light of the torch filled the passage, and Kinison began to breathe a little easier. The path had been dug through the bedrock until it reached a great cavern under the citadel. The sheer drop on his left went down beyond the reach of his torchlight, and the path was only a few feet across. Kinison took slow, measured steps, though even then he only just caught himself before he would have tumbled down into the chasm.

Suddenly a pair of gleaming red eyes appeared on the path ahead of him. Kinison stopped dead in his tracks, placing a hand on the hilt of his sword. The eyes stared menacingly as the outline of a huge wolf emerged from out of the gloom. The wolf stopped just outside the range of his torchlight.

"The master knew you might try to sneak into the citadel," the wolf growled.

"You can speak?" Kinison gasped, stepping back and gaping at the beast. "How?"

"The master gave my pack and I intelligence and speech. We are his servants, bound to him forever."

"Who are you?"

"I am Bodulf, once leader of my pack, but I lost the boy."

"The boy?" You mean Corin?"

"The dark-skinned man killed my friends. When the master learned of my failure, he sent me here."

"Who is your master?"

"We are unworthy to speak the master's name." The wolf growled menacingly at Kinison. "I weary of this. I was ordered to kill any who tried to pass this way, and I shall not fail my master again."

At that, the massive wolf lunged at Kinison, who just barely dodged the attack. The wolf turned and lunged again, this time knocking Kinison to the ground and causing him to drop the torch, extinguishing its light. Kinison now had to fight in complete darkness, and his only clue to the location of his foe was the gleam of its red eyes.

"Your end is nigh," the wolf growled, springing at him once again.

Kinison didn't have time to even draw his weapon before the wolf was on top of him. The weight of the massive wolf drove him into the stone floor, and the beast's breath reeked. He pushed against the wolf's snapping jaws, praying for a miracle. Just as Kinison's arms felt as though they might give out at any moment, a sudden idea came to him. He slid his left leg out, feeling for where he guessed the wall lay. His foot soon hit the wall about a foot away. The wolf made a powerful lunge at his throat, and Kinison punched the beast in the nose. The wolf yelped but did not retreat. Kinison maneuvered his knees so that they were directly under the wolf's stomach. He pushed up with his knees then put his feet on the wolf's stomach and kicked up as hard as he could. The wolf flew to Kinison's right, and the gleaming red eyes disappeared over the edge of the chasm. He heard the wolf let out a howl, but it too was soon lost in the darkness.

Kinison lay there, panting for a few minutes and collecting himself. Then he slowly stood up with his hand on the wall both for direction and support. He had no idea where the torch lay nor had he any way to reignite it. There was but one choice. He placed his hand on the wall again and slowly felt his way along. Each step was terrifying as Kinison fought to subdue his fears. Soon the path began to climb, and about fifteen minutes later, Kinison reached a wall of stone blocking his path. He moved his hand across the

- R.S. GULLETT -

wall, feeling for the same type of indentation as before. He found
it and pushed his hand into it. A gap in the wall appeared, sending
blinding light into the dark passage. Kinison squeezed through the
gap and closed it behind him. Kinison found himself in a little-
used corridor across the courtyard from the Great Hall. The moon
had disappeared beyond the horizon, leaving everything in
darkness. Kinison knew that his only hope of saving Sarah was by
enlisting the help of his once friend Sir Ren Gables. Though he
remembered that Sir Ren had participated in his removal from the
Guardians, he had a hard time blaming the man for deciding to try
and protect his family. He knew that Sir Ren's family resided in the
city, and he also knew that Noliono would not hesitate to threaten
or even kill his family if Sir Ren had opposed him.

Kinison stealthily made his way across the courtyard, aiming for
the west tower, which was the location of Sir Ren's office. The
only problem would be if Sir Ren decided not to help Kinison. In
that case, Kinison might have to kill him in order to save his wife,
Sarah. He earnestly hoped it would not come to that. He reached
the door leading to the west tower and found it unguarded. This
was troubling as this door was always guarded during his tenure as
Lord Commander. He took a deep breath, turned the handle, and
knew no more.

✳   ✳   ✳   ✳

When Kinison came to, he found himself in a dimly lit room.
He was seated, and when he tried to move, he found his arms and
ankles bound to a chair. He also felt pain on the back of his head
and suddenly realized that he'd been attacked from behind. They
had been waiting for him the whole time. He looked up and saw
Sir Ren Gables seated across from him behind a large wooden
desk. Kinison looked at his old friend and noticed several more
gray hairs than the last time he had seen the man. He was also
skinnier, and his face appeared more careworn. Kinison was struck
at how much his friend had changed in the span of just two

months. At the moment, Sir Ren was staring at Kinison. His expression was one of pity and sorrow.

"Leave us," Sir Ren said to the men standing at the door.

Kinison watched them leave then turned back to Sir Ren.

"Kinison Ravenloch," Sir Ren said, opening a bottle of wine and pouring himself a cup. "Of all the people...ha," he said with a dark laugh. "Would you care for some wine?"

"No, thank you," Kinison said sternly. "Since when do you drink, Ren?"

"A habit I've picked up since you left," Sir Ren replied, tossing back the cup's contents in a single go. "Helps calm the nerves. The job has become more demanding since...well, since you left."

"I didn't leave, Ren," Kinison said, his anger bubbling up inside him.

"I know," Sir Ren said, pouring himself another cupful. "Shame how everything turned out—you exiled, Greyfuss dead, kingdom torn apart by civil war. It's a shame."

Kinison watched Sir Ren, realizing that this was not the same man who'd served under him for so many years. Somehow, over the course of a few months, the Ren Gables he had known had been purged of his very soul.

"What happened to you?" Kinison finally asked.

"What happened?" Sir Ren asked incredulously. He stood up and walked over to the window. "After you were exiled, Noliono decided to purge the city of anyone who might oppose him. He told us it was necessary to preserve the wellbeing of Alethia." He poured another cup of wine and drank it without looking at Kinison. "You remember Mikel Greyvan?" he asked, turning toward Kinison, who nodded. "After Princess Aurelia's escape, Mikel began opposing Noliono's new decrees for the city. Noliono ordered Lord Kludge and I to arrest him and anyone who supported him. I tried to argue, but Kludge threatened my family. What was I supposed to do?

"We found Mikel with fifty other members of the City Watch and surrounded him with over one hundred Guardians. Kludge demanded his surrender, Mikel refused. What he didn't know was that Kludge had sent archers to the walls above Mikel, and at his signal, the archers opened fire on Mikel and his followers. More than half of them were killed with the first volley, including Mikel. Any who tried to flee were cut down by those of us on the ground. It was a bloodbath. I lost a friend that day, and I've been losing more every day since."

Kinison could not hide his shock and disgust of this man he'd once called friend. Sir Ren must have seen it on his face, for he looked away quickly.

"Kinison, I..." he began, returning to his seat behind the desk. "I know you came here looking for my help, but I'm afraid I'm going to have to hold you until Lord Kludge returns."

"Ren, you must know why I'm here," Kinison said quickly. "I'm here for Sarah. Please help me!"

"I can't, Kinison," Sir Ren said, pain on his face. "He'll kill them, Kinison. He'll kill my family."

"Ren, please," Kinison pled. "Help me save Sarah, and we'll get your family out too."

"I can't risk it. I helped Princess Riniel and Sir Jordan Reese escape, and somehow Noliono and Kludge found out. They moved my family to the Fortress of Noland and threatened to have them killed if I defy them again," Sir Ren said, slamming his fist on the desk. "Guards!"

The guards returned, and Sir Ren motioned for them to take Kinison away.

"Ren, you were a good man once. How can you do this?"

"Kinison, there are no good men anymore. I'm just a man trying to protect his family."

"No, Ren, please!" Kinison yelled as the guards stood him up and began dragging him away. "Don't do this!"

"I have no choice," was the last thing Kinison heard Sir Ren say before he was pulled out the door.

✳   ✳   ✳   ✳

The guards dragged Kinison down to the dungeons and hurled him into one of the cells. As the guards locked the door and moved away, Kinison was left in complete darkness. He sat up against the hard stone wall and fumed with indignation. His mind raced with angry and desperate thoughts. *How could Ren do this? Is Sarah all right? How could I escape from here? Is there any hope now?*

Kinison stood up and felt along the walls until he located the door. He yanked and pushed, shook and pounded, banged and kicked, and at last when all his energy was spent, he sat back down and wept bitterly.

"I warned you that this would happen," came a voice from the darkness.

Kinison stood up, his eyes desperately trying to pierce the blackness.

"Who's there?" he asked, a hint of anxiety in his voice.

"After all this time, you still do not know my voice, Kinison?" asked the voice.

Kinison thought he recognized the voice but could not be sure.

"Where are you?"

"I am always with you, even when you think you don't need me," the voice answered.

"Are you the man who keeps visiting me in those visions or whatever they are?" Kinison asked, finally remembering.

"I am."

"Well, what do you want with me?"

"I am here to encourage you, Kinison. Do not lose heart or your faith in me."

"Don't lose heart!" Kinison exclaimed. "How can I not lose heart? I'm locked in the dungeon, my wife has been taken and might even be dead, my friend has betrayed me again, and I'm hearing voices and must be going mad."

"You are not mad, Kinison. I've come to guide you if you will at last do as I say and trust me."

"How can I trust you when I don't even know you?"

"As I have said before, you know of me, but you don't know me. If you wish to know me, you must confess your sins and mistakes and surrender your will and obey mine. Will you surrender, Kinison, to my will and stop trying to always do things your way?"

Kinison was silent for several moments, his mind trying to make sense of this. All that the man had said Kinison had heard before, only this time Kinison was listening. He sighed heavily.

"Fine. What must I do?"

"Sarah has but one chance to live. If you wish to save her, you must obey my instructions completely. If you choose not to do exactly as I say, Sarah will not survive."

"Are you saying you will let her die if I don't do exactly..."

"It is up to you to save her, Kinison. She was given to you and you to her. She is your responsibility to honor and protect. I will help you, but you must do as I instruct you."

"Very well, I will do what you say," Kinison said, and for the first time he really meant it.

"First, a chance will come for you to escape, and your friend's life will be in your hands. You must spare him and help him escape."

"Why?" Kinison interrupted.

"Second," the voice said, ignoring the interruption. "You will discover where Sarah is being held, but you must not attempt to rescue her alone."

"What?" Kinison exclaimed. "How can I not try and save my wife?"

"You must do as I instruct, Kinison," the voice said simply.

Kinison sighed again.

"You will see the very place that Sarah is being held, and you will also see a young lord fighting for his life. You must save the young lord, or all will be lost. Once you save him, he will help you save Sarah. These things you must do. What will you do, Kinison Ravenloch?"

"Why must I do these things?" Kinison asked, but there was no answer. "Tell me more. I must know more! Why do you always have to be so cryptic!" Kinison pounded his fist into the hard stone wall. This was so infuriating. Why was he always left in the dark, waiting?

After several hours of going over all the things that had happened, Kinison realized that each time he had chosen his own way, things had gone horribly wrong. He remembered something; one of the bishops had said, "There is a way which seemeth right unto a man, but the end thereof are the ways of death."

His entire life he'd been so confident that his way was the right way; now, as he sat in the darkness of his cell, he began to consider if there was a better way.

24

NOLIONO

Noliono awoke to find himself tied to a chair, his bindings digging into his wrists and ankles. His head was spinning. Struggling against the ropes, he let out a roar of anger. There was laughter coming from his right. Noliono turned and saw three men in heavy fur coats, bearing battle axes. Noliono knew them to be warriors from the kingdom of Nordyke. Their normally grim faces twisted into evil grins. The foremost man bore a long scar across his left eye. The one to his left wore a helmet, and the one on his left had a large mustache. It was to him the others seemed to look for direction and affirmation.

"Release me, now!" Noliono shouted.

"Squeals like a stuck pig," the one with the mustache said.

"Perhaps we should stick 'em and see what he squeals to us about the fortress, Deofol," the man wearing the helmet commented, addressing the man with the scar.

"No, I have a better idea," Deofol said with an evil grin. "Bring in the woman and the two boys. Let's see what he is willing to tell us."

One of the men left, and Noliono struggled harder at his bonds. *No! No! This can't be happening!*

The man returned shortly, carrying a woman. Two more men followed close behind, carrying two young boys.

"Brenna! Kade! Jacob!" Noliono shouted, pulling with all his might. "Let them go!"

"Or what?" Deofol laughed.

"I'll kill you!" Noliono shouted, his body pulsating with rage.

"Ha-ha! Empty words from a helpless fool," Deofol retorted, walking over to Brenna.

Noliono watched in horror as Deofol grabbed his wife's beautiful dark-brown hair and forced her head back, exposing her slender neck.

"Now tell me what I want to know, my lord, or watch your dear wife die," Deofol said, sliding a wicked-looking knife across her throat.

"What do you want to know?" Noliono gasped, straining violently against his bonds.

"You would try my patience while I hold a knife to your lovely wife's neck?" Deofol said, pressing the knife into Brenna's throat. A small drop of blood ran down the blade. Noliono froze.

"Please, don't," he said, his heart racing. "I'll tell you whatever you want to know."

"Tell me how to enter Ironwall Fortress. Tell me its weaknesses."

"I don't know," Noliono said quickly. "I am not from the north. I don't know anything about this part of Alethia."

"You still try my patience," Deofol said, pressing the knife again into Brenna's neck enough to draw blood.

"*Please!* I don't know anything!" Noliono shouted.

"You think I'm a fool?"

"I don't know, Deofol!"

"Does your wife's life mean nothing to you?"

"I don't know!"

"You are forcing me to do this!"

"*I don't know!*"

"Tell me how to enter Ironwall, or your wife dies!"

"Don't you think I would if I knew!" Noliono screamed. His wrists were bleeding from his straining against his bonds. "I don't know! I don't know anything! Please!"

Deofol looked away and sighed. Then his knife raked across Brenna's neck. Noliono screamed and screamed, his heart bursting in agony. Time seemed to stop as he locked eyes with her one last time, a look of shock and terror etched on her face. He strained with all his might to free himself. If only he could get to her, he could fix this. That was what his mind was telling him. Tears flowed from his eyes as he watched his beloved wife fall to the ground.

"*Brenna! Brenna! No! Brenna! No!*" Noliono continued to scream. He could not believe it. She couldn't be dead. This could not be happening. His entire body thrashed in pain and agony. He looked from his wife's body to Deofol's grinning face and back. Waves of pain and hatred were surging over him.

"*I'll kill you!*" *I'll kill you!*" Noliono yelled as he jerked upright in his bed.

Noliono's head swam in a blur of color as the room spun around him. He was covered in sweat, and his heart was racing. Noliono looked about him and realized he was still in his tent. He and his men were encamped only a day's ride north of Abenhall. He covered his face with his hands, trying to regain composure as two men entered his tent, followed by Kludge.

"Are you well, Your Majesty?" Kludge asked with a bow.

"Just a nightmare," Noliono said, gasping. Then looking up he said, "Prepare to leave in one hour."

❋　❋　❋　❋

As Noliono rode, his mind carefully considered all that had transpired since Greyfuss's death, and he realized that everything he hoped to accomplish now depended on his next move. His army had sacked Rockhold and Estelhold, effectively annihilating the House of Aurelia. The House of Rydel had been destroyed by his pawn, Anson Thayn. The city of Abenhall and House Eddon was all that stood between him and final victory. His army, made up by House Noland, Thayn, Farod, and Nenlad had besieged the city. His victory and claim to the Throne of Alethia hinged on the outcome of this siege. Once Abenhall had fallen, he could turn his attention to his true target.

Noliono's blood began to boil at the thought of Deofol and the kingdom of Nordyke. How long had his wife and sons gone unavenged? He cringed involuntarily as images from the vivid dream of the night before came rushing into his mind. He had been rescued, but Deofol had escaped. He gritted his teeth as the memory of his demand for war with Nordyke was quelled by King Greyfuss.

He had begged for a chance to avenge his family's murder, but the king decided to sign a truce with Nordyke. He still had a hard time believing it. That day he had withdrawn from the Council of Lords, leaving Kaleb Jorrah from Norhold, to serve in his place. It was during that time that he'd been visited by Methangoth, the dark sorcerer. It had been he who helped Noliono devise a plan to seize control of Alethia and destroy Nordyke. In exchange, Noliono promised to obtain the *Book of Aduin*. He still wasn't sure why Methangoth wanted the old book, but what did he care? Greyfuss was dead, and the only thing standing in his way was Abenhall.

Several hours later, Noliono and his men arrived at the army camp, situated in the foothills surrounding Abenhall. As Noliono dismounted, he gazed down at the Bay of Ryst, where the ships of Nenlad and Farod lay. He smiled despite himself. It would soon be over, and Abenhall would be his.

He entered the main tent and found Lords Anson Thayn, Gaven Soron, and Atton Nenlad debating strategy. They stopped abruptly and bowed upon his appearance. Noliono noted Lord Anson's arm was in a sling and he appeared to have several lacerations on his face that were not quite healed.

"Your Majesty," Lord Soron said with a growl. "What brings you from Ethriel?"

"I would think that was obvious, Gaven. I am here to bring an end to this rebellion. The final stroke that will unite Alethia is about to fall, and I am going to deliver it personally," Noliono said, picking up a report and glancing at it. "This siege had gone on long enough. I intend to end this once and for all."

"Your Majesty," began Lord Anson. "The forces of Abenhall are great, yet they cannot hope to hold out for much longer. If we wait them out, they will surrender, and we will not suffer any loss of life."

"Without bloodshed the lesson of war is wasted and this kingdom will learn nothing from this rebellion," Noliono said calmly. "Tomorrow we shall attack and take this city, and you, Lord Anson, shall lead the attack on the north gate personally."

Lord Anson looked defiant.

"Need I remind you the cost of disobedience, Lord Anson?" Noliono asked with a meaningful look.

Lord Anson's mouth tightened, but he remained silent. He bowed and left the tent without another word. Lords Soron and Atton followed in Lord Anson's wake as Kludge came up behind the king.

"Shall I take care of Lord Anson, sire?"

"There will be no need, Kludge," Noliono whispered with a smile. "Tomorrow we shall silence all our enemies."

Dawn found Noliono upon the heights above the city as the sun first peeked over the Iron Hills. Down below, just out of bowshot of the city walls, stood over ten thousand soldiers. Noliono took in the scene for a moment before signaling to his page. The boy raised the banner of Alethia, and a roar went up as the mass of men surged forward toward the city. Flaming arrows flew high, setting alight the wooden palisade along the walls.

Ladders were brought up along the eastern and northern walls. The dust flew into the air, and the ground was covered with the bodies of men.

Noliono smiled to himself, and he signaled to his page. "Tell the captain of the catapults to prepare to bombard the north gate with a full barrage. He may open fire when ready."

Lord Soron approached the king as the boy ran off to relay the orders.

"Your Majesty, may I point out that Lord Anson and his men are presently attacking the north gate? The bombardment will undoubtedly weaken the wall and kill our men at the same time, possibly even Lord Anson himself."

"The price of failure, Lord Soron," Noliono said with a meaningful look. "Do you wish to join Lord Anson?"

"No, sire," Lord Soron said, bowing low.

In a few moments, the catapults released a salvo of boulders and jars of flaming oil aimed at the north gate. There was a moment of silence as both sides stopped fighting and gazed in horror at the sky. Then there was only darkness and screams as the salvo rained down upon them. The smoke and dust rose high into the air, blocking from view the result of the bombardment. The tumult rose to a deafening roar as the gate itself exploded in fire and smoke.

"Tell the captain to cease fire!" Noliono shouted at his page.

The bombardment ceased after a few more minutes, and a hush fell upon the battlefield. Noliono gazed intently at the cloud of dust, attempting to pierce through the obstruction. Then as the wind picked up, the smoke and dust began to clear. Noliono smiled wide as a great breach appeared where the north gate had once stood. Dozens of bodies littered the ground nearby.

"Forward!" Noliono cried, and his army surged toward the gaping hole in the wall. Victory was his at last.

✳   ✳   ✳   ✳

Two days later in the king's tent, Noliono was seated at his desk, reviewing reports. He was pleased with the information he was gleaning from them. According to one of his captains, Lord Anson's body was found along with several hundred men of House Thayn near the ruins of the north gate. Another report stated that Lord Markus Eddon and his three sons had been slain defending the west gate. With no one to lead them, House Thayn and Eddon would fall, allowing the lands to revert to the crown. Noliono could then award the lands to a more loyal family who would also support his future war with Nordyke.

Noliono reached for his wine goblet and sat back with an irrepressible grin. *It was all falling into place.* He was given only moments to revel in his victory, for Ramond Kludge and two others abruptly entered the king's tent. Noliono rose as apprehension suddenly hit him.

"Report, Lord Kludge."

"Sire," Kludge began with a bow. "I bring news from Elengil."

"What is Lord Renton Myr's answer? Will he bend the knee and offer his fealty?"

"He refused, sire."

"What!" Noliono cried, anger and hatred filling him. *Not another siege!*

"There is more, sire," Kludge said apprehensively.

"Then speak!"

"There is word coming from Elengil and from all the lands around that the last son of Aranethon has come forth."

"Impossible!"

"They say that he has been crowned king, and there is a rumor that he is engaged to Riniel Aurelia."

"This is madness!" Noliono exclaimed, beginning to pace. "The last descendant of Aranethon was killed almost twenty years ago. This must be an imposter."

"These men with me come from Ytemest and Ironwall in the far north. They say Barons Warde and Astley have sworn their allegiance to this new king."

"What of Renton Myr?"

"He also has sworn fealty, giving this new king Elengil itself."

"This cannot be happening!" Noliono shouted in rage and threw the goblet at Kludge, who ducked. *How could all my carefully laid plans now be unraveling before my eyes?* He stood rooted and pondered in silence.

"Sire?" Kludge said after Noliono was silent for several minutes.

"Gather our forces, Lord Commander, and be prepared to march by nightfall. We march on Elengil. Perhaps we can destroy this new threat before he has time to consolidate his forces."

"As you wish, Your Majesty," Kludge said, bowing and leaving with the other two men.

He had come too far and sacrificed too much to lose everything now. This usurper and any who followed him would share the same fate as the rest of his enemies. *One last obstacle and then Nordyke.*

25

AZKA

The tavern was growing darker and quieter by the minute. The midnight hour had come and gone, and most of the patrons had left. Azka sat in a corner, mulling over the day's events. He had been sent by King Corin to the towns along the western edge of the Forest of Roston to gather more men for the army. Most answered the king's summons eagerly, but the inhabitants of the small town of Rein flat refused.

"The only king we recognize is the late Greyfuss Aurelia and his daughter Riniel," one old man had said, with many of the townsfolk murmuring their agreement. "We answer to no other summons but theirs."

Azka had tried to reason with them, telling them that Riniel had renounced her claims and had joined King Corin, but the townspeople refused to listen. He chose to remain in the town another day and tried to convince some of the other men to go with him to Elengil, but he only found heightened hostility by his presence. He had now decided to wait until morning then ride south to another village and try his luck there. He was just about to retire to his room above the tavern when another man suddenly sat down across from him. Azka was startled but did not show it. His calm, stoic face and demeanor revealed nothing of his true feelings. It was a trait that he had used to his advantage many times.

Azka studied the newcomer—a man with sharp eyes, a black goatee, and red hat with a long red feather sticking out of it.

"Your luck at gathering forces for the young king seems to have dried up," the man said with a sneer.

Azka stared back at the man without a word. He was pleased to see it unnerved the stranger.

"I can see you're a man of few words, so I will make this simple," the man said after a long silence. "I've been sent by King Noliono to deliver a message to a man with dark skin named Azka. Seeing no other dark-skinned men about, I concluded that you must be him."

"Deliver your message, then be gone," Azka said irritably.

"Manners, good sire," the man scolded, wagging a finger at Azka. "You would not dismiss me so quickly if you know my name. I am Silas Morgan."

Azka, who had truly never heard that name before, looked blankly back at the man.

"Silas Morgan?" the man repeated after a pause. "Don't tell me you've never heard of Silas Morgan?"

"I have not," Azka said, suppressing a grin.

"This is absurd!" Silas said, almost shouting. "Even people across the Sea of Aear know my name. How do you not know it?"

Azka stared at Silas, again without a word.

"Apparently your people lack basic conversation skills, which explains your ignorance," Silas said irritably after another long pause. "I will save my breath and just simply tell you the message. Noliono has your sister, Aylen. He will return her to you in exchange for the assassination of Corin Stone. You have three days. If Corin is not dead by the end of the third day, she will be executed."

Azka attempted to hide the turmoil this news brought to his heart. "You have fulfilled your task, messenger," Azka said, struggling to remain calm. "Now be gone."

"Gladly," Silas said, leaving Azka to his thoughts.

After a few moments, Azka got up and went to his room above the tavern. Sitting down on the bed, he put his face in his hands, struggling not to howl in rage. For many years he had searched the whole of Alethia for any news of his sister, always hiding in the shadows. Now that he had come forth into the light of day, he at long last knew of her whereabouts and that she was being held captive. He shook his head in disgust. How could he kill Corin after sparing his life and swearing to protect him? He could not break his word even if it meant his sister's death. Could he save them both? There had to be a way.

Azka lay down on the bed, and no sooner had he closed his eyes than he heard a noise. He sat up quickly and saw a man standing in the middle of the room in a dark-gray cloak.

"You!" Azka exclaimed, recognizing the man at once.

"Yes, I am He," the man said, sitting down. As he did so, his cloak slid off his right knee, revealing an inner robe of brilliant white. The robe shone with a dazzling light that filled the room, blinding Azka.

"Here, let me fix that," the man said, adjusting his cloak. Immediately the light was extinguished. "As I have told many others, most cannot stand such light. Instead, they prefer the darkness."

"Who are you?" Azka asked, bewildered.

"Who do you think I am?"

"If I knew your name, I would not be asking you for it," Azka said irritably.

"I am the Light."

"Then why do you hide it under your cloak?"

"Is an infant child able to eat the same food as a grown man?" the man asked, looking hard at Azka, who dropped his gaze because of the intensity of the man's eyes. "So it is with most men concerning the light I bring."

"I do not understand what you mean."

"That is why I am shielding you from what would only confuse you further."

"Why are you here?"

"I have come to warn you."

"Warn me? Warn me of what?" Azka asked angrily.

"You cannot save your sister alone. You must return to serve your king."

Azka stared at the man for a moment. "How do you know of my sister?"

"I know much about your family, Azka. You must heed my words, or you will cause much suffering."

"How?"

"Heed my words, Azka."

＊　＊　＊　＊

Azka awoke with a start. He sat up and looked about the dark room. It was empty. *It must have been a dream. There is no other explanation. Why would anyone tell me I cannot save my sister?* A sudden thought crossed Azka's mind. *Silas knows where my sister is being held.*

Azka stood up, ran across the room, down the stairs, and out to the stables. He woke the stable boy and had him saddle his horse. Azka tossed the boy a silver lion for his trouble and rode off into the darkness. He somehow knew this Silas would return to the ruins of Rockwicke to report to his superiors. Azka had noticed a small garrison of Noland soldiers encamped near the refugee camp. He had to catch him before he could reach the ruins.

Azka urged his horse to a fast gallop and hoped the road did not run rocky or make any sharp turns. The only hope of catching Silas was his horse's speed. One hour passed, then two, and then three. He had to lessen his pace or risk killing his poor horse.

He finally stopped and dismounted about four hours hard riding from Rein. He unsaddled his poor beast and led him to a small stream near the edge of the forest.

Azka struggled to contain his anger and frustration. He had seen no sign of travelers along the road. Azka was beginning to fear that Silas had not returned to the ruins when he spotted a faint light through the trees in the distance. He was sure it must be the light from a campfire. He left his horse tied near the stream and quietly moved toward the distant light. It took him half an hour to make his way through the underbrush. When he finally reached the source of the light, it turned out to be a large campfire. Two dozen or so men sat around the fire, and most were wearing tunics bearing the crest of House Noland. Azka moved in closer to see if Silas was among them. He found a place just outside the ring of firelight, where he could observe but not be observed. It was then he overheard the conversation taking place.

"The target was in the town of Rein, Lord Kludge," said a voice Azka recognized as Silas's. "I've made it clear to the townsfolk that if even one man joins him, the whole town will be burned to the ground."

"Do you think he will go through with it? Do you think he will kill the usurper?" asked Kludge.

"How should I know?" Silas said noncommittedly. "All I care about is getting paid."

Azka watched as Kludge threw a small bag of coins at Silas, hitting him in the chest.

"Take your money and go, slime," Kludge barked.

Some of the men with Silas rose and drew their weapons.

"This is barely half what I was promised," Silas said angrily.

"You'll take it and go if you know what's good for you," Kludge growled.

"Do you think I'm a coward, Kludge?" Silas asked, rising and drawing his own sword. "I am Silas Morgan, and I do not suffer insults lightly. I demand the pay I was promised, or I will exact it from your corpse. These men are not mere mercenaries. They are Méce from Eddynland. Few can match their skill with a blade."

"Put your faith in a few foreigners if you wish, but I've got the numbers to best you, Morgan. Get 'em, boys!" Kludge yelled, lunging at Silas.

For several minutes there was pandemonium. Azka soon found himself in the midst of the fight as the combatants moved beyond the ring of firelight. Two of Kludge's men caught sight of him and charged. Azka dispatched them easily enough, but not before both Silas and Kludge saw him.

"There he is!" roared Kludge.

"Get him!" Silas yelled.

In half a heartbeat, Azka was surrounded.

"You are either incredibly brave or incredibly foolish." Kludge said, leering at him. "Drop your weapon."

Azka glared at him, but did not lower his guard.

"He must have followed me here from Rein. Thinking of convincing me to reveal your sister's whereabouts, eh?" Silas asked with an evil grin.

"You've decided to decline the king's offer, I take it?" Kludge said with a laugh. "You know your sister is quite beautiful. It would be a shame to have to kill her. Perhaps I will make her my wife instead."

"You will not touch her!" Azka roared, lunging at Kludge.

The other man parried the blow and sent Azka reeling into a tree. Azka had chosen to act on emotion, a choice he knew he might not live to regret. He righted himself but found several men almost upon him. His sword flew through the air, striking and parrying. Yet even his skill was no match for so many. He was overcome within seconds, pinned to the ground, and his sword wrenched from his hand.

"You've some skill, dark one, but that will not save you or your sister," Kludge said, breathing heavily. "I'll offer you one last chance. Will you die by my hand here, or will you take the king's offer and save yourself and your sister? Choose now!"

26

NOLIONO

Noliono sat in his chambers facing the Donian ambassador, Zar. He eyed the other man with masked annoyance and frustration. Here he was negotiating trade agreements with this snide, stoic man with a strong Donian accent, which he found gruff and unsettling, while his kingdom was under threat.

"I asked a simple question, Ambassador Zar," Noliono said, trying to mask his irritation. "Why has your king decided to cancel Donia's trade agreement with Alethia?"

"Donia's agreement vas with Greyfuss Aurelia. Since he und his entire house are dead, und Alethia ist torn by civil var, King Kalem has decided to vithdraw from Alethian affairs. Perhaps ven you haf sorted out your own kingdom's issues, ve can discuss renewed relations between Donia and Alethia."

"Perhaps your king should reconsider his position. My reign has just begun, and once this minor insurrection is at an end, I will remember who supported me and who turned his back," Noliono said with a dark look.

"Ve shall see," Zar said, standing. "I vill relay the contents of this meeting with King Kalem. I'm sure he will take zee appropriate measures."

"I'm sure he will," Noliono said, also standing and motioning to the door.

Ambassador Zar left his chambers, and Noliono rubbed his forehead in frustration. His gaze fell on a report that was sitting on his desk. It stated that the army had arrived at Elengil and found the city heavily fortified and prepared for a long siege. Noliono crumpled the parchment in anger and threw it into the fire.

"Where is my book, Noliono?" said a deep, menacing voice from the right corner. Noliono spun around in surprise as a tall man in a black cloak emerged.

"Methangoth," Noliono said bitterly. His jaw was set, and his eyes burned with anger. "How did you...?"

"What news of the book?" Methangoth said with a covetous look in his eyes.

"Last report, it was in Elengil," replied Noliono, turning back to his desk. "Is this why you summoned me back here to talk about your obsession with this book and to meet with a treacherous Donian ambassador?"

"Watch your tongue, fool!" Methangoth shouted. "Or your reign will be the shortest in Alethian history."

Noliono fought to mask his anger, though it still burned fiercely below the surface.

"Donia is nothing," Methangoth said, eyeing Noliono with a burning anger to match his own. "So long as you obtain for me the book, none shall stand against us."

There was a knock at the door.

"Say nothing of my presence," Methangoth said, stepping back into the corner. The darkness hid him so completely that Noliono actually wondered if the man had disappeared.

"Enter," he said through gritted teeth.

Ramond Kludge and Silas Morgan entered, both looking anxious.

"What news, Lord Kludge?" Noliono asked, trying to remain calm. "What of Azka?"

"I delivered your message, sire," Silas said with a bow. "Yet your minion refused to pay the amount we agreed upon."

"Is that so?" Noliono asked, unabashed.

"Sire," Kludge interrupted. "The dark one followed us to the ruins of Rockhold and attempted to kill us."

"That is not quite true, sire," Silas corrected. "Azka seemed to want to extract information from us rather than kill us."

"Be silent, knave!" Kludge roared, grabbing hold of Silas's tunic. "I should have killed you back when..."

"Enough!" Noliono ordered. "Kludge, release him."

"Yes, sire," Kludge said, releasing Silas and with a look on his face not unlike a chastised schoolboy.

"Did Azka escape?"

"No, sire. We captured and released him on the western bank of the Rockwicke River," Kludge said proudly.

"You released him?" Noliono asked, his voice barely betraying his annoyance.

"Yes, sire."

"And will he kill the usurper as planned?"

"I don't know, sire," Kludge replied with a slight grimace.

Fools! Why must I be surrounded by such incompetent men? "Very well, I must put my contingency plan into motion," Noliono said, pulling out a sheet of parchment and handing it to Silas. "Your services are required, Silas. You will find your instructions and the amount you can expect to receive on this parchment."

Silas read over the piece of parchment then looked up, bemused. "You want me to break into a besieged city for this same book you hired me to steal from Stonewall? Why?"

"The *Book of Aduin* is the only evidence the boy has to prove his claim to the throne. Without it, his followers will desert him," Noliono answered condescendingly.

"What assurance do I have that you will pay me this time?" Silas said bluntly.

"The only thing you can be sure of is this: if you fail to complete the assignment this time, you will be hunted down and executed."

"Your Majesty, if you expect me to work for free..."

"You will receive one hundred gold crowns for the *Book of Aduin*. Satisfied?"

"Yes, sire," Silas said with a bow and he turned to leave.

"And Silas," Noliono called after him. "Don't fail me again."

Silas left, and Noliono turned to Kludge.

"What if he fails, sire?"

"I expect him to, Kludge, which is why I am also putting this plan in motion," Noliono said, going back to the parchments on his desk and handing one to Kludge.

"But, I thought the House of Thayn was destroyed at Abenhall, sire?"

"Follow me, Kludge," Noliono said, walking out into the corridor. "For the most part, the House of Thayn was destroyed, Kludge, but Anson Thayn's third son was not at the battle."

"You mean?"

"Yes, Ardyn Thayn still lives," Noliono said, stopping in front of a door guarded by two sentries.

"I thought he died when the princess escaped."

"No, Kludge. Despite your best efforts, the boy lived. If I can convince him to join us, he will help us to end this war."

"Is that even, possible?"

"I will soon see. The physicians say he has finally regained consciousness. Take your leave, and I will see if I can persuade our young friend."

"Yes, sire," Kludge said, bowing and leaving.

Noliono opened the door and found a young man lying on a bed. Another man was nearby examining him.

"Is he awake?" Noliono asked.

"Yes," the man replied, looking up at Noliono. "He awoke two hours ago. You may speak with him, sire, but I caution you not to upset him. He is very weak."

"I understand. Thank you, doctor," Noliono said with a nod toward the door. The physician took his meaning and left.

When he had gone, Noliono sat down in the chair near the bed. Ardyn turned toward him.

"Your Majesty," he said timidly.

"Yes, Ardyn. I am here, and you are lucky to be here too," Noliono said kindly.

"Yes, sire," Ardyn said, looking away.

"You betrayed me, Ardyn."

"Yes, Your Majesty."

"Yet those you tried to help ultimately betrayed you."

Ardyn did not respond.

"Riniel and the others you helped escape left you for dead."

"I would have given my life for hers," Ardyn said, staring at the ceiling.

"I know you would, but do you know how she repaid you?"

Ardyn did not respond.

"She left you to die, and now she is to marry Corin Stone, a young man from Stonewall pretending to be the lost heir of Aranethon. He has declared himself King of Alethia and adopted the crest of House Aranethon: a crimson rose on a field of white."

"What!" Ardyn said angrily. "Corin Stone?"

"You know him?" Noliono asked, surprised.

"He and I were friends at one time. My father helped him get a job at the academy."

"Then he has betrayed you as well, for his army marched on Abenhall and attacked us. Ardyn, your father and brothers were slain by Corin and his men at Abenhall."

"My father and my brothers are dead? All of them?" Ardyn cried, tears welling up in his eyes.

"I'm sorry, Ardyn."

"No, no, no..." Ardyn said, trailing off as tears poured from his eyes.

Noliono resisted the overwhelming urge to smile. He knew Ardyn was overwhelmed with grief now, but he could turn that grief into loyalty to him and his cause.

"Ardyn, my army is currently laying siege to Elengil, where Corin is hiding. If you agree to help me, I will pardon your crimes and give you back your house and titles. You will be known as Lord Ardyn Thayn."

Noliono watched as Ardyn looked up, momentarily bewildered, but Ardyn's eyes suddenly became hard and his jaw set.

"I pledge myself to the true King of Alethia," he said, extending his hand.

"I accept your fealty, Lord Ardyn," Noliono said, shaking the young man's hand. "Rest now. When you are well enough, you will return to Stonewall and muster your forces."

"Yes, Your Majesty."

An hour later, Noliono was descending the winding stairs into the deepest part of the citadel, the dungeons. It was here in the pitch blackness that the worst criminals in the kingdom were held, and it was here that Noliono hoped to remove a thorn in his side. According to Silas, it was Kinison, the former Lord Commander of the Guardians, who had managed to find the lost heir of Aranethon and helped him amass an army large enough to hold Elengil. It was Kinison who had caused Noliono all this trouble, and now that he was Noliono's prisoner, it would be Kinison who helped him defeat this would-be king.

The guards opened the cell door, and the torch illuminated a depressing sight. There sat Kinison, his hair unkempt, a full beard growing on his face. If Noliono had not known better, he'd have sworn the guards had led him to the wrong cell. Noliono was slightly amused when the man hid his face from the light, and he wondered how long it had been since Sir Ren Gables reported Kinison's capture. Had it been two weeks or three?

"What do you want?" Kinison growled. "How the mighty have fallen," Noliono said sagely as he stepped into the cell. The stench of the place almost forced him back into the corridor, but he hid his disgust. "Kinison Ravenloch, former Lord Commander of the Guardians turned rogue. You seem to have chosen the wrong side."

"Any side is better than yours!" Kinison tried to yell.

"I'm leaving for Elengil in the morning to dispose of the usurper and his followers. This rebellion will be crushed, and all who do not swear fealty to the true King of Alethia, me, will be dealt with accordingly. I give you this one last chance, Kinison, to save yourself and your wife, Sarah."

"Sarah?"

"If you would tell me the weaknesses of Elengil, you and your wife will be released and taken to Abenhall. You may then take a ship to whatever kingdom you desire so long as you never return to Alethia."

"And if I refuse?"

"Oh, please, Kinison!" Noliono said irritably. "Must I spell it out for you? Will you tell me what I need to know or not?"

"I want to see my wife," Kinison said bluntly.

"Tell me, and you will be brought to her."

"No," Kinison answered after a long pause.

"You refuse," Noliono said, turning to leave. "Then Sarah will be told you are dead and married to Sir Kludge."

"What!" Kinison said, rising quickly.

"You had your chance, Kinison," Noliono said as the door was closed and locked. "May you find solace in your choices."

"Wait! Please!" Kinison shouted.

Noliono paused at the door.

"You swear to deliver me and my wife to Abenhall after I tell you?" Kinison asked quickly.

Noliono smiled broadly. "Tell me Elengil's weaknesses, and I will deliver you and your wife safely to Abenhall."

Kinison stared back at Noliono with deep conflict in his eyes.

"This is your only chance, Kinison." Noliono sneered. "You must choose a side. Which is it to be?"

27

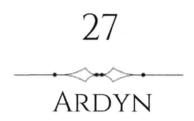

ARDYN

Stonewall, the greatest city in the north. After a perilous journey through Oakwood Forest, Ardyn Thayn now beheld the city of his forebears. Generations of Thayns had ruled from Stonewall since before the first kings. He checked his horse at the far end of the bridge that spanned the great chasm separating the city from the forest and gazed upon its grandeur. The gray stone walls and towers gave the city a somber appearance in the early morning light. Above the towers and over the battlements flew black banners. Ardyn supposed the black color was in honor of the deaths of his father and brothers. He sighed and reached inside his saddlebag. From its depths, Ardyn pulled a blue banner bearing a large white eagle, the banner of House Thayn. Ardyn hung the banner on his spear and held it up for those on the walls to see. A moment later, horns sounded, and the gates opened wide. From within, a dozen armed men emerged on horseback, all wearing the same blue tunics bearing the white eagle. They rode out to Ardyn and checked their horses about five feet from him. The lead man, whom Ardyn recognized as Sir Simon Moore, the captain of the City Watch, dismounted and walked over to him.

"My Lord Thayn," he said with a bow. "You have returned to us."

"You have heard then, Sir Simon?" Ardyn said somberly.

"The city mourns the loss of your father and brothers," Sir Simon replied, his face downcast. "We feared you had fallen as well, my lord. The people feared for their future, since all the men of House Thayn were thought dead."

"Why do they still fear?" Ardyn said, confused. "When the king sent word that I would return, I assumed the city's inhabitants would rejoice."

Sir Simon was silent. He looked uncomfortably at his men.

"What is it, Sir Simon?"

"I am no longer the captain of the City Watch, my lord."

"What!" Ardyn exclaimed.

"Sir Simon," said one of the men with him. "What of our orders?"

"What orders?" Ardyn nearly shouted. "Sir Simon what is going on?"

"Your father's advisor, Zul Voss, declared House Thayn fallen and made himself Lord of Stonewall."

"I...I don't believe this," Ardyn said, his voice shaking in anger.

"My Lord Thayn," Sir Simon said somewhat timidly. "I must take you into custody."

"Oh?" Ardyn said, placing his hand on his sword hilt.

"Lord Voss has ordered anyone claiming to be a member of the House Thayn to be brought to him at once."

"Very well," Ardyn said after a moment's consideration. "Lead on."

After remounting his horse, Sir Simon shot Ardyn a meaningful look. A sudden fear gripped Ardyn, and he briefly considered running for it. As they rode into the city, Ardyn saw that a crowd had gathered.

A man in a black hood and cloak stood in the middle of the street, holding a staff and blocking the way forward.

"Stand aside," Sir Simon commanded.

"I would speak with the Lord Ardyn Thayn," the man said loudly.

At the mention of Ardyn's name, the crowd became alive with whispers, and every eye seemed to stare into him. Ardyn shifted uneasily in the saddle and saw Sir Simon look just as uneasy. Not waiting for permission, the man walked over to Ardyn and removed his hood.

"My Lord Ardyn," the man said in a whisper. "I am Galanor."

"I have heard of you," Ardyn responded in shock. The man's deep blue eyes seemed to bore into him. He had heard of Galanor from his father. He was a wandering historian and councilor to kings.

"I have come to offer counsel," Galanor whispered ominously.

"I would have it," Ardyn said eagerly.

"First, if you wish to live, you must address your people."

"If I wish to live?"

"Yes. Zul Voss means to kill you before the whole city knows you are here. Appeal to them for support. Do not demand it."

"I see."

"Enough, old man!" one of the soldiers shouted at Galanor. "Away with you!"

Ardyn looked at Sir Simon, who nodded slightly. This was it. He squelched his fears and turned to address the crowd.

"People of Stonewall," he began, his voice gaining strength with each word. "You know me as Ardyn Thayn, third son of Lord Anson Thayn. I have returned to claim my inheritance. I confess that I do not yet possess the wisdom of my father or the strength and courage of my brothers, but I am a Thayn and rightwise lord over this city. Despite my right to rule, I do not demand it. Rather, I appeal to you, the people of Stonewall. Would you have a Thayn as lord over this city again, or have you found a new lord?"

There was silence for a moment, then a man shouted, "We would have House Thayn!"

The shout was echoed by others, and soon everyone was shouting it. Ardyn turned to Sir Simon.

"Well said, my Lord Ardyn," he said with a smile.

"Indeed," said Galanor. "But this is not over."

"What now?" Ardyn asked in a whisper.

"Have Zul Voss meet you here with the people looking on rather than at the castle where he might ambush us."

"Very well," Ardyn said then turned to Sir Simon. "Send one of your men to invite Zul Voss to meet me near the fountain in the square at midday."

Sir Simon obeyed, and the rider was dispatched at once. Ardyn's stomach was full of butterflies. He knew his life and his future would be decided in the next few hours.

✳   ✳   ✳   ✳

As the sun reached midday, Ardyn's anxiety grew stronger, and the crowd gathering nearby grew larger. During the morning hours, Galanor had been coaching Ardyn on how to deal with Zul Voss and how to appeal to the people as they sat near the fountain in the square.

"Remember, Ardyn," Galanor said for the tenth time. "You must appeal to the people as if you are giving them the choice between you and Voss."

And for the tenth time, Ardyn found himself asking, "And how do you know they will choose me?"

"As I have said before, the people fear Voss. They do not love him. If you stand up to him, the people will follow you."

A trumpet blast drew their attention. The crowd parted, and several guards entered the square, followed by a short, fat man with a grim face. He wore a blue tunic, but without the white eagle of House Thayn. He also wore a long black cape.

"Zul Voss," Galanor said as he and Ardyn stood to face the newcomer.

"Galanor," Voss said with a false smile. His voice was high pitched and whiny. "What commotion are you stirring up in my streets now? Rumor has reached my ears that a member of House Thayn has returned to the city."

"For once, the rumors are right, Zul. This is Ardyn Thayn, third son of the late Anson Thayn."

Voss squinted at Ardyn, his eyes looking him over as if sizing him up.

"No, no, this is not Ardyn Thayn," Voss said, turning to the crowd. "As you all rightly know, I was advisor to his lordship, the late Anson Thayn, for many years. Lord Anson's third son was younger and scrawnier. This man cannot possibly be Ardyn Thayn."

"Excuse me," Ardyn said, feeling both flattered and insulted. "I am Ardyn Thayn, and I can prove it."

"Indeed," the fat man said in a singsong voice. "And what proof do you bring?"

"This," Ardyn said, extending his right fist. On his hand was a large golden ring bearing the crest of House Thayn. "Behold, my father's ring, bearing the crest of House Thayn."

Ardyn looked out across the crowd as shock and surprise covered every face. His gaze finally returned to Zul, whose expression was of utter delight. The smile on his face made Ardyn's skin crawl.

"Ardyn!" the fat man exclaimed, clapping his hands. "I see the resemblance now. You have grown so much since last I saw you."

"Then you recognize my lordship of Stonewall?" Ardyn asked, lowering his arm and looking surprised.

"Your lordship?" Zul said with a sneer. "House Thayn has fallen, Ardyn. The people chose me as their new lord."

"Have they indeed?" Galanor asked angrily.

"People of Stonewall!" Ardyn shouted, trying to sound more confident than he felt. "You have heard my claim and seen my father's ring. By rights, I am Lord of Stonewall. Yet I do not come before you to force your fealty. I ask only that you would choose me as your lord. If you have truly chosen Zul Voss as your new lord, I and my family will leave forever, but if you choose to give me the right to rule this city, I promise to bring peace and prosperity back to this city."

Voss clapped his hands loudly. "Very nice speech, young Ardyn. You have inherited your father's gift with words, but the people have made their choice."

"What say you, people of Stonewall?" Galanor shouted at the crowd. "Would you have Ardyn or Zul as your lord?"

Silence answered Galanor, and Ardyn's anxiety grew into fear.

"I would have Lord Thayn," said a voice.

"Thayn," said another voice.

"Thayn," said a third.

Soon the whole crowd was shouting "Thayn," and both Ardyn and Galanor turned to Voss, who was glaring at them.

"My Lord Ardyn," he said, bowing reluctantly. "Your people have spoken. May your humble servant take your lordship to the castle?"

Ardyn looked at Galanor and then nodded. The people followed them, cheering all the way to the castle gates. Ardyn's apprehension should have ebbed, but instead it had grown with every step. By the time they were within sight of the castle gates, Ardyn's hand was resting on the hilt of his sword. Galanor must have noticed this for he moved toward Ardyn.

"Do not enter the castle," he whispered.

Ardyn tried to stop, but Galanor subtly pulled him forward.

"On the threshold of the castle, address the people," Galanor whispered as they walked forward.

"Why? What do you want me to say?" Ardyn whispered crossly.

"Thank Zul for his service, but tell the people you are replacing him with Sir Simon Moore."

"Why?"

"If you enter the castle with Zul still in office, I fear you will never walk out alive."

"You think he means to kill me?"

"I am certain of that."

"Very well," Ardyn said, realizing that they had reached the gates of the castle at last. He stopped and turned to the people.

"People of Stonewall, I thank you for your support, and I would also like to thank Zul Voss for his willingness to serve as steward in my absence," Ardyn said, motioning Voss over.

Voss hesitated for a moment then reluctantly joined Ardyn. The fat man was almost a head shorter than Ardyn.

"Please, let us thank Zul Voss for his service to this city," Ardyn said, clapping.

The crowd hesitated, then several people clapped weakly.

"Now that I have returned, Zul, I can now relieve you from your post."

"My lord?" Voss asked with a whine. "What do you mean?"

"I am relieving you of your post and releasing you from my service," Ardyn said, trying to sound confident.

"My lord, you cannot do this!" Voss protested. "I have served your family for years."

"Yes, and I thank you for that. Yet I must demand you relinquish your post immediately."

"You, you stupid boy!" Voss cried. "Guards, arrest this imposter!"

"Sir Simon, arrest Zul Voss!" Ardyn commanded, drawing his sword.

Sir Simon did not hesitate but drew his weapon and advanced on Voss. His men, however, seemed unsure. This gave Voss's men the advantage as they surged forward toward Ardyn, Galanor, and Sir Simon. Voss disappeared into the castle amidst the chaos, and Ardyn heard the great wooden doors slam behind them. They were trapped between Voss's men and the gates.

"What now?" Ardyn asked anxiously.

"We fight!" Galanor shouted. "People of Stonewall, arise!" Your city is besieged from within. Down with the tyrant Zul Voss! Down with the agents of tyranny! Arise and defend your lord, Ardyn Thayn!"

At once the crowd surged forward, and Voss's men were quickly subdued.

"Now to capture the beast in his lair," Galanor said, turning to the castle.

"And I think I know just how to do it," Ardyn said with a sly grin.

✳   ✳   ✳   ✳

Ardyn's heart was beating fast. This was his first real test as leader of the people of Stonewall. Following the incident at the gate, Ardyn had called a meeting with the elders of the city to discuss plans to retake the castle. Six of the elders now sat at a table in a tavern called the Eagle's Nest. Along with these men sat Galanor and Sir Simon Moore.

"Men," Ardyn began with as much confidence as he could muster. "We have but one option here. We must retake the castle and deal with the traitor Zul Voss. We cannot wait him out, for I must leave again to go to the aid of my king, and all men who are able must ride with me."

"How can we do what you say, my lord?" Sir Simon asked. "The castle of Stonewall is impenetrable."

All eyes turned to Ardyn, who swallowed hard. "What I am about to tell you must not leave this room."

The men shifted nervously in their seats.

"There is a secret entrance into the castle known only to the members of House Thayn. Not even Zul Voss knows of its existence. My plan will have a small force infiltrate the castle using this secret entrance and open the gates for the remainder of our forces. Then we can seize the castle and arrest Zul Voss."

"Where is this secret entrance, my lord?" Sir Simon asked skeptically.

"Near the peak of Mount Arryon," Ardyn said.

"What?" Sir Simon nearly shouted. The elders murmured their shared disbelief. "None have scaled Mount Arryon in over a hundred years."

"I have," Ardyn said quickly. "A former friend and I scaled the mountain just before I left for Ethriel."

"How?" one of the elders exclaimed.

"There is a secret stair that climbs the mountain. It is steep and treacherous, but if we can gain entrance to the castle, we can unlock the gates. The rest of our forces can then storm the castle and capture Zul Voss."

"This is a dangerous plan," interjected Galanor. "One filled with peril. The fact that you are willing to undertake such a journey for the sake of your people proves you are the son of Anson Thayn."

The elders murmured their reluctant approval.

"My lord, I must accompany you on your quest," Sir Simon said.

"No, Sir Simon. You must stay here to lead the rest of our forces. Only I can find the secret entrance and lead a small company through the dark tunnels within."

"But, my lord..." Sir Simon began to protest.

"It is decided, Sir Simon," Ardyn said, ending the discussion. "You must be ready to take the castle once we open the gates."

"What will be the sign?" Sir Simon asked.

"The banner of the House of Thayn waving over the gatehouse."

28

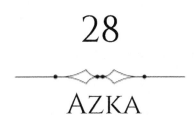

AZKA

Azka was not an impatient man, nor did he easily become anxious. Despite years of training and facing many dangers without fear, he now paced anxiously, awaiting an audience with the king. He had only been the young man's personal guard for a little over a month, yet somehow he felt more loyal and devoted to him than any other man he'd ever met. This young man, who had given him the benefit of the doubt even when he'd confessed his true purpose in finding him, was now his king, and he resolved to serve him. Now he stood in anteroom to the king's chambers awaiting his return.

The door opened, and the king entered, followed by Lord Myr and Barons Astley and Warde. Azka would have preferred to speak with the king in private, but under the circumstances...

"Your Highness," he said with a bow.

"Azka," the king said, seating himself at his desk. His advisors flanked him. "You requested this meeting and said it was urgent."

"Yes, sire," Azka began meekly. "I must confess to you, my King, that I have withheld information from you regarding my mission to recruit men from the villages along the Ryparian River two weeks ago."

"Go on," the king said following a brief pause.

"I was approached by a man named Silas Morgan in the town of Rein."

"Silas Morgan!" the king nearly shouted. "What'd this man look like?"

"His most defining feature was the large red hat and feather."

"Yes, that's him," the king said, anxiety on his face. "What'd the rogue want?"

"He delivered a message from Noliono. It seems that he is holding my sister hostage and offered to release her if I killed you."

There was a sudden intake of breath as each man eyed Azka suspiciously.

"Why would you keep this from me, Azka?" the king asked, hurt etched on his young face.

"I was afraid, Your Highness, that you would nullify our agreement and that I would lose my sister forever," Azka replied, realizing for the first time that he was being honest and open with someone. It shocked him.

"Your Majesty," Lord Myr interrupted, glaring at Azka. "You may know this man best, but I recommend he be disarmed and imprisoned. At the very least, he should be exiled from this city at once."

Azka did not look at Lord Myr, but his gaze remained fixed on his king. He waited as the king appeared to be considering carefully before speaking.

"Lord Myr, I do know this man well enough to know that if he wanted me dead, I would be so," the king said with a slight smile. Azka took heart at this. "Nevertheless, Azka, you have kept important information from me—in time of war, no less."

"Yes, sire."

"I am forced to test your loyalty, Azka."

"Sire!" Lord Myr interjected. "This man was your personal guard, trusted above all others. This is the man who lied and kept the truth from you. Why should you test his loyalty to you when he has so obviously failed?"

Anger burned inside Azka. For this man, who was descendant of the very family who'd murdered the Aranethons, to accuse and condemn him was almost too much to bear. Yet Azka retained his composure and did not allow his anger to even reach his expression.

"Yes, Lord Myr, I know his crime, but I also knew yours and your family's," the king said with a gleam in his eyes. "Have you forgotten so quickly the mercy I granted you? Would you deny the same for someone else?"

"Your Majesty is very gracious," Lord Myr said with a bow. "I suppose each man deserves a chance to redeem himself."

"My feeling exactly, Lord Myr," the king responded kindly.

Azka could not help but feel impressed at how quickly the young king had learned how to manipulate his vassals.

"Azka, you are relieved as my bodyguard, and I am sending you on a dangerous mission. At nightfall, you will leave this city and infiltrate the enemy camp. You will learn their strategy and strength. Once you have completed this task, you will return and report your findings. I will then pass final judgment on your conduct."

"Yes, sire," Azka said with a bow. He turned to leave, but the king called him back.

"Azka, good hunting," the king said with a noticeable pain in his voice.

"Thank you, Your Majesty," he said with another bow.

As he left the king's chambers, Azka made for his own room to prepare for his mission. For the first time in his adult life, he felt a determination to succeed that was driven not by material gain but by a sense of duty and a desire to prove himself to another person, his king.

* * * *

At nightfall Azka was released from the city. The enemy camp surrounded the city, and the king and his advisors had no idea where the main tent might be located. The night was brisk, and the cloudy overcast blocked out almost all light—a perfect night to infiltrate the enemy's camp. The problem was the empty field between the city walls and the camp. Azka had to choose the best way to approach. Even with the cloud cover, to cross that distance without being seen was almost impossible. He needed a plan. Azka's eyes scanned the enemy camp, noting the location of the campfires. They were approximately forty feet apart. Azka gauged that if he moved between the fires, he might be missed by the guards around the fires. It was his only chance. Azka sprinted, his robes whipping and billowing behind him. Despite his training and physical stamina, he was already breathing hard at the halfway point. He realized he'd never run this fast in his life. His muscles were becoming fatigued. At a hundred yards from the camp, Azka could see the small silhouettes of the guards passing in front of the fires. At fifty yards out, his body ached with the effort he was forcing upon it. At twenty-five yards away, the number of guards could now be clearly seen in the nearest fire. Ten more yards; he was almost there.

"Who goes there?" came a voice from the nearest fire.

He'd been seen. Azka had but one chance. He made for the nearest tent and dove under the canvas. The inside was lit by a lantern hanging from the main pole. A single soldier was reclining on his bed. He and Azka stared at one another for a moment, then they both reacted simultaneously—the man reaching for his sword and Azka lunging at the man and quickly placing his hand over the other's mouth and nose. They struggled silently for several moments until the man's eyes rolled back, and he passed out. As he lowered the man back onto his bed, Azka had a sudden thought. Just a few short weeks ago, he would have dispatched this man without a second thought. Yet with this man, he'd opted for a nonlethal method. He stood for a moment in silent contemplation, then the noises from outside drew his attention back to the present. He quickly extinguished the lantern and knelt by the tent entrance.

He could hear the men outside shouting and running from tent to tent in an effort to find him. He had to move, or he would certainly be caught. Azka pulled back the tent flap just enough to see the other tents nearby. The guards were searching the one across from his, but the way was clear to the one right beside it. Azka darted across and dove into the other tent. It was empty. Azka breathed a sigh of relief then moved over and pulled the canvas up to peer at the next row of tents. More guards were searching here. This was going to take a while.

✳   ✳   ✳   ✳

It was not until around midnight that the camp quieted down enough for Azka to move about without drawing too much attention. He spotted a nearby watch fire near the eastern edge of the camp. Four men sat around it. Azka edged closer and overheard the conversation.

"You hear about the intruder a few hours ago?" one man asked the other three.

The others shook their heads.

"Some of the guards said a man managed to break through the line. They said he was dark skinned, maybe from the land of Kusini."

"Kusini?" one of the others asked. "Where is that?"

"Somewhere far to the south, I think," answered the first man.

"Why'd a man from Kusini be here in Alethia?" asked a third man lackadaisically.

"Who knows?" answered the first. "Add it to the list of things we don't know."

"You know," the second man cut in. "I think I saw a dark-skinned woman entering the king's tent last night."

Azka froze.

"Maybe the king made an alliance with Kusini or something," the third man offered.

"Doesn't matter," replied the first man, standing up to leave. "We can win this war without any help. I'm back on watch. See you later."

The man began walking straight toward Azka's hiding place. As soon as he was close enough, Azka grabbed him and threw him to the ground. He landed on his back, and Azka was on top of him in a moment, covering the other's mouth and holding a knife to his throat.

"Call out and you die," Azka growled, removing his hand from the other's mouth.

The man just stared in disbelief.

"Where is the king's tent?"

The man hesitated, and Azka saw his eyes dart in the direction of the watch fire.

"Tell me the location of the king's tent, and I will let you live."

"It's t-two h-hundred yards north of here. There's banners and flags all around it, but you'll never get close. There are too many guards."

"How many?" Azka said, pulling him up and glaring hard at him.

"I...I don't know, fifty maybe," the man said, fear etched on his face.

Azka let him go, and the man fell back to the ground.

"One last question," Azka asked with a small smirk. "Are those guards anything like you?"

The man was dumbstruck, and Azka quickly knocked the man unconscious. He looked down at his handiwork and laughed softly to himself. In the old days, he'd have killed this man as well. Azka wondered to himself what this change meant as he picked up the man and placed him in an empty tent nearby. He then turned toward the direction of the king's tent.

＊　＊　＊　＊

As it turned out, the guards around the king's tent were much like the man he'd just interrogated. He easily avoided the sentries and reached the area just outside the king's tent. The giant pavilion stood out from among the other tents merely by its size and color. The other tents surrounding it were the plain tan color, while the king's tent was a crimson red. Flags and banners flew over the tent, all crimson and all displaying the black wolf of House Noland. Azka flattened himself against the nearest tent and peered around the corner. Two guards stood at the entrance, and two more patrolled the perimeter. Azka noticed that none of the guards were members of the Guardians simply by the absence of the silver shield, which was the badge of office. The absence of any Guardians meant that the king must not be in his tent. This puzzled Azka as he wondered what could possibly be more important to Noliono than consolidating his power and putting down this rebellion.

Azka darted around to the rear of the huge tent. He knelt down, pulled out his knife, and cut a small slit about two inches long in the canvas. He replaced his knife and peered through the slit. At first the light within blinded him, but as his eyes adjusted, Azka could make out a figure seated and another standing on the far side of the tent. He gasped as he recognized the two people. One was Ramond Kludge, and the other was his sister, Aylen. He had not seen her in years, but as she turned and her face became visible, Azka knew it to be her. Why was she here and with Kludge? What did Noliono hope to accomplish by bringing her here? He watched as Kludge turned and approached Aylen. Azka tensed, but Kludge only handed Aylen a cup. Azka was already working on an escape plan, but his mind froze as he saw his sister give Kludge a weak smile. What happened next made Azka's stomach turn, for Kludge moved toward her, and he kissed her. Azka stared in disbelief, his mind befuddled.

Though still bewildered, Azka still possessed enough wits to notice two others had just entered the tent. It was Noliono and another man Azka did not recognize.

"Your Majesty," Kludge said, bowing. "You, of course, know Aylen."

"Your Majesty," his sister said, bowing also.

"Welcome, Aylen," Noliono said, moving over and kissing her hand. "I trust you are being treated well."

Azka saw Noliono wink at Kludge, and his anger burned inside of him.

"You remember Kaleb Jorrah, Baron of Norhold," Noliono said, beckoning the other man over.

"It is a pleasure to meet you," Jorrah said, also kissing Aylen's hand.

"Jorrah, please escort Aylen to her quarters. Lord Kludge and I have matters to discuss in private."

"Yes, Your Highness," Jorrah said, offering his arm to Aylen, who took it with a smile.

Azka watched them leave and was suddenly torn between rescuing his sister and honoring his king. If he followed his sister, he might be given the opportunity to rescue her, and they could escape together. If he remained where he was, he might overhear Noliono's plan and be able to report back to his king. He struggled with what to do for a few moments. Then as his sister and Jorrah exited the tent, he knew what he must do. Azka shook his head and turned toward Noliono and Kludge, who were standing on opposite sides of a large table.

"Elengil is surrounded, sire," Kludge reported proudly. "No one can enter or leave without our knowing."

"That is good, Kludge, but I wish this matter to be dealt with quickly," Noliono said without looking up. "I cannot afford a long siege. I want the city taken and this usurper dead soon."

"Sire," Kludge said timidly. "The city is impregnable. I have sent scouts throughout the lands about. There is no way in save a direct assault, which would cost many hundreds of men."

"Men I cannot afford to lose if I am still to invade Nordyke as planned," Noliono said earnestly. "I will be avenged upon those accursed barbarians."

"Nordyke?" Azka whispered to himself.

"We cannot afford a lengthy siege or a direct assault," Noliono continued. "There must be another way to conquer this city. What about the assassin?"

"No word yet, sire," Kludge said quietly.

"He knows we have his sister?"

"Yes, sire."

"What of the rogue, Silas Morgan?"

"Our men saw that he was able to enter the city, but I have not heard anything further."

"It may be inevitable then," Noliono said, sighing heavily. "Prepare your men for a feigned assault on the eastern gate to gauge their defenses."

"Yes, Your Majesty," Kludge said, bowing and heading for the exit.

Azka turned and quickly made for the city in the distance. He must get back to King Corin at once and warn him of all he'd heard.

29

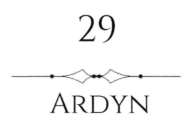

ARDYN

Mount Arryon, the tallest of all the mountains of Eodar. Its snow-covered peak rose high and menacing in the waning light of the late afternoon. Ardyn and twenty of Sir Simon's choice men stood outside the gate near the eastern slope of the mountain. Ardyn watched as the men gazed apprehensively at their goal. He had given the best motivational speech he could, but now it was up to him to lead these men up the mountain, find the secret entrance, brave the dark tunnels that led into the castle, succeed in opening the gates for the rest of his men, and take the castle. No small feat for any man, but Ardyn wondered if it was even possible. *Who am I to attempt such an impossible quest?* He pushed aside such thoughts, realizing that he could not afford such doubts. This demonstrated just how far Ardyn had come over the past several months. The weight of so many people depending on him coupled with the hard lessons he'd learned in Ethriel had worked a positive change on Ardyn. He felt the change, but he still had to fight his doubts. It was more than that though. He wasn't doing this just for himself or even the people of Stonewall. He was doing all this for his father. Though in life his father had only shown disappointment in him, Ardyn had always loved his father and would have done anything for him.

He looked at the men that would accompany him on this quest and saw Jon and Kabe, two trusted members of Sir Simon's company. Sir Simon told Ardyn he could trust these men, and Ardyn hoped he could. His love for his family strengthened his resolve, and as he took his first step toward the daunting task ahead, Ardyn somehow knew his men would follow.

They climbed for hours up the steep slopes of the mountain. Several of his men had slipped in their footing and slid several feet back down the mountain. Often when one man slipped, he took a few of the others with him. Ardyn pushed forward, earnestly searching for the hidden stair. He was trying to retrace the journey that he and Corin had made together, yet his attention was constantly drawn to what Noliono had told him about his father and brothers' death, how Corin had ordered their assassination at the Battle of Abenhall. The inner rage that Ardyn felt toward his former friend was almost overwhelming. Hadn't his father been kind to Corin and even arranged for a position at the academy? He just could not fathom why Corin had turned on him and his family.

Ardyn shook his head and continued to climb. About an hour later, they reached the hidden stairs. The company gazed up in awe as their eyes followed the stairway as it wound its way up the mountainside. Ardyn steeled himself for the climb, but sensed the other men's courage was waning. He turned to them and looked at each man in turn. Every man there was his senior by ten or more years, and Ardyn's sense of inadequacy surged to the forefront of his mind. He hesitated for a moment, but the faces of those men looking to him for direction overcame his feelings of self-doubt.

"Men," Ardyn began, his voice gaining strength with each word. "We are charged with opening the gates of the castle so that our brothers-in-arms can help us free our city from the tyranny of Zul Voss. We cannot allow our fears to deter us from succeeding. We cannot fail our brothers, our families, our city. Who will still follow me?"

The men shouted as one, "For Stonewall!" Then the company began its long climb up the mountain.

✳   ✳   ✳   ✳

After several more hours of climbing, the company reached a wide ledge at the end of the steep stairway. The ledge looked out toward the west, high above the city. The mountainside adjacent to the ledge was sheer and gave no indication of a door or opening of any kind. Ardyn heard some of the men grumbling about a waste of a climb and the oncoming of night, so he took action. He approached the mountainside, feeling along the rock face. The men watched him anxiously. Finally, after several minutes of this, Ardyn's left hand came across a small indention about the size of the tip of his index finger. He pushed his finger into the indention, and there was a loud crack that echoed into the valleys below. Ardyn stepped back, and they all watched in wonder as the outline of a door gradually appeared in the rock face.

"Push!" Ardyn cried, stepping forward and throwing his weight against the door. Several others joined him, and slowly the door swung inward, revealing a winding set of stone steps leading into the black heart of the mountain.

"What is this place?" one of the men asked.

"Hand me a torch," Ardyn said.

One of the men lit a torch and handed it to him. He peered into the darkness, which seemed to sneer at his pitiful light.

"My father once told me that this ledge was once a watch post in the days before the king, when the lords of Stonewall were often assailed by the wild men of the north," Ardyn replied, turning to look out on the ledge again. "This stair leads down into several hidden storerooms behind the castle, which were once well stocked in case of a long siege."

"How far is it down to the castle?"

"I don't know," Ardyn admitted. "None of my family has entered this hidden passage in over a hundred years."

Ardyn could sense the failing courage of his companions.

"I don't blame any of you for not wanting to go with me into this unknown danger, but I at least must go," Ardyn said, trying to sound courageous, while his insides squirmed vehemently. "Whoever will accompany me will be rewarded once we retake the city. Follow me, men of courage."

With that, Ardyn turned and began descending the stairs. He heard the sound of many feet behind him and breathed a sigh of relief. Whatever dangers lurked in the blackness below, at least he would not be facing it alone.

After descending the stairs for over an hour, Ardyn and his men reached a landing that led to a large wooden door. The hinges were rusted and the wood was decaying, but with some effort, Ardyn and several others managed to pull the great door open a crack. Ardyn squeezed through first, followed by the rest of the company. Even with the light of over a dozen torches, the far walls and ceiling remained shrouded in darkness. As they proceeded into the dark chamber, Ardyn felt his heart pounding in his chest. Despite his lack of experience, something told him that they were being watched. The other men with him seemed to sense it too, for they were constantly looking about, waving their torches in every direction. They took several more steps inside. Everyone was on guard and looking all about the chamber for the source of their uneasiness.

Suddenly, from the far side of the chamber came a low growl. The men all turned, holding their torches toward the sound. Whatever it was remained hidden in the darkness beyond the torchlight. The growl came again, this time from behind the company, and they all turned toward the new sound, brandishing their weapons. Ardyn began to fear that he'd led all these men to their deaths. Suddenly, from within their ranks, a bright light erupted. Ardyn turned to see Galanor standing in the midst of the company, a bright light coming from his staff. The company could now plainly see their situation. There were two creatures guarding the way forward and the way back. They were massive gray wolves with dark fur and glowing red eyes. The wolves bared their teeth and shrunk before the light of Galanor's staff.

"Wolves of Ardaband!" Galanor shouted.

"How did you..." Ardyn began, but Galanor interrupted.

"I knew such dangers may lurk in these old tunnels," Galanor said simply. "I decided to secretly join your company in case you needed my help."

Ardyn nodded his thanks then turned toward the wolf in front of him.

"They will not come near the light. Press forward and be ready to strike!" Galanor shouted.

The company slowly moved across the chamber. The wolf before them shrank back, while the wolf behind followed the company closely.

"Steady, men," Ardyn said, feeling his heart pound in his chest.

"They had almost reached the far side of the room. The beast was backed into the left corner, leaving the door wide open. Then it happened. The two wolves attacked at once, knocking the men into one another and sending Galanor to the ground, unconscious. As the old man fell, his staff was extinguished, leaving only the light of their torches to keep the beasts at bay.

"Pick him up and get ready to run for it!" Ardyn shouted, swinging at the pair of glowing eyes not five feet from the company.

"What do we do?" Jon asked anxiously.

"Jon and Kabe will remain with me. The rest of you will carry Galanor out of the chamber and down the stairs beyond. Do not stop or return for us."

"My lord," one man protested.

"No arguments!" Ardyn retorted. "Now go!"

One of the stronger men picked Galanor up and swung him over his shoulders. Ardyn nodded at him, and the rest of the company ran for the door, leaving Ardyn and his two companions against two wolves. He guessed that the odds of their survival were slim, but Ardyn comforted himself with the knowledge that the rest of the company would make it. Sir Simon would be able to retake the castle, and Stonewall would be safe.

He and his companions retreated to the door opening, holding their swords and torches in front of them. The wolves paced back and forth, snarling and looking for a weak point in their defenses. Suddenly, one of the wolves lunged at Ardyn. He dodged its attack and brought his sword around to slash through its hind leg. The creature crashed into the wall, knocking it senseless.

"Mind the other one!" Ardyn shouted at his companions, dispatching the fallen beast.

The other wolf roared in fury as the first breathed its last.

"Watch yourself, men!" Ardyn said, rejoining the other two. "This one will not likely make the same mistake."

The standoff continued for several more long minutes, and then Ardyn had an idea.

"Are either of you carrying a bow?"

"I am, my lord," Kabe said, producing the weapon.

"Fit an arrow to the string and be ready," Ardyn said, moving away from the other two. "I will draw it away."

As Ardyn had hoped, the wolf began moving toward him. A single arrow would not bring down such a large beast, but it might injure it enough to allow him to deliver a killing blow or, at the very least, drive it away so they might escape. The wolf drew closer to Ardyn. Now was the moment. He could see the wolf was preparing to pounce.

"Now!" Ardyn shouted as the creature sprang at him.

Ardyn dodged to the left as the beast missed him by inches. He could not see the arrow in the darkness, but he knew Kabe had found his mark. The wolf let out an ear-piercing howl. It rose on its hind legs, giving Ardyn his chance. He turned and plunged his sword into the beast's chest. The wolf let out another howl then fell dead at Ardyn's feet.

"Nice shot!" Ardyn said, rejoining his companions. "Now for it. Let's go find the others."

* * * *

An hour later, Ardyn, Jon, and Kabe met up with the rest of the company at the end of a long tunnel that dead-ended into a rock wall. Galanor was awake, and his staff lit the whole tunnel with a brilliant white light. They all stood waiting as Ardyn searched the wall for a way to pass through. He ran his hand from top to bottom all across the rock face, but to no avail.

"I cannot find the means to open the entrance to the castle," Ardyn confessed to Galanor in a whisper.

"Perhaps the tunnel itself holds the answer," Galanor suggested.

They each took a side and began feeling along the walls. Surprisingly, Ardyn's right hand found the indention in the wall almost at once. He pressed it, and there was a sharp snapping noise behind him. The outline of a door appeared in front of Galanor, who quickly dimmed his staff.

"Push together," Ardyn ordered, and everyone pushed against the door. It gave way, and the men were greeted with the soft glow of moonlight. They had reached the courtyard of Stonewall Castle.

"Douse the lights," Ardyn whispered. "We cannot be seen, or all will be lost."

When the lights were out, Ardyn moved cautiously into the empty courtyard. Nothing moved in the darkness. He turned to Kabe and pointed toward a corridor to the right, which led to the gatehouse. Kabe nodded, and he, Jon, and half the men broke away from the group and made for the corridor. The rest remained with Ardyn and Galanor.

"It is for us to capture Zul Voss," Ardyn said earnestly. "I will not be able leave Stonewall should he escape."

The men nodded their approval.

"He should be in the treasure room," Galanor continued. "He always loved counting the gold and silver kept there. Your father always thought he was just keeping an accurate tally, but now you know it was because he believed it to be his."

"He is sure to have plenty of bodyguards. We cannot risk a pitched battle," Ardyn said.

"You know there is only one way into the counting room, Ardyn. We have no choice," Galanor said a bit condescendingly.

"Then we need a plan."

"We have little time, Ardyn," Galanor retorted irritably. "Your men will arrive at the gatehouse soon, and Sir Simon is waiting to storm this castle. If we don't capture Zul before then, he may escape in the chaos."

"Then we have but one choice." Ardyn sighed. "Men, follow me to the counting room."

❋   ❋   ❋   ❋

Several long minutes later, Ardyn and his men arrived outside the corridor leading to the treasure room. Ardyn peered around the corner. The corridor dead-ended into a large wooden door guarded by four heavily armed men. He conveyed this information to his men and instructed two of them to fit arrows to the bowstring.

"Fire if they advance," Ardyn whispered. "You must take two of them down immediately for this to work."

The two men nodded, and Ardyn stepped out into the corridor and drew his sword. The guards peered at him, hesitating.

"I am Ardyn Thayn, son of Anson Thayn," he said, trying to sound bolder than he felt. "I have come to arrest Zul Voss and to claim what is rightfully mine. Surrender and your lives will be spared."

At this the guards laughed, and two advanced on him.

"Now!" Ardyn yelled, and his men joined him in the corridor. The bowmen found their marks, and two of the guards crumpled to the ground.

"Attack!" Ardyn yelled as he and his men ran down the corridor.

The two remaining guards were so overwhelmed that they dropped their weapons and ran into the counting room. They tried to close the door behind them, but too late. Ardyn threw his full weight against the door, keeping it from closing. The rest of the company joined him, and they forced the door open. As they surveyed the room, Ardyn and his men were stunned by what they saw.

"Welcome Ardyn," came the sneering high-pitched voice of Zul Voss.

Ardyn glared at the little man surrounded by a dozen or more men all armed with crossbows and aiming at the doorway.

"I have been expecting you," Zul said with an evil smile. "You've caused quite an uproar in my city, but that is over now. Drop your weapons and surrender."

Ardyn turned to Galanor, who nodded.

"Men," he said with rage building within him. "Attack!"

30

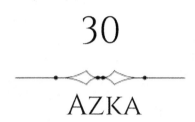

AZKA

"So once he is finished with us, Noliono plans to invade Nordyke to satisfy a personal vendetta?" the king asked incredulously.

Azka was standing in the Great Hall once again. The king was seated on his throne, and his advisors were standing on either side of him, all eager to discuss Azka's report.

"Yes, sire," Azka said, his mind still on what he saw in Noliono's tent.

"That's preposterous!" Lord Myr shouted in disgust. "Noliono is foolish, but not enough to risk the kingdom to satisfy his own need for revenge. "The fact that I am more interested in is that your sister is cavorting with the enemy!"

"How can this be?" the king asked, shaking his head.

"I do not know, Your Highness," Azka admitted, his face bowed in shame. "I can only think she has been bewitched or succumbed to torture."

"Or she is simply in love with Ramond Kludge!" Lord Myr suggested with a nasty look at Azka. "After all, some women are attracted to power like flies to..."

"That's enough, Lord Myr," the king said, his voice rising slightly. "His sister's allegiance is in question, but we shall not impugn her honor without further evidence."

Azka glared at Lord Myr, who returned his expression.

"Your Majesty, I have a suggestion," Baron Astley interjected.

"Proceed," said the king.

"I would suggest a parley with Noliono."

"To what end?" the king asked, his brow furrowing.

"My plan is to call for a parley, which will intrigue Noliono because he believes he has already defeated us. We shall meet in a pavilion halfway between the lines, and Azka shall accompany us. His presence will provoke Noliono and Kludge, who is sure to be in attendance. We shall offer to meet Noliono on the battlefield to decide who is King of Alethia, and in exchange, we shall demand the return of Azka's sister."

"This is madness, sire!" Lord Myr nearly shouted. "To risk the kingdom over a man's sister is absurd!"

"We would not be risking the kingdom, sire," Astley retorted. "Noliono will accept the challenge, but we will demand to see her. We can gauge her attitude when she is brought to the parley and sees Azka. What's more, we can also try to manipulate Noliono into revealing his true intentions and strategy by playing to his ego."

All were silent as the king considered this. Azka noticed the king's expression only revealed a hint of uncertainty and marveled at how far this young man had come since they had first met. It had only been a month since his coronation, yet Corin wore the crown with more care and wisdom than a man twice his age.

"Baron Warde," the king said, turning to the man next to Baron Astley. "What say you of this plan?"

Warde looked at Astley for a moment then looked at Azka before turning to the king.

Azka saw the hesitation in the man's eyes and wondered what it meant.

"I support Baron Astley, sire," Warde said, finally. "I think this will help reveal Noliono's true intentions."

"What of Azka's report?"

"I believe that Noliono wishes to end this civil war, but I do not think he'd plunge the kingdom into war with Nordyke so soon after."

"Very well," the king said, standing. "Firstly, Azka you have infiltrated the enemy camp, returned and reported, and provided an opportunity to undermine their strategy and resolve. I declare, in the presence of Lord Myr and Barons Astley and Warde, that you are pardoned from *any* crimes you may have committed against the crown."

"Thank you, sire," Azka said with a low bow.

"Furthermore," the king continued, drawing his sword. "I dub you, Sir Azka, and make you the Captain of the King's Garrison."

"I am honored, Your Majesty, but I do not seek titles," Azka said humbly.

"Nevertheless, you are recognized before this court for your valor and loyalty to my person. Rise, Sir Azka."

Azka stood and noticed the king was holding his own sword.

"As Captain of the King's Garrison, you will be the leader of my personal bodyguards. If you are to defend me, you shall need this back," the king said, handing Azka his own sword.

"Thank you, Your Highness," Azka said, taking the sword and bowing.

"Now, we shall see what Baron Astley's plan yields," the king said, turning to face his advisors. "Lord Myr, send a messenger to Noliono. Tell him that I wish to hold a parley."

"Yes, sire," Lord Myr said, bowing and exiting the Great Hall.

Azka wished he knew more about his sister's situation. Could she really be in love with Ramond Kludge? The idea seemed ludicrous, and yet he could not shake the fact that he'd seen her kiss him. He felt a hand on his shoulder.

"I am sure your sister is being coerced," the king said quietly. "Have faith in her, my friend."

"I have little to put faith in, Your Highness," Azka admitted without looking at the king.

"All will be made clear in the next few hours."

This, of course, was what Azka feared most.

✳   ✳   ✳   ✳

It was midday. A pavilion had been set up halfway between the city and the enemy camp. A large table sat in the middle of the pavilion with five chairs on each side. On one side sat Azka, Lord Renton Myr, King Corin Aranethon, Baron Peter Astley, and Baron Alaster Warde. On the other side sat Baron Kaleb Jorrah, Lord Gaven Soron, King Noliono Noland, Lord Atton Nenlad, and Lord Ramond Kludge. No other guards were allowed within a hundred feet of the pavilion, and each man was only allowed a sword for protection. Each side eyed the other suspiciously.

"You have called for a parley," Noliono began after several awkward minutes of silence. It was a statement, not a question. "I am intrigued by this since your city is completely surrounded and my forces outnumber yours quite substantially. What could you possibly have to offer me to parley?"

Azka turned and looked at Corin. He seemed nervous. Azka hoped Noliono had not noticed.

"I have called for this parley to determine a battlefield to decide who will rule Alethia," Corin said, trying to sound confident.

"A battlefield!" Noliono laughed derisively. "Fine! Choose whatever field you think will avail you most. I know my forces outnumber yours at least three to one, thanks to a certain spy. Perhaps you've heard of him? His name is Silas Morgan."

Azka watched as Corin's face grew red in anger.

"He also got a look at a certain book in your possession, the *Book of Aduin*. Seems you think it will legitimize your claim to the throne. Pity your guards found him before he could relieve you of such a potent piece of evidence," Noliono said with an evil grin.

"Yes," Corin replied, his eyes narrowing. "I received word that the guards found a man trying to steal the *Book of Aduin*. The real tragedy is that he escaped before my men could give him a proper welcome."

"I also see a new face at this table," Noliono said, changing the subject. His eyes were resting on Azka. "You should be careful, my young friend. Some of your sheep are really wolves in disguise."

Azka remained calm on the surface, but his anger raged within.

"Azka has been open regarding your attempts to use him," Corin retorted, his face still red in anger. "It interests me how you planned to accomplish this."

Azka silently studied Noliono's face as Corin continued.

"You have captive a certain woman named Aylen, whom you know is the sister of Azka."

Noliono sat back and put his fingers together. He looked from Corin to Azka and then back again. "I have a woman under my care who is named Aylen, yes, but she is not a captive.

"Please bring her forward that we may see her."

"And why should I do that?"

"Because her safety is a term of this parley," Corin said quickly. "We know you do not wish to tarry here long and that you have plans for Nordyke."

Noliono stared, dumbstruck.

"You would plunge the whole kingdom into war just to settle a personal vendetta!" Corin shouted accusingly. "Or is it simply a means to retain control of the throne? Either way, it shows how low you will stoop to usurp my throne."

"Don't test me, boy!" Noliono growled, his smile quickly changing into a scowl. "I am the one in control here, not you."

Corin sat wordlessly, glaring at Noliono. Everyone at the table was silent for a few minutes.

"I tire of this farce," Noliono said, standing up. "You called for this meeting to decide a battlefield, so decide."

"Bring Azka's sister here," Corin said obstinately.

Noliono considered the young man for a moment then turned to Ramond Kludge. "Send for your companion, Lord Kludge."

Kludge bowed and left the pavilion. He was gone for less than ten minutes, but it seemed like hours to Azka. He knew that sister's fate could well be decided in the next few minutes. Then Azka spotted two people walking toward the pavilion. His heart sank when they got closer and could see they were arm in arm. He recognized his sweet sister's face, though she gave no indication she recognized his. Kludge led her into the pavilion, and she bowed to Noliono. Azka wanted to call to her but thought better of it. He watched as she met each person in the tent, then her eyes fell upon Azka. He watched as recognition flashed across her face, a look of utter bewilderment.

"Azka!" She gasped.

"Aylen," Azka said softly, nodding in reply.

She stood for a moment, dumbstruck. The entire tent was absorbed in the exchange between the two siblings, wondering what would happen next. Suddenly, Aylen tried to run to Azka, but Kludge caught her by the arm.

"Azka, help me!" she screamed. "They are holding me captive, forcing me to..."

"Silence!" Noliono shouted. "Take her away, Kludge!"

Azka, along with everyone at the table, rose from his seat. Noliono and his cohort drew their swords as did Corin and his party.

"You will release Azka's sister at once, Noliono," Corin growled.

"Oh?" Noliono said in mock surprise. "And why would I do that?"

"You have proven your dishonor here today, Noliono!" Corin cried in anger. "Rest assured, I will meet you in battle, but you will not die there. I will make sure you are captured and brought forth to answer for your crimes before the whole kingdom."

"Empty words." Noliono sneered. "Send word of your chosen battlefield. I await your envoy."

Azka glared after them as Noliono and his party backed away from the table to a safe distance then turned and walked back to their camp. Now both he and Corin knew his sister was not a collaborator; she was a prisoner. He silently vowed, no matter what the cost, that he would rescue his sister and make Noliono and Kludge pay for what they'd done.

31

CORIN

Corin sat at his desk, his face in his hands. Behind him on a large table lay a large map of Elengil and the surrounding region. Enemy troop positions were designated by small red blocks, while friendly troops were designated by blue ones. Even to the ignorant, the strategic situation was obvious. Reports cluttered the edges of the map, and there was evidence of a mass exodus from the room as the chairs around the table were left in disarray and several stray pieces of parchment littered the floor around it.

Corin had been trying to choose a battlefield that afforded them the best chance for victory, but the constant bickering between his advisors had pushed him beyond endurance. He ordered them to leave him for a few hours so he could clear his mind and think. That was over an hour ago, yet his mind was still frazzled. Corin stared down at the map for several seconds and then shook his head. A sudden thought occurred to him that a walk around the grounds might clear his mind. He had just reached for his staff and was getting up when he heard a soft knock at the door. He sighed loudly, assuming that one of his advisors was interrupting him early.

"Enter," he said, standing with an effort.

The door opened, and to Corin's surprise, Riniel Aurelia entered the room. He smiled, and so did she. He was not sure that Riniel saw him as anything more than a friend, but he was hopeful that one day she might. Corin was sure of one thing: that her presence brought him comfort.

"Welcome," he said, trying to mask his exhaustion. "Please don't mind the mess."

She smiled again, and Corin's heart leapt into his throat.

"I heard you dismissed your advisors for a few hours, and I thought you might like some company," Riniel said with a mischievous look in her eyes.

Corin smiled at her and then looked away.

"You are troubled," she said softly. It was a statement, not a question. Corin was surprised at her discernment and nodded. He knew to deny the obvious was pointless.

"I know little of war," Corin admitted, sitting down with a heavy sigh. "Yet it falls to me to make a decision that will decide the fate of an entire kingdom. I look to my advisors for guidance, but they are conflicted at the moment. Barons Astley and Warde advocate a battlefield on the hills east of the city because the enemy's numeric advantage will count for less, but Lord Myr, who knows this land best, says that the hills will make little difference against so many."

"What strategy does Lord Myr suggest?" Riniel asked knowingly.

"He urges me to remain in the city and wait for winter, but if I did that, I'd be breaking my word and condemning Azka's sister to death."

"What do Azka and Galanor say?"

"They have been absent since the parley with Noliono," Corin said with more than a hint of frustration. "We used the parley as a distraction so Galanor could escape the city unnoticed."

"Why?" Riniel asked quickly.

"He would not say," Corin said, frustration evident in his voice. "Azka left soon after the meeting to journey north along the eastern edge of Oakwood Forest."

"I see," Riniel said. Corin could tell she didn't know what else to say.

"I am truly glad to see you, Riniel," he said with a smile.

She smiled back.

"With all this conflict and turmoil, it helps me to know there is still good in this world. It gives me hope and something to fight for," Corin said, reaching for her hand.

She flinched slightly at his touch but did not recoil. Her hands were soft, and she was so beautiful. He locked eyes with her, and it was as if time stood still. Corin breathed a sigh of momentary contentment, wondering if she felt the same.

Suddenly there was a loud knock at the door that interrupted Corin and Riniel's moment.

"Enter," Corin said, releasing Riniel's hand.

The door opened, and several people pushed their way inside. At the front was Galanor, followed quickly by Azka, Lord Myr, and Barons Astley and Warde. A quick look of bemusement crossed each face as they took in the scene.

"Our apologies, Your Majesty, for interrupting," Lord Myr said with a smile and a wink.

"It is fine," Corin said though admittedly annoyed at the interruption.

"Sire," Galanor said, stepping forward. "We bring important news."

"I will excuse myself," Riniel said, standing.

"No," Corin said a bit too quickly. He saw everyone exchange knowing looks, and his face grew red in embarrassment. "I would have you stay."

Corin was relieved to see Riniel was blushing also as she sat back down.

"Sire," began Azka with a bow. "I bring news of a large force riding from the north. They bare the banner of House Thayn."

"I thought House Thayn fell at the siege of Abenhall," Corin said, bewildered.

"It is commanded by Ardyn Thayn, Your Majesty," Azka continued.

"Ardyn?" Corin and Riniel asked at the same time. They both exchanged looks.

"A friend of yours?" Corin asked, searching her face.

"Yes," Riniel said, dropping her gaze. "I thought he'd been killed during our escape from Ethriel." There was a moment's pause, then Riniel looked up at Corin. "Wait, how do you know him?"

"We were friends in Stonewall," Corin said, as sadness fell on his face. "Inseparable we were, until his father decided to take him to Ethriel. I have not seen him since."

"There is more, sire," Galanor said, redirecting their attention. "Kinison was captured trying to enter the Citadel of Ethriel."

"No! Is he still alive?" Corin asked earnestly.

"Yes, but he's been held in the citadel for over a month."

"How did you come by this information?"

"One of my contacts in the city saw Kinison and sent word as soon as he could."

"Why the delay?"

"Noliono has forbidden travel from Ethriel until the war is over," Galanor said patiently. "It was not until a week ago that my friend had an opportunity to get word to me."

"Who is this informant?" Corin demanded.

Galanor hesitated.

"Galanor, I demand to know."

"His name is Ren Gables, Your Majesty," Galanor answered after a moment's consideration. "He is a lieutenant in the Guardians of the Citadel."

"Can we trust him?"

"Yes," Galanor answered simply.

R . S . GULLETT

"So, Kinison is in prison, and Ardyn's forces are nearing Elengil. Do we know their intentions?" Corin asked, his hands clenched into fists.

"Anson Thayn fought for Noliono from the beginning of the war," Galanor answered gravely. "It is likely his son will remain loyal to him."

"No," Riniel said softly.

Corin looked at her questioningly.

"He helped us escape Ethriel," she said almost pleadingly. "He could not side with Noliono."

"Sire, we cannot base our strategy on a hope that House Thayn will side with us," Lord Myr interrupted. "We must assume he is an enemy for the time being."

"The news you all bring is grievous indeed," Corin said, his face downcast. "It seems our plight becomes worse and worse."

There was silence as every person in that room waited for the king's decision—his decision. Minutes dragged on as Corin stared blankly at the map upon the table.

"I must now divulge a plan that Galanor and I put in place to draw at least a part of Noliono's army south," Corin said with some trepidation. The room was completely silent. "A month ago, I sent a messenger to the King of Eddynland, Wilhelm Sunderland, to ask for his aid."

"How can Eddynland help when they are so far to the south?" Lord Myr asked suspiciously.

"I have given King Wilhelm my leave to lay siege to Fairhaven," Corin said softly.

"Sire!" Lord Myr nearly shouted in protest.

"The House of Farod is allied with Noliono, is it not, Lord Myr?" Corin asked, his voice rising. "That means he is in rebellion, and therefore his lands are forfeit to the reigning King of Alethia. If Eddynland invades, Noliono will be forced to send aid or risk losing his most powerful ally, Lord Gaven Soron. If he does send aid, we can expect at least a third of his forces to be sent south. If he refuses, Lord Soron will forsake Noliono and march south, taking at least half of Noliono's army with him. In either case, this will benefit us."

"What of Eddynland?" Lord Myr said incredulously. "What if at the end of all this, they refuse to return Fairhaven?"

"King Wilhelm and I will negotiate the terms at a later time," Corin said bluntly.

"The House of Aranethon and the House of Sunderland were allies before the War of Ascension," Galanor said, stepping forward. "Even a rumor of an invasion of Farod will draw Lord Soron south, with or without Noliono. Eddynland shares no love for House Noland or Farod. They will remain loyal to King Corin, and their loyalty at a time like this is worth one city."

"When do you expect to hear from your messenger, sire?" Baron Astley asked in a placating tone.

"He arrived last night," Corin answered, causing a wave of shock and expectation to spread through the room.

"And what word did this messenger bring?" Baron Warde asked anxiously.

"Eddynland's army crossed the Waterdale River a week ago," Corin said with a small smile. "Even as we speak, King Wilhelm's forces surround Fairhaven. Word of this will reach Noliono and Gaven soon. Even still, we need a battle plan."

"Your Majesty," Baron Warde said with a bow. "I think I have an idea."

"If your ploy is successful," Baron Warde began. "Noliono's forces will be diminished, but our best hope is that they will be reduced by half. Even if our best hopes are realized, we will still be outnumbered."

"We know all this, Alaster," said Lord Myr irritably. "Get to the point."

"The only hope we have is to meet them on the plains before the city," Warde continued, unperturbed.

"Have you lost your mind?" interrupted Baron Astley.

"How can open plains give us any advantage over such a massive force?" Lord Myr demanded.

"Our forces will be arrayed in front of the city, with archers in the battlements above," Baron Warde said, pointing to the map before them. "The three nights before, the cavalry will leave the city in three separate groups under my banner. Noliono will assume I have deserted you and let them go. At dawn on the fourth day, when the battle lines are formed, the cavalry will attack their right flank."

"They will think the army of Eddynland is attacking them," Corin said, nodding his head in agreement.

"Or at the very least, we can turn their right flank and route them," Lord Myr added excitedly.

"I approve your plan, Baron Warde," Corin said, standing. "Prepare to leave at once."

Baron Warde bowed and left the room. Corin turned to Azka and ordered him to deliver word to Noliono that the battle will be met before the city in four days' time. Azka bowed and left the room.

When both men had left, Corin sat back down in his chair.

"Your Majesty," came the voice of Baron Astley. "If I may speak to you."

"You may," Corin said, motioning for the others to leave.

"Please, sire," Astley interjected. "What I have to say affects all of us."

"Very well," he said with a nod.

"Sire, I feel I would be negligent not to mention that this plan for Baron Warde to feign like he is deserting you may in fact be Warde's true intention."

Corin looked at Galanor, shocked by this sudden realization. The older man's face was expressionless, yet Corin saw the anxiety in his eyes. He turned back to Baron Astley.

"Do you have any evidence to support this accusation?"

"Nothing substantial, sire," Astley admitted. "Yet, as I said, I would be negligent not to say anything."

"Explain," Corin demanded with some frustration in his voice.

"He has appeared of late anxious to return to Ytemest," Astley answered. "Though I understand the desire to return home, I do not speak of it as often as he."

Corin was silent for a few moments. If he trusted Warde with his cavalry and he deserted, there was no hope for victory. Yet he could not hope to win this battle without using Warde's plan.

"I will lead the cavalry," he said abruptly.

Lord Myr and Baron Astley looked at him in amazement.

"But sire, you are..." Baron Astley began, but he trailed off without finishing.

"I realize that," Corin said, knowing the others' thoughts. "I can still ride, and Captain Jon Grehm was appointed over the cavalry. He comes highly recommended by Galanor and Kinison. He can make up for any lack of experience on my part."

"Sire, this plan will only succeed if Noliono believes Baron Warde has deserted you." Astley interjected.

"I will ride out under Warde's banner and head northeast. On the second night, we will turn south and make for the town of Rein. There we will wait for word."

"And who shall speak for you in your absence?" Lord Myr asked expectantly.

Corin thought for a moment then turned to Riniel.

"Princess Riniel will speak for me," he said with a smile.

32

RINIEL

Did she hear him right? Did the king just say that she, Riniel, would speak for him in his absence?

"You heard me correctly, Lord Myr," the king continued after everyone in the room looked bewildered at him. "I have come to trust Riniel, and therefore I reinstate her title of Princess of Alethia, and she will serve as my regent. If there is nothing more, you all have work to do."

There was a finality to the king's last words that all those in the room took to heart. They did not speak but began filing out in complete silence. Riniel, still stunned by the king's decision, moved to join the others.

"Riniel, please remain," said the king.

Riniel turned back and stood before the king as everyone else walked past and exited the room. When the door closed and they were alone, the king stood and moved toward her.

"I know my decision to make you regent must come as a shock," the king began without making eye contact. If Riniel had not been so wrapped up in her own feelings of anxiety and amazement, she would have realized that the king was anxious as well. "I know I was harsh with you when we first met, but the past two months have shown me your loyalty, and I have come to enjoy your company."

"Thank you, Your Highness," Riniel said, not knowing what else to say.

"As I have said before, please call me Corin," the king said with a smile.

She smiled and nodded.

"I have come to trust you, Riniel, and I..." He paused. Riniel glanced at him again and saw his cheeks redden. She grinned at him.

"I really enjoyed your company, Riniel," he said awkwardly. "I'm sorry for any pain I've caused you, and I hope you can someday forgive me."

Riniel hesitated but nodded.

"I don't know how to do this, but..."

Riniel's heart began to beat fast as she watched Corin kneel down with a great effort. She started forward to help him, but he held her back.

"Riniel Aurelia," he said, pulling a beautiful ring from his pocket and holding it up. "I know we have not known each other for very long and that we still have much to work out between us, but I have come to love you. I do not understand what that means, but I know that I do love you. I also have come to love this kingdom and its people, as I know you do also. I ask for myself and for the good of the kingdom..." He paused as if struggling to speak the next words Riniel knew he was building toward.

She felt faint and gripped the chair next to her. Could this be happening? Was he really about to ask for her hand? What would she say?

"Will you marry me and become queen of Alethia?"

✳   ✳   ✳   ✳

Riniel left the king's chambers in complete shock. Had she really just been asked to become King Corin's bride, and what's more, had she also just been made Regent of Alethia? This was all too much for Riniel to handle. She could not believe it. A month ago this man had stripped her of all her titles and lands, embarrassed her in front of a hundred people, and now he was declaring his love for her and asking her to become regent in his absence. How could he trust her so soon? How could he love her so soon? Could she forgive him for what he'd done?

Riniel had made it halfway down the corridor when she stopped, feeling her head starting to spin. She reached out with her right arm quickly to brace herself on the cold stone wall. She knew that Corin had feelings for her, and truth be told, she had feelings for him, but marriage! She didn't know if she was ready for that. Corin had asked her to make a decision soon, but Riniel was riddled with uncertainty. She walked down the rest of the corridor, turned the corner rather quickly, and ran into something solid.

"Pardon me," she began but stopped as she recognized the tall middle-aged man standing before her. "Sir Jordan!" she exclaimed, embracing her former guardian.

"Just Jordan, my lady," the man said, smiling and chuckling.

"Well then, call me Riniel," she said, releasing him and laughing.

"As you wish," he answered with more chuckling.

"I haven't seen you in weeks."

"My unit was sent to scout out the enemy's movements to the north. I only just got back," Jordan said with a sigh. "How have you been?"

"I, um..." Riniel stammered. "I was just made regent."

There was a long silence.

"Why would King Corin make you regent?"

"That's not all, Jordan," Riniel said quickly. "He also restored my title and...proposed."

"He did?" Jordan said after a long silence. Riniel saw a twinkle in his eye and turned away. "And what was your answer?"

"I didn't," Riniel said, turning and pacing up and down the corridor. "He asked so suddenly and I...I just don't know."

Jordan continued to smile at Riniel, which only increased her feelings of embarrassment. "Stop looking at me like that!" she said, frowning. Then changing the subject, she said, "You were scouting to the north right?"

"Yes, why?"

"Follow me," she said, leading him down the corridor and into a vacant room. They closed the door and sat down in some nearby chairs facing each other.

"What news of Ardyn?" she asked in a whisper. "I heard he approaches from the north with men ready for battle?"

Jordan hesitated, looking hard at Riniel as if deciding what to tell her.

"Please, Jordan," she said earnestly.

"Yes, my Princess. It is true," Jordan answered, inclining his head momentarily.

"Do you know whom Ardyn will support?"

"The House of Thayn, as you know, supported Noliono at the start of this war," Jordan answered with a long pause.

Riniel nodded eagerly.

"I believe Ardyn remains loyal to Noliono," he answered finally.

"Why would he support Noliono?" Riniel nearly shouted, standing and pacing. "Why would he be loyal to Noliono after all that man has done?"

"I don't know," Jordan replied, shaking his head.

"Jordan," Riniel said, choosing her words carefully as a plan formed in her mind. "I need a favor."

"You have but to ask, Princess," Jordan said, inclining his head once again.

"I need you to find Ardyn's camp. Find it and confront Ardyn regarding his loyalty. And if possible, ask him about my father's murder. He told me whom he believed murdered my father."

Jordan hesitated then nodded. "I will leave at once."

"And Jordan," Riniel said as he moved toward the door. "If he is still loyal to Noliono?"

"I will take care of it," Jordan answered gravely. He bowed and left.

After Jordan left, Riniel sat in the empty room in silence. Her mind wandered back to her father, and her eyes filled with angry tears. For months now, she'd been seeking to uncover her father's killer to no avail. Her only source was Ardyn Thayn, a young man who'd betrayed her, saved her life, and was now threatening her king, the man who'd asked for her hand. Riniel shook her head, stood up, and left the room.

※　　※　　※　　※

Riniel had wandered about the castle of Elengil all afternoon. She had to make a decision regarding the king's proposal, but she was still so conflicted. So much had happened in such a small amount of time. To make matters worse, she had just ordered one of her most trusted friends to confront and even assassinate Ardyn Thayn, a young man she'd once trusted and about whom she cared a great deal

As if coming out of a haze, Riniel realized her walk had brought her to the Great Hall. Taking it as a sign, she proceeded to the main doors, and the guards ushered her inside. She saw Corin sitting on his throne surrounded by his advisors. Corin spotted her at once and motioned her forward.

"Princess Riniel," Corin said with a smile when she'd reached the foot of the dais. "I had just sent a messenger to summon you here so that we can finalize plans. Galanor believes the army under Ardyn Thayn will support Noliono."

Riniel's heart fell at these words. She shook her head in disbelief.

"I know how you feel, but we must prepare for battle," the king said with a grim look. Then turning to his advisors, he said, "My lords, you know what must be done. I must now discuss preparations for the city's defenses with Princess Riniel."

The others bowed and dispersed to carry out their roles in the upcoming battle. It was a moment before Riniel realized she and the king had been left alone again. She looked up at Corin, who smiled and motioned her to join him on the dais.

"I know my proposal caught you off guard," Corin began softly.

Riniel smiled weakly. Being caught off guard was an understatement.

"I was hoping you might feel the same way about me as I feel about you," Corin continued. His face was flushed, which made Riniel feel compassion for him. "Given all that has happened, including the betrayal by my former friend Ardyn Thayn, I felt the need to ensure that I would not lose you as well. I have truly come to love you, Riniel, though I admit that I am still coming to know what that means."

At the mention of Ardyn's name, Riniel felt a vindictive anger burn inside her. She suddenly wanted to hurt Ardyn in the cruelest way possible. She then found herself saying something that surprised herself as much as it surprised Corin.

"I will," she said suddenly.

"You will what?" Corin asked, confused.

"I will marry you," she said.

33

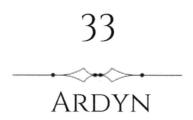

ARDYN

Ardyn was seated in his tent, reading a report from one of his scouts. Honestly, had it not been for the advice of Sir Simon Moore, he would not have even thought of using scouts. He shook his head, realizing for the hundredth time how inexperienced he was in warfare and leadership in general. Before this war, Ardyn's father had two other sons, Ardyn's older brothers, on whom he could depend to govern and lead Stonewall and House Thayn. Now it had fallen to Ardyn, the last surviving member of his house, save his uncle Kelhem Thayn. After the capture of Zul Voss and his followers, Ardyn had freed his uncle and left him to govern Stonewall in his absence. Ardyn had ridden out at once for Elengil with as many men as could ride. He was now only two days' ride from the city, and with every mile closer, Ardyn became more uneasy.

His mind drifted as he read over the scout's report of the conversation he'd had with Galanor before riding from Stonewall.

"Ardyn, you must believe me," Galanor had said earnestly.

"It is simply not possible, Galanor," Ardyn had retorted. "Noliono would not have killed my family only to save me."

"It is all a part of his scheme," Galanor had insisted. "Noliono seeks to destroy all but those loyal to him alone. You told me yourself that Noliono blackmailed your father into helping him by holding you captive. Or have you forgotten?"

At that, Ardyn had become angry.

"I could never forget the dark cells under the citadel. Not if I spent a hundred years in the light of the summer sun!" Ardyn had shouted.

"Then how can you believe Noliono's lie that Corin, your best friend, killed your father and brothers?"

"My best friend!" Ardyn had retorted angrily. "Best friends do not betray each other!"

"How has Corin betrayed you, Ardyn?" Galanor had said with a heavy sigh.

"Enough!" Ardyn had said, his face becoming red. "I have made my decision, Galanor. I have seven hundred men ready to ride at dawn."

At that, Ardyn had excused himself and left. He would never admit to anyone his true hatred for Corin stemmed from his unreturned love of Riniel and his jealousy of Corin's engagement to her.

He shook his head, completely absorbed in his own thoughts.

At that moment, the door of the tent opened, and a man in a dark cloak entered.

"Declare yourself," Ardyn said, standing and placing his hand on the hilt of his sword.

"We have spoken many times, yet you still do not know me?" the man said, taking off his hood.

Ardyn recognized the man at once. The long brown hair to his shoulders, short brown beard, and kind brown eyes were apparent to Ardyn as the features of the mysterious visitor who was constantly inserting himself into Ardyn's life.

"I do know you," Ardyn said in astonishment.

"And you have nothing to fear from me," the man said, coming and sitting down across from Ardyn.

"Why are you here?" Ardyn asked, his voice shaking in surprise.

"I am always with you, Ardyn," the man said simply. "But I appear to you now in order to dissuade you from the course you have chosen."

"What course is that?" Ardyn asked, sitting down without shifting his gaze.

"You believe that Corin and Riniel have betrayed you," the man said, his eyes looking intently at Ardyn.

The power and wisdom in those eyes was overwhelming, and Ardyn looked away, unable to bear the man's gaze.

"I do," Ardyn mumbled. He was suddenly overwhelmed with feelings of guilt and shame for his actions.

"Why do you believe this?"

Ardyn was silent for a few moments. He felt like a child being asked to explain his misbehavior. He resented being made to feel this way but felt compelled to answer.

"I helped Riniel escape from the citadel, and I was a friend to Corin when he had no friends," Ardyn answered quietly.

"Ah, but did you not also betray her trust and help Noliono imprison Riniel in the first place. And Corin was a true friend to you when you also lacked friends."

Ardyn put his face in his hands and shook his head. "I loved her," he finally admitted. "But she left me to die. Corin killed my father, my brothers, my whole family."

"Ardyn," the man said, his voice gentle but firm. "The man who told you these things you know to be a liar. Does your memory fail you?"

"What must I do?" Ardyn asked softly and without looking up.

"You must turn away from this jealousy," the man replied, his voice softening. "You must forgive those you believe to have hurt you and let go."

"But how..." Ardyn began, looking up. He stopped short as he realized he was alone. The man had gone.

Ardyn stood up and ran out the door of the tent. The bright morning sun blinded him momentarily. When his eyes had adjusted, he forgot about the strange visitor as his gaze fell upon a slew of men approaching. They were led by Sir Simon Moore, and they brought with them a man bound in chains. It took a moment, but Ardyn recognized the man as Jordan Reese, Riniel's personal bodyguard.

"My lord," said Sir Simon with a bow. "Our scouts caught this man riding toward our camp from the south. He bares the crest of a rose, but none of us knew the house it represents."

"The crest is known to me," Ardyn said in an undertone as he and Jordan stared at one another.

"He claims that Riniel Aurelia sent him to speak to you."

"Take him to my tent, Sir Simon," Ardyn said with a look of interest. "I would speak to him there."

※　※　※　※

When Jordan had been brought into Ardyn's tent and bound to a chair, Ardyn dismissed Sir Simon and the guards and sat down opposite his prisoner. Jordan looked at him, a hint of anger in his eyes.

"So," Ardyn said, breaking the silence. "Why have you come, Jordan?"

"I was sent by Princess Riniel to deliver a message to you, Ardyn," Jordan replied in almost a growl. "She is concerned about you and was very happy to know you are still alive after everything that happened."

"I thought I was dead," Ardyn said, looking away.

"We all did," Jordan said gravely. "I saw your wound and believed it to be a mortal one. If I had known..." He trailed off.

Ardyn looked at Jordan and realized he was being sincere. The anger and betrayal he'd felt toward Jordan vanished suddenly. "I forgive you, Jordan," he found himself saying.

"Thank you, Ardyn," Jordan said with a slight inclination of his head. "When we heard you were still alive, Riniel and I both wondered how you survived."

"I woke up weeks later in the citadel," Ardyn said, looking away again as if reliving the past events. "Noliono had me nursed back to health and informed me that my family had been murdered by Corin."

"That's a lie, Ardyn!" Jordan nearly shouted.

Ardyn eyed him suspiciously and then asked, "Why should I believe you?"

"Why did you decide to help Riniel after turning her over to Noliono?" Jordan asked with a knowing look.

"I felt guilty for betraying her," Ardyn said, turning away again to hide his embarrassment.

"Think about it, Ardyn!" Jordan said earnestly. "You betrayed Noliono. Why would he just overlook that and then save your life?"

"To use me..." Ardyn whispered after a moment's pause. The realization for Noliono's kindness toward him hit him hard in the face.

"Corin was nowhere near Abenhall when your family was killed, nor did he have the strategic resources to order any sort of attempt on your family's lives. It is all a lie."

"I am such a fool!" Ardyn said, bowing his head and placing his face in his hands. He was overwhelmed with feelings of disgust regarding his own stupidity. "It must have been Noliono who killed them."

"We all make mistakes, Ardyn," Jordan said reassuringly. "But you are only a fool if you fail to learn from them."

Ardyn looked up at Jordan then nodded. He stood, walked over to Jordan, and unbound him.

"Thanks," Jordan said, rubbing his wrists.

Ardyn nodded and clapped his hands. At once Sir Simon and several guards entered, looking surprised that Jordan was standing and free of his restraints.

"Sir Simon, please remain. The rest of you, stand guard at the door."

The others bowed and left. Sir Simon looked at Ardyn inquiringly.

"Sir Simon, this is Jordan Reese, a former member of the Guardians."

Sir Simon inclined his head but eyed the man suspiciously.

"He had brought word of Noliono's duplicity," Ardyn continued. "It seems Noliono lied to me about Corin murdering my family."

"Forgive me, my lord, but how can you trust him?" Sir Simon asked, still eying Jordan.

"He and I knew each other when we were both members of the Guardians of the Citadel. He was the personal bodyguard to Riniel Aurelia, which more than vouches for his character."

Sir Simon paused for a moment then nodded his assent.

"Good," Ardyn said with a smile. "Now, we have some planning to do."

"Planning, my lord?"

"If we are to help defeat Noliono, we will need a plan, Sir Simon," Ardyn said with a cunning smile.

34

NOLIONO

Noliono was riding south with over a dozen members of the Guardians. His eyes were narrow and his jaw set in frustration. He'd been summoned to the ruined Fortress of Deadwood to meet with Methangoth. He was irritated at the summons. He was King of Alethia, after all. It should be Methangoth riding to meet with him.

He was also frustrated at the timing. Here he was about to deal the final blow upon his enemy and put an end to this pointless rebellion, and he was being summoned away from his army to meet with some sorcerer. Noliono sighed heavily as they approached the gatehouse of the ruined fortress.

It was dusk as they dismounted. The crumbling towers loomed menacingly over their heads. Made of dark stone mined from the nearby Iron Hills, the Deadwood Fortress was originally built to guard the road between Abenhall and Elengil over four hundred years ago by King Henry II. It also served as the political prison for King Kelbrandt Aurelia, following the War of Ascension. The fortress's menacing exterior meant to strike fear in all those interned there.

The fortress was dark, save for a single light coming from the least decrepit-looking tower.

"Sire," one of the men closest to him said. "You cannot go in there alone."

"Enough," Noliono said as the other men murmured their assent. "I must go alone. Wait here."

Noliono left his disgruntled men and entered the fortress. He carefully made his way up multiple dark staircases to the lit room above. Upon reaching the landing outside the door, Noliono paused for a moment, swallowed hard, and knocked.

"Enter," came a deep, commanding voice from beyond the door.

Noliono entered the room and closed the door behind him. The room was lit only by the large fire in the hearth. Ancient tomes filled the dusty shelves that ran along the perimeter of three-quarters of the room. A large window dominated the far wall, with a large desk sitting before it, littered with more books and parchments. In the corner nearest the door, a small table sat with two chairs sitting opposite each other. On the table sat a chessboard. Noliono stared at it for a moment, noting the placement of the pieces. It appeared to be nearing the end, with the black player having the advantage. The white player seemed to have a pawn in a promotion position, but few other options.

Noliono's gaze shifted to the hearth where a man stood, shrouded in black robes, silhouetted against the flames.

"You are late," the man said with a growl.

"Your summons came only a day ago, Methangoth," Noliono replied, the frustration and irritation replaced by trepidation and growing fear. Noliono had to admit the man was very intimidating. "I came as soon as I was able."

"I assume you've heard the news from the south?"

"What news?"

The man turned, and Noliono beheld his face. Methangoth's black eyes flashed in the firelight. Noliono could not long hold the other's gaze.

"You have been king for less than three months, and your kingdom is on the verge of collapse."

Noliono remained silent, though a surge of indignation rose within him.

"Your focus on the rebels in Elengil has blinded you to the danger from the south."

"Speak your news then," Noliono said, his voice shaking slightly.

The man made a low growl then moved to the desk and picked up a piece of parchment.

"This," the man said, brandishing the parchment. "This is a report from one of my informants in Fairhaven! It states that the King of Eddynland has crossed the River Waterdale and laid siege to the city!"

Noliono looked at the sorcerer blankly.

"You knew?" Methangoth asked, his eyes flashing.

"I received the same report before I left Elengil," Noliono said calmly.

"And Lord Soron?"

"He does not know yet," Noliono admitted. "And the longer I stand here, the greater the chance he will learn of the news."

Methangoth growled, striding back over to stare into the fire. There was a long moment before either man spoke.

"What is your plan, Noliono?" Methangoth asked, clearly trying to contain his frustration. "Lord Soron will undoubtedly move his army south when he learns of this, and Alethia will be at war with Eddynland instead of Nordyke. You will also be unable to crush the young usurper without Soron's forces."

"I still have a piece yet to be played," Noliono said confidently. "I have sent to Ethriel for Kinison Ravenloch."

"The former Lord Commander of the Guardians?" Methangoth asked skeptically. "What value could he have to sway the young king?"

Noliono's face contorted at Methangoth's use of the title of "king" to describe Corin Stone, but he resisted the urge to correct him.

"Kinison and Corin are friends, as is his betrothed, Riniel Aurelia," Noliono said with a small smirk. "I will call for a parley and demand Corin surrender in exchange for his friend."

"He will refuse."

"Of course he will, but his betrothed will undoubtedly insist he be rescued. I will then remind him that I also have in my custody Azka's sister, Aylen. With these two bargaining chips, I will insist he surrender himself to me in exchange for my captives, and I will offer a full pardon to everyone who followed him. When the noble-minded boy opens the gates, I will have a group of soldiers ready to infiltrate the gatehouse while the rest of my army storms the city."

"A nice plan," Methangoth admitted, though he continued to glare at Noliono. "You'd better pray it works."

"Understood," Noliono said gruffly and turned to go.

"Remember, Noliono," Methangoth called just as Noliono's hand touched the door. "Should you fail, you will lose more than just the kingdom."

Noliono did not answer but opened and closed the door, descended the stairs, and walked quickly from the tower as fast as he dared. When he reached his men, he did not speak. He simply mounted his horse and rode off north at breakneck speed. His men quickly followed in his wake.

✳ ✳ ✳ ✳

When Noliono arrived back at the camp, he found Ramond Kludge waiting for him just outside his tent entrance.

"Sire," Kludge said with a bow.

"What is it, Kludge?" Noliono asked irritably as he dismounted.

"Perhaps it would be best to talk in private, Your Majesty," Kludge said, looking about at the men with Noliono.

"Perhaps," Noliono said, walking past him and into the tent. Kludge followed in his wake.

When they were inside, Noliono walked over and sat down at his desk. "What news, Kludge?"

"Lord Soron knows, Highness."

"You're sure?" Noliono asked, anxiety clear in his voice.

"Yes, sire. He requested an immediate audience, and his forces are already breaking camp as we speak."

"Send for him," Noliono said, waving Kludge away.

No sooner had Kludge exited the tent than Lord Gaven Soron entered, looking extremely bothered.

"Highness," he said without even the slightest inclination of his head.

Noliono ignored Gaven's lack of decorum.

"You've heard then?" Gaven asked, looking at the map on Noliono's desk.

"I have," Noliono said shortly.

"And?" Gaven said, turning to Noliono. He was breathing hard, clearly struggling to contain his anger. "How can you be concerned with this boy when a foreign invader marches openly through our lands!"

"Lord Soron," Noliono said calmly. "*We* will deal with the invasion, but we must first end this rebellion. Only a united Alethia can hope to defend itself against a foreign enemy."

"The boy is contained in Elengil!" Gaven nearly shouted. "My lands are under siege by an army from Eddynland numbering in the thousands."

My spies indicate King Wilhelm will not move past Fairhaven," Noliono retorted, his irritation with Gaven beginning to show.

"So Fairhaven is expendable?"

"Lord Soron!" Noliono said, rising from his seat. "Whatever the King of Eddyland does to our lands will be repaid tenfold once this rebellion has ended."

"My forces are breaking camp and *will* march south within the hour."

Noliono and Gaven glared at one another across the desk for a moment when Ramond Kludge returned, gasping for breath.

"Sire!" Kludge gasped. "Hundreds of riders...leaving through the north gate...banner of House Warde...most already through our siege lines...not attacking!"

"House Warde is abandoning the boy?" Noliono asked skeptically.

"It would seem so," Kludge said, still breathing hard.

Wanting to see this with their own eyes, Noliono and Gaven rushed outside. They saw as the last of the riders crossed the siege lines, the banner of House Warde clearly visible, even from a distance. Noliono considered this for a moment then turned to Gaven.

"In light of this, Lord Soron, you have my leave to march south and defend Alethia from its enemies. Once the rebellion has been crushed, I will march south to aid you against Eddynland."

Gaven Soron bowed and left without a word.

*　*　*　*

An hour later, Noliono was again seated at his desk, studying the latest reports from his informants. The door of the tent opened, and Ramond Kludge entered, followed by Azka.

"Azka," Noliono said, a smile spreading across his face. "To what do I owe the pleasure?"

"I bring word from King Corin," Azka said in his deep, impassive voice.

"Speak then."

"The king has chosen a battlefield," Azka said calmly. "He will meet you on the plains below the city at dawn two days from now."

"So be it," Noliono said, his jovial attitude intended to unnerve Azka, who turned to depart. "Azka," Noliono called after him. "My offer still stands. Your sister's life for the boy's."

Noliono watched as Azka paused for a moment to turn back

and glare at him, then Azka left. Noliono sat back in his chair and placed his fingers together on his chest. "So it begins," he whispered to himself.

"And so it will end," said a voice from the corner of the room.

"Who's there?" Noliono said, standing and placing his hand on his sword.

"You know my voice, Noliono Noland, though you often choose to ignore me," the voice said.

"Come into the light, that I might see you," Noliono said, his heart pumping rapidly.

A man wrapped in a dark traveling cloak emerged from the shadows. The man had long brown hair to his shoulders and a short brown beard. Noliono gazed at the man's face, which seemed to glow slightly, even in the dim light of the lamps.

"You!" Noliono said, his face contorting with rage. "I thought I told you never to visit me again!"

"I have come to give you one last warning, Noliono," the stranger said calmly. "This is your last chance. If you continue down this path, only destruction will you reap."

"I am done with your riddles!" Noliono shouted. "Be gone from me!"

The man looked at Noliono with pity and sorrow. Noliono was about to shout at him again when the man disappeared. Noliono stared at the place where the man had been for a moment then turned away.

"Nothing will stand in my way," Noliono whispered to himself. "Nothing!"

35

KINISON

The noonday sun found Kinison Ravenloch astride a horse, riding westward toward Elengil. His hands were bound, and the reins of his horse were in the grip of his captors. Thirty members of the Guardians were escorting five prisoners, including himself, to Elengil. For what purpose, Kinison did not know. He suspected that he and his fellow prisoners would be used as bargaining chips. The Forest of Roston rose up on their right, cutting across their path in the distance. The River Rockwicke flowed southwest through the forest until it converged with the River Ryparian near the southern end of the Forest of Roston. There the river rushed both deep and wide toward the southwest until it flowed into the Deadwood Marshes far to the southwest near the Iron Hills.

They were now two days out from Ethriel, and Kinison sat astride his horse pondering all that he'd witnessed in the past two days. The streets of Ethriel had been deserted as they'd left the city. Businesses and homes were dark, and the whole city had an abandoned feel about it—the legacy of Noliono, no doubt. The lands about the city were no better. Many inns and farms were also abandoned as their owners sought refuge from the war elsewhere.

The Dancing Lion Inn, where Kinison had first met Galanor and Sam Brandyman, was now a smoldering ruin. Kinison had gazed sadly at the once proud inn as he and the others had ridden past.

Sir Ren Gables had avoided Kinison the entire journey, though Kinison had caught site of his former friend several times from a distance. He often would stare angrily at Ren when he appeared for lack of anything else to do during the monotonous journey.

After the long day's ride, Kinison and the other prisoners were thrown to the ground and their feet bound. Sir Ren personally bound Kinison's feet, making eye contact only once. Kinison saw pain in Ren's eyes but also a resolve to obey his king. Eventually food was brought to them in the form of broth. Kinison didn't bother with a spoon but drank it straight from the bowl. When he'd finished, his attention was drawn to his left where two guards were conversing nearby about their journey.

"Thought we were safe guarding the citadel, but now the king makes us ride with prisoners to Elengil, and at the end of September, no less," one of the guards complained.

"You mean the middle of October," corrected the second guard. "You lost count as you always do. It's the fourteenth of October."

"The fourteenth?" Kinison whispered to himself. He could hardly believe it. His birthday had come and gone, and he hadn't even realized it. He was thirty years old. Kinison shook his head as the realization of reaching his thirtieth birthday hit him. Thirty years old, and what did he have to show for it. He'd lost his career, his wife, his freedom, and his faith. He laid his face in his hands. How had it come to this?

"Oh, Sarah," Kinison whispered sorrowfully. "I'm so sorry I failed you. It *was* all my fault. It was never God's fault, it was mine. My decisions and my consequences."

It was then that Kinison remembered the vision, or whatever it was, where the visitor had told him, "A chance will come for you to escape, and your friend's life will be in your hands. You must spare him and help him escape."

Kinison shot a glance at Ren, who was several dozen feet away talking to one of the other Guardians. How could he spare Ren's life after all he'd done?

Suddenly to his left, two cries came from the guards who'd been standing there talking. Kinison turned and saw them lying on the ground with arrows in their chests. More cries erupted from all around him as more Guardians fell, pierced with arrows from unseen archers. The camp was in uproar as the remaining Guardians attempted to find the direction from which the arrows were originating. The company had left Ethriel with over thirty Guardians; now only half of them remained.

"Surrender or die," came a voice from the night. "Throw down your weapons, and you will not be harmed."

Kinison was surprised at how quickly his captors surrendered. The sound of clattering steel echoed all across the camp. Kinison watched as dark figures emerged from the underbrush all around them, moving into the light of the fires. There were at least a dozen men, all armed with bows and short swords. The one closest to Kinison came over to the prisoners. Kinison recognized the man at once because of the red hat with a long red feather sticking out of it.

"Silas Morgan!" Kinison nearly shouted.

"Kinison Ravenloch, Lord Commander of the Guardians." Silas roared with laughter. "My, how the mighty have fallen. It's been a long time since Stonewall. How's that young lad, Corin, I think his name was?"

Kinison glared at Silas.

"I see you and the new king don't get along," Silas said, continuing to leer at Kinison.

"We have our differences," Kinison said through gritted teeth.

"Enough to get you dishonored and imprisoned, I heard," Silas said with a snide grin on his face. "I don't suppose you'd care to join my humble band of raiders?"

Kinison glared at the man.

"I thought as much. Still you should know that I bear you no ill will," Silas said then turned to one of the raiders next to him. "You, untie the prisoners. Then tie up the remaining Guardians."

Kinison's bonds were quickly cut, and Silas leered at Kinison as he stood rubbing his sore wrists. The other prisoners were also freed, and yells of glee filled the camp. As he stood there, Kinison watched as Silas's men bound the remaining Guardians and dragged them into a group to Kinison's right. He looked over to see Ren Gables thrown into the group of Guardians. Ren met Kinison's gaze, and for some unknown reason, Kinison's hatred and fury melted away.

"You!" Silas shouted, pointing at Ren. "Bring him here!"

One of Silas's raiders brought Ren over to them and threw him down on the ground at Kinison's feet. Ren gazed up at him in fear.

"A gift," Silas said to Kinison.

Kinison looked away from Ren and turned to Silas. "What do you mean?"

"Isn't it obvious?" Silas asked with a ringing laugh. "This man was one of your lieutenants, right? Well, I assume he betrayed you. Otherwise he'd be a prisoner too." Kinison looked from Silas to Ren and back again.

"Here," Silas said, throwing a dagger to Kinison.

Kinison caught it and looked from the dagger to Ren.

"Do it," Kinison heard Silas say as a shadow of terror fell on Ren's face.

Kinison was silent for a moment as he considered all that had happened over the past three months. Ren Gables, his most trusted friend and lieutenant, had betrayed him and aided in sentencing him to exile. He'd supported the tyrant Noliono, captured Kinison, and imprisoned him. Worst of all, Ren had stopped him from saving Sarah. As this last thought crossed Kinison's mind, his brow furrowed, and his eyes narrowed. His anger built to a crescendo, and for a moment Kinison truly wanted to kill Ren for all the pain he'd caused.

Then, as quickly as the anger had come, it faded and was gone. Kinison stared down at the terror-stricken face of his friend, and pity filled his heart. He realized that Ren Gables was not an evil man but a man who'd been forced to do all these things because Noliono had held Ren's family hostage. Kinison sighed and let the knife fall from his hand.

"I knew you didn't have it in you!" Silas exclaimed, to a roar of laughter from his raiders. "You noble-minded fools are too weak. No sense of vengeance."

Kinison turned to look at Silas and considered his options.

"I suppose I should kill you both. Make quick work of you and move on," Silas said with a knowing grin.

"How many men do you have, Silas?" Kinison asked, a sudden idea coming to him.

"Why do you want to know?"

"We both hate Noliono. If we work together, we can help King Corin defeat him."

"Help you!" Silas laughed, joined again by his raiders. "Why would I want to help one king of Alethia defeat another? While you fight among yourselves, my men and I will collect the spoils."

"For how long?" Kinison asked ominously, and he was pleased to see Silas's grin falter. "Noliono will defeat King Corin without aid, then Noliono will come for you and your men. You will lose everything."

Silas considered this for a moment, pulling on his goatee.

"What can I expect in return from King Corin?"

"I will get you and your men a full pardon and possibly lands in the south."

"A pardon and lands?" Silas asked, and Kinison saw that he was intrigued.

Kinison looked briefly down at Ren, who looked anxiously back at him.

"Come with me to Elengil," Kinison said, looking back at Silas. "Come help us defeat Noliono."

After a long pause, Silas nodded his agreement and held out his hand. Kinison took it.

"We have an agreement," he said with a dark look. "See that your king remembers it afterward."

"What of the Guardians?" Kinison asked, motioning toward the prisoners close by.

"What would you suggest?" Silas asked slyly.

"Free them and let them choose," Kinison answered with a glance at Ren.

"Are you certain?" Silas asked disbelievingly, but Kinison merely nodded. Silas sighed and then turned to his men. "Very well, release the prisoners, and prepare to move out."

Ren's bonds were cut, and he stood up, rubbing his hands. Kinison walked over to him, but Ren would not look up.

"I am sorry, Kinison," he said finally.

Kinison didn't know what to say, so he simply stood quietly for a moment.

"I owe you my life," Ren said at length, finally looking up at Kinison. "And I will repay that debt. I swear it."

Ren held out his hand, and Kinison took it. Despite all that had happened, Kinison was overcome with a sense of satisfaction and contentment. He realized that somehow, he'd forgiven his friend.

"I forgive you, Ren," Kinison said, smiling. "Will you come with me to Elengil?"

"Across the western sea and back if you ask it of me," Ren said with a small smile.

"For Alethia," Kinison said, turning to the west and walking toward the horses. He'd dealt with his friend's betrayal. Now it was time to deal with Noliono's.

36

CORIN

Corin watched the last light of the setting sun fade behind the western horizon as he sat on the ground before the fire. As he sat anxiously awaiting Baron Warde's report on the enemy's movements, he reflected on the past few days' events and on the plan to defeat Noliono. They had ridden out four days ago from Elengil under Baron Warde's banner, over seven hundred men. As they had neared the enemy lines, Corin had expected a battle, but Noliono's forces were taken completely by surprise. They simply stared as Corin, Warde, and all his men rode past without a word.

They continued riding northeast for several hours. Then as the sun began to set, they stopped and made camp near the Forest Roston. The following day brought a heavy rain, which hindered their progress as they rode south. They were supposed to reach the point where the River Rockwicke emerged from the Forest of Roston by the second day, but the sun set on Corin's forces miles away from their goal.

The following day brought more rain and more delays. Corin began to fear the plan would fail and his forces in Elengil would be overrun. Now three days out and they were still struggling to reach their original goal. He stared into the flames, pondering what to do. In the morning, his forces within Elengil would march out to meet Noliono's army in battle. Without their aid, the city would be overrun, and there would be no one to stand against Noliono's tyranny.

Corin looked up as Jon Grehm and Baron Warde walked up out of the twilight.

"Your Highness," they both said with a bow.

"Join me, gentlemen," Corin said, gesturing to the area across from him. "What word from Elengil?"

"No word, sire," Warde replied gravely. "I've sent two scouting parties northwest to track enemy movements. It seems Noliono has chosen not to track us."

"The rain delayed us long enough for any of Noliono's scouts to find us and report back," Jon added. "The fact that our scouts report nothing out of the ordinary suggests that Noliono has decided to let us go for now."

"Which means our plan may still work?" Corin asked with more surprise than he meant to reveal.

"It would seem so, Highness," Warde said with a small smile. "It will all become clearer tomorrow. If our raid disrupts the enemy's attack on our main force, then we have a chance."

They sat in silence for a few minutes, then Warde stood up.

"I beg your leave, sire," he said quickly. "I have preparations to make for the morning."

Corin nodded and watched Warde as he walked away into the gloom. When he was a sufficient distance away, Corin turned to Jon.

"Tell me the truth, Jon," Corin whispered quickly. "What is our situation?"

"I noticed two of Noliono's scouts following us from a distance both yesterday and today," Jon replied gravely.

Corin sighed heavily. "I suppose a more important question is why Warde is lying to me."

"Most of the men here are retainers of House Warde," Jon said a bit anxiously. "If they were forced to choose between you and Warde..."

"Let us hope it does not come to that, Jon," Corin said, shaking his head and dismissing the terrible idea. He gazed out into the encircling darkness.

"Has there been any word from the King of Eddynland?" Jon asked, breaking the silence.

"None," replied Corin. "Though the army under Gaven Soron is not large enough to defeat King Wilhelm, the battle will not be easily won either."

"Even should Eddynland prevail, can you really trust its king?"

"Galanor seems to think so," Corin replied, trying to sound more certain than he truly felt.

It seemed good enough for Jon, for he let the matter rest. They remained in silence for an hour or so. Corin continued to stare into the fire until Warde came running up out of the darkness.

"Sire," he said, puffing heavily. "The rain has ceased, and the way is clear. I recommend a night march across the plains."

"A night march?" Jon asked skeptically.

"We can reach Elengil in the morning before the sun rises."

"If we move in the dark, won't some of our men become lost or left behind?" Corin asked pointedly.

"A chance we must take, Highness," Warde answered urgently. "We have no choice if we hope to reach Elengil in time."

Corin considered Warde for a moment, glancing at Jon, whose face bore an expression of caution and apprehension.

"Very well," Corin said at length. "Prepare to move out."

Warde bowed and moved off, while Jon came and sat beside Corin. They watched Warde until he was out of sight.

"Your Highness, this may be Warde's plan—to abandon you during this march."

"If he wished to abandon me, Jon, he could have done so during the storm that has plagued us for the past three days,"

Corin replied. "A night march is the only way to reach Elengil in time."

✳ ✳ ✳ ✳

Corin and Jon rode cautiously all night. Corin had placed Jon in command of his personal guard, and they all watched for any sign of treachery from Warde's men. As the sun rose over the mountains behind them, it became clear that a large number of Warde's men were missing.

They stopped behind a group of hills about a mile from the city. Corin and John rode up to the top where Warde stood overlooking the plains below. Corin and Jon dismounted and beheld the vast army that was laying siege to Elengil; thousands of men, most under the red banner of House Noland.

"Your Majesty," Warde said with gusto, greeting Corin with a small bow. "We made it."

"Yes, Baron Warde, but not all your men did."

Warde looked uneasy, and Corin and Jon exchanged looks. Jon had his hand on the hilt of his sword.

"Warde," Corin began sternly. "What is going on?"

"Sire, I am afraid I've not been completely honest with you," Warde began, making a point of not looking at Corin.

"Speak quickly, Alaster!" Corin said with a mixture of anger and apprehension. *Is this what it meant to be king? To never know who could be trusted?*

"Your Majesty, from the time we rode out from Elengil, Noliono's scouts have tracked us," Warde said, continuing to gaze out at the enemy. "Last night, I sent half my men north in the hopes that the scouts would be confused."

"I know we are being tracked, but why did you keep this from me?" Corin asked irritably. "I've known about the scouts for days."

"The Council was unsure of you, Highness," Warde answered, finally looking at him. "We decided that due to my experience,

I should be in command of the cavalry, not you."

"You decided?" Corin said quietly, his face contorting with anger. He was enraged by this blatant betrayal. *How could he have been so naive as to think these men could have any faith in him as a leader?* Corin felt like such a fool, which only made his anger boil even more. Corin took a deep breath and chose his words carefully.

"You speak as if the Council has the right to make such decisions without my knowledge or leave to do so. I should have you and the rest of the Council arrested and executed for this betrayal, Baron Warde," Corin began through gritted teeth. "Yet at present, I need your expertise and the loyalty of your men. Fight well today, and I may yet forgive this transgression."

Warde bowed and remounted his horse. Corin and Jon watched as the baron rode off to rejoin his men.

"After today, perhaps the Council will have more regard for you, Your Highness."

"Honestly, Jon, I feel I have little reason to hope these men will ever see me as their king," Corin answered darkly.

"What will you do then?"

"We must first defeat Noliono, Jon," Corin answered at length. "Then I will deal with the Council."

＊　　＊　　＊　　＊

The next morning dawned bright and fair. The air was crisp and the sky devoid of clouds. It was as if the day was unaware of the bloodshed and sorrow that was about to occur. Corin, Jon, and Warde stood on the hills to the south of the city since dawn, waiting to play their part in the coming battle. Corin gazed across the plains below, watching as his forces within the city marched out in formation to meet the enemy. As per the plan, his forces broke into three groups to cover the slopes below the main gate. He could not see from this distance, but archers were supposed to be positioned on the battlements above. Noliono's forces were already arrayed along the slopes below the city, waiting for the battle to be joined.

Jon turned to Corin, who nodded. They mounted their horses, and Corin lifted the banner of the king. Across the plains, high on the tallest tower of the keep, his banner was hosted high in the morning breeze. The signal had been sent and received. His forces before the city gave a shout as the trumpets rang out, and then his men rushed toward the enemy. Corin drew his sword and turned to Jon and Warde, who also drew their swords.

"Charge!" Corin cried, and he and the entire cavalry host tore down the hill. The wind shipped across his face as the enemy lines grew closer. They cleared the hills, and Corin glanced to the right to see Warde's second group crossing the plains to the northeast of them. Corin turned back to see the enemy lines reform on the right flank. Spearmen knelt down with their spears pointed outward toward the oncoming cavalry. Enemy archers fired over the spearmen when the horses drew close enough. The arrows fell behind Corin and the front line of horsemen. Just before they crashed into the line of spearmen, Corin saw many of the enemy break ranks and flee; then their lines met in a tangle of horse, man, and steel.

The front line gave way almost at once. The charging horses carried Corin and his men through the enemy's entire right flank before they turned outward upon reaching the city. Corin glanced across the battlefield as he rode onward. The right flank of the enemy was in disarray, but the left was falling hard on his forces near the city. The middle was turning to reform on the right. His heart fell as he realized their charge had only momentarily stalled the enemy's advance on the city. His cavalry line was now disorganized, and his men were being surrounded and their horses killed from under them. There would be no second charge.

37

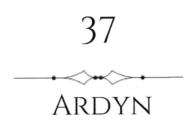

ARDYN

Smoke rose from the south as Ardyn and his men rode across the hills north of the city of Elengil. They rode east around the edge of the eastern hills, keeping out of range of the city's defenders. Sir Simon Moore and Jordan Reese had warned Ardyn that the defenders might mistake them as foes. When they reached the hills, Ardyn ordered a halt. He rode out to the edge and surveyed the battlefield. Sir Simon and Jordan joined him.

"The new king is hopelessly outnumbered, my lord," Sir Simon said solemnly. "It is as we feared."

"Even with our forces, the young king cannot hope to defeat Noliono's army."

"Perhaps, Sir Simon," Ardyn said, still surveying the battlefield. Movement from the east and south caught his eye. "Perhaps not. Look there!" he shouted, pointing at two hosts of cavalry riding up from the east and south toward Noliono's forces.

"They mean to turn Noliono's right flank, my lord. We must join them!" Jordan cried imploringly.

"Not yet," Ardyn answered. Something inside him made him hesitate.

"But, my lord!" Jordan protested. "If we do not aid him now, the charge may fail!"

"And if we join the battle too soon, we may all be slaughtered, Jordan," Sir Simon said warningly. "My lord, I agree that caution is the best course of action. Let us wait and see when we might be of most benefit."

Ardyn let out a deep sigh as he watched Warde's men ride into the enemy. His heart leapt as Noliono's right flank began to crumble, but as soon as the right fell into disarray, Sir Simon pointed at the middle as it formed a new line.

"Warde's forces are too disorganized, and the right is reforming to the south."

"They mean to crush them between the two sides like a giant pincer!" Jordan exclaimed in dismay.

Ardyn hesitated. He knew his men would help Warde's men, but he still was too novice in the art of war. If he made the wrong decision now, all of them might be killed. He stared down into the fray, and his eye caught a lone white banner in the midst of Noliono's red and Warde's blue and black.

"What banner is that?" he asked, pointing.

"That is the king's banner!" Jordan cried. "The king is under attack!"

"Are you certain?" Sir Simon asked, peering out across the field.

"I recognize his banner even from here!" Jordan interjected. "He is beset. The middle is advancing, and the right has reformed. We must ride to his aid!"

Ardyn watched in horror as the banner suddenly fell to the ground.

"To the king!" he exclaimed without waiting to think. He drew his sword and drove his spurs into his mount. The horse reared and flew down the hill. His men fell in behind as they reached the bottom and turned west. They fell upon the enemy's unsuspecting right flank, crushing most and routing the rest.

"To the king! To the king!" Ardyn cried, forcing his men

onward. He knew he had to reach Corin. He must.

Ten heartbeats later, Ardyn arrived at the place where the white banner had fallen. He reined in his mount and ordered Sir Simon and Jordan to reform the line. As he did so, he scanned the ground for Corin.

"There!" he called, dismounting and running over to the body of a young man whose head was red with blood.

"You stupid fool of a boy!" came an all-too-familiar voice.

Ardyn spun around, bringing his sword up just as Ramond Kludge brought his sword around at Ardyn's head. The steel rang as the two swords met.

"You just couldn't do as you were told!" Kludge yelled, pushing Ardyn away and forcing him to the ground. "The king gave you your father's land and titles, and still you turn and betray him."

Ardyn jumped up and dodged Kludge's next attack. The two men then began circling one another. Jordan rode over and dismounted.

"My lord," he called, but Ardyn shook his head. This was his battle.

"Proud fool!" Kludge shouted with a rancorous roar. "You think you can defeat me?"

Ardyn glared but did not let his emotions rule him. Kludge attacked again, this time bringing his sword down with all his strength. Ardyn brought his sword up, but the force of Kludge's blow knocked him to the ground again. Kludge's blade was inches from his head. Ardyn pushed back with all his strength, but Kludge's blade continued inching closer. Ardyn, remembering his legs, kicked up hard at Kludge's stomach. Though he was wearing chainmail, the blow winded Kludge, and Ardyn was able to roll away and get to his feet. Kludge stood wheezing for a moment, glaring at Ardyn, then Kludge lunged forward without regard to defense. Ardyn saw his opportunity. Ardyn parried Kludge's wild attack and knocked the sword from his hand. Kludge fell to the ground and glared up at Ardyn.

"Finish it!" he yelled.

Ardyn looked down at Kludge with malice in his eyes. Hate and anger bubbled up from deep inside him. He wanted so badly to end this man's life, to exact revenge for all this man had done. The man who...then suddenly Ardyn saw the man for what he was—a fanatic minion of Noliono, the true villain. Kludge was just a follower, a tool for Noliono to use to bring hurt upon the world. Ardyn hesitated then hit Kludge over the head with his sword hilt, knocking him unconscious. He looked down at Kludge for a moment then ran over to Corin. He checked his hand and felt a pulse.

"Help me!" he called to Jordan, who ran to his side. They hoisted Corin up and carried him to Ardyn's horse.

"Signal another charge!" Ardyn shouted at Sir Simon after remounting his horse. "Jordan and I will ride to the city with the king's body."

"Sire, the city defenders will mistake you for a foe!" Sir Simon protested.

"There, Jordan, hand me that banner," Ardyn ordered after scanning the ground nearby.

Jordan picked up the broken staff bearing the king's banner and handed it to Ardyn, who brushed off the dust.

"We will ride under our king's banner," Ardyn answered with a smile. "Now ride."

Ardyn did not wait for Sir Simon to argue but rode at breakneck speed toward the city, holding the king's banner high in the air. As he neared the city, the defenders moved to the side as he rode on to the gates, which opened to receive him and Jordan.

He reined in his mount as he heard the gates slam shut behind him.

"Help me!" he called out, dismounting his horse.

Just then several hands grabbed hold of Ardyn and forced him to the ground.

"What is the meaning of this!" Ardyn heard Jordan demand.

"Orders from the regent," one of the guards said. "This man bares the crest of House Thayn, enemy of our king."

"You fool!" Jordan exclaimed. "Why would an enemy of the king risk his life to rescue him?"

"He is to be brought before the regent," the guard said, ignoring Jordan's protests.

Ardyn was disarmed and marched off toward the castle of Elengil. Ardyn wondered what fate awaited him there and if he'd made the right choice.

38

RINIEL

Riniel burst through the door and ran over to the bed where Corin's body lay. She knelt down, bewildered, as everything about her began to spin.

"No," she whispered, tears welling up in her eyes.

Galanor, Lord Renton Myr, and Baron Peter Astley arrived a moment later, gazing down at their young king.

She looked up at Galanor. Tears were now streaming down her face.

"Is he...?" she began, but she could not bring herself to finish her question.

"No, princess," Galanor said consolingly. He knelt down beside her and took her hand. "He is still with us."

"How do you know this?" she asked, looking back at Corin through the tears.

"The doctor just told me Corin is going to be fine. He took a nasty blow to the head, but the doctor believes the king will fully recover."

Riniel gave a small smile of relief, wiping the tears from her eyes. She reached out and took Corin's hand, realizing for the first time just how much he meant to her. After a few moments, Riniel stood up and turned to Galanor and the others.

"I want to know who is responsible for this," Riniel said, trying to make her voice measured and calm.

"Two men entered the gates, bearing the king's banner," reported Astley.

"Who were they?" Riniel pressed.

"One was Jordan Reese and the other was Ardyn Thayn."

"Ardyn Thayn!" Riniel exclaimed. Her heart began to race. This was her chance to finally know who had killed her father. "I demand that Ardyn Thayn and Jordan Reese be brought to the Great Hall at once."

"Princess Riniel, there is a battle going on," Lord Myr interjected condescendingly. "Ardyn's men are fighting alongside our own. I hope you are not about to endanger..."

"Lord Myr, please return to the walls and see to our defenses," Riniel said. Her voice was calm, but her eyes flashed dangerously. "I will see Ardyn and Jordan in the Great Hall immediately."

Lord Myr bowed and left, followed by Baron Astley. Riniel looked back at Corin. She was not going to let this chance pass her by. She was going to learn who'd killed her father. No one was going to stop her.

* * * *

Ten minutes later, Riniel was standing on the dais in the Great Hall. Her heart was racing as she waited for the arrival of the very person who could finally reveal her father's killer. The doors opened on the other side of the hall, and a slew of men entered, leading Ardyn Thayn and Jordan Reese. Riniel watched anxiously as they crossed the hall, stopping at the foot of the dais.

"Hello, Princess," Ardyn said quietly with a bow.

Riniel looked hard at Ardyn for a moment then spoke to Jordan Reese.

"Your mission was a success?" she asked, her voice shaking slightly in anticipation.

"Yes, Your Highness," Jordan answered with a bow. "Ardyn and his men aided us in the battle."

"You have our thanks, Jordan," Riniel said with a smile. "I will make sure the king is informed of your courage when he awakes. Please report to Lord Myr and aid in our defenses."

When Jordan had left, Riniel turned to Ardyn.

"Ardyn Thayn, you rescued the king and risked your life to bring him back. For this you have my eternal gratitude," she said, her heart pounding in her chest in anticipation of her next question. "Ardyn, you once told me that you knew who killed my father. I ask that you finally reveal to me who it was."

Riniel watched as Ardyn's face fell.

"Princess, I thought you knew, but..." Ardyn began but stopped short.

"You told me you knew. Was this a lie?" Riniel asked, anger boiling inside her.

"No," Ardyn said quickly. "At the time I believed Noliono had killed your father with Ramond Kludge's help. Since then..."

"So you are saying that you do not know who killed my father," Riniel said, trying to control her anger and frustration. "So if it wasn't Noliono, who was it?"

"I don't know," Ardyn said, looking down at his feet.

It was as if the dam that held all the frustration, fear, guilt, and rage that Riniel had been holding back for the past three months finally gave way. She shook with rage, and her eyes filled with angry tears. Her hands clenched into fists as she still fought to contain her emotions.

"Guards," she said through clenched teeth. "Take this man to the dungeon until he decides to tell me the truth."

"What?" Ardyn exclaimed as the guards grabbed hold of him and started dragging him away. "Wait, you can't do this! Riniel, I have told you all I know. Please, you have to believe me! Riniel!"

The doors of the Great Hall slammed shut, and Riniel was left alone on the dais. She stood resolutely, still shaking with rage, tears flowing down her face. She wanted to scream. She fell to her knees as she was overwhelmed with all the anger and despair of the past three months. Would she ever know who had killed her father? Would she ever be able to bring her father's killer to justice?

＊　＊　＊　＊

It was late when Riniel awoke. She was in the king's chambers, kneeling next to Corin's bed, her head lying on the bedsheet. When the door opened, she turned quickly to see Baron Warde enter, followed by Lord Myr, Baron Astley, and Jordan Reese.

"Princess," Warde began, breathing hard. "I came as soon as I was able. I bring word from the battle."

"Yes," Riniel said, wiping her eyes and standing. "Please tell me everything."

"The attempted cavalry raid has failed," Warde said solemnly. "Nearly half my men and horses were killed. If not for House Thayn arriving when they did, we'd all have been killed."

"What of the rest of the army?" Riniel asked, turning to Lord Myr.

"We managed to withdraw most of the army behind the city walls, but we lost many today," Myr replied gravely.

"What of the enemy?" Riniel asked, hopeful for some good news.

"Many were lost on both sides, Princess, but they still outnumber us greatly," Warde answered. "We have few options. Do we fight them on the field, or do we remain inside the city?"

"Leave me, my lords, and allow me to consider this," Riniel said softly.

"But Your Highness," began Warde, but Astley put a hand on his shoulder.

"We await your decision, Princess," Astley said with a bow.

Lord Myr led the others out, but Jordan Reese, who appeared to want to say something, lingered for a moment. She shot him a look, and he bowed and left with the others.

She turned back to Corin, who still slept. Anger and grief began to surge up from within her again. She knelt on the floor with her hands over her face.

"Why has all this happened?" she asked aloud. Tears were again sliding down her cheeks. "Why must I be the one who must make all these decisions?"

"The king chose you because he trusts your judgment," said a familiar voice.

Riniel looked up.

"You," she said, recognizing the man who'd visited her previously. "Why are you here?"

"I have appeared in your hour of need. As I have told you before, I am always here."

Riniel suddenly felt a peace that had been absent in her life since her father had left on his journey several months ago. She breathed deeply and gazed up into the man's warm, smiling face.

"Riniel," the man said calmly. "You must release Ardyn."

Riniel's face changed in a moment from serene to confused.

"I can't," she said as if pleading with the man. "He's the only one who can tell me who killed my father."

"Riniel," the man said sternly but consolingly. "Ardyn never knew who killed your father."

"Never?" she asked, her resolve breaking.

The man shook his head.

"Ardyn saved the king's life," the man said, his voice growing louder. "Jordan Reese told you himself. The king lives because Ardyn risked his life to save him, just as he did for you."

Riniel was suddenly overwhelmed with guilt and shame.

"What have I done?" she said, beginning to sob, but the man reached down and pulled her to her feet.

She looked up, expecting to see anger and condemnation in the man's eyes. Yet all she saw was forgiveness and understanding.

"Free Ardyn," he said simply. "He will still fight for your cause. Free him, and your forces will be victorious."

Riniel hesitated then nodded. She turned to look at Corin for a moment.

"What about Corin?" she asked, turning back, but the man was gone.

She stood there for another moment, then making up her mind, she crossed the room to the door. She opened it and instructed the guards to bring Ardyn up from the dungeons to the king's chambers. Though she was only recently acquainted with him, Riniel had made her decision to trust the visitor. Though he'd not said his name, Riniel was now sure she'd known it all along.

❋ ❋ ❋ ❋

Ardyn was brought to the king's chambers a mere ten minutes later. The door opened, and two guards brought him inside, bound in chains.

"Remove his bindings at once!" Riniel exclaimed. "And leave us."

The men quickly did as she'd commanded and left. Ardyn stood in the middle of the room, rubbing his wrists and looking confused and a bit angry.

"Ardyn, I..." Riniel began, but her words caught in her throat.

"It's okay," he said, holding up a hand. "I get it."

"No, you don't," Riniel said, crossing the room and hugging him. "I'm so sorry for the way I've treated you."

"I'm sorry too," Ardyn said, hugging her back.

"If I didn't know any better, I'd say Ardyn Thayn is trying to steal away my fiancée," said a voice from the bed.

Riniel and Ardyn broke apart and turned quickly toward the bed to see Corin raising himself up on his pillows.

"Corin!" exclaimed Riniel, running over and throwing her arms around him. They embraced one another for a long, happy moment.

"It is good to see you, Ardyn," Corin said when he and Riniel finally broke apart.

"Your Highness," Ardyn said with a bow and a smirk.

"Riniel," Corin said, turning back to her. "Tell me all that has happened."

Riniel told Corin and Ardyn everything that had happened since the king had fallen on the battlefield.

"So the raid failed and the siege continues," Corin said almost to himself. "I will need to meet with the Council and find out what our options are."

"Release me, and my men will fight for you," Ardyn declared.

Riniel and Corin looked up at him, and Riniel was suddenly struck by how quickly Ardyn had changed since she'd first met him in the citadel gardens.

"I give you leave to return to your men, my friend," Corin said, extending his hand.

"I'm sorry I ever doubted you, Corin," Ardyn said, clasping Corin's arm.

"And I you, Ardyn."

"I'm also sorry," Riniel murmured.

Ardyn took her hand and smiled. "I will attack at dawn," he said, bowing and turning to go.

"We will be ready," Corin said.

Riniel watched Ardyn leave, knowing she'd made the right choice. Now she wondered what tomorrow might bring now that they had an ally in Ardyn Thayn.

39

KINISON

"What do you mean he's not here?" Kinison asked impatiently.

Kinison, Ren Gables, and Silas Morgan were standing just outside the main tent in the camp of House Thayn. Blue banners bearing the white eagle waved in the early morning breeze. The sun had not yet risen.

"As I said before," the sentry stated irritably. "Lord Ardyn Thayn and Jordan Reese took the body of Corin Aranethon back to Elengil. He's been gone ever since."

"Corin's body?" Kinison asked anxiously. "The king is dead?"

"I don't know, sir," the sentry replied gravely.

"If your king is dead, then we've ridden here for nothing," Silas said, glaring at Kinison. "All your promises are meaningless, and Noliono will surely hunt us down and kill us."

"Watch yourself, rogue!" Ren shouted at Silas. "The king may yet be alive, but even if he is not, I still choose to fight against Noliono's evil."

"Then fight you will," came a voice from the darkness.

They all turned and watched two figures emerge from the gloom. Kinison recognized them both at once.

"The king lives. We have seen him with our own eyes," Ardyn declared, striding forward. He held out a hand to Kinison. "Will you fight with me?"

"For King Corin," Kinison said, taking Ardyn's hand.

"What about your companions?" Ardyn asked, turning to Ren and Silas.

"Sir Ren Gables," Ren said with a bow. "Formerly of the Guardians. I have pledged my sword to Kinison Ravenloch. Where he leads, I follow."

"Silas Morgan," Silas said, with a smirk. "I fight for the new king simply due to my hate of the old one. My men and I await your command."

"Welcome, Ren and Silas," Ardyn said, shaking each man's hand. Kinison thought he saw mistrust in Ardyn's eyes when he shook Silas's. "Now, let's plan our attack."

Kinison spent the next hour with Ardyn, Jordan, Silas, and Ren planning their attack on Noliono's forces.

"In summary," Ardyn said, gesturing at a crude map he'd drawn on the ground. "We will skirt the hills east of the city then cut across the plains and attack Noliono's right flank."

"If we can turn it, the city defenders should be able to capitalize on it and route Noliono's main force," Kinison said confidently. It was a good plan, but Kinison also knew it was risky.

"When do we begin?" Silas asked quickly.

"At sunrise," Ardyn replied, turning to the east and gauging the time. "We've planned long enough. Prepare to ride out at once."

❊   ❊   ❊   ❊

They rode hard and fast, skirting the hills east of the city. Ardyn called for a halt on the hill just above the battlefield. The sun was just beginning to peer over the Gray Mountains behind them. Kinison looked out over the battlefield, realizing for the first time how powerful a force Noliono had mustered. Even after Ardyn reported yesterday's losses, Noliono's army still numbered over ten thousand. Jordan reported the city's defenders numbered only about two thousand now. Kinison wondered to himself what Ardyn's and Silas's force of less than seven hundred men could hope to do against so many.

Ardyn signaled to form a line and drew his sword. Kinison and Ren followed suit. In the measure of a heartbeat, Kinison was suddenly struck by the importance of this moment. He closed his eyes and said a brief prayer for safety and deliverance then he heard Ardyn sound the attack.

The whole host raced down the hill toward the enemy's right flank. Kinison saw the outer line of spearmen bracing for the attack, spears and shields facing outward and arrows flying overhead from the archers right behind the spearmen. Kinison breathed in and out once, and then Ardyn's host crashed into Noliono's forces.

At once, Kinison knew the attack had been a mistake. They broke through the outer wall of spears only to find a second and third wall prepared for them. Ardyn's line was soon broken, and man and horse were being slain. Just as Kinison checked his horse and was preparing to double back, a spearman suddenly leapt in front of him and speared his mount. The horse reared, throwing him to the ground. Kinison was momentarily dazed but got to his feet just as the spearman came at him. He parried the initial blow, knocking the man backward, and prepared to follow up his attack but found his assailant unconscious. Kinison looked about and found himself alone in the midst of the enemy. He grabbed the spearman's fallen shield and prepared to defend himself.

"Leave this one to me," came a familiar voice over the din.

Kinison turned and glared as Ramond Kludge advanced on him. Kinison brought up his weapons in a defensive posture, while Kludge stopped short and stood a mere ten feet away.

"I was hoping I might one day get the chance to kill you, Kinison Ravenloch," Kludge said with an evil grin.

"Here's your chance, Kludge," Kinison said, smiling in turn. "Make the best of it because you only get one chance."

Kludge brought up his blade and crossed the distance between them, bringing his blade down hard. Kinison dodged the attack and swiped at Kludge's legs. Kludge leapt backward, and he and Kinison began to circle one another. Kludge was bigger and stronger than Kinison, but Kinison knew he was smarter. He also knew that Kludge would continue these heavy attacks, so all Kinison had to do was wait until Kludge tired himself and then move in for the final blow.

As if on cue with Kinison's thoughts, Kludge lunged at Kinison again, and once again Kinison dodged the attack. They circled one another several more times, broken by Kludge's heavy attacks and Kinison's agile dodges. He smiled slightly upon seeing Kludge's heavy breathing, knowing his moment was quickly approaching. Kinison dropped his guard to prepare a sudden attack. Just as he did so, Kludge rushed forward, throwing his whole body weight against Kinison, knocking him to the ground. Kinison looked up just as Kludge prepared to deal the final blow, when from somewhere on his right, Kinison saw Ren Gables rush forward, knocking Kludge away just in time.

Kludge righted himself and roared in anger. Ren stepped in front of Kinison, bringing his sword into a defensive stance.

"You fool!" Kludge roared. "How dare you defy King Noliono! When I'm done with you, I will personally kill your wife and children for this betrayal!"

Kludge rushed forward, swinging his sword at Ren's head. Kinison stood up quickly, helping Ren parry the blow. Ren was knocked back by the force of Kludge's swing, giving Kludge an opening at Kinison. Kludge dealt him blow after blow, pressing his attack until Kludge managed to knock his sword from his hand. Kludge roared with glee as he thrusted his sword at Kinison's unguarded chest, but his blade never touched him. At the very moment Kludge had stabbed at Kinison, Ren had leapt forward, taking the deadly blow and plunging his own blade into Kludge's chest. Kinison watched as Kludge's expression faded from glee to shock as he fell to the ground and did not move again.

Kinison caught Ren as he fell back and lowered him slowly to the ground. Ren looked up at him.

"Ren," Kinison began, but the words caught in his throat, and tears welled up in his eyes.

"I guess now we're even," Ren said, trying to laugh. He coughed several times, each one more strained than the last. "I'm so sorry, Kinison, for everything."

"All is forgiven, my friend," Kinison said, shaking his head. "You are once again the honorable man I knew."

Ren smiled, then his eyes grew dim. He grabbed Kinison's tunic and pulled him closer.

"Promise me you will rescue my family. Promise me you will protect them."

"I promise, Ren," Kinison said, holding his sword hilt to his heart.

Ren smiled again for a moment, then his grip on Kinison's tunic released, and the light faded from his eyes. Ren Gables was gone. Kinison lowered his friend's body to the ground and closed his eyes for the last time. He bowed for a moment over the body, and then he turned to rejoin the battle.

40

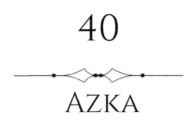

AZKA

Azka stood beside his king on the battlements of the city wall, which overlooked the southern plains. Below them, the second day of battle was unfolding. He stole a glance at the king, noting the look of anxiety expressed there as well as a looking of longing. Azka could plainly see that Corin wished to be in the midst of the battle, not watching it from the walls of the city while he waited for his body to heal.

"I should be down there," Azka heard Corin murmur. It surprised Azka at how quickly the young man had gone from an awkward, whiny young man to a leader that even inspired himself to follow.

"I have not forgotten my promise to you, Azka," the king said, turning to him. "If Ardyn's attack is successful, fifty horsemen are waiting in the courtyard outside the main gate. They've been ordered to raid Noliono's camp and to rescue Aylen."

"May I have your leave to accompany them, sire?" Azka asked, suppressing the anxiety he felt for his sister. He had buried his desire to rush off and rescue her only because his king had promised to do whatever it took to save her.

"You have my leave, Azka," the king answered, shaking Azka's hand. "Good hunting."

A trumpet suddenly rang out, and both Azka and the king turned back to the battle. The enemy's right flank was in full retreat.

"Ardyn's done it!" the king exclaimed. "Go, Azka! Tell them to ride at once!"

Azka did not wait but turned and ran across the battlement, down the spiral staircase and out into the courtyard. Fifty horsemen, mounted and ready, awaited him.

"A horse!" Azka commanded, and one of the men dismounted and handed Azka the reins.

"Do we ride?" Jon Grehm asked, riding over to him.

"Ardyn's men have succeeded. The king commands we ride at once," Azka replied.

"Open the gates!" Jon yelled, moving to the front of the party. "You all know our mission. Avoid combat until we reach the enemy's camp. Ride hard, and once we reach the camp, search for Azka's sister, Aylen. Once searched, burn every tent and kill all who take up arms to stop us. Ride now for King Corin! Ride for freedom! Ride for Alethia!"

A cheer went up as the gates opened, and the whole host rode out into the fray.

※　※　※　※

Azka, Jon Grehm, and fifty horsemen tore out of the gates and down onto the plains. They then turned toward the enemy's right flank, where Ardyn and the men of House Thayn were fighting. They rode into an area of the battlefield where the fighting had subsided. Azka spotted a single man standing alone amongst the fallen and recognized him at once.

"Kinison!" Azka exclaimed, riding over to him, followed closely by Jon.

"Azka, Jon," Kinison said with a looked of detachment.

"Where is Ardyn?" Jon asked.

"They continued the charge after I was unhorsed. Ren Gables, my friend, is dead," Kinison responded without looking at him.

"I am sorry," Azka said, bowing his head in respect.

"He saved my life," Kinison continued as if reciting a story from a book and not events that he'd witnessed personally. "He even killed Kludge."

"Kludge?" Azka exclaimed, his heart racing. "Ramond Kludge is dead?"

Kinison nodded.

"Then your friend is a hero!" Azka said, smiling for the first time in months. "Come, Kinison, we ride for Noliono's camp."

"Noliono's camp?" Kinison asked, suddenly looking up at Azka. "My wife is being held there."

"Then we ride with a common purpose, for Noliono also holds my sister," Azka said quickly. "Give him a horse, and let us be off."

One of the horsemen dismounted and handed the reins to Kinison. Once in the saddle, Kinison and Azka led the company of men as they rode hard and fast, skirting the enemy's right flank. Azka noticed the enemy's formation nearest to them was on the verge of collapse. When they reached the camp, they found a few soldiers guarding it, and even they gave little resistance. Azka and Kinison dismounted and entered the first tent, but it was empty. They moved on to another tent but still found no sign of Aylen or Sarah. They reemerged and surveyed the search effort. The raiding party was darting in and out of the tents, burning them as they went. Azka and Kinison both ran on, passing the rest of their men, and entered an area yet to be searched. They circled around a large tent and almost ran headlong into a slew of Noland soldiers. Upon seeing Azka and Kinison, they charged forward at the two men. Even for the seasoned veterans that they were, Azka and Kinison were hard-pressed. Three men attacked Azka at once, forcing him back from Kinison. He parried a blow from one and hurled him to the ground. The other two both leapt at him, but Azka dodged, bringing his blade up just in time to block their wild attacks. They came at him again, but Azka dodged and used their momentum to send both of them flying into a nearby feed trough. Both men were knocked unconscious.

Azka turned just in time to see a group of Noland soldiers exit the large tent with two women in tow. One of the women was dark skinned and the other light.

"Aylen!" he roared, but a yell from his right drew his attention. Kinison was fighting five men at once, barely keeping them at bay. Azka was torn between rescuing his sister and helping Kinison. He stood rooted in indecision until another cry from Kinison forced him to choose. Azka ran toward Kinison, tackling two of his attackers to the ground. He flipped onto his back and onto his feet just as another man came at him, brandishing his weapon. Azka parried the man's wild swing then drove his sword hilt into the man's head. He fell to the ground and didn't move again.

Azka turned back to find Kinison had dispatched the other two men.

"Kinison, I found them!" Azka called, gasping for breath. He pointed in the direction the Noland soldiers had taken his sister and Sarah. "Come on!"

They raced on, dodging in between tents. Azka wondered why there were no Noland soldiers trying to waylay them, and every so often, he caught a glimpse of a red tunic. They rounded a large tent surrounded by many smaller tents. A small group of enemy soldiers were standing guard at the larger tent's entrance. Azka and Kinison let out a bloodlust roar, which sent them scurrying off in every direction. Azka could not help but laugh as they raced on until they reached a cluster of tents pitched close together. They formed a corner, leading to the right. Azka and Kinison were running full sprint when they rounded the bend, but the scene that greeted them stopped them dead in their tracks.

They had entered a wide open area several dozen yards across, tents surrounding the area like a wall. A hooded figure in black robes stood before a slew of Noland soldiers, all armed and prepared to attack. In the midst of the soldiers, Azka saw Aylen and Sarah were bound and held by several guards.

"Welcome, Azka and Kinison," the figure said, drawing back his hood to reveal a long mane of black hair. His face was fierce, and his eyes were black as midnight. "I have been expecting you."

"And who are you?" Kinison asked, bringing up his blade in a defensive posture.

"I am Methangoth," the man said with an evil grin. "No doubt you've heard of me."

Azka and Kinison exchanged looks but kept their guard up.

"Indeed," Azka said, seemingly calm. "You are the monster who orchestrated this war."

"Indeed, dark one. This kingdom is under my control, and soon I will become more powerful than either of you can possibly imagine." Methangoth laughed then gestured behind him. "No doubt you've noticed the two women standing here are none other than your sister, Aylen, and Kinison's wife, Sarah. Azka, I give you the choice: choose one to be freed and one to die. Choose now."

Azka looked at Methangoth with a mixture of rage and apprehension. How could he make such a choice? He glanced at Kinison and saw his panic mirrored in the other man's eyes.

"Choose, dark one," Methangoth said, clearly enjoying the conundrum he'd created for Azka. "Choose, or I will kill them both."

"Neither!" shouted a voice from behind Azka.

He and Kinison spun around just in time to see Corin and a host of men ride past them and into the Noland soldiers. The men holding Aylen and Sarah released them and fled behind the wall of tents. Azka and Kinison rushed forward at Methangoth, but before either of them could reach him, he turned and cast a burst of red flame at Aylen. It was like watching events in slow motion. The ball of fire left Methangoth's hand and flew at Aylen, but just before it hit her, Sarah jumped in front of her. Azka and Kinison watched in horror as Sarah burst into flames and fell to the ground. She shrieked and writhed in agony for a moment then was gone. Kinison roared with rage and rushed at Methangoth in full fury, but his wife's killer took a handful of black powder from his robes and cast it to the ground. The powder burst skyward, enveloping Methangoth in a black pillar of smoke, and then he was gone.

Kinison reached the place where Sarah had been killed, dropped to his knees, and howled in agony. Azka moved over to Aylen and embraced her. She was shaking from head to toe in utter shock. He held her close but found his joy mixed with sorrow. Methangoth had taken Sarah from Kinison, something Azka knew he'd never be able to forgive or get over. Corin came over to Kinison and spoke to him in a low voice. Kinison stood and walked away from the king. Azka wanted to go after him but thought better of it. He wondered what Kinison would do now.

41

NOLIONO

Noliono slammed his fist down on the table. Several parchments and maps went flying into the air. How had it come to this? He was King of Alethia with an army several-thousand strong. The city had been surrounded and the enemy severely outnumbered. He'd even lured the stupid boy out from behind his walls and onto the battlefield, and still Noliono had lost. Not only had his forces been driven from the field, Noliono had been forced to abandon the siege and retreat half a day's march from the city in order to reorganize his forces and avoid pursuit. Noliono stood up and began to pace. How could the boy beat him? How!

A sudden movement by the door of his tent drew his attention. There Methangoth stood, the evil wizard who'd led him down this twisted path.

"What do you want?" Noliono asked, shooting him a look of irritation.

"Watch your tone, Noliono," Methangoth warned. "Remember your place. You may be king, but don't forget who gave you that crown."

Noliono put his hand on his sword hilt, wanting to draw it and cut the disrespectful villain's head off, but he knew how quickly the wizard could react. If Noliono ever tried anything, Methangoth would reduce him to a pile of ash without a second thought.

"What do you want?" Noliono asked, fighting to suppress his anger.

"You know why I am here!" Methangoth said, advancing on Noliono in unsuppressed anger. "I handed you a kingdom, and in less than three months, you have all but lost it!"

"I've lost nothing," Noliono said through gritted teeth. "A single battle was lost, but I still outnumber his forces, and he will not venture far from Elengil to pursue me."

"The siege went on for weeks," Methangoth growled. "Your army was three to four times larger, yet even in a pitched battle, you are bested by this orphan boy with a crown."

"Don't forget it was you who killed Kinison's wife, and it was you who lost Azka's sister," Noliono retorted. "You lost us our only bargaining chips."

"I eliminated the only reasons Kinison and Azka are loyal to the boy. Now they will desert him, leaving the boy weak and vulnerable," Methangoth said dismissively.

Noliono bit back his retort, seeing no point in arguing further.

"And you still haven't retrieved the book," Methangoth said after a long pause.

"What is it about this book that is so important!" Noliono shouted in exasperation.

"The book is more important than any battle or any crown!" Methangoth shouted then, almost to himself, he said, "I must have it."

"I will defeat this boy and get your book," Noliono said with a look of annoyance.

"I have my doubts," Methangoth retorted with disdain. "Perhaps it is time I join you on the battlefield."

"You!" Noliono exclaimed, looking at Methangoth in surprise. "You're joking! Why join us now?"

"I grow weary of your failures. It may be time for me to take the field."

Noliono considered Methangoth suspiciously before speaking. "No," he said finally.

"You would refrain from using your most powerful ally?"

"I will win this without you. I will kill the boy, destroy Elengil, retrieve your book from the ruins, and you and I will part ways."

Methangoth gave a low growl, or was it a chuckle?

"Now leave me," Noliono said, turning his back on Methangoth.

He heard the tent flap open and close. Noliono put his hands on the desk and closed his eyes.

"You reap what you sow," came a voice from behind him.

Noliono spun around to see a man in gray robes standing in the doorway. The man had brown hair that fell to his shoulders, a short brown beard, and Noliono would have sworn the man's face glowed slightly. His eyes were brown, and there was a kindness in them. Noliono recognized the man at once and was filled with immediate hatred.

"Behold the man!" Noliono mocked. "I thought I told you never to visit me again!"

"Even so, I have come to you this last time, Noliono, to implore you to turn from the path you have chosen."

"I will hear no more of this!" Noliono cried, covering his ears. "I have endured your constant appearances and warnings, your message always alluding danger and to my demise. I am King of Alethia, about to destroy my enemies and secure my kingdom."

"You rule because My Father allows it," the man said, becoming stern. "You rule a kingdom of sand, and tomorrow the kingship will be taken from you, Noliono, and handed to Corin Aranethon."

Noliono stared at the man as if he'd just been slapped.

"If you go to Corin now and surrender yourself and your forces, he will show you mercy. If you renounce your sins, My Father will also show you mercy, even now."

"Surrender?"

"You will be freed and sent into exile."

"Exile!" Noliono spat, barely containing his outrage. "You would have me give up all that I have achieved and beg this boy for my life?"

"Your pride will doom you, Noliono," the man said softly.

"*Get out!*" Noliono shouted angrily. "I never wish to see your face again."

"Do not harden your heart against me, Noliono. If you will not turn from this evil path and repent of your sins, you will die tomorrow and never see your family again. Your kingdom will be taken from you, but your life may be spared. Consider my words."

"I said, get..." Noliono began, but the man disappeared. He stared in disbelief and outrage as the man's words seemed to echo in his mind. "No one is taking my kingdom from me!" he yelled. "Tomorrow I will crush this boy and end this pointless rebellion! And then I will have my revenge!"

✳   ✳   ✳   ✳

Noliono sat astride his horse the next morning. The battle lines had been drawn. The boy and his forces were arrayed on the other side of a wide open plain between two sets of rolling hills. His main force was set in a wedge formation to his left, while he led the cavalry charge. Across the plain, he could see the enemy's cavalry waiting. Noliono smiled at the situation. The boy may have won the battle below the city, but here on the plains, Noliono's overwhelming numbers were going to crush the rebels once and for all.

Noliono signaled to begin. Trumpets sounded the attack, and his forces began marching forward. Noliono's cavalry waited for several long minutes until the main force was almost upon the enemy.

"Charge!" Noliono cried, drawing his sword and spurring his horse. The rest of the cavalry unit roared and spurred their own horse, and they were soon galloping across the plains. Ten heartbeats later, the battle lines were joined. Noliono led his cavalry in a wide turning motion then split in two. One sent to draw the rebel cavalry out of position, the other to encircle them. Then the two would ride together and crush the rebels in the middle. As Noliono's horsemen split, he spotted the boy. The cripple was actually leading his own cavalry charge. Noliono turned his group in sharply to pursue the boy, but too late. The rebels turned inward and rode into Noliono's right flank.

"No!" Noliono shouted, realizing his mistake.

The boy had predicted his strategy and outmaneuvered him. Noliono's cavalry was now out of position, leaving his right flank completely unprotected. The boy was scattering his men, and the right side of the wedge was partially routed. Noliono signaled a full pursuit, enraged that the boy had outsmarted him again.

Noliono pushed his horse onward, but to no avail. By the time he and his horsemen reached them, the right flank was in full route, and the rebel horsemen were turning the wedge inward. The battle would be lost if Noliono did not stop the boy. He turned his horse and signaled his cavalry forces toward what remained of his right flank. They tore across the field toward the rebel infantry, scattering them in all directions. Yet Noliono's eyes never wavered. He was locked on to the white banner. Noliono was so overwhelmed with hatred and rage that he broke ranks despite the objections of his men nearby. The boy's back was turned, and his horsemen were all distracted. This was his chance. Noliono grabbed his bow and fitted an arrow. This was it. He was finally going to put an end to this pathetic rebellion. He held his breath and released the arrow. Noliono watched as it soared through the air, his face breaking into a smile as the deadly missile seemed to be on target, but just before it hit the boy, the arrow burst into flames. Noliono stared, stunned for a moment, then saw Galanor ride in between himself and the boy. The old man held up his staff, and Noliono felt himself leave his mount, go flying through the air, and fall to the ground. He picked himself up, drawing his sword, and saw all his horsemen had also been unhorsed and thrown to the ground.

They now faced the rebel horsemen on foot. Noliono did not like their odds. The men backed away from one another, creating a wide open area; Galanor had ridden out into the middle. A black pillar of smoke suddenly appeared in the middle of the field. When the smoke cleared, Noliono saw that Methangoth stood a mere ten feet from Galanor. The two men stared at one another.

"This seems all too familiar," Noliono heard Galanor remark. "Your attempt to seize power has failed yet again, Methangoth."

"The game is not over yet, old man," Methangoth retorted. Noliono could not see his face, but could hear the sneer in Methangoth's voice. "I've waited until now to draw you out for a final conflict of wills. Today, Galanor, our game will finally come to an end."

With that, Methangoth cast a ball of fire at Galanor. Though the fireball bounced off an invisible barrier, leaving the older man unscathed, the sudden attack spooked Galanor's horse, which reared and threw the older man to the ground. In the blink of an eye, Methangoth was on top of Galanor, and Noliono saw a sword wreathed in red flames appear in Methangoth's hand.

"The game has been fun, old fool!" Methangoth roared, bringing the sword down hard.

The barrier that stopped the fireball also stopped the flaming sword, but even from this distance, Noliono could see Galanor was weakening. He was surprised by a sudden pity he felt for the older man. It was as if he did not want Methangoth to win, which was absurd. Noliono looked around the open field at all the men as they watched the two wizards dueling. The epic battle for the kingdom was forgotten as all those present beheld the power of these two men. He turned and saw the boy, still astride his horse, watching and waiting. Hatred burned inside him.

The duel, the battle, even the kingdom was forgotten as Noliono made his way through the men toward the boy. A stray fireball caught his attention about halfway across the field as

Galanor and Methangoth continued dueling. Noliono hoped they'd keep both sides occupied while he made his way through their midst. When he was in range, he checked the men around him, but their attention was still focused on the duel. Noliono slowly drew an arrow from his quiver and fitted it to his bowstring. His hands were shaking with anticipation. This was it. He was going to kill the boy, and this time Galanor would not be able to stop him. He drew the bowstring back, took a deep breath to steady his shot, and released. The arrow soared through the air true to his mark. It seemed to take an eternity for the arrow to reach his target. As Noliono watched, a smile began to spread across his face. Yet a sudden movement to the boy's right caught his eye. Someone was moving toward the boy. Noliono's smile was replaced by a look of shock and outrage as Kinison Ravenloch dove in front of the boy and took the arrow in his chest. A cheer went up from the rebels, and Noliono glanced over to see Galanor standing over Methangoth, pointing a sword of pure light at his heart.

"It is over!" Galanor shouted with a fierceness that even Noliono could respect. He watched as Methangoth tossed something small up to Galanor.

"For now!" He heard Methangoth shout before he disappeared in a whirl of black smoke.

As if coming out of an enchantment, both sides realized where they were and looked around at one another in confusion.

"You fools!" Noliono shouted. "Attack them!"

"Peace!" came the boy's voice. "There has been enough Alethian bloodshed.

"No!" Noliono shouted, drawing his blade.

He started to run at the boy, but someone hit him from behind. Noliono fell on his face, rolled over, and looked up just in time to see Azka standing over him with a sword in his hand pointed at Noliono's throat.

"Yield," Azka commanded with a rage Noliono had never before seen in his eyes.

Noliono stared disbelievingly. Azka pressed the sword point into his throat.

"I said yield!" Azka shouted.

Noliono looked at him for a moment longer then nodded.

A cheer erupted all around him, and Noliono sank back to the ground in despair. It was over.

42

CORIN

Corin sat alone in his chambers. The night was overcast, leaving the room in darkness save the fire in the hearth and the candle on the desk in front of him. He sat staring at the wall, his face blank. It has been two days since Noliono had surrendered. Corin's forces had disarmed Noliono's men, and Lord Atton Nenlad had even sworn fealty to Corin before relinquishing his sword and signet ring; another of the great houses of Alethia to fall because of this war. Events were transpiring almost too quickly for Corin to handle. Since the battle ended, Corin's mind had been preoccupied by Kinison's sacrifice. The first person he'd really trusted, save Galanor, was lying in the infirmary with no guarantee of recovery. Corin was overcome with grief and the desire for revenge. If Kinison died, his killer was none other than Noliono himself. The fate of the monster who'd killed so many now rested in Corin's hands. That was why he secluded himself, even from Riniel, to think. There was a part of him that wanted to execute Noliono without even a trial. The man's crimes were evident, and not even history would question Corin's decision to execute the man.

There was a sudden knock at the door.

"Enter," he said as he shook himself out of his contemplation.

The door opened, and Galanor entered.

"Highness," Galanor said, quickly turning and closing the door.

"I thought I told you to call me Corin."

Galanor managed a small smile as he sat down, though Corin could see concern and anxiety etched in the old man's face.

"Corin, there are two things I wish to discuss with you."

"What's on your mind?"

"I wanted to discuss Noliono's trial with you."

"If there is a trial," Corin said darkly.

"Corin, I've reached out to my contacts all over Alethia. The realm is on the verge of collapse. Of the great houses that have ruled Alethia for centuries, only House Thayn remains. As you know, Lord Myr was hit by an arrow atop the southern battlements. Since Renton Myr has no heir, that leaves his lands in disarray. You declared House Nenlad disbanded, and Houses Eddon, Aurelia, Rydel, Farod, and Noland have all fallen. Most of the provinces are now without any leadership. They look to Elengil for direction. You swore to uphold the law. Will you turn so quickly from your oath?"

"What do you suggest?" Corin said somewhat irritably.

"I suggest instituting a new Council of Lords and give Noliono his trial," he answered without hesitation.

"What!" Corin exclaimed, shooting Galanor a look of disgust.

"You will need someone to lead each province, and you will need advisors in these early years of your reign," Galanor said gently.

"The same type of men who undermined me during the war?" Corin asked condescendingly. "I have shared with you what Astley, Warde, and Myr plotted to do because they lacked faith in my abilities. They undermined my authority, Galanor. What if I appoint this council you suggest and another lord like Noliono arises and tries to seize power?"

"You must be cautious, Corin," Galanor answered as a teacher answers a student. "You must choose people loyal to you, someone who will uphold the law and put the people before personal ambition. There are a few trustworthy men who have served you."

Corin sighed, turning away. He was wearied by the constant bad news. Who would have thought being king was so difficult?

"Corin," Galanor said as if trying to keep his attention. "If you fail to uphold even the most basic rights of your citizens, you set a precedent of tyranny that your descendants will exploit."

"You are right, as always, Galanor," Corin admitted after a long pause. "Who will serve as counsel for Noliono?

"I will."

"You!"

"I am qualified, and I feel responsible, as I shared with you previously, because Noliono was merely a pawn of Methangoth."

"Your old apprentice?"

"Indeed," Galanor said, and Corin saw a shadow of guilt pass across the man's face. "Methangoth is my responsibility. I believe the true blame lies with Methangoth, not Noliono. His actions—"

"Are his actions, Galanor," Corin interrupted. "Not yours."

"By the way, what did Methangoth throw to you just before he vanished?"

Galanor reached inside his robes, pulled out a small object, and handed it to Corin, who gazed at it in surprise. It was a black queen from a chess set.

"I don't understand."

Methangoth considers this entire war as a chess game between him and me. He was letting me know he was relinquishing his most valuable offensive piece but that the game was not over."

"He thinks all this is just some game?"

"Yes, and the people as mere pieces to be used and sacrificed," Galanor said with a weariness Corin had not expected. "Methangoth is a twisted man with a desire for power."

"What of the *Book of Aduin*?"

"He believes it to contain powerful spells that would make him able to control the world."

"Does it?" Corin asked eagerly.

"It does not," Galanor said flatly. "It contains the power of knowledge and wisdom. Knowledge of the past so that we may shape the future."

"Is that why it has been hidden away?" Corin asked quickly. "To keep Methangoth from being able to control Alethia's future?"

"You are indeed wise, young Corin," Galanor said with a small chuckle. "You see why I feel so responsible for my former apprentice. Methangoth learned much from me. What he chooses to do with the knowledge I chose to give him falls partially upon me."

"That is unfair!" Corin insisted.

"Much about life is unfair," Galanor replied gently. "Yet the Almighty is with us through all of it."

"I know," Corin said, remembering all the times the visitor had appeared to him.

"I know you do," Galanor said with a knowing grin. "You know what you should do."

Corin sighed then nodded. "Noliono shall have his trial, and I shall appoint new members to a Council of Lords."

✳   ✳   ✳   ✳

At dawn the next day, Corin had summoned the gold- and silversmiths to craft new signet rings, for at noon the court would convene in the Great Hall, and he would appoint a new Council of Lords. After giving much consideration to all those who had pledged their loyalty and lives to him during this conflict, he'd decided on Ardyn Thayn, Jon Grehm, Alaster Warde, Peter Astley, and Kinison Ravenloch as the new members of the Council of Lords. Since Kinison was still in the infirmary, Corin retained the lands belonging to House Myr in the hopes his friend would recover. Because Corin had promised Riniel that he would maintain Ethriel as the capital of Alethia, he personally took up the stewardship of the lands once belonging to House Aurelia. Riniel was already making plans to return to Ethriel.

Corin sat atop the dais with Riniel seated by his side. Galanor stood on Corin's other side as his assistant for the ceremony. The four men stood at the foot of the dais in their new trappings. Each man bore the new heraldry given to them by Corin before the ceremony. Ardyn Thayn retained his blue tunic bearing a white eagle. Jon Grehm wore a dark-green tunic bearing a white griffin. Alaster Warde's black tunic bore a white wolf, while Peter Astley's crimson red tunic bore a black falcon.

"Loyal Alethians!" Corin said, standing with an effort. "I welcome you to witness the forging of a new era in our history, a chance to rebuild Alethia and end the tyranny of past rulers!"

The crowd shouted and cheered. Corin was still not used to the acclamation and wondered if he would ever be.

"As your king, I hope to lead you into that bright future, but I cannot do it alone. These four men standing before me have been carefully chosen to help rule Alethia. They shall vow before you to rule justly and maintain the laws of God in their respective provinces," Corin continued, gesturing to the men standing before him. "Please, Galanor, call forth the first man."

"Come forth, Ardyn Thayn," Galanor called. His voice echoed around the hall.

Ardyn came and knelt before Corin, who drew his sword from its sheath.

"Ardyn Thayn, son of Anson Thayn, do you swear to cause law and justice, in mercy, to be executed in all your judgments?" Galanor asked.

"I so swear," Ardyn answered.

"Then I restore to you the lands of your fathers and add to them the lands once belonging to House Rydel. Your title shall be High Lord of Alethia, and you shall retain your heraldry. Receive the ring of your father, Anson, as a symbol of your office. Arise,

Lord Ardyn Thayn," Corin said, tapping him lightly on each shoulder.

Ardyn stood up smiling as Corin handed him the signet ring of Ardyn's father to him. The crowd cheered as he put the ring on, turned, and descended the stairs to the foot of the dais.

"Come forth, Jon Grehm," Galanor called as Ardyn reached the bottom.

Jon ascended and knelt before Corin.

"Jon Grehm, son of Reese Grehm, do you swear to cause law and justice, in mercy, to be executed in all your judgments?" Galanor asked.

"I so swear," Jon answered.

"Then I bestow the lands once belonging to House Eddon. Your title shall be High Lord of Alethia, and you have received your heraldry. Receive this ring as a symbol of your office. Arise, Lord Jon Grehm," Corin said, tapping him lightly on each shoulder.

Jon stood up with a look of bewilderment on his face as Corin handed him the signet ring. The crowd cheered as he also put the ring on, turned, and descended the stairs to the foot of the dais.

"Come forth, Alaster Warde," Galanor called as Jon reached the bottom.

Warde ascended and knelt before Corin.

"Alaster Warde, son of Alexander Warde, do you swear to cause law and justice, in mercy, to be executed in all your judgments?" Galanor asked.

"I so swear," Warde answered.

"Then I bestow the lands once belonging to House Noland. Your title shall be High Lord of Alethia, and you have received your heraldry. Receive this ring as a symbol of your office. Arise, Lord Alaster Warde," Corin said, tapping him lightly on each shoulder.

Warde stood up with a look of pride and accomplishment on his face as Corin handed him the signet ring. The crowd cheered as he also put the ring on, turned, and descended the stairs to the foot of the dais.

"Come forth, Peter Astley," Galanor called as Warde reached the bottom.

Astley ascended and knelt before Corin.

"Peter Astley, son of Reginald Astley, do you swear to cause law and justice, in mercy, to be executed in all your judgments?" Galanor asked.

"I so swear," Astley answered.

"Then I bestow the lands once belonging to House Farod. Your title shall be High Lord of Alethia, and you have received your heraldry. Receive this ring as a symbol of your office. Arise, Lord Peter Astley," Corin said, tapping him lightly on each shoulder.

Astley stood up with a look of achievement on his face as Corin handed him the signet ring. The crowd cheered as he also put the ring on, turned, and descended the stairs to the foot of the dais.

"To my friend, Kinison Ravenloch," Corin said over the cheering crowd. "I will award the lands formerly held by House Myr at a later date. He is a just man and will oversee this city with the same justice as I have. He shall be granted the heraldry formerly held by House Aurelia." Then with a look of uncertainty, Corin turned to Galanor.

"Come forth, Silas Morgan," he cried as the crowd grew silent.

Every eye turned as Silas Morgan strode up the center aisle, his hat bearing his signature red feather and a broad smile on his face. He ascended the steps and knelt before Corin.

"Silas Morgan, son of Silas Morgan, do you swear to cause law and justice, in mercy, to be executed in all your judgments?" Galanor asked.

"I so swear," Silas answered with a smile.

"Then, in accordance to the promises made to you by Kinison Ravenloch, I grant the city of Nenholm into your care. Your title shall be Baron of Nenholm. May you turn that city into a center of trade and culture. Your heraldry will be a white star centered on a blue field, opposite a plain white field," Corin said after a brief hesitation. "Arise, Baron Silas Morgan."

Silas stood up and gave Corin a big grin. "Thank you, Your Highness," he said, bowing and taking off his hat so that the feather almost swept the ground. Then he turned and descended the stairs. The crowd did not cheer, but it did not seem to faze Silas. Corin began clapping, and some others joined in, but it quickly died away.

"Come forth, Azka," Galanor said.

Azka approached the dais and bowed.

"Azka, my friend and protector," Corin began with a smile. "I would reward you most generously. Name what you will, and if it is within my power to give, it will be yours."

"Highness," Azka said with another bow. "I do not desire lands or titles. I only ask leave for my sister and me to return home."

Corin felt a wave of sadness sweep over him, and he fought to keep his voice even.

"If that is your wish, though it pains me deeply, you and your sister shall be sent home."

Azka and Aylen bowed and joined the crowd.

Corin beckoned the new Council of Lords to join him on the dais. They filed up and took their places on either side of the throne. Corin turned to Galanor and nodded slowly.

"Bring forth the accused," Corin called, sitting down on the throne with a sigh of relief.

The crowd turned to the great front doors at the far end of the hall. As they opened, a slew of soldiers entered with Noliono, bound in heavy chains, in their midst. When they reached the foot of the dais, Corin ordered Noliono's bonds removed, and Galanor moved to stand beside him. Corin saw Noliono stare up at him in defiance.

"Noliono Noland, once King of Alethia, you stand accused of atrocities and crimes against the people of Alethia, of which the most heinous are the murder of Anson Thayn and his sons at the Battle of Abenhall, the massacre of the Ethriel City Watch, and the attempted murder of Greyfuss Aurelia," Corin said. He saw Riniel stiffen at the last charge, and the crowd began to murmur.

"Who speaks for the accused?" Corin asked in a voice loud enough to carry over the din.

"I, Galanor, will speak for—" Galanor began, but Noliono cut him off.

"No one speaks for me." Noliono spat. "Corin Stone, the supposed heir of House Aranethon. You are just some orphan boy from the streets of Stonewall. You have no authority over me nor any right to rule Alethia!"

Several members of the Council stepped forward at Noliono's last words, but Corin held up a hand. He braced himself on the arms of the throne and, with significant effort, he stood.

"By right of blood and conquest, I am the rightful ruler of Alethia. Whatever your intentions were, you usurped the throne and began a reign of tyranny. Your crimes are evident, supported by a host of people who personally witnessed your crimes and cruelty."

At that moment the doors of the Great Hall opened, and a young man came running down the aisle and to the foot of the dais. He handed a roll of parchment to Galanor, who took it and read it. Corin watched as a smile spread across the old man's face. He handed it back to the boy and pointed to Corin. Corin struggled to his feet as the boy nervously ascended the dais. He handed the parchment to Corin, who took it and read these words aloud.

> To Corin Aranethon, King of Alethia, greeting.
>
> I, Wilhelm Sunderland, King of Eddynland, write this message to you in hopes that it finds you victorious over the tyrant, Noliono.

Corin paused as Noliono swore and spat at the last few words, then he cleared his throat and continued.

> We met Gaven Soron and his forces on the field of battle near Farodhold and were victorious. I am pleased to inform you that Soron is dead and his forces scattered. I have taken Farodhold, Fairhaven, and will soon march north on Norhold. As per terms of our alliance, I will hold the southern lands of Alethia in my keeping until you or your representative arrives.
>
> Your friend and ally,
> King Wilhelm Sunderland

Corin looked up to see Noliono fuming.

"You stand accused before this court, Noliono Noland. How do you plead?"

"I stand in contempt of *your* court, boy!" Noliono shouted. "I enter no plea, nor do I recognize your right to issue judgment upon me. I know after this farce, you will execute me."

Noliono sprang forward and grabbed a nearby guard's sword, brandishing it at anyone who moved toward him. Noliono turned to Corin, glaring malevolently.

"You mean to kill me, but I will not give you the satisfaction!"

With that, Corin watched in horror as Noliono turned the sword and fell upon it. The whole hall rang with shouts of shock and dismay. Galanor ran over to Noliono's side and turned him over. He pressed his hand to Noliono's neck then bowed his head.

"He's dead," Galanor said as the uproar from the crowd grew.

Corin fell back into his throne, bewildered by a man so fanatic that he would take his own life rather than submit to anyone. Corin was filled with pity and remorse for a man whom he'd once feared and hated. The kingdom had lost two kings in less than a year. Corin said a silent prayer for strength and wisdom to guide Alethia through this period of grief and upheaval.

✳ ✳ ✳ ✳

Later that night, word came that Kinison had awoken. Corin made his way to the infirmary and opened the door to find Galanor, Azka, Riniel, and Ardyn seated around Kinison's bed. He smiled as they all looked up. Here gathered were the handful of people he could truly trust, who'd come through the fire with him and had helped him secure his throne.

"Corin," Kinison said weakly. "About time you got here."

"Sorry, got a kingdom to run and all that," Corin said, grinning as he made his way over to the bed. Ardyn gave up his chair, and he sat down next to Kinison. "Glad to finally find you awake, my friend."

"Not sure I'm glad," Kinison said, his face darkening. Corin knew why but could not bring himself to say it.

"I have retained the lands once belonging to Lord Renton Myr," Corin said, changing the subject. "When you are well, you will be granted his titles and lands."

"I must respectfully decline, my King," Kinison said after a moment's hesitation. "I have no desire to take any further part in leadership."

"But Kinison," Riniel began softly.

"My wife died because of my decisions," Kinison said firmly as tears welled up in his eyes. "The Visitor told me what I should do, and I chose my own path. I will not allow any more to die because of my pride or arrogance."

"Visitor?" Corin asked with a sudden realization. "What'd he look like?"

"A man with a pleasant face with kind brown eyes, brown hair that fell to his shoulders, and a short brown beard," Kinison said with a far-off look. "He also wore a gray hood and cloak that hid a blindingly white robe underneath."

There was a sudden intake of breath from everyone in the room except Galanor.

"It appears we have all seen this Visitor," Corin said with surprise and excitement.

"He may have seemed like a 'Visitor' to you," Galanor said wisely. "Yet he is always with you."

"You know him, Galanor?" Corin asked.

"Who is he?" Riniel asked.

"He is the Son of the Almighty," said a deep voice.

Everyone turned to see Azka with a small smile on his face. Even Galanor looked surprised at Azka's statement.

"It seems strange hearing you say that, Azka," Galanor said, unable to contain his happiness as the careworn lines on his face seemed to smooth in a wide smile.

"I, like all of you, have come to know Him, the same Jesus found in your Bible. Though I am confused as to why he chose to appear to each of us, we can know without a doubt that He loves us and desires for us to prosper in His will," Azka said confidently.

"I too heard His warnings and chose not to heed them at first," Corin said, looking at his crippled leg.

"We all did," Ardyn added.

"The question is," Galanor interjected, "what will you do now with your newfound knowledge?"

EPILOGUE: GALANOR

"And so, the five friends parted ways. I, Galanor, returned to Elmloch Castle with the *Book of Aduin*. Corin and Riniel returned to Ethriel, where they were married and ruled in the city of her ancestors with justice and mercy. Azka departed with his sister, Aylen, for the land of Kusini, and Ardyn returned to Stonewall to take up his father's charge to rule his lands with wisdom and strength." Galanor paused for a moment.

He was in his study in Elmloch Castle, the *Book of Aduin* open before him, his pen hovering over the page on which he was writing. It was night, and the only light came from the candle on his desk. He looked up briefly at the black queen chess piece on the shelf above his desk then returned to the page.

"Of Kinison, I know not where he travels. Grief-stricken, Kinison took his leave of King Corin and headed south for Abenhall and lands unknown. May the peace of the Almighty go with him and with us all."

A harsh wind blew through the open window, snuffing out the candle. Galanor lit his staff and prepared to defend himself, but the room was empty. A sudden thought crossed his mind, and he turned again toward the shelf above his desk. The black queen was gone, and in its place was a pawn and a small piece of parchment. Galanor took the parchment and read:

> You took my best piece, but while you were preoccupied, one of my pawns crossed the board. With my best piece restored to me, I declare the game not over, and this time the victory will be mine.

ABOUT THE AUTHOR

R. S. Gullett is a proud alumni of Stephen F. Austin State University and currently teaches United States history at a community college in Houston, Texas. As a historian, he loves to mingle the historical with the fantastical and places an emphasis on faith in all his writing.

Made in the USA
Middletown, DE
22 January 2021

31725799R00209